# Vampire Charming

## Cassandra Gannon

Text Copyright © 2014 Cassandra Gannon
Cover Copyright © 2014 Cassandra Gannon

All Rights Reserved

Published by Star Turtle Publishing
www.starturtlepublishing.com

Visit Cassandra Gannon and Star Turtle Publishing's website or on Facebook for news on upcoming books, behind the scenes details, trivia and promotions! If you enjoy our books, be sure to sign up for our mailing list!

Or email Star Turtle Publishing directly:
starturtlepublishing@gmail.com

We'd love to hear from you!

## Also by Cassandra Gannon

The Elemental Phases Series
*Warrior from the Shadowland*
*Guardian of the Earth House*
*Exile in the Water Kingdom*
*Treasure of the Fire Kingdom*
*Queen of the Magnetland*
*Magic of the Wood House*
**Coming Soon**: *Destiny of the Time House*

A Kinda Fairytale Series
*Wicked Ugly Bad*
*Beast in Shining Armor*
*The Kingpin of Camelot*
**Coming Soon**: *Happily Ever Witch*

Other Books
*Love in the Time of Zombies*
*Not Another Vampire Book*
*Vampire Charming*
*Cowboy from the Future*
*Once Upon a Caveman*
*Ghost Walk*

## You may also enjoy books by Cassandra's sister, Elizabeth Gannon.

The Consortium of Chaos series
*Yesterday's Heroes*
*The Son of Sun and Sand*
*The Guy Your Friends Warned You About*
*Electrical Hazard*
*The Only Fish in the Sea*
**Coming Soon:** *Not Currently Evil*

*The Mad Scientist's Guide to Dating*

*Other books*
*The Snow Queen*
*Travels with a Fairytale Monster*
*Everyone Hates Fairytale Pirates*
*Captive of a Fairytale Barbarian*
***Coming... Eventually****: The Man Who Beat-Up Prince Charming*

# Chapter One

EXT. INFINIA- NIGHT

Scene opens with a horrific battle scene. Supernatural beings of all kinds fight desperately on a vast green field. Trees burn. People scream. Weapons flash. Lots of quick *Gladiator*-like shots. Pieces of hacked up torsos sail through the air. Then, amid the smoke and raining blood, we see our villain striding over the bodies of the fallen. FANG is really, really bad and the audience needs to understand his villainy from the first. In fact, we should probably add some kittens to the battlefield and he can stomp on them as he passes by. With boots. Because sinister guys wear boots, and hate little kittens, and this guy is waaaay sinister.

The camera lingers on FANG'S amazingly handsome (but sinister) face as he climbs atop a small hill, triumphantly raising his evil-looking sword. He lets out an evil-sounding roar of victory as his army of evil Goblins wins the battle. The good citizens of Infinia weep as FANG claims the kingdom for his own evil purposes.

It's all very *Lord of the Rings*-ish. Only more awesome. And evil. And with more hot guys.

*Opening Scene of Film- "From Here to Infinia"*


"My Eternal-One left me for a Werewolf." Slade, King of the Vampires, stood in the sterile supermarket aisle and pinpointed the exact moment his life went to hell. "That was the start of all my troubles."

The small human beside him was rearranging racks of

ice cream in a freezer case. She glanced up like she thought she'd misheard him. "Did you just say a *werewolf?*" She asked in a dubious tone.

"It's unbelievable, I know." Slade certainly understood her confusion. "Who would choose a Werewolf over a Vampire? But I assure you it's true. As we speak, the two of them are living in my castle, having stolen all of my followers, my fortune in rubies, and even my formerly faithful horses." Slade shook his head, careful not to muss his golden hair. Even in this backwards world, he refused to give anyone the satisfaction of seeing him in a disreputable state. He was royalty, after all. "Obviously, I could no longer stay on the Vampire Isle."

"Obviously."

His audience was a plain girl, who wore rectangular glasses and a strikingly unattractive blue apron. Her nametag read "Jane Squire: Stock Clerk." She looked like any number of unremarkable servants who did servant-y things, so Slade couldn't quite explain his compunction to converse with her. Kings didn't talk to maids, after all. Not unless they were ordering their suits pressed.

Something about the woman drew his notice, though. Possibly it was her hair. The shade was unexpectedly lovely, with streaks of burnished bronze mixed into the toffee-colored curls. Or maybe it was Jane Squire's unique citrusy fragrance. The scent of her wrapped itself around Slade's enhanced senses, soothing some of the unrest he'd been feeling for far too long. Or perhaps it was the girl's buxom shape. She had admirable curves for a human and they were easy to see in the unseemly pants all the women of this time period seemed to favor. Slade had to work to keep his eyes off her lush body.

Vampires were gentlemen, after all.

Whatever the reason he'd been drawn to her, Slade found that he *liked* having someone new to talk with about this ordeal. Though she was just a peasant, Jane Squire was a good listener.

"I should have seen it coming." Slade could now view his doomed relationship with the wisdom of twenty/twenty hindsight and spot all the warning signs. "Melessa and I were not compatible. From the minute we began planning our wedding, it was clear. She wanted the color scheme to be orange and pink." He looked at Jane Squire, still outraged over the horrible clash of shades. "Orange *and pink!* Can you imagine? Right then, I should've known it was hopeless."

The human didn't respond to that. No doubt she was too appalled by the cruelty he'd faced to form the adequate words. She flashed him an odd look and knelt down to load cartons of Rocky Road into the freezer beside him.

Slade took her silence as encouragement. "Melessa insisted we hire the supernatural world's most famous wedding coordinator to plan the event. *Viktor.*" He spat out the name. "Never trust a Werewolf, no matter what his references. Remember that, Jane Squire."

"I'll certainly try."

"I've warred with Werewolves for centuries, driving most of them from our lands. In my mercy, I allowed some to stay, but I should have ensured they were *all* gone. Their entire species is rotten to the core. Had I listened to my better judgment, this wouldn't have happened and I'd still have my kingdom."

"Uh-huh."

"Two weeks after the wedding ceremony, I walked in on Melessa and Viktor doing unmentionable things in our royal bathtub. Victor was wearing only my sacred Crown of Mikinlouse. Melessa wore even less than that." Slade scowled at the memory. "Far from being repentant, she told me it was *my* fault that she'd given herself to another. Apparently, I'm conceited and selfish, with no idea what a woman really desires."

Jane Squire looked over her shoulder as if she expected someone to be hiding behind her. Not seeing anybody else that Slade could be talking to, she turned back to him. "Is this some kind of performance art thing?" She demanded. "Is the theater group pranking me, because I told them I hate all the crappy vampire scripts they're trying to produce?"

Slade frowned at that foolishness. "Vampires are the noblest of all species. Nothing written about us is 'crappy.'"

"If you say so."

"I do say so. I am Slade, King of the Vampires, and I am *always* right."

"Well, *your majesty*, your 'noble' kind has been screwing me over ever since season one of *Dracula, Ph.D.*, so I'm going to stick with my opinion."

Slade frowned. "I know of no Vampire doctors named Dracula. If such a man upset you, be assured he was not part of my kingdom."

"No. *Dracula, Ph.D.* is a TV show about Vampires. In grad school. A nighttime, soapy, teen-drama deal. I played Clarissa, the undead wife of Johnathan, but he was in love with Mina..." She stopped and waved it aside. "Well, it doesn't matter. My character got beheaded after six episodes. Vampires are like my kryptonite. Every time I land a role with them in the script, it all goes south."

Slade didn't have a response for any of that. In fact, he didn't even understand most of the words. Rather than admit his confusion, he quickly went on with his story. Over the past month, he'd noticed that humans hated answering logical questions such as: "Are there no zombies in this land?" "Where can I find fresh blood?" and "Why are you summoning the police?" It seemed best not to risk inadvertently driving Jane Squire away by asking her to explain her odd words. He wished her to continue talking to him.

"In any event, after sleeping with the Werewolf, Melissa reported that she was divorcing me and claiming the Vampire Isle for her own. Then she laughed." It was hard to remember that part. "It was as if she couldn't stand the sight of me."

Jane Squire's expression changed. "I'm sorry. Getting dumped sucks."

Slade heard compassion enter her voice. It sounded close enough to pity that he flashed her a frown. No human should ever pity him. He was the greatest and most important being ever born.

"The *hard part* came when that idiot judge granted all her demands." He informed the presumptuous woman. "I should've known my enemies would take advantage of the divorce and strip me of my power. Because of Melessa, I lost *everything*." He hesitated. "Except, obviously, for my incredible good looks and humble nature."

"Obviously." Jane Squire said again and moved onto the cartons of Butter Pecan. Her tone had gone back to being bland, instead of sympathetic.

Slade could deal with that.

"Rather than follow *Viktor* as my new king, I left my homeland in disgrace. I traveled to this backwards dimension to find my good friends. The two people I knew would support me in this trying time. It was difficult, but what choice did I have?" Slade gave a fatalistic shrug. "Now, I am stuck in a strange world, directionless and without a clear destiny." He hesitated. "Also, I am unsure where to find the apples in this accursed store."

"Aisle one, passed the salad dressings." She pointed to the left. "Listen, it can take a long while to heal from a breakup. You just have to hang in there and forget about your ex, okay?"

"It's not the loss of Melessa that haunts me. It is the loss of my kingdom. Viktor is a *Werewolf*." Slade slammed a fist against the freezer in agitation. The links of his massive silver bracelet clanged against the steel. "How can a *Werewolf* be King of the Vampires? It doesn't even make any sense. Why am I the only one who sees that?"

"It's good that you realize this story isn't very logical..." Jane Squire trailed off, looking at the fist-sized dent in the side of the metal case. "Hang on, did you just...?"

"Of *course* I realize it's illogical!" Slade interrupted. "Where is the logic in Melessa dumping me for that crown-stealing golden retriever?" He gave a disparaging wave of his hand. "I'm not surprised, though. The woman was always difficult. I should never have married her, regardless of our entwined fates. I felt that something was wrong, nearly from the first."

Jane Squire was quiet for a moment. "Did you love

her?"

Slade was surprised by the question. "Melessa is the most beautiful woman in the universe." He said automatically.

"That's not what I asked."

Jane Squire didn't understand. The poor human seemed wholly uneducated about the supernatural, so he tried to explain. "Unlike your species, Vampires have only one perfect match. Our Eternal-Ones are the brides that destiny selects for us. Melessa was my one true mate. She was supposed to give me my soul and bring me happiness." He frowned. "For some reason, that didn't seem to happen. Perhaps because we never fully bonded."

"I don't think you can rely on someone else to bring you happiness. You have to find it for yourself."

Slade crossed his arms over his chest. "For lesser beings like you, perhaps that is true. But I'm King of the Vampires. Happiness should be *given* to me. It is my right." No, there was only one explanation for the disastrous state of his life. "I believe a Dark Fairy has hexed me. They are treacherous creatures, often in league with Werewolves."

"Well, that's certainly an exciting theory." Jane Squire moved to open another cardboard box full of ice cream cartons. "Okay, I'm going to humor you and give you some real advice. I get that you feel like your heart and soul are missing. Breakups are hard."

"My heart is still in place. It is my soul that remains lost." And likely always would be, since he'd divorced his Eternal-One and no one else could restore it.

"Uh-huh. Well, I think this Melessa girl leaving you might be for the best. Obviously, you two weren't meant to be. Maybe this crisis is going to lead you to some bigger plan."

"Bigger plan? What could be bigger than being King of the Vampires?"

"I'm not sure." She admitted. "It does sound like a pretty cushy job. But when bad stuff happens, I like to think that there's a greater reason for it. Like maybe we have to deal with all these problems, in order to find our *real* purpose." She turned to nod at him. "For instance, I didn't plan to be working the nightshift at Iverson's when I was thirty. I always wanted to be an actress."

Slade looked around at the dingy linoleum and endless rows of human food. "This is a dismal place." He agreed. "It's no wonder you wished to flee. But your appearance is too ordinary to be an actress."

Gray eyes narrowed. "A lot of casting people agreed with you." She said stiffly.

"I have much wisdom."

"Jesus, why am I even talking to you?"

"I was wondering why I graced you with my presence, as well. I saw you here and I felt compelled to approach." It was like he'd already known her. Like he'd been looking for her, in fact. Slade couldn't explain it. "It's most unusual for a human to capture my attention."

"Wow, aren't I a lucky girl?" She muttered. "Anyway, my point is, I'm stocking shelves instead of being a movie star, but that's okay. I know that I can work here and save up my money and buy a house. That's what I *really* want."

Slade frowned. "You have no home? Nowhere to belong?" He knew that feeling well.

"Well, I have an apartment, but one day I'll have a *real* house." She brightened. "It's something I've been working towards all my life. A home. I can close my eyes and picture it in my head." To demonstrate, she shut them tight. "It will have a walk-in closet, and flowers lining the walkway, and a bedroom big enough for a queen-sized bed."

"In my castle, I had an elevator to reach the top stories of my closet." Slade told her, studying the long length of her lashes against her cheeks. "My bedroom was large enough to accommodate my indoor ski jump and the fountain in my garden sprayed pink water to nourish my collection of giant butterflies. How could I ever picture a better home than *that?*"

Jane Squire's eyes popped open again and she flashed him a glower. "Giant butterflies? *Really?*"

"In the springtime, they flutter their wings and create rainbows so beautiful that all who see them weep with joy." He sighed. "They were the most treasured of all my pets. Of course, they fled the Vampire Isle when Fang took over. They only follow *true* kings."

The woman didn't seem impressed. "*Anyway*," she repeated pointedly, "sometimes unexpected things happen to us and we have to deal with them. *That's* what I'm saying. It's not always fun. For instance, occasionally arrogant customers pester me with their insane stories and I have to pretend to be nice to them."

"Many humans are oblivious to how annoying they are." Slade concurred.

"But I just bite my tongue and remind myself of what I'm working towards. Besides, things could be worse. At least, I haven't gone crazy, yet." She shot him a sideways look. "Not like *some* poor bastards."

"You have simple desires, Jane Squire." Slade envied her lack of greater calling. "Most humans do. It's part of the limitation of your species. But I am so much grander. I am a *king*. No amount of stacking food items will satisfy my true destiny."

"Well, I'm sorry I couldn't be more help, then." Jane Squire finished arranging the ice cream and got to her feet. Dusting her palms together, she gave him a dismissive smile. "Have a great evening, sir." She headed off passed the frozen pizzas.

Where was she going?

Slade quickly fell into step beside her. "I come from a long line of kings, you know." He announced. "Both sides of my family were the highest in their lands. My father ruled the Vampire Isle for millennia. My mother was a princess from the Enchanted Realm of Melody, before she was lost forever in the Sea of Silence."

"Some silence would be good, right now."

"It was not good for Mother. We never saw her again." Slade barely remembered the woman, but she must have been amazing. She'd contributed half of his DNA, after all. "In any case, majesty is in my blood. And, to a Vampire, blood is all."

"Uh-huh." Jane Squire said.

It wasn't much of an answer, but Slade would take what he could get. He was unwilling to let Jane Squire end the conversation. This unexceptional human was the first person who'd really *listened* to him in ages. Karalynn and Damien tried, but how could two people so blissfully in love understand Slade's misery?

Jane Squire's life seemed adequately dreary enough to comprehend his despair, though. This store was filled to the brim with depressing people and things. Perhaps that was why Slade felt driven to speak with her.

"I am also a hero." He continued, awaiting her impressed reaction to that happy news.

She gave a dismissive snort. "Sure ya are."

"You don't believe me?"

"I don't believe in heroes."

Slade didn't know what to make of such a preposterous statement. "How can you not believe in heroes?"

"Because I live in the real world and not inside a fairytale."

"There are no heroes in this world?" Dear gods. No wonder everyone here was so unhappy. "Without heroes, how do you...?"

"Jane." A rat-like man in a blue apron interrupted Slade's baffled question. The human male glowered disapprovingly, the flickering, buzzing lights overhead reflecting off his bald head and giving it a moist sheen. Slade was unsure why the citizens of this world wanted their buildings filled with electricity. Most of them looked better in the dark. "You can't be hanging out with your friends during business hours." The man complained, gesturing towards Slade. "We pay you to do a job around here."

"He's not my friend, Mr. Anderson. He's a *customer*."

"No, I have decided you are worthy of my friendship." Slade offered magnanimously. He gave the other man a decisive nod. "I am Slade, King of the Vampires, and Jane Squire's dearest friend."

Jane Squire closed her eyes like she was in pain.

Mr. Anderson jotted something down on his clipboard,

his pointy face still set in a sour pinch. "This is the last time I'm warning you, Jane. Keep your freeloading theater buddies out of here or you're fired."

Slade felt the need to defend the woman. "There is no need to be so harsh, human. She has organized much ice cream for you and worked hard this night. Apologize to the lady."

Jane Squire shot him a strange look.

Mr. Anderson's beady eyes somehow squinted up even smaller. "Watch it Fabio or I'll boot your pretty-boy ass right out the door." He went stomping off towards the cash registers.

"Dickhead." Jane Squire muttered under her breath.

Slade's eyebrows soared. Surely that tiny male hadn't just threatened the greatest Vampire warrior ever born. He glanced down at Jane Squire, thinking he must have misunderstood. "What is a Fabio? Did he just challenge me to a duel?"

All Vampires possessed a more primitive side that they had to suppress. Unlike so many supernatural creatures, Vampires overcame their animalistic impulses through reason and intrinsic honor. It was a constant struggle, though, even for someone of Slade's remarkable abilities. The Dark Instincts didn't care about his innate nobility. They just told him to chase after Mr. Anderson and break his bones, one by one, for the insult.

And for mistreating Jane Squire.

"Ignore Anderson. He's just jealous that you're so," she scanned Slade up and down, "*shiny*, while he's just an ugly, bitter, little troll."

"He's a Troll?" Slade relaxed. "That explains it, then. They are always disagreeable creatures."

Jane Squire let out a tired sounding sigh and led the way into the produce section. "Do you mind if I ask you a personal question, sir?"

"You may call me Slade, human. I have honored you with my friendship."

"Are you under a doctor's care, Slade?"

Slade brightened. "Damien is a doctor. We used to be

mortal enemies, but now I'm staying at his home."

"And I'm guessing his 'guest room' has padded walls, right?" She pinched the bridge of her nose, knocking her glasses askew. "Do you know your doctor's cell number or should I call the hospital or...?"

"Damien has given me the number for his wireless phone machine." Slade searched his pockets. "His wife, Karalynn, wrote it down for me, along with their address." He handed Jane Squire the yellow slip of paper. "She was concerned that I would become lost in this city. I have been to Chicago before, but not in this century. Where I come from, it is 1894."

"That's a new one." Jane Squire studied the row of numbers. "Well, why don't I give Doctor Damien a call and he can come get you, before you lose me my job."

Slade would think she'd welcome an opportunity to find employment elsewhere. He'd only known the woman ten minutes and he already saw that she was wasted here. After all, some instinct had pushed a man as mighty as himself to talk to her. He still didn't know the precise reason, but it surely meant she was more important than the rest of the humans in this tedious place.

"I have no wish to return to that small apartment." He informed her. "It has naught but six bedrooms. I am used to more palatial living arrangements." He hesitated. "Besides, I needed to get out into the night and escape those 'commercials.' Buying human food seemed a welcome distraction."

"TV commercials?"

"Yes, one came on the picture box, showing photographs of sad kittens and asking for money to save their small lives. The sorrowful music and broken whiskers were heartrending. Of course, I wished to help." Slade shook his head. "I called the kittens to pledge many rubies, but they only take donations from a Card Master. I do not qualify as a Card Master."

"They wanted your Master Card number?" Jane Squire guessed.

He nodded. "I explained that I was a King, which *must* be a higher status than whatever a Card Master is, but it was to no avail. My spirits were much dampened. No doubt the poor kittens have starved to death by now. Your world is filled with so much misery."

"That's true." She studied him for a moment, looking like she wanted to say something else. "You like cats, huh?"

"Oh yes. My grandmother is a cat."

Jane Squire gave a startled laugh at that statement. She quickly tried to hide it, casting a wary glance towards the front of the store and Mr. Anderson, but she couldn't contain her mirth. Her gray eyes danced with amusement, her mouth spreading into a wide grin. It completely changed her unremarkable face. When she smiled, her ordinary features were transformed into something approaching pretty.

Slade felt a surge a satisfaction that he'd made the woman happy. He wasn't sure *how* he'd done that, but it was still a triumph. So many times, people smiled at him without meaning it. They just wanted something from him. Jane Squire was genuinely delighted.

"Sorry." She struggled to regain her composure. "I just didn't expect you to say your grandmother was a cat. I probably should have, given the rest of our conversation, but it caught me off guard. How does that work exactly?"

"She is a shape shifter from beyond the stars. Not many know of her secret identity."

"I'll bet."

"Though she has forsaken me to live in my ex-palace with my ex-wife on the ex-isle of my birth, I still love my grandmother and her feline brethren." He paused. "Traitor that she is."

"That's very generous of you."

"I know." Slade agreed.

She shook her head. "You really should join a theater company when they release you from the hospital, because you're great at improv."

Slade had no idea what improv was, but he was confident Jane Squire was right about his skill. There had never been anything he wasn't "great" at. He gave a gracious nod, accepting the compliment.

Jane Squire focused on opening boxes of fruit and Slade focused on her.

"Do you have a mate?" He asked, once again noticing the woman's toffee-colored locks. They were drawn back in a ponytail with spiraled tendrils looping to her shoulders. Supernatural beings didn't have curls, so the feature was always appealing and exotic. Many creatures coveted humans for their hair, desperate to possess females with such blessings. Looking at Jane Squire, he understood why.

"You mean am I married? No." Gray eyes watched him suspiciously. "Why do you ask? Because, I don't date actors… or Vampires."

"I am not asking to date you." Slade scoffed. "Kings don't court peasants."

She snorted sardonically. "Tell that to Prince Charming."

Slade disregarded that odd statement. He had met no royalty in this world, so he wasn't certain who this "Charming" man was. Surely no one important. He kept his attention on Jane Squire. "If you worked at it --perhaps buying suitable dresses, and wearing lipstick, and getting rid of those gods-awful glasses-- I think you could find a tolerable stable boy or bell-ringer to claim you. Then you could leave this life of drudgery. You're a plain girl, but you're not as unattractive as you first seem."

"Thanks. That's very encouraging."

"You're welcome." Slade was pleased that he could help. He began selecting some apples and dropping them into a brown paper bag. "I am an expert on this subject of physical perfection, you know. I was voted the handsomest Vampire in the world every year for the last millennium."

"Really?" She sounded surprised.

Wait… why did she sound surprised?

"Yes, *really*." He snapped, affronted by her apparent shock over what should be obvious to all. "It was barely even a contest."

She gave a noncommittal nod and sorted through a large carton of bananas, piling them on a display.

Slade scowled. "You think another male should have won?" He interpreted. The woman was out of her mind to claim such a thing. It was nearly laughable.

*Nearly.*

"Who could even compare to me?" He demanded.

"Well, I've never met another Vampire. If you say you're the best looking one, I guess I have to believe it."

He wasn't appeased. "You *should* believe it. If we were back on the Vampire Isle, you'd see for yourself." He brooded for a beat. "Not that I ever wish to see the Vampire Isle, again. Let them all rot with their usurping Werewolf king. I will find another land for myself."

"Good idea. In fact, you should probably get started on that, right now."

"Get started?" He repeated blankly.

"Yeah. Go out there and conquer yourself a new kingdom, Slade. Don't let anything keep you from your destiny. ...Which is *out* of my store."

Slade blinked, amazed by the perception of her words. The woman toiled in this life of squalor, yet she alone understood his grand purpose. He saw now why fate had brought him to this supermarket and placed this nondescript creature before him. No doubt this was why Jane Squire had been born in the first place. So she could be here to guide Slade, King of the Vampires, to his glorious future.

This was the moment where he made the leap from mere king to *legend*.

It was about time.

Deep inside, he'd begun to question everything he'd always believed. Doubts plagued him. Telling him that he was unworthy. Destined to fail. Stupid and weak. Now he realized that his recent misfortunes were all part of a larger design, leading him to a better path. Talking to the human, Slade suddenly saw the truth.

The Vampire Isle had been too small. Too safe. Of *course* the gods would have bigger plans for a man such as himself. Slade was made to take risks and inspire timeless tales. Why had he not thought of that before? This was his opportunity to prove he was worthy.

This was his only chance.

"You are right, Jane Squire." He whispered, filled with a renewed sense of purpose. "I must find a new kingdom to rule."

"Great. Good luck with that. And thanks for shopping at Iversons."

# Chapter Two

INT. ROLAND'S BLACKSMITH SHOP- NIGHT

ROLAND, the hero of our story, manfully does blacksmith stuff by torchlight. He's shirtless and looking yummy. His dark hair is sweaty, but in a sexy way. His dark eyes are soulful and dreaming of bigger things. Above all, he's got a smoking hot body. The subtext should tell the audience that this kid is way too handsome to be poor. He should be played by someone in his thirties, who's portraying someone twenty-two, who's behaving like he's sixteen.

ROLAND
(In a Scorsese-like voiceover)
As far back as I can remember, I always wanted to be a king. I was born a lowly blacksmith, but I somehow sensed that I was destined for immortal royalty. At first, I thought I'd achieve it with my music. I had a really awesome band going, with these other two guys and an Orc named James. (Actually, James was kind of a dick, but whatever.) We were called "Roland and the Infinites." Or maybe "The Blacksmyths." We hadn't completely decided on a name. But --I'm serious, man-- we coulda been huge.

Anyhow, then I learned that killing the Werewolf was my sacred calling or some shit, so I said, "Sure, dude, sign me up." I was all about the questing. It's just the kind of hero I am.

But why take the risk, you ask? Why challenge Fang when I was already so close to rock super-stardom?

Well, wait until you check out the killer rack on the princess I *get to bang, bitches!*

*Film Script- "From Here to Infinia"*

"Where the hell have you been?" Damien, last of the male Wizard-Warlocks, was waiting to pounce as soon as Slade entered the apartment. "I told you not to wander off, didn't I? This Chicago isn't like the old one. You don't understand how things work in this world."

"I am not a child." Slade retorted. "I am stifled in this box and the night beckoned me. I sought refuge in it, as any Vampire would."

Damien scowled, his black eyes missing nothing. "You were watching those damn Humane Society commercials again, weren't you?" He guessed.

Slade didn't want to dwell on the poor kittens. "Your sister recommended that I go to the grocery store to clear my head." He informed Damien, striding towards the kitchen with the brown paper sack. "We were out of taco supplies and apples."

"What do you care? All you eat is holy water and blood."

"I was being helpful and gathering them for *you*." Slade shot back. The sorcerer was endlessly frustrating. No wonder so many people had tried to kill him. "I am a perfect, selfless, and thoughtful houseguest. How many times have I told you this?"

"About as many times as *I've* pointed out that houseguests are usually *invited*. You're more like a squatter." Damien scanned the small bag in Slade's hands. "So where is the taco stuff?"

"I forgot it." Slade waved aside such petty concerns. "I was distracted by a vision of my future." He smiled. "Amalie was right. My brief sojourn to the supermarket has opened my eyes to my greater destiny."

"Let's hope it involves you moving into a hotel." Damien stomped after him. "And why the hell would you listen to my sister? You *know* Amalie's always up to something. If she sent you to the store, she probably has some spell up her sleeve."

Damien's younger sister was a Witch. She was forever plotting some new trick, but Slade found her to be a sweet girl. Amalie always had negative things to say about Werewolves, which was a definite mark in her favor.

"Your sister simply made the suggestion." He defended gallantly. "She asked me to fetch tacos for dinner and some apples for her new project. Which I've done. ...Except for the taco part."

"Close enough, Slade. Thanks." Amalie skipped into the kitchen, her black hair twisted into two braids. Her bright green shirt read, "Still Kissing Frogs." She snagged one of the blood red apples from him and took a large bite. "These are about to come in *super* handy."

"I don't even want to know *how*. I'll just pretend that you're baking a pie." Damien checked his watch and swore. "Hang on." He pulled out his small phone box to send a "text."

Damien had been in this world for months and had picked up on many human habits. Much to Slade's consternation, the sorcerer seamlessly blended into the twenty-first century. Working as a doctor... Expecting a child with his loving mate... Rarely blasting anyone into goo with his powers, anymore... Damien was right where he belonged.

Slade wasn't.

He doubted he would ever get used to the baffling technology and the staggering lack of magicks here. His Vampire abilities weren't welcomed, yet he had no human skills to attain suitable employment, either. Each day he searched the want ads, but no positions were available for "Beloved Monarch of a Mystical Land." What else was he qualified for?

Even if he could find a worthy role in this world, he wouldn't want to stay. He disliked the noises of this future Chicago. Everything was so loud and mechanized. "Cars" were especially annoying. They spewed smoke and honked their horns at him. Where did all the horses go?

And why did no one speak to each other? Aside from

Jane Squire, the humans here went out of their way to avoid conversing. Who wouldn't want to talk to Slade? He was majestic and fascinating and kind to all! Instead, these humans scurried from place to place, shunning contact that wasn't conducted over a computerized screen. Back home, all the supernatural beings knew Slade. They waved as he passed in the street or gratefully welcomed him when he joined them for some rousing war. He was used to being surrounded by his people.

Now he was the only Vampire in the world.

It was lonely.

"Wonderful." Damien muttered at his phone box. "Because of you, I'm going to be late meeting Kara Lynn at Lamaze."

"Why do pregnant humans need classes on how to breathe?" Slade would never understand that, but much of this place was a mystery. "And why is your scheduling mistake my fault?"

"Because, you're the *reason* I'm late, dumbass. I was out looking for you. *Again*." Damien shoved the small contraption into the pocket of his black suit. "I just hope you didn't tell anyone you were a Vampire this time. There are only so many clean psych evaluations I can fake for you."

Slade was silent.

Damien's eyes narrowed. "You told someone, didn't you? Damn it! I'm suddenly remembering why I spent several centuries trying to behead you, Slade."

"Well, I *am* a Vampire. Did you wish me to lie?"

"Yes, I wished you to lie! I've explained fifty times, they don't *have* supernatural beings here. Not unless they've hitchhiked in from another world. The humans think you're insane when you tell them the truth!"

Slade shook his head. Damien, like most sorcerers, had been born slightly evil. Slade forgave him for his weaknesses. Not all creatures could suppress their Dark Instincts and rise to the level of Vampiric enlightenment. Still, Slade had to abide by his own superior moral code.

"I must be forever who I am, Damien."

"I swear to gods, if I could come up with a plausible story to explain your disappearance to Kara Lynn, I'd just leave you on a street corner." Damien snapped. "Since I'm stuck with you, though, the least you can do is not get the Men in Black after us."

Slade had no idea who the Men in Black were. Not that it mattered, since he *did* know Karalynn Donnelly. Damien's mate was the undisputed ruler of their household. She was the one who'd invited Slade to stay when he'd shown up on their doorstep the month before. Damien would never gainsay his treasured mate and Karalynn adored Slade. All women adored him.

Except Melessa.

Slade found himself thinking of Jane Squire's earlier question. No, he'd never loved Melessa and she'd never loved him. How strange that fate had made them Eternal-Ones, then. Had it been some kind of punishment? Why would anyone seek to punish Slade? He was flawless.

Perhaps there was a deeper reason for the mix-up that he was missing.

In any case, their divorce had actually been a relief. Melessa had annoyed him long before the marriage and spending an eternity with her would have been unbearable. Pink and *orange*, for gods' sake. He would never recover from that atrocity. At least, she was out of his life. Slade was just angry that she'd *taken* so much of his life when she'd gone. He missed his grandmother, and his people, and having a place where he belonged. He even missed his giant butterflies. But his beloved pets could flit between realms, so they would return if he called.

Maybe.

They only followed kings and, deep inside, he wasn't sure he qualified anymore. Slade was no longer sure of anything. Especially not himself.

He tried to project an image of confidence to the world, but his hidden doubts were getting louder all the time. That's why this new opportunity for greatness was so important. Somewhere deep inside, he was very afraid he was the loser that everyone on the Vampire Isle believed. He needed to do something to silence his insecurities.

"Look, I have to go." Damien told him. "You just stay *right here* with Amalie and don't do anything stupid, alright? He jabbed a finger at Slade. "I'm not bailing you out of jail, again. I mean it."

Slade scowled. The week before, he'd spent three hours in a human prison cell and it still annoyed him. He tried to help weaker beings and act heroically, but this world didn't appreciate his efforts. Maybe Jane Squire was correct. Maybe no one here believed in heroes.

"I was *saving* a woman when those policemen arrived. I explained many times that she misunderstood my intentions..."

"You slayed her Vespa with a broadsword." Damien interrupted. "You're an idiot. Don't leave the house."

Amalie rolled her eyes at her brother. "Just go already, Damien. Slade and I will be fine. I have our evening all planned."

Damien gave an exaggerated groan at that announcement and slammed the door on his way out.

Slade made a face. "Your brother is no longer a villain, but he is still a difficult man."

"He's an ass." Amalie agreed cheerily. "You have no idea the trouble I went through to save the big doofus from himself."

"Actually, I do." Slade sat down at the chrome and glass table, seizing the opening. "Witches have access to many different dimensions, correct?" He'd certainly paid one enough to get him there. What Melessa hadn't stolen in the divorce went to travel expenses so he could escape his old world. At the time, he'd marveled at how easy it had been. Almost like some greater force was guiding him. Now that he'd seen this place, it was clear he'd overpaid.

"Correct-*ish*. I can fiddle with the spaces between the different dimensions." Amalie dropped onto the chair across from him. "Why?"

"Because, I need to leave." Slade leaned closer to her.

"I must find my real spot in the universe, Amalie. I do not belong here."

She propped her chin in her hand. "Totally picking up on that." She commiserated.

"I can't stay in this world and I can't go back to the Vampire Isle. That leaves only one choice: You must help me get to a *new* land. One that's in need of a mighty king. Where I can lead my people with valor and strength. Where I will find my true purpose. ...And a large castle."

Amalie thought about that. "Well..." She let the word trail off. "There is *one* thing I could do to help, I guess. It won't be easy, though."

"No challenge frightens me." It was an undisputed fact that Slade could do anything. He'd simply been born superior in every way. He needed to believe that. "Tell me what I must do and I shall see it done."

"Well, a lot of my power comes through my Witches' Writing Circle. We kind of peek into other worlds and write down observations and sometimes... fiddle with stuff." She shrugged. "I mean, it's all *real*. We're not controlling anything or *making* people do things. We're just giving them some... opportunities."

"You did that to our old world." Slade nodded. "It is how Karalynn and Damien found each other."

"Right. Theoretically, I could plop you into some other world, using a Witches' Writing Circle manuscript as a doorway. But..."

"But what?" Slade prompted impatiently.

She bit her lower lip. "Well, some of the things we write aren't very good. There is one screenplay about a king questing for a throne, but it's kind of lame. Like *Dragonheart* meets *The Dark Crystal* meets *Beastmaster 2*. Trust me, you do *not* want to go to that world."

Slade wasn't so sure about that. He didn't recognize any of those things she was comparing it to, but at least these people were in need of a king. "This kingdom is searching for a new ruler? It has magicks and supernatural beings and no automobiles?"

"Yeah. Hang on. I have the story right here." Amalie picked it up and handed it to him. "It's like a swords-and-sorcery thing. I think the movie would rely a lot on special effects and monster makeup. See, the land's been overtaken by this jackass Werewolf named Fang."

"Fang?" Slade scowled. "I expelled him from my world many years ago. He was a cruel and twisted man, like most of his species. He enslaved thousands before I singlehandedly defeated him. I would have killed him, but he can only be slain with the fabled Silver Sword and I did not possess it."

"Well, he found a new kingdom to oppress. Now, the people there need someone to valiantly fight him, free their beautiful princess from his evil clutches, and restore peace to their enchanted land." She shrugged. "It's not something *you'd* be interested in..."

"Yes, I am!" Slade interjected excitedly. "I can do *all* of that." He wasn't sure why Amalie already had the script sitting beside her at the table, but it seemed like fate. "Yes!" He fanned through the pages, quickly scanning words like "knights," "magick spell," and "crown." "*This* is where I belong."

"Are you sure? Because there's this kid called Roland who thinks *he's* the one who will save Infinia..."

Slade cut her off. "No one will keep me from my destiny. Certainly, not a lad named Roland. Send me here immediately." He pointed at the red folder. The title typed on it read: *From Here to Infinia*. "I will gather the rubies you need for payment. Anything you ask. No matter the cost, I can..."

"Don't be silly." Amalie interrupted with a flick of her hand. "I'm happy to help *pro bono*. I feel partially to blame for the whole Melessa thing. I knew that she wasn't your true Eternal-One. We'll get it right this time."

Slade barely heard her, his eyes on the folder. "They have horses!" He pointed to that paragraph with great enthusiasm. "This is truly where I am meant to be. I can overthrow Fang again and give these peasants all they seek."

"And maybe someone's going to help you figure out

what it is that *you* really seek." Amalie hopped to her feet. "Speaking of which, I'd better get the door."

Slade hadn't heard the bell ring, but he gave a vague nod. He flipped through the script, learning more about his new homeland. This "Infinia" seemed a wonderful place. Once he arrived, he would immediately begin rallying loyal subjects. It should be quite simple. All peasants loved him.

"*Where is he?!*"

Slade's head snapped up at the sound of shouting, unexpected happiness filling him as he recognized the voice. "Jane Squire!" He breathed in the unique citrusy scent of her skin, his Vampiric instincts humming at the tart fragrance. How could an ordinary human smell so good? "How did you find me?"

"You left your doctor's address, you moron." Jane Squire wadded up the yellow paper with Damien's contact information and threw it at him. "Way to be a criminal mastermind."

"Criminal?" Was this about killing that ridiculous "Vespa" creature, again? The monster was defeated and *still* they harassed him about it. "What have I done besides make this world safer for all?"

"You got me fired, *that's* what you've done!" Jane Squire pointed at the apples on the counter with an outraged finger. "You didn't pay for those. And who do you think got blamed for your shoplifting? *Me*. So, you're going right back to Iversons and telling Mr. Anderson that we *aren't* friends and that I had nothing to do with your aggravated fruit theft."

"But we *are* friends. I cannot lie. Vampires are innately noble. Have I not mentioned this?"

Jane Squire looked ready to explode. "I need that job, you delusional lunatic!"

"Why? It seems quite thankless." He shrugged. "Any worthwhile establishment would be pleased to give Slade, King of the Vampires, a few paltry apples." It actually hadn't occurred to him to pay. He'd never had to pay at any shop he visited. Why would he? "Truly, I've done you a favor by freeing you from such miserly people, Jane Squire."

"The last thing I need is favors from *you*." She grabbed one of the apples and threw that at him, too. "Now, I don't care if you think you're King of the Vampires or an orangutan, you're going to fix this or I'm going to fix *you*. Got it?"

Slade's eyes widened at the passion on her face. High emotion lit her plain features from the inside. Why was she not like this all the time? It was much preferable to the wallflower monotonously stacking ice cream cartons. She was a woman who needed to be freed from the shackles of this tedious existence, if she was ever going to find her full potential. She needed to take risks and have adventures. Like Slade, Jane Squire didn't belong in this drab world.

Inspiration struck.

He had only found his new path because of this human. Why shouldn't she benefit from his good fortune? Slade was a generous ruler, who always strove to help the little people. Besides, he did not want to see the last of this woman. The doubts that plagued him of late were silent around her. Jane Squire was the one thing he was suddenly sure of. The one person who made him feel less alone.

"You do not need to work in that gloomy market any longer." He informed her, rising to his feet. "I've found a new kingdom and you shall come with me as my trusty servant." Surely, she would see the great honor he'd just bestowed and be thankful.

Instead, another apple bounced off his head.

Slade frowned.

"You're insane!" Jane shouted at him.

"Oh, I think he's making a lot of sense. A king *does* need a squire." Amalie said, strolling back into the kitchen. "Don't worry, this is going to work out just like it's supposed to. I'm kind of an expert." She handed Slade a set of golf clubs. "You're going to need these, so don't lose them."

He had no idea what she was talking about, until he saw she'd hidden his sword in the tall bag. No doubt she hadn't wanted him to upset Jane Squire by brandishing a weapon in the kitchen. Slade was resigned to the fact that humans tended to react badly when they spotted a broadsword. They were such a high-strung group.

"An expert at what? Golfing?" Jane Squire retorted skeptically, glowering from Amalie to the clubs. "Yeah, that makes me feel a lot better." She rolled her eyes and looked back at Slade. "Look, I'd rather live in a dumpster than be your servant. Just drop the curtain on your little play and let's go back to the store. That's the only way things are going to *work out*."

Amalie ignored that and gave Slade a jaunty wave. "Bon voyage, Vampire. Do yourself a favor and listen to something deeper than your ego." She glanced over at Jane. "And, Jane, learn to take a risk, huh? It's the only way you're going to find your real home."

Jane Squire frowned. "What?"

Amalie winked and began chanting some words of magicks.

Slade nodded in thanks, bracing himself for the trip to Infinia. "Tell your brother and Karalynn that I will think of them often, Amalie. We part the best of friends. They are welcomed in my new kingdom anytime. And if they wish to name their child after me, it would be honored."

"You're on drugs, aren't you?" Jane Squire demanded.

He decided to rise above her ingratitude and fruit throwing. She could *still* accompany him on his mission of destiny. Now that she was here, he was in no hurry to see the last of her. For some reason, the ordinary little human still seemed... special.

Jane Squire gave her head a clearing shake, her eyes on Slade. The woman did have lovely eyes, even covered with the absurd square glasses. "Look, just march down to the store or I will drag you back there by your pretty blond hair." Her index finger jabbed into his chest. "I don't care if you *do* look like a shinier version of Thor, you are *not* going to..." She broke off mid-word, her gaze darting in shock as the kitchen spun around them.

It was as if Slade and Jane were standing still while the rest of the world began twirling down an invisible drain. The apartment faded, melting away so that, for one moment, he could still see the outlines of the appliances and the next they'd vanished. The kitchen became fainter and fainter, until it was suddenly gone and they were surrounded by nothing but trees that towered hundreds of feet in the air.

Slade and Jane were no longer in that chaotic and confusing "modern" world. They'd been safely transported to Infinia. No oversized building, or noisy machines, or interchangeable humans rushing in all directions. Just a dense green forest that stretched out in all directions and a wonderful, welcoming silence.

Slade gave a slow smile.

Jane Squire looked around in astonishment. "What the hell just happened?" She yelped. "Where *are* we?" She whirled back around to Slade, her voice edging towards hysteria. "*What did you do?*"

"I have brought us to our new homeland." He told her proudly and shouldered the golf clubs. "No more will you suffer at the hands of aproned humans or be surrounded by the annoying sounds of Earth. Today, we begin again, here in the realm of Infinia." He inclined his head in modest acknowledgement. "You may thank me later."

"*What!?*" The woman was clearly overcome with appreciation. She didn't seem able to even find coherent words.

Slade gave her arm an understanding pat. "I am glad I could do this small thing for you, Jane Squire." He assured her in a grave tone. It seemed *right* that she be beside him. For whatever reason, he sensed that this human's small fate was linked to his own grand destiny. He couldn't explain it, but her mere presence made him happier. With her along, his mission would succeed. He knew it. "Together we shall..."

He didn't get to finish that sentence. From out of the underbrush, a deadly foe launched an attack. Slade instantly recognized it as a Wood Elf. He wasn't surprised to see such a monster here. They were the lackeys of the underworld, feeding off misery and unrest.

Like all of its unholy kind, the Wood Elf was genderless and spindly. It was dressed in an elfin green cloak that matched its bulbous eyes and clashed with its electrified mop of purple hair.

"Vampire!" It shrieked and sprinted forward. Its jaws stretched opened at a wide, inhuman angle, jagged black fangs gleaming. One bite put victims into a thrall, their will lost and their mind no longer their own.

"HOLY SHIT!" Jane Squire bellowed as the Wood Elf barreled straight towards them.

Slade shoved her backwards, already reaching for his sword. He pulled it free of the golf bag, giving the blade a practiced twirl. "Stay back, Elf." He warned, standing in front of Jane Squire. "Else I'll part your head from your shoulders."

Jane Squire gaped at the sword like she'd never seen one before. The woman was clearly a sheltered being. "What the *hell* is going on?!"

"Vampires are forbidden in this land." The Wood Elf hissed, but it warily stopped its advance. Its body was deceptively thin, its head seemingly too big for its bony shoulders. That was all a facade. They were among the strongest and fiercest fighters in the supernatural world. "We have orders to kill your kind on sight."

Slade marveled at the creature's impudence, his confidence rushing back now that he had a familiar foe to vanquish. He was the mightiest warrior ever born! "I welcome you to try." He offered with a laugh. "I have killed many of your species."

The Wood Elf's eyes narrowed in rage. "And we have killed many of yours." It gave a shrill whistle and the forest was suddenly alive with a dozen more of the skeletal demons. They poured out of the bushes, their thin bodies poised to attack.

Jane Squire sucked in a panicked breath and Slade instantly felt his arrogant amusement fade. Not because he was now outnumbered, but because the human was scared. He spared her a quick glance over his shoulder, his chest tightening as he realized the extent of her vulnerability. She was braced to defend herself, but the woman was helpless and this world was completely foreign to her. All his life, Slade had shouldered the responsibilities of the Vampire Isle and its people, but this was different. More personal. Jane Squire safety depended on him. Just him.

Not on the King of the Vampires, but on *Slade*.

He felt a sudden sense of purpose that had nothing to do with ruling a kingdom. He could do this. He could keep her safe. "Have no fear, Jane Squire. I shall let none harm you."

"What are they?" She breathed in terror.

Slade would have been happy to answer that, but the Wood Elves didn't give him an opportunity. They rushed forward in a mob, which was their preferred method of attack. It made them predictable. Slade's sword swung out in a practiced arc. He cleaved their oversized heads from their shoulders, refusing to allow any of the monsters closer to Jane Squire. They fell to the forest floor in a wide circle around the woman, but more kept coming.

"Goddamn it." Jane Squire seemed to shake herself from her frightened trance and grabbed a fallen tree branch from the ground. Refusing to be intimidated, she began battling alongside Slade, beating the Wood Elves with the wooden club. "God*damn* it." She caved in one of their skulls and cringed at the gush of green blood. Still, she kept fighting. It was impressive courage for a human. "*Goddamn it,* what are these things?"

"They are Wood Elves. They no doubt work for the Werewolf usurper of this land."

"*Elves?* Like fucking Santa Claus?!"

Slade had no idea what that meant and he was too busy slashing through the torrent of vile monsters to ask. The first Wood Elf must have been the leader of the group. As the others kept Slade busy, it skittered closer, looking for an opening. It found one with Jane Squire. The creature lashed out at her as she swung her branch.

The Wood Elf latched onto her arm and Jane Squire gave a cry of alarm. She tried to push it away, but the Wood Elf was unrelenting. It drove her to the ground. Poisonous teeth bared in a snarl, it prepared to rip into her flesh.

"Slade!" Jane Squire screamed.

Slade felt his Dark Instincts come over him as she cried

out his name, his own fangs lengthening and his fingernails sharpening into daggers. Seeing Jane Squire in danger let loose the inner animal that Vampires usually suppressed. For once, he didn't try to stop the bloodlust. He grabbed for the Wood Elf, a roar leaving his throat. He pulled it away from Jane Squire, intent on killing it for touching her. His claws shredded the creature's lanky body, tearing open its neck.

"I should've been a contender for... something." It gasped and finally stilled.

Jane Squire scrambled backwards from the fountain of gore, her eyes huge in her face.

"You are safe now." Slade dropped the creature's body to the ground, breathing hard. "Fear not. I shall protect you from the monsters of this world."

Jane Squire stared at the carnage, wheezing and dazed. "Was it misquoting Brando?" She got out weakly.

"I do not know who that is." Therefore, the man couldn't have been very important. Slade stood still for a moment, taking stock of the battlefield. With their leader dead, the other Wood Elves quickly scattered back into the trees. He could feel his teeth and claws returning to normal and the adrenaline fading as the danger passed.

In all, that had been the most interesting fight Slade had engaged in since he and Damien used to try and slaughter each other. Far more satisfying than hunting Vespas. And Jane Squire had battled beside him. His new servant was a worthy partner on his quest and far more hardy than most humans. He couldn't imagine Melissa facing down Wood Elves, in such a way. His petite ex-wife would have fainted at the sight of so much green blood. Jane Squire had bravely killed three of the fiends. She was a sturdy lass.

He glanced down at her, smiling widely. "The enemy has retreated! Our campaign is off to a splendid start." He saw that they were standing on a wide path, so he even had a trail they could follow out of the forest. Clearly, this was all part of destiny's great plan.

Jane was still on the ground, looking shell-shocked. "You're really a Vampire." She blurted out.

Slade's eyebrows drew together. "Yes." He agreed. "I have repeatedly told you as much."

"*But you're really a fucking Vampire!*"

Had the woman bumped her head? She seemed very confused. Perhaps a recap was in order.

"I am Slade, King of the Vampires." He reminded her in a slow voice. "You are my trusted servant, Jane Squire. We are in the enchanted realm of Infinia, where I shall defeat the Werewolf overlord and claim the kingdom as my own."

"Oh." She whispered and swallowed hard.

Slade frowned at her faint tone. "Are you alright?" He demanded, crouching down beside her. "You look unwell."

He rested a hand against the top of her head, reluctantly noticing the feel of the toffee-colored strands touching his palm. The Vampire Isle had the most luxurious silks imaginable, but even they couldn't compare to the softness of Jane Squire's hair. Like most supernatural beings, Slade had always been fascinated by humans' curls and Jane Squire's seemed purposefully designed to tempt him.

His mind was instantly filled with captivating images of the shiny tresses sliding against his body. Sliding *down* his body. The beautiful spirals dancing across his skin as her lips sealed around him. His fingers tangling in the tight ringlets as he thrust into her suckling mouth...

Slade swallowed hard, trying to focus. The fantasy was not like him. She was a small and delicate creature under his protection. He should not be imagining all the brazen things he wanted to do to her small and delicate body. Vampires were gentleman.

He cleared his throat. "Have you need of something, Jane Squire?" He prompted when she just sat there in a stupor.

She nodded vaguely, her gaze still locked on the decapitated Elf. "Yeah, I seriously need a drink."

# Chapter Three

INT.- DRUNKEN DRAGON TAVERN- NIGHT

It's been a hard day of doing whatever it is blacksmiths do all day. ROLAND is looking forward to having a drink and maybe picking up the bartender. (Note: It's important that we show ROLAND sleeping with other women, besides just the heroine. This proves to the audience that he's very manly and awesome. She, of course, can't sleep with anybody but him or she'd be a slut. That's just how movies work.) Anyhow, as ROLAND works his blacksmithy charms on the locals, little does he know that destiny is about to come knocking...

There is a knock at the door. Everyone turns as a stranger stumbles into the tavern. He's a DYING OLD KNIGHT GUY, with a bunch of arrows in him. Looking around the bar, his eyes fall on ROLAND.

> DYING OLD KNIGHT GUY
> Roland, you are the last of a mysterious, beautiful, but tragically extinct royal clan. You were hidden among peasants for your own safety, but you are far better than them.
> You are a hero.

> ROLAND
> I *knew* it!

> DYING OLD KNIGHT GUY
> I have come to give you the enchanted Silver Sword. Use it to defeat Fang and save the kingdom.
> Also marry Princess Allandrina.

ROLAND
(Taking the Silver Sword, which is silver and about the size of a letter opener)
It's kind of small isn't it?

DYING OLD KNIGHT GUY
We had to think about its marketing potential in toy store aisles.

ROLAND
Whatever.  Look, this is cool and all, but I got a band to think about, man.  Once we figure out the instruments, we're really going to go places.
I can't be tied down to some princess chick.

DYING OLD KNIGHT GUY
You know that Allandrina was the centerfold in last month's *Waxed and Wet Wenches*, right?
But she's definitely *not* a slut.  That needs to be explicitly stated, even through my agonizing pain.
The nude photo shoot was part of a royal sorority initiation.  Allandrina is very free-spirited.
…But, not a slut.

ROLAND
(Recalling that picture in the men's magazine)
That hottie with the killer rack?  Oh fuck…I *totally* have to save her!

DYING OLD KNIGHT GUY
I knew you would do the right thing, Roland.  You are destined to help reshape Infinia's future.
It is now unclear what role you will play, but…

ROLAND
(Cutting him off)
Unclear?  How is my role unclear?  You just said I'm the

> *damn hero!*
>
> DYING OLD KNIGHT GUY
> (With Yoda-y wisdom)
> It seems there is another...
>
> ROLAND
> Hang on? Another? Which another? Where'd he come from? What the hell are you talking about?
>
> The DYING OLD KNIGHT GUY gurgles and dies. It's way sad, but also dramatic. Like with violin music in the background and stuff. (Note: He should totally be played by ANTHONY HOPKINS or that dude who's ALFRED in the Batman movies.)
>
> *Redrafted Film Script- "From Here to Infinia"*

Jane sat on a barstool and glared at Slade. She'd been doing that for half-an-hour.

The good news was Slade was damn easy to look at. At six foot eight, with shiny golden locks brushing his wide shoulders and a face straight out of a fairytale, the guy was undoubtedly the handsomest nut job in Chicago. She'd been surreptitiously gawking at him ever since he'd shown up in aisle five of the grocery store.

Slade was so damn... *shiny*.

Yeah, he dressed like a pirate, with tight black pants and an open-neck white shirt. Yeah, he probably spent all his waking hours admiring himself in the mirror or working out at the gym. Yeah, he expected roses to be thrown at his feet, just for walking into a room. But none of that distracted from the pretty, pretty view.

Slade glowed with vitality and flawless masculinity. He could land the lead in any summer blockbuster just by smiling at the casting director. He was *perfect*.

Then he started talking.

The bad news was Mr. Perfect registered off-the-scales crazy. "I'm the Vampire King of an enchanted island" crazy. And the *worst* news was he didn't seem to be morphing into a cute surfer, or an astronaut rabbit, or a bumblebee who talked backwards. Ergo, she wasn't going to wake-up and forget this even happened over her second cup of coffee... Because this *wasn't* a dream.

So, maybe Slade wasn't so crazy.

Except, he had to be crazy, because if *he* wasn't crazy then *Jane* was crazy and Jane didn't want to be crazy. She had enough problems. Except, if she was sane, then Jane had been magically transported to a creepy forest filled with killer Elves. That was an even *bigger* problem. Was it better to be crazy *yourself* or to be stuck in a galaxy far, far away with a crazy person? Assuming Slade *was* crazy. Maybe he wasn't. It was kind of hard to deny that something a *teeny* bit weird was going on.

So maybe neither of them was crazy.

Except that would mean that this was *really happening* and that was the worst possibility of all. If neither she *nor* Slade was a raving lunatic, then she was stranded in some alternate dimension with an egomaniacal Vampire and monsters who were trying to kill her. How the hell was she supposed to deal with *that* possibility?

Jane wasn't even sure what to hope for. Her mind was racing, trying to think of some reasonable explanation for all of this. So far, it was just a jumble of panic and confusion and fury.

And Slade's jabbering wasn't helping to clear things up.

He stood in the middle of the woodsy, folksy, old timey pub, weaving that dumb story of his destined crown, and the grimy looking locals were actually buying it. Creatures of various unknown species stared at Slade with enraptured expressions, eagerly nodding at each ridiculous detail. Wasn't it lucky for his majesty that everyone here spoke English and had the IQ of a doormat?

"I'll have another round of the strongest one." Jane

told the blonde bartender, finishing off a glass of unidentified liquor. "Make it a double. In fact, just leave the bottle."

Jane's short term coping strategy was to get as hammered as possible. Hopefully, they took debit cards here in "Infinia," because she fully planned to rack up a tab in the triple digits. Unlike the size two actresses who got cast in all the best parts, Jane was big enough to hold her alcohol, so getting blackout drunk might take a while. It would totally be worth it though, because she didn't want to remember *anything* about today.

Especially not that freaking Vampire.

She'd spent hours walking through the forest, listening to Slade talk about some stupid movie script he'd used to travel here, and how "magicks" existed, and how this wasn't Earth anymore. ...And damn if she wasn't almost plastered enough to believe it.

Try as she might, Jane couldn't come up with another explanation for what she'd seen. She'd always been a pragmatic girl and there didn't seem much point in denying reality. A degree in preforming arts might have rendered her virtually unemployable, but it did give her a high tolerance for the bizarre. She knew an Elf when it tried to bite her on the arm. Jane kept trying out different scenarios, but they all led back to the indisputable fact that she was sane and this was actually happening.

If that didn't call for getting wasted, then nothing did.

"Wonderful news!" The golden-haired cause of all her problems came bounding over, looking like a model from a cologne ad. All he needed was a horse, a beach to ride it on, and a French-accented voiceover promising that seductive passion awaited all those who bought his perfume.

Jane pretended he wasn't there.

Slade didn't notice the snub. He leaned in closer, his body language shouting that he considered them united in this madness. Hell if she knew why. "These men know of the rebel forces who seek to overthrown the evil Werewolf Fang." He told her happily.

"Fang?" Jane repeated dubiously. Ignoring Slade was

impossible when he said shit like that. She poured herself another drink. "Jesus, there's just not enough booze in the world to deal with this."

"Fang is a nefarious villain. I've faced him before and I've seen his cruelty firsthand."

"Uh-huh."

The bartender smiled enticingly at Slade, posed so her ample bosom was shown off to best advantage. "Can I get you something, my lord?" She cooed. "I know that supernatural patrons don't imbibe alcohol, but we have a nice selection of holy water."

"No, I'm fine." Slade didn't even glance her way. As usual, his Caribbean blue eyes watched Jane as if she was the only person in the room. It was like being under a brilliant, cerulean spotlight.

Jane refused to be impressed, no matter how unique it felt to be the center of someone's attention. Slade probably didn't even realize he was so focused on her. The man's personal charisma was off the charts, but he was also a complete and utter idiot. No wonder he wanted to get into politics.

"I'm Tegan." The bartender told Slade. "Call if you need *anything*." She bounced away, giving him one last come-hither wink.

Slade barely seemed aware she'd been there, at all. "This is our only chance, Jane Squire." He grinned at her, his teeth far too white and even. No fangs were evident, but they'd sure been there when he'd killed the Elf who'd attacked her. "We shall meet with these rebels, secure their help, and together we will claim this kingdom as my own." He banged a triumphant fist down on the countertop, launching Jane's drink in the air with his irritating Vampire strength. "It's all as you said it would be."

She caught hold of her glass. "As *I* said it would be?" Jane might have been above the legal limit, but she didn't recall saying anything that stupid.

"Yes. You told me I should find a new land to rule and I have. I just need to fight for it."

"And what about me?" Jane demanded.

"You shall fight for my kingdom, too." He slung a companionable arm around her shoulder. The son of a bitch smelled like magic. "You'll be by my side. And when we win this land, I will grant you all that you desire."

"I desire to go home." She shoved him away. "You brought me here. You can send me back. Do it. *Now*."

Seeing as how he was an actual, genuine, for real, holy-God-how-is-that-possibly-*possible?* Vampire, she should probably be wary of Slade. She'd seen the guy behead about a dozen scrawny little monsters back in the forest and rip one apart with his bare hands. Upsetting him was a lousy idea.

Jane had never been very good at watching what she said, though. Thoughts just popped out before she even finished thinking them. Especially around conceited jerkoffs who'd basically kidnapped her. No way could she even pretend to be civil to the guy. Every word out of his mouth made her want to punch him. Slade was like the worst of all possible ex-boyfriends. Sickeningly handsome, emotionally oblivious, and apparently immortal. Everything that had gone wrong today was *his* fault and she had every right to blame him for it.

Besides, retractable fangs or not, Slade wouldn't hurt her. Growing up on the Southside, Jane had been around plenty of tough guys. She knew how to spot the dangerous ones and Slade wasn't dangerous. Not to her. It was impossible to fear a man who tried to donate to homeless kittens and stood in front of you when Elves attacked.

...Even if he was armed with a sword and a fully loaded golf bag.

Slade had the audacity to look hurt by her words. "Send you back to what? That dreary world, where men in aprons shout at you? I've freed you from that life, Jane Squire. Now, you serve a *higher* purpose." He splayed a hand over his annoyingly muscular chest. "You serve *me*. Together we shall write an epic tale for the ages."

Jane snorted at that idea. She wasn't destined to be the star of any epic tales. She was too plain-looking for the role. Too large. She wasn't so much overweight as she was "sturdy." At least, that's what her Aunt Maybelline had called it. Jane didn't play the delicate or beautiful heroine. She was the character who made the wisecracks and encouraged the film's stars to follow their dreams. Jane got cast as the servant, who helped the spunky heiress flee her stifling life of tiaras and dukes. The anonymous computer geek, who cracked the code for the adventurous spies. The faceless extra, who held the knight in shining armor's helmet, while he kissed Sleeping Beauty awake.

And it pissed her off.

"I'm not going to be your sidekick, Slade. Aside from the fact sidekicks usually die in these kind of movies, *I don't even like you*."

"Don't be ridiculous. Everyone likes me. I am the hero of my people."

"I don't believe in heroes."

"That is an absurd thing to say. You might as well not believe in Vampires."

Jane barely resisted the urge to strangle him with her bare hands. "Look, I just want to go home. I don't belong inside *The Black Cauldron*. I never even saw *The Black Caldron*. As soon as I'm sober, I'm pretty sure I'm going to have a total fucking breakdown. Understand? We're talking rocking-in-a-fetal-position-until-all-the-scariness-stops *freak out* of epic goddamn proportions. So just send me back to Chicago, before I lose it!"

He blinked at the vehemence in her tone. "I cannot."

"Can't or won't?"

"Can't. I haven't the magicks necessary to cross realms. Only a Witch can do that. But fear not." He nodded wisely. "If this is truly what you wish, I know where we can find such a woman."

Jane closed her eyes. "Please say she's in this bar."

"No. She is a princess, held prisoner by Fang, the Werewolf overlord who has seized Infinia. She is also a mighty Witch of untold powers. When we save Princess Allandrina, she will fling herself into my mighty arms in gratitude. As we embrace, I will ask her to grant your request."

Jane squinted at him. "So we're doing all this so you can get laid?" She translated.

Slade shook his head. "Allandrina will be my bride." He explained like he already had it all figured out. "Together we will rule these lands in supreme splendor and magnificence."

The arrogance was breathtaking. "So it's *her* kingdom and you're just going to take it? What kind of sexist crap is that?" Why did female characters in movies always have to be props for men? "Besides, you've never met this girl. What makes you think she'll even *want* you?"

"Of course she will want me. All women want me."

Jane scoffed at that. "Except for me, your cheating ex, and anyone else with higher brain functions."

"Melessa doesn't count. Neither do you, since you are inebriated and not thinking straight. Allandrina will be far more reasonable, especially since I am her only path to reclaiming her kingdom. Even if she does not like me as a person, she will like that I can give her back her crown. Trust me, we will quickly reach a mutually beneficial understanding."

"Very romantic. Use those exact words when you propose. She'll be putty in your hands."

"I am through with romance." Slade declared. "For millennia, I longed for my Eternal-One. Having found Melessa, I now realize that the tradition is highly overrated." He firmed his jaw. "My next bride will be chosen without regard to my Vampiric instincts. It will be a straightforward business arrangement between us. Like one of the shallow 'marriages' you humans have."

Jane still wasn't drunk enough to deal with him.

He frowned as she poured some more liquor. "You are part of a weaker species, Jane Squire. This much alcohol is sure to affect you. If you continue on this way, you will no doubt pass out soon."

"Here's hoping." She raised her glass in a mock toast and downed it in one swallow.

Slade's brows drew together. "You seem upset." He finally decided. "But there is no reason to despair. Our path is clear. This could be a great new start for us both."

"You're here because you're on the rebound." Jane told him. "You're trying to get over Melissa..."

"Melessa."

"Like it matters. The point is, you're having some kind of emotional crisis because you got dumped. I *haven't* got dumped. My life is just fine the way it is. I don't need a fresh start."

"I believe you do. That is why fate has brought us together."

Jane rolled her eyes. "Iverson's Grocery brought us together. Speaking of which, thanks to *you*, I have to go job hunting in the morning. Not only am I stuck on a different planet, but I'm going to be hung over for the interviews."

Focusing on her unemployment seemed preferable to dealing with the rest of this nightmare. Even if Slade went back to the store and explained that he was solely responsible for the great apple caper, odds were good that she wasn't going to be rehired. Not when she'd dealt with her unwarranted firing by punching Mr. Anderson right in his ratty little face. Damn it, this was why she didn't take risks. Whenever she did something impulsive, disaster struck.

Still, she was pissed off that Zapp Brannigan didn't even care that he'd lost her her job. Not that he seemed to care about *anything* that wasn't directly related to Slade, Sladeness, or Sladeiocity.

"You are a vital part of my quest, Jane Squire. I feel it. Our futures lie in the same direction."

"Bullshit." She turned to meet his eyes. "Why did you really drag me into this?"

Men who looked like Slade didn't strike up random conversations with women like her. Even in sappy *Lifetime* movies, the "plain" girl was always TV plain. The kind of plain where she took off her glasses and she suddenly looked like Grace Kelly. Jane was *regular* plain. The kind of plain where she took off her glasses and nothing happened, except she couldn't see. She was overlooked and passed by, because there was just nothing particularly memorable about her.

"Why did you even start talking to me, Slade?" She persisted when he remained quiet.

"I..." For the first time ever, he looked unsure. "I cannot explain it, but when I saw you, I felt as if I had... *found* you after a long search. I *know* that we must complete this journey together." He regarded her with hopeful sincerity. "All my Vampiric instincts tell me that you are important to my success."

Jane rolled her eyes. "Then we're both screwed, because I've got nothing to offer right now." She was used to taking charge, but this was *way* above her coping threshold. "I'm barely holding myself together, in case you haven't noticed."

"*I* will hold you together. You support me and I support you. That is how it should be. We are *partners* in this."

She glanced over at him, unexpectedly touched by that offer. She'd never had a partner before. It sounded almost nice.

His Caribbean blue gaze held hers steadily, sensing her hesitation. "Trust me." He urged and, for one second, she nearly bought into the fairytale.

Christ, she really was loaded.

Jane looked away and pinched the bridge of her nose. "Just leave." She ordered tiredly. She wasn't getting sucked into his insanity. She couldn't take that kind of risk. "You're a big, shiny disaster area. I'll find my own way home."

Slade sat down beside her, refusing to give up. "You are overwrought." He diagnosed in a wise tone. "It is a common ailment of lower species. If you would just heed my greater..."

"Go *away*, Slade! I'm staying right here and figuring this out alone." As usual, the only one she could count on was herself.

He blinked, amazed that she didn't want him hovering around and spreading more chaos. "You're being unreasonable." He sputtered. "You need me."

"*Need you?* For what?" Getting far away from him was the logical choice. Jesus, she was basically babysitting the big doofus. "I can get home by myself." With *him* leading the way, she'd end up retiring in this shithole dimension full of refugees from a *Monty Python* skit. God only knew what mess he'd lead them into next.

What she really needed was more liquor.

Slade's frown deepened. "You need me to look out for you, Jane Squire. You are young and entirely helpless. You have no magicks, so I do not think you fully understand the situation. Inter-dimensional travel is very difficult. It can only happen with the aid of a Witch."

"So you've said."

"Then you should *listen*. You cannot get back to your world without me finding Allandrina first. It's impossible."

"Watch me."

He sighed as if he was disappointed by her attitude. "I believe you are in denial about our circumstances. It isn't healthy."

"I'm *not* in denial. I'm well aware of the fact that you've ruined my life." She waved a hand towards the exit. "Go back to Asgard and battle Frost Giants, alright? I want no part of your crazy Stan Lee fantasies."

"There is no such world as Asgard. And Frost Giants are pleasant creatures, who I would *never* battle..."

"Would you please stop talking and just leave me alone?"

"You are supposed to be my trusty servant!"

"Then consider this my resignation!"

The two of them glowered at each other for a long moment.

Finally, Slade straightened with grave dignity. "I do not accept your resignation. As your caring and wise employer, I have no wish to upset you, though. Therefore, I have decided that you may remain in this safe and well-lighted tavern, futilely drinking to escape reality."

"That's the plan."

"Meanwhile, I shall go meet with the rebels at their hidden base and formulate the next step of our plan."

"Best of luck. I *really* mean that." She didn't mean

that.

He wasn't done. "I shall return for you in two hours."

Jane's jaw ticked. "Then I won't *be* here in two hours."

"Then I will *find* you in two hours and five minutes." He leaned in even closer, his nauseatingly handsome face serious. For once, he actually seemed like a badass Vampire King. "I am a thousand years old and the greatest tracker of my kind. No one can evade me, so don't bother to try."

"Are you threatening me, you son-of-a-bitch?"

"No. I am *protecting* you. This is a dangerous land for small humans. We must remain together."

Hang on... Did he just call her small?

Granted, Slade was massive, so *everyone* probably seemed small to him, but the unprecedented comment still mitigated her desire to drive a wooden stake through his heart. No one ever thought Jane was small.

No one ever wanted to protect her, either. In her neighborhood, life was sink or swim. Jane's parents had both split when she was a baby. She'd been raised by an elderly aunt who'd passed away when Jane was still in high school. Since childhood, she'd been looking out for herself. Some of her anger faded as she realized that Slade was actually trying to *help*. Kind of.

Jane took a deep breath and considered her options. Slade was a dick, but he was basically harmless and bizarrely fixated on keeping her with him. He also seemed pretty gullible for someone who'd been alive for ten centuries. Playing along with his lunacy was probably the best choice.

"Jane." She finally said. "Stop using my last name and just call me Jane. The 'Jane Squire' thing is annoying me."

Slade inclined his head, taking that as a victory. "Of course." His disgustingly shiny teeth gleamed in a triumphant smile. "I shall return soon, Jane. Stay here and regain your strength."

He patted her head with a condescending brush of his hand, his fingers lingering for a beat in the tangle of curls. Jane had tried every straightener on the market, but her hair was beyond help. Slade seemed to notice, damn him. His eyes stayed on the unfashionable mess, like it fascinated him.

"This journey has clearly been hard on your feeble human constitution." He murmured. His thumb absently wound through one of spirals and he let out an odd sigh.

She tried hard to ignore the feel of his palm smoothing over her unruly hair. No *way* was she drunk enough to be attracted to this jackass. She refused to be that pathetic. Jane hated him with a festering passion. She just had to keep reminding herself of that fact.

She also wasn't going to wait around this bar for him, because she was better off without the big oaf. There was no sense in *telling* him that, though. Jane gave a "Yeah, you betcha" sort of nod. "Yeah, you betcha."

Slade grinned and let his hand slip from her curls. "That is more like it! Here." He dropped a red folder on the counter. "While I am gone, peruse *From Here to Infinia* and familiarize yourself with our new kingdom. We have much to accomplish."

He headed off, satisfied that she would obediently stay put. Kings were probably used to people following orders. Four bearded men with hairy goat legs pranced after Slade, no doubt leading him towards the hidden rebel base or whatever *Star Wars* crap this "script" was plagiarizing.

Jane rubbed her temple. Against her better judgment, she flipped through the thick binder. Page after page of barely coherent sci-fi bullshit and some punk named Roland. Not to mention the Endless Woods… And the Magma Pits of Maldondorr… And the Obsidian Fortress… Who the hell had written this garbage? Christ, *From Here to Infinia* was everything wrong with modern films.

Jane slammed the folder shut, again. Maybe she *was* in denial, because no *way* could this really be happening. No *way* were Slade and some little horned guys really conspiring against a Werewolf king. No *way* was she stuck in some God-awful fantasy movie. No *way* was her only ticket home some kidnapped princess-witch who Slade wanted to seduce. Jane just wouldn't accept that this was her life, now.

No. fucking. way.

She was going back to her shoebox apartment, ordering a pizza she could no longer afford, and throwing darts at pictures of Barnabas Collins. Goddamn Vampires were *not* going to...

"Is your Vampiric master leaving with the Satyr brothers?" Tegan the bartender whispered in horror, interrupting Jane's silent pep-talk.

Jane slowly raised her eyes to look at the woman. "You did *not* just say 'Vampiric master.'" For the sake of her tip, blondie better start back-peddling.

"The Satyr brothers cannot be trusted." Tegan continued with theatrical dread. "Like all of Fang's followers, they prey on anyone who is naive enough to believe their lies. If your lord has fallen into their clutches, he is in grave danger"

"Wait..." Jane began piecing that gibberish together. "Those fuzzy guys who just left aren't rebels? They're working *for* King Werewolf?

"The Satyr brothers are mercenaries. They work only for rubies and Fang offers massive rewards for anyone who can bring him Vampires. He *hates* them. They say a strong and noble Vampire drove him from his last world. He's never forgiven their race." Tegan clutched her palms to her massive chest. "If Fang gets his hands on your handsome master, I shudder to think what he might do."

"Can you stop calling him my *master*, please?" Still, Jane found herself looking towards the door, scanning for Slade's golden head.

He was gone.

Her jaw tightened. It wasn't her problem. Jane had long ago learned to avoid unnecessary risks and Slade was *incredibly* unnecessary. What did she care if he was walking into a trap? The Vampire King was nothing but a royal pain in the ass.

Besides, he'd be fine on his own. To hear Slade tell it, he was the greatest warrior, strategist, leader, and polo player the world had ever seen. He rattled off his spectacular accomplishments by the dozen. With an ego like that, he should be able to easily pick off those chubby little imps, in between saving some elderly nuns from a fire and organizing a canned food drive for baby seals.

Except, with an ego like that, he wasn't *expecting* those chubby little imps to attack.

Slade anticipated that everyone in Infinia would welcome him as their big, blond savior. He wouldn't see the Satyr brothers' betrayal coming until it was too late. The guy might possess superpowers, but he had all the streets smarts of one of his precious forlorn kittens.

On the other hand, Jane had grown up in places like this. A little less medieval looking, but filled with the same kind of amoral opportunists. It was probably the reason she was able to at least *semi*-adjust to this craziness. Jane was a survivor. She'd never had the luxury of daydreaming about happy endings.

Prince Charming only showed up to save the *heroine* of the story. Day-players like Jane learned to save themselves.

She might be confused and panicked and not sure how this nightmare had happened, but she could quickly adapt to all kinds of bullshit. It was what kept her alive through her crappy childhood and an endless string of professional failures. She was *going* to find a way out of this mess. Jane was a pragmatist.

Slade wasn't.

If she didn't intervene, her new "boss" would be staked out in the sun by morning. Something inside of her jolted at that idea. Shit. She couldn't just let Slade die. …No matter how tempting it was.

Jane blew out an irritated breath and looked over at Tegan. "Alright, *fine*." She muttered, feeling grouchy and put upon. "Where are they taking him?"

"To the forest caves, no doubt. They often hide there." She leaned closer to Jane across the counter. "You're not planning to go after them, are you?" She sounded simultaneously enthralled and scandalized by the idea. "Perhaps, you should forget about the Vampire. Your problems don't amount to a hill of beans in Infinia."

"Oh for God's sake, that is an incorrectly quoted line

from *Casablanca*." Jane picked up the folder again and fanned through it. "Is this just one stolen movie quote after another? Is that why that stupid Elf was screeching paraphrased dialogue from *On the Waterfront* as it died?" She made a face. "That is so typical. I swear, I'm almost glad I was never cast in a major film. All modern scripts are just inferior rehashes."

"You must listen to me!" Tegan cried. "It would be suicide to follow the Satyr brothers. They are the most feared people in this whole town."

Jane tossed aside the screenplay, just tipsy enough to be dangerous. "Well, that's because no one's met *me*, yet." She polished off the last of her drink and slammed it down on the bar. "Now, which way to the caves?"

Tegan swallowed, seeing her resolve. "Follow the path. *Always* follow the path. It's the only way to get *anywhere* in the Endless Woods."

"Really? Is it made of yellow bricks?"

"Please listen. This will save your life. Don't leave the trail, because it's impossible to navigate without it. The forest is enchanted. It plays tricks on you and leads you in circles. People have been lost forever in the Endless Woods."

Jane looked around the creepy bar and snorted. "Not enough of them."

# Chapter Four

EXT. THE OBSIDIAN FORTRESS-NIGHT

ROLAND rides his horse towards massive gate, knowing that this will be his first meeting with FANG. Everything that comes later will build off of this decisive moment. The cinematography should be done from a helicopter, so we can get a feel for the grand scope of it all. ROLAND is riding fast and looking incredible. Also, he's shirtless. He draws the Silver Sword and screams FANG'S name at the glassy, black walls of the palace. It all begins now...

> ROLAND
> (Screaming)
> Fang! Come out and face me like a man, Werewolf!
> It all begins now!

> SENTRY ON WALL
> (Apologetically clearing his throat)
> Ummm... Fang's not here, kid.
> He just left.

> ROLAND
> (Confused and pissed)
> He *left?*
> He can't do that.
> We're supposed to have a confrontation!
> Damn it, this is totally fucking up my plans, dude.
> Where'd he go?

> SENTRY ON WALL
> (Shrugging)
> He's out looking for some Vampire.

*It all seems kinda weird, if you ask me.*

*Redrafted Film Script- "From Here to Infinia"*

Slade didn't have to see the woman to know she was nearby.

His heightened senses lit up whenever Jane came close. The incredible scent of her drifted passed him and his body jolted. Gods, that citrusy aroma would be the death of him. No other being smelled as good as Jane Squire. She was just a human, but something about her was unnaturally appealing.

He looked off to the left, spotting Jane peeking into the mouth of the cave. Slade was sitting around the Satyr brothers' fire, waiting for the rebels to arrive. The horned siblings were getting increasingly tense as Slade told them of his plans for Infinia. He wasn't sure what was troubling them, but their uneasy shifting was dampening the victorious mood.

The sight of Jane lifted his spirits.

Slade had been torn about leaving her alone in the tavern earlier. On the one hand, everything Vampire within him had revolted at the idea of letting her out of his sight. On the other hand, he could clearly see that Jane was close to the breaking point. Inter-dimensional travel had been more difficult for her than he'd imagined. If Slade had tried to force her to come with him to meet the rebels, she might have bolted.

He didn't want that.

Even if he could've quickly tracked her down after she fled, Slade wanted her to stay with him because she believed in him. More and more, his Dark Instincts told him that Jane Squire was vital to his epic destiny. That he couldn't succeed without her. That he'd been led to that dreary grocery store for some greater purpose. He couldn't explain it, but the feeling was growing stronger. Keeping Jane happy was paramount. So, he'd reluctantly allowed her to stay behind in the safety of the bar and now she'd come to her senses, rejoining his journey.

She was moving closer, quietly edging towards him like she didn't want to be spotted by the men drinking from tankards. When she realized she had his attention, she put a silencing finger to her lips and made an emphatic "Get over here!" gesture with her free palm, still staying hidden from the others.

The woman was so odd.

But --Christ-- he'd missed her in the hour they'd been separated.

Slade had never actually missed anyone before and the feeling was uncomfortable. It was wrong to desire his second-in-command. Their working relationship would suffer. Rationally he knew that, but his Dark Instincts didn't care. They just wanted to drown in the tart fragrance of her hair and the infinite color of her stormy eyes. The longer he was around Jane Squire, the more insistent their wanting became. Never had his Dark Instincts been so hard to ignore.

It was also difficult to ignore the rocks hitting him.

Pebbles rained down when Slade didn't move fast enough to suit her purposes. Jane Squire delighted in heaving small objects at him. She had no idea how a subordinate was supposed to act.

"Jane, what are you doing?" He demanded, rubbing a sore spot on his skull. "Stop pelting me with stones and come sit by the fire."

Jane Squire's palm slapped against her forehead in frustration.

All four Satyr brothers turned to look at her, their beady eyes narrowing. "Who's that?" Cal hissed. Or possibly it was Hal. Or Val. Or Al. All four of them looked identical, so it was hard to tell.

"That is my second-in-command, Jane Squire." Slade waved her forward. "Welcome, Jane. We are discussing our battle strategy. What know you of Werewolf weapons?"

She stepped forward, staring up at the ceiling like she was praying for patience. "Werewolf weapons?" She said tightly. "Not much. But at least you still have the golf clubs.

They're *bound* to come in handy. God only knows when your rebel forces might need to caddy for you."

"That's true." He patted the bag beside him. "I don't think golf clubs are made of silver, though." He turned back at the Satyr brothers. "Are golf clubs made of silver?"

The four goat-men exchanged confused glances, like they had no idea what to say to that perfectly clear question. They often looked that way when Slade spoke.

"I was being *sarcastic*, Slade. Do they look like fucking golfers to you?" Jane snapped. "Why do you even still have that stupid bag?"

"Amalie told me it will be useful and I trust her word. She is a powerful witch."

Jane let out an agitated breath, like she was trying to calm down. "We need to talk." She bit-off in an exaggeratedly level tone. "Like *a lot*."

"Of course!" He smiled at her, pleased that she always called him "Slade." Most beings addressed him as "your majesty" or "King Slade," as was proper with underlings. But Jane was his *friend*. He enjoyed the fact that she used his given name. Her voice gave it a sultry sound that fed into his bloodstream. "I am always eager to hear your ideas." He patted the rock next to him. "Come here."

"I meant alone." She persisted with a determined expression on her face. "You and me. Outside. *Alone*."

"Yes, but..."

"*Now*."

Several of the brothers frowned at each other, apparently concerned that a mere servant would speak to their new monarch in such a disrespectful way. Slade understood their feelings, but he was too content to care about Jane's continued impertinence. The insecurities that had plagued him of late went silent when she was beside him. Jane was the one person he was totally sure of. She would guide him to his destiny. He knew it.

Plus, she smelled *incredible*.

"Uh, Vampire." Hal or possibly Al began in a worried voice. "I mean, *King* Vampire. I don't think it's such a good idea for you to leave. Stay here and let us make you an offer you can't refuse."

Jane made a scoffing sound. "Jesus, if this becomes some kind of *Godfather* porno, you're on your own, Slade."

He wasn't sure what to make of that or of Hal/Al's proposition. "It's fine, minion." Slade assured the man. "Wait here." He bounded over to Jane, even though he should've moved at a more aloof and regal pace. He'd *missed* her while they were separated. How did she make him miss her so much? And was he going crazy or did she not look so plain in the moonlight?

"What did you wish to speak about?" He lowered his voice. "Women troubles?"

"Get over here, you gigantic moron." Jane seized hold of his arm and tugged him into the night. "Have you completely lost what little mind you have?" The cave was set on a small incline. The golf clubs clattered as she dragged him down the hill.

"No, I..."

Jane herded him passed the tree line, so they were hidden from view. "Did you ever consider that the strange men who pick you up in bars *aren't* people you want to go home with? Huh?" She gestured back towards the cave. "You can't trust them. They're working for the Werewolf. And --Jesus-- I cannot *believe* I just said that."

Slade's eyebrows compressed. "No. The Satyr brothers support the rebels. They wish to defeat Fang and help me claim the throne. They are very interested in my plans to unite Infinia."

"Says who? Them? Because the half-naked bartender says they're notorious bad guys. They've lured you here to sell your pretty, empty head to that Fang guy's soldiers."

Slade considered that possibility. "You believe she's right?"

"Yes! It's *easy* to believe people are rotten, because they always fucking *are*."

"That's not true." Slade found it sad that she'd say such a thing. Jane Squire was too young to be so cynical.

"Most people are good. Not as intrinsically honorable as Vampires, but…"

Jane interrupted him. She did that a lot. "You're so naive, you shouldn't be allowed to roam free in the world." She jabbed a finger at him. "For whatever reason, I seem to be stuck with you, so just do what I say, alright? We're *leaving*."

Slade crossed his arms over his chest. "You're being unduly suspicious. The Satyr brothers are our first link to the rebels. If we abandon them, how will we begin our quest?"

"It won't be much of a quest if you're dead."

Slade shook his head. "I cannot allow pessimism and fear to influence my choices. This is my *destiny*."

"King Slade?" One of the Satyr brothers called from the cave's entrance. It might have been Val. "Where are you? Why don't you come back inside and buckle your saddle belt? It's going to be a bumpy night."

Slade turned to answer him, but Jane slapped a hand over his mouth. "Don't you dare." She warned. "At least it's not Brando this time, but *All About Eve* should still sue them for screwing up that quote so badly. It just sounds ominous and sleazy."

Slade couldn't think of a single response to that. The feel of Jane's fingers over his lips sent a fire flickering through his system that shorted out his brain. He blinked at her, stunned by the passion that ignited when their skin met. The instant heat was like nothing he'd ever experienced. He had to shift his hips to hide the intensity of his reaction. If she was a Witch, he'd swear that she'd cast a spell on him. The lust he felt for her was spiraling out of control and all she'd done was touch him.

Jane yanked her hand back and gave her head a clearing shake. "Okay." She swallowed hard. "Right. Look… The brothers are tricking you." She dropped her gaze like she was uncomfortable with the way Slade was staring at her. "Can't you see that?"

Slade tried to concentrate on her words, but it was nearly impossible. Did she feel the heat between them, too? How could she miss it? He had to clear his throat before he could talk. "Success can only come through risk, Jane."

"You know what else comes through risk? *Death*. Taking risks is almost always a bad idea."

Slade slowly shook his head. "You're wrong." He said simply. "Unless you take risks, you'll never have anything that matters."

Jane looked at him again, studying his grave face. "Okay, we'll try this another way." She gave him a tight smile. "You think I'm your loyal sidekick, right?"

"You are my most trusted friend." He agreed. His Dark Instincts had more faith in Jane Squire than he'd ever had in anyone. He had no idea why, but he didn't question it.

"Then listen to me." She leaned closer to him. "We're trapped in some cheap knock-off of *Willow*. And *Willow* was *already* kind of a knock-off. If we're going to survive this crappy movie, we need to be smart. Now, I don't have your experience at potentate- ing, but I doubt the current ruler is looking for any kingly competition. Fang isn't going to welcome you with open arms."

It was hard to dispute that logic. "Werewolves are so selfish."

"The point is, stealing his crown won't be easy." She shook her head. "And don't you think this all seems *way* too easy? You just walk in a bar and some random hooved guys are instantly setting you up on a date with the super-secret underground? Even for a movie, that's too big a coincidence."

Slade pondered that. He hated to admit it, but Jane Squire made a small bit of sense. Obviously, the people of this land would be thrilled to have him as their majestic leader. But Fang's henchmen would be everywhere, trying to stop Slade's ascension with all sorts of chicanery. It never paid to underestimate the duplicity and avarice of his enemies. Perhaps he should…

Jane suddenly grabbed his arm, again. "Get down." She tugged him lower, ducking behind a strange shrub with bright orange berries shaped like dominos.

The woman enjoyed manhandling him, but Slade didn't mind. In fact, it just made him think of *other* ways she could touch his body.  Wicked, hot, wonderful ways… Jane inspired very un-gentlemanly thoughts about kings and pretty little servant girls.  He'd never had those kinds of fantasies before, but with Jane his mind was filled with all sorts of startling new ideas.

"You see?"  She hissed at him, oblivious to the fact he was picturing her fingers stroking every inch of his skin.  "I *knew* it was a set-up."

"What?"  Slade dragged his attention away from her and blinked over at the clearing.

Armed soldiers began arriving, carrying massive swords and obsidian shields.  Riding beasts that looked like a cross between a rhinoceros and a dinosaur, they thundered closer.  With wart-covered skin and hideous, oversized bodies, the men could only be Goblins.  The species was amoral and dangerous, often hiring on as mercenaries.  Moving down the wide path, they surrounded the hill.

Slade's eyes narrowed when he saw the howling wolf painted on their armor.  These were no rebels.  These men fought for Fang.  Slade recognized the dreaded insignia, which had struck fear into the hearts of beings throughout his former homeland.

Jane was right.  This was a set-up.

"If we don't live through this, I told you so."  She muttered.  "Remember that."

Slade ignored her complaints, quickly running through battle scenarios.  His first instinct was to attack the Goblins.  Even greatly outnumbered, he could sweep the field.  He'd done it before.  If something went wrong, though, he'd leave Jane all alone at the mercy of their enemies.  He might have lectured Jane on the importance of taking risks, but even a one percent chance of endangering her was too big a gamble.

That feeling of purpose returned, so different than his uncomplicated desire to rule Infinia.  Keeping the small human beside him safe trumped his need for a quick victory.  Slade put a hand on her shoulder, easing her behind him.

Jane looked up at him in surprise, like she wasn't used to being protected.

In the clearing, one rider pulled away from the others. From the golden regalia on his uniform and the enchanted creature he was riding, he was clearly the leader of the group. He removed his helmet, glossy black hair falling to his wide shoulders. "Where is the Vampire?" He demanded in a deep voice.

Even from the distance separating them, Slade could see the lupine yellow of his eyes and the savage angles of his face. There was no mistaking his old enemy. "Fang." He snarled.

"He's here, your highness." Al or Val called from the mouth of the cave, his voice shrill and nervous. "He just stepped out for a moment."

"Holy buckets." Jane breathed. "*That's* Fang? Because... *wow*."

Slade flashed her a glare.

"Oh come on. *Look* at him." She pointed towards the false king. "You know he's gorgeous. I mean, it kind of makes sense actually. If this place is supposed to be some lousy film, of *course* the human-ish characters are going to be Hollywood beautiful. Even Tegan the bartender looked like a *Playboy* centerfold."

Slade didn't have a clear recollection of that woman and he had no idea what *Playboy* was. He also didn't care. He glowered down at Jane, angered at her disloyalty.

She questioned his status as handsomest Vampire ever born, yet she drooled over that mangy dog? He wasn't sure why that surprised him. Wolves were irresistible to women, as Melessa had so graphically proved in the royal bathtub. For some reason, Jane's interest in Fang pissed him off even more than his ex-wife's affair.

"You cannot *seriously* find that animal attractive."

"I have eyes, don't I?" Jane arched a brow. "For real, are you sure your prospective fiancée isn't *happy* being held prisoner? There's probably a line of princesses waiting to be kidnapped by that guy."

"You're still drunk." Slade decided. "Fang is as hideous outside as he is within."

"Keep telling yourself that."

"The Vampire *stepped out*." Fang repeated in a dangerous tone. "You mean you *lost* him." The Werewolf dismounted from his irritatingly lovely mount and swept forward, his black cape billowing. "You let him escape."

"And is Fang really riding a unicorn?" Jane asked quietly.

Slade made an annoyed face. "It's a pegasus." Not even Slade had ever owned such an exquisite animal. The beautiful creature was pure white, with glossimer wings and the unmistakable look of a thoroughbred. It made Slade miss his own mighty steeds. He really should have had a better lawyer in the divorce.

"The Vampire didn't escape, King Fang." Val or Al stuttered out. "A human woman came and asked to speak with him. He just went outside to talk to her. He'll be back any moment. He would have to be crazy to wander off into the Endless Woods."

"You furry fool." Fang spat. "You let some bitch steal the Vampire right out from under you?!"

Jane's eyes narrowed. "Okay, you're right. I'm suddenly thinking this guy's a dick."

"I am Slade, King of the Vampires. I'm always right." Still, he was delighted to hear her come to her senses. "And Werewolves are *always* dicks. It's one of the reasons they hate Vampires. We are popular and likable, while they are the cruelest and most deceitful creatures in the supernatural world."

"Not that you're biased or anything."

Fang stalked up the small hill, his boots crunching on the gravel. "Fan out and locate them." He ordered. "Do what you want with the woman, but I want the Vampire alive. We need to discover if more of his kind are in hiding. Fucking Vampires won't contaminate my land." He scowled out into the darkness, like he was trying to see through the dense trees. "And don't underestimate him. This bloodsucker has already killed a dozen Wood Elves."

"It was fifteen." Slade told Jane smugly.

"Yeah, but a couple of them were mine." She watched Fang with deepening concern. "Can he --like-- sniff us out or something?"

"Only in his wolf form. When he shape-shifts, he possesses heightened senses."

She looked up at the sky. "Does he need a full moon?"

"No, of course not." The woman clearly knew nothing of Werewolves. "Just the night. He will not change in front of his men, though. The transition leaves him vulnerable for several moments."

"I can find him, sire." One of the other Satyr brothers interjected. "King Slade couldn't have gone far off the path…"

Fang cut him off. "Slade?" He echoed, his eyes narrowing into slits. "The Vampire is named *Slade?*"

"*King* Slade. He repeated it about fifty times." Cal or Hal muttered. "We found him in the Drunken Dragon Tavern, rambling about how he was going to take over the kingdom. The dude's a weirdo. If we just wait a few hours, it will be sunrise and he'll have to…"

"*Find him!*" Fang roared, whirling back to his men. "I don't care what it takes, you find Slade and you bring him to me! *Now!*"

"I think he remembers you." Jane muttered. "Only people who've met you can get that pissed." She tugged on his sleeve. "We should go."

Slade hated to retreat, but she had a point. Without the Silver Sword, he could not yet kill Fang and staying here longer would endanger Jane. This was a war, not a single battle. "Head into the woods." He couldn't stop himself from running a hand over her amazing toffee-colored hair. "I'm right behind you."

"Good. Then *you* can take the first hail of bullets as they chase after us. Or arrows or whatever the hell they use in this dump." She headed through the forest, her ponytail bouncing.

No one followed them.

The Endless Woods were a vast place and they no longer had the path to guide them. It became a maze of trees.

Slade and Jane walked ceaselessly without seeing anything but strange looking foliage. Sometimes he thought they'd passed the same area several times, but he couldn't be sure. Even his Vampiric senses were affected by the woods. He didn't know which direction they were traveling in.

Hours passed. Slade watched the shadows move across the undergrowth, gauging the time. The unidentified Satyr brother had been correct about the dawn. It was approaching far too quickly. Vampires couldn't be in the daylight for more than a few moments without burning to cinders. Slade was going to need to find shelter soon.

"Would this be a bad time to tell you that we weren't supposed to leave the path?" Jane batted aside a branch with leaves that spilled down like cooked pasta. "I think that's why we got away so easily. No one else was dumb enough to come in here."

"You mean no one else was *brave* enough."

"No, I mean *dumb*. Tegan said these woods are dangerous. That it's impossible to find your way without the trail."

"A Vampire can find his way through any amount of danger."

"Can you find your way through any amount of *trees?* Because that would be awesome."

Slade disregarded her snarking. As leader of their quest, it was up to him to keep up morale. "My Grandmother is one of the universe's greatest warriors and prophets." He announced.

Jane did not seem inspired. "You mean the cat-lady grandma?"

"Yes. Granted, Dawnyah-Zanabriah is a shape shifter from beyond the stars and not a biological Vampire, but she fears nothing and this aids her in her endless string of victories. We must follow her example and press onward."

"Didn't she help exile you from your island? If we're following her example, the *getting rid of you* part is what I'd like to emulate." Jane arched a brow. "Hey, what made her side with Melessa in the break-up, anyhow? I mean aside from the fact that everyone who's ever met you seems to hate your guts."

"I do not know." Just thinking about Grandma Dawn's unexpected betrayal irritated him. Why *had* she sided with Melessa? The question triggered all his secret doubts. Slade tried hard to be a worthy king, but he always seemed to fall short. "And barely anyone hates my guts." He muttered, although he wasn't sure that was true. "Most people adore me."

"Which is why we're on the run from all your many admirers."

The woman was difficult to motivate. Slade cast around for another way to boost Jane's spirits and to change the subject. Discussing his lack of popularity depressed him. More importantly, dwelling on the fact that everyone else had left him might encourage Jane to leave, too. That was the last thing he wanted.

"So… Do you happen to have any anti-Werewolf talismans on you?" He ventured. It seemed like a far safer topic.

Jane fixed him with a flat look. "Shit." She deadpanned. "They're all in my other wizard's hat."

Slade took that as a "no." "You really should not leave your home without the proper talismans, Jane. They are as imperative as shoes and swords." He unfastened his silver bracelet and held it out to her. The treasury of the Vampire Isle held untold riches, but this piece was the one he always wore. It hadn't left his wrist in over a century. "Here. You will wear this."

Jane wrinkled her nose at the elaborate piece of jewelry. Thick links were hammered together, covered with engravings of dead Wolves and triumphant Vampires. "It's hideous." She announced.

"It's an amulet to repel Werewolves. It is not meant to be pretty." Since she didn't seem eager to put it on, Slade did it for her. The massive chain was big on her hand, but he felt a jolt of unexpected pleasure at the sight of it on her arm.

Jane seemed less delighted. She glowered down at the

bracelet and then at him. "Whatever." She grumbled.

...But she didn't take it off.

Slade found himself smiling. Knowing Jane Squire, she would've thrown the talisman into the weeds if she didn't secretly like his gift. Maybe she sensed the same thing Slade did: The bracelet belonged to her. In an odd way, he felt as if he'd been wearing it for so long because he'd been waiting for this moment. Waiting to give it to her. Waiting *for* her.

"That bracelet was given to me by the Merpeople of the Hidden Lake." He said proudly.

"Merpeople of the Hidden Lake?" She echoed. "Jesus. Your autobiography must read like a *NeverEnding Story* fan-fic. Especially, the *never ending* part."

Slade wasn't sure what that meant, but he doubted it was a compliment. "My epic tale is all true." He insisted, seeing her doubt. "The Merpeople are an enchanted race. Few ever look upon them, but they *do* exist."

"If you say so."

"I *do* say so. You see, I had defeated a legion of monstrous bats, which had been sweeping in and picking off their young. The Merpeople bestowed that amulet upon me as a symbol of their thanks." He paused. "They also offered me my choice of their most beautiful women as my bride."

"How thoughtful."

"Of course, I turned them down. I was awaiting my Eternal-One. Not even a topless Mermaid could tempt me to marry another." He grunted at how stupid he'd been. "Had I known Melessa was the destined bride awaiting me, I surely would have accepted the comely Mermaid and enjoyed her underwater agility."

"Look, I'm sobering up and it's hurting my head to listen to your weird stories, so..."

Something moved in the thick brush beside them, cutting her off. Before Slade could call warning to Jane, they were surrounded by a dozen warriors in green camouflage. Not that a warning much mattered. Armed with wooden spears and slingshots, they weren't a particularly intimidating force.

"What the hell is this now?" Jane demanded.

"Frigging Ewoks?"

"Are you free citizens of this land or slaves to that bastard Fang?" One of the men demanded, waving his homemade weapon around like a flyswatter.

"Surrender or die!" Another one squawked in a voice that would've been more threatening if it was three octaves deeper and not shaking in terror.

Jane rolled her eyes towards the heavens. "Tell me these twerps aren't the rebels."

Slade smiled over at her. "Splendid news, Jane. We've found my army."

# Chapter Five

## BACKGROUND NOTES ON THE REBELS' MOTIVATIONS

The rebels are motivated by various stuff. Probably. And other stuff. And lots of assorted whatever.

Seriously, this part is a waste of time.

These nobodies probably want *something*, but does anybody really care about what it is? They're just supposed to be the dead bodies on the battlefield that Fang steps over to show us what a badass he is. It's not like they actually matter. In fact, we should probably just skip all their whining and do this whole next part as a training montage.

Or a musical number!

*Redrafted Film Script- "From Here to Infinia"*


Apparently, *From Here to Infinia* had some kind of "innovative soundtrack" thing going on. A minstrel-y version of *We're Not Gonna Take It* blared as Slade and Jane were led into the rebel village. Even *Dracula, Ph.D.* had more dignity than this crappy film. Also, the plot made more sense. And the sets were better.

The rebels' secret forest hideout looked exactly like filmdom's secret forest hideouts *always* looked. Lots of little huts with straw roofs and wooden walkways spanning the trees. *From Here to Infinia* had plagiarized the backlot from every Robin Hood movie ever made. And --of course-- the second-rate Merry Men clones populating the unimaginative village were dirty, supernatural looking, and liked jabbing pointy sticks at Slade and Jane.

It was seriously pissing her off.

The Vampire genius beside her didn't seem to notice that anything was amiss. Slade smiled broadly, walking through the village like he owned every tree. Probably because he thought he *did*. "Greetings, peasants." He stopped in the center of Jungleville and looked around. "Be at ease. I have come to lead you."

*That* was sure to win them over.

"We have no leader here." One brave soul piped up. "Not yet, anyway."

It was hard to tell which of the rebels was talking. Extras were always pretty faceless. Jane knew that firsthand. She'd been an Under-Five most of her career. For some reason the lack of respect for her fellow day players suddenly annoyed her. Couldn't *From Here to Infinia* at least focus on the kid talking? Didn't everyone deserve some of the spotlight?

"We are awaiting someone strong enough to take charge of our glorious mission to defeat Fang." Some other random villager added. Or maybe it was the same guy. It was impossible to be sure. "*He* will be our leader."

"Well, your long wait is over." Prince Valiant assured the huddled mass of nonspeaking parts. "I have arrived." He posed with his hands heroically planted on his hips. "I am Slade, King of the Vampires, and this is my second-in-command, Jane Squire. We shall guide you to victory."

Jane rolled her eyes as the rebels all turned to look at her. "Hi, how are ya?" She muttered and leaned closer to Slade. "We have to get out of here before they eat us or something." She whispered fiercely. "I think that kid over there was in *Deliverance*. Trust me, *From Here to Infinia* is bad enough. You *don't* want to wander into *Deliverance*."

Banjo kid smirked at her.

"Worry not, Jane." Slade surveyed the rebels with the same confidence the captain of the *Titanic* must have felt just before that iceberg attacked. "I know how to inspire troops."

"Oh obviously. That's why you're still ruling the Vampire Isle."

He slanted her an irritated look.

Jane almost smiled. It was probably the horror of the situation affecting her mind, but Slade was cute when he glowered. Hell, he was *always* cute. If she was stuck in this Alan Smithee nightmare at least she had someone pretty to look at. Someone who wasn't *that* horrible to be around, all things considered.

Jane was a loner by nature, but Slade's presence wasn't *quite* as suffocating as she would've thought. Even when he was irritating her, he was still kind of amusing. And it was nice to have somebody to talk to, for a change.

Sometimes, her life got a *little* lonely. Jane could admit that. Being independent was safer, but it meant she lived with a lot of silence. There was no such thing as silence when Slade was around. In fact, Jane hadn't felt lonely even once since she'd met the King of the Vampires. He was always very, very *there*. Talking, and smiling, and taking up space with his shininess.

And she'd *never* had anyone pay so much attention to her before. Not ever. At first, she'd assumed Slade watched *everybody* with the same level of interest he aimed at her, but... he didn't. The longer she was with him, the more Jane saw that it was just *her* he focused on with an off-the-scales amount of glowing blue concentration. Like she was *important* to him. It was sort of disconcerting. Jane wasn't used to that kind of intensity being aimed her way. She was supposed to be a background character and Slade was born to be the star. Didn't he understand that?

"How do we know he's not a spy for the Werewolf?" A token woman rebel demanded. Every fantasy movie needed some poor girl dressed in a fur bikini, after all. "Fang will stop at nothing to crush us. We all know that. I stood against him and he killed my parents in retaliation. He kills the bakers who smuggle us bread and the barkeeps who send us mead. He even kills the priests who bury the victims he slaughters. Would he stop at sending a Vampire into our midst?"

"He refused to let my fiancée marry me." Someone else called. "Instead, he took her for himself and then threw her from the roof of the Obsidian Fortress when she resisted."

"Fang burned my house down, with all my children inside." Another man agreed. "He locked the door and lit the match, with a smile on his face. His men held me back as my babies screamed for me."

Holy *shit*.

Jane looked around as more rebels shouted out their Werewolf horror stories. Tears and anger and terrible blank expressions filled the crowd. As ridiculous as *From Here to Infinia* was, the people here actually felt the suffering Fang inflicted on them. Their anguish was genuine.

For the first time, Jane realized that this place was *real*. It wasn't just a film. Fang was actually torturing people. *Real* people. And he was so powerful that no one in this whole kingdom could stop him.

Except...

Her gaze very slowly traveled over to Slade. Back in reality, the idea of a hero was complete bullshit. She believed that with every pragmatic bone in her body. But when she looked at this big, shiny Vampire, it was very hard to remember that logic even existed.

"I am not in league with Fang." Slade said, his eyes on the rebels. "I will kill him and save Infinia. I am meant to be king of this land and you are meant to follow me."

"If you seek to lead us, then you must prove your worth." A guy with feathers interjected. Fifteen hours in makeup and this was probably his only line in the film. "You must enter... The Cage." He swept a wing towards a large enclosure that seemed to be constructed out of crisscrossed tree limbs and human skulls. "You must defeat ten of our bravest warriors at once."

"Eleven men enter. One man leaves." The crowd obediently chanted.

Oh Jesus. They were ripping-off *Beyond Thunderdome*. That was just the final straw. Technically, Infinia might be real, but it was also a pain in the ass.

"No." Jane snapped, grabbing hold of Slade's arm before he could agree to this lunacy. "Don't even *think* about it. Yeah, fine, *Mad Max*-era Mel Gibson was hot, but all remakes suck. It's like a law. You can't get in that cage and beat up ten men."

Slade scoffed at that. "Of course I can. Look how small they are."

The man was unbelievable. "Someone will get seriously hurt, Slade!"

"Well, unless they possess a blue diamond blade, that 'someone' will not be me." He arched a brow, when Jane blinked at him. "Have I not explained that Vampires are quite hardy? Only enchanted blue diamonds can kill us in a fight. The weapons can cut through magicks, but they are rare and expensive for peasants to buy, so there is no need to be concerned for me."

"I'm not concerned for *you*, idiot." She waved aside the Vampire biology lesson. "My point is, reenacting *Battle Royale* is a terrible way to win support for your cause. If you want the rebels on your side, you can't get their loyalty through force. Aren't you listening to their stories? They've seen enough bloodshed."

They hadn't, however, seen enough singing.

To Jane's horror, at least half of the assembled rebels launched into an elaborate dance routine. Even Slade's eyebrows soared as they spun around in complicated choreographed kick lines, flipping and sweeping through the forest. Yeah... definitely the "innovative soundtrack" thing. The song was a ridiculously modern pop confection about their rage towards the cage in an age of drage. What the fuck was "drage?" Were they just making up words now?

She shook her head in utter disgust and glared up at Slade. "Great. Now we're in a musical number. You see what you did?"

"I did not cause this! I merely wanted to prove my valor by killing some warriors. How else will they be convinced to follow me?"

"Why don't you try *talking* to them? It would certainly beat the singing, don't you think?"

Slade seemed confused by the idea. "Talking?"

"Yes! Explain why you're a better choice for monarch than the Werewolf. How hard could that be? They already detest Fang and you're," she waved a hand up and down Slade's perfect form, "*you*. Go campaign for the job, like a normal person."

"I do not know how to *campaign* to peasants." He shifted out of the way of a breakdancing Gremlin, looking doubtful about this whole idea. "I have never had to convince anyone to follow me before. They just *did* it. I was born with a crown and they respected my exalted position. That is the system I prefer."

"Do you have amnesia or something?" Jane's character on *Dracula, Ph.D.* had a storyline about a forgotten husband, so Jane knew the symptoms. "Your last group of 'respectful' peasants overthrew you, remember?"

"That was an aberration." Slade insisted stubbornly.

"An aberration? The whole Vampire Isle dumped your ass, even your grandmother the cat. You told me so yourself."

Slade's expression darkened, even as multicolored lizard-people pirouetted past. "You don't need to remind me of my grandmother's treachery. All my life, she was the one I trusted most. She was *always* in my corner. But, in the end, Grandma Dawn turned against me and helped banish me from my homeland. I don't even know why."

Jane paused, considering Slade's uncharacteristically bitter words. It occurred to her that his unflagging confidence hid a lot of hurt and doubts. How could it not? Everyone really *had* turned against this guy. Slade's own family had sided with his cheating wife in the divorce. It had to be hard for him to swallow that kind of betrayal, especially when he seemed to be loyal to the point of stupidity.

"Why did your grandmother…?"

Slade cut her off. "I do not wish to discuss Grandma Dawn. None of that is relevant to this situation. The rebels *wish* me to fight. It is their custom. I understand that you have a soft heart and do not wish me to destroy…"

"I do *not* have a soft heart."

Slade's mouth twitched as though he found her

indignant interruption adorable. "Yes, you do." He said quietly. "It is why you are here."

Jane resisted the urge to slug Conan in his soft head. "I *don't*. I'm a pragmatic, bitchy, cynical person. Everybody who's ever met me knows that. And I'm being completely rational about this. *You're* the one not thinking straight."

"Nonsense. I am being eminently rational. With the sun coming up, we do not have time to waste on protracted negotiations. Gaining power will be far easier if I kill a few rebels and prove I am the strongest."

She raised her voice so he could hear her over the music. How in the hell did they have electric guitar riffs in a world without electricity? "Do you want them to follow you because you're strong or because you're *right?*"

"I am Slade, King of the Vampires. I'm always right."

The urge to hit him was almost irresistible now. "Would you just shut up and listen? Intimidation is a terrible way to run a kingdom. Fang seized control through killing. Is that who you are, too? Someone who scares people into obedience?"

His head tilted, his expression going gentle. "I would *never* harm you." He vowed, as if he thought that must be her concern. "I have no desire to force your compliance. That would gain me nothing. I want you to stay with me willingly." One large palm came up to touch her hair and he gave a strange sigh as the curls slipped through his fingers. "I want you to *want* to be with me, Jane."

Jane should've batted his hand away. It was the sensible thing to do and she was a sensible girl. Instead, she shifted closer to him, her whole body tingling. It was always like that. The guy generated some kind of electricity that zinged through her whenever they touched. She knew it was a bad idea, but she couldn't bring herself to break the contact.

His thumb briefly brushed across her cheek. "I would do whatever you ask, if you'd only choose to remain at my side." He whispered. "I want you to *like* me, Jane."

She did like him.

Shit. Why the hell would she like such a lunatic? It

was an even stupider idea than the rebels building a cage and wanting them to participate in the Seventy-Sixth Annual Hunger Games. No possible good could come from sticking with Slade and she was smart enough to know it. So why wasn't she running for the hills?

Maybe she was still drunk.

"I'm not worried that you'll hurt me. Not like that." Jane shook her head, breaking the spell. "Look, I won't help a king unless he's fair to *everyone* in his kingdom. Even the unbilled peasants. These extras are the ones suffering and they should have some say in the story."

Slade stared down at her for a long beat and Jane felt her insides dip. As much as she should run away from the lunatic, she could seriously get used to the way he looked at her. Slade might be actively working to ruin her life, but he watched Jane like she was the only thing that could *save* his.

The dance number ended with a dynamic flourish of random fireworks. Confetti drifted down from someplace. The music crescendoed and the rebels all stopped in "ta-da!" poses, like they were expecting thunderous applause.

Jane and Slade ignored them.

"You will help me?" He sorted through her statement and came up with the one part that interested him. "*Really* help me? With no more angrily sitting at bars or slipping away when my back is turned?"

"I never tried to sneak away. I just threatened it. In fact, when you were in trouble, I came looking for you. I've been pretty damn helpful so far, buddy. I'm even wearing this ugly bracelet without complaint." She held up the anti-Werewolf accessory, even though she kinda *had* been complaining about the damn thing.

A lot.

"But you are not yet committed to our journey." Slade clarified. "I feel like you are just looking for an opportunity to leave me."

Probably because she *was*. The Vampire did his best to hide it, but he wasn't a *total* moron. "Tell me why I should stay, then." Jane arched a brow. "Why should I follow you?"

"Because you wish Allandrina to send you back to your gloomy world and I am going to marry the woman."

The reminder of Slade's princess didn't improve her mood. "Not good enough. I've *met* you. I figure there's only a fifty/fifty shot of this girl being dumb enough to say 'I do.' I don't like that kind of risk."

"You seem to dislike *all* risks."

"Because, I'm not an idiot. And the smart money says I can hire a Witch easier than I can take over a kingdom. This is a fantasy movie and fantasy movies *love* Witches. There *has* to be some scantily-clad enchantress wandering around Bartertown." She leaned closer to him. "So, if you want me to spend even one more hour in a land without potato chips, *Variety*, and tampons, tell me *why* you're worth taking a chance on. Why should the rebels and I vote Team Slade? Convince us. Convince *me*."

Slade angled his jaw at the challenge and turned back to the rebels. They didn't seem to know what to do now that the music had stopped. Aside from more scattered calls of "Eleven men enter. One man leaves," the whole army was silently waiting for them to finish their argument. Why wouldn't they? It wasn't like they had storylines of their own to worry about. They were just the red shirts who died in the trenches, while the stars preened at center stage.

"I will not fight in the Cage." Slade declared, brushing passed the feathered guy. "Neither will any of you. Today, we begin anew."

That line sure as hell hadn't been in the script. "What?" Chicken Man squawked. "Wait, you can't…"

Slade ignored that and stepped up on the wooden platform where the Middle Ages' version of *Twisted Sister* waited for their next cue. The music died away and Slade stood there like he was spotlighted on Broadway. Dawn began to peek through the clouds, washing him in an otherworldly glow. No lighting tech could've created that effect. It was as if the sun was shining down multicolored beams of magic just for Slade. If the dim rays burned him, he didn't show it. Instead, he braced his legs apart and looked out at the rebels.

"I am Slade, King of the Vampires." He announced loudly. "And I know what it is to have my home stolen from me."

Just that quickly, he won the crowd.

The rebels stopped chanting for the Cage and started listening like Slade was delivering the Gettysburg Address. Clearly, no one had ever bothered *talking* to them before. Their awe would've been annoying, except Jane sort of understood their reaction. It wasn't so much Slade's words as it was his *presence*. It was like he knew everything you'd been through and now he was there to help solve all your problems. Two sentences into his speech and Slade was already the greatest public speaker she'd ever seen. Any political party would have sacrificed small children to have this guy on their ticket.

"I know what it is to be cast aside." He continued, his voice echoing through the woods. "To be hated. To be forced from your old life and thrown onto the mercy of fate." He paused. "To be alone."

Jane couldn't have looked away if her life depended on it.

"All of us are the same here. We are all unwanted and forsaken." He shook his head. "But we are not beaten, or hiding, or prepared to give into our fears. *All* heroes must struggle. It is what makes them great. And, friends, *we* are the heroes of this tale. *We* are the ones who wish to make this world better. And we are just *beginning* our destinies."

People started nodding.

Even a pragmatist like Jane could feel the electric pull of Slade's optimism. It was like hope and shininess came together to create this one perfect savior of the downtrodden. Slade's face reflected confidence, and strength, and so many *ideas* that you wanted to join his crusade without even knowing where he was headed.

"The paths we *intended* to walk would not have led us to this point, it's true. But I do not question the wisdom of the gods. *This* was where we were needed and *this* is where we must fight." His gaze glowed with absolute sincerity. "You've heard the stories of Fang's cruelty. People here are suffering and scared. If justice for all the citizens of Infinia matters to you," he looked straight at Jane, "then you *must* help them. You must help *me*. It is who you are."

"You son of a bitch..." She whispered, seeing where this was headed.

"If you think a king should be fair to peasants and lords alike, then you *must* do all in your power to overthrow the Werewolf. Would you turn your back on misery, because it is safer? Would you allow a monster to kill the innocent, because you fear the risk?" Slade arched a brow. "No. I think you are so much braver than that."

Jane stared at him and knew he'd just fucked up her whole life.

"There is a deeper purpose at work, bringing us together." Slade made an emphatic gesture with his hand. "I believe that. We are here, because our old lives were stifling all we are truly meant for. We were *chosen* to save this world. And we must do it *together*."

The rebels gave a brief cheer and Slade glanced at them in surprise. Maybe he'd forgotten they were there. The speech was aimed at Jane.

"*Together*." Slade repeated, more forcefully. "Together, we shall overthrow Fang. Together, we shall free Infinia. Together, we shall build *new* homes and a *new* kingdom for the people we love. You are not faceless extras in this story." He looked right at Jane. "You *are* the story. This is our legend and we are writing it *right now*. Together."

Against her better judgment, she felt her lips curve.

Slade's eyes gleamed, seeing that she appreciated that line. "It will not be easy. Great quests never are. But I ask that you join me in building a better future. The future we were meant to have. The future you deserve." His gaze stayed locked on hers. "Stay with me and you will not be sorry. I swear it."

In that second, Jane saw the truth. She gazed up at the lunatic in front of her and knew that he really *was* a king. His destiny *was* huge and important. Slade was the star of this film.

Not because he was good looking or charismatic, but because he believed that he could solve all of Infinia's problems before the credits rolled. He was asking her to save this whole stupid world, because he believed they were the only ones who could do it.

    And he was right.

    Crap.

    Jane let out a long sigh.  She wasn't going home today.

# Chapter Six

INT. OBSIDIAN FORTRESS- DAY

Open with a tracking shot along a sinister corridor of the palace. The forbidding Obsidian Fortress looks like Castle Grayskull mixed with the Death Star. The rest of Infinia is terrified of the place and with good reason: Its owner is a mean, dangerous, (but super-hot) Werewolf. All sorts of creatures cower in the darkened corners, fearful of FANG'S wrath. Some of them are crying. Some are praying. There's a close-up of a scared baby covering its eyes.

Then we see FANG. He's looking super-hot and majorly pissed. Ominous music plays, something with BIG sound and BIG drums and maybe some creepy chanting. (Note: We should definitely hire JOHN WILLIAMS to write an evil sounding score for this part.) FANG approaches a hidden door ...and the scene fades to black, leaving the audience wondering what this super-hot villain is planning next.

*Redrafted Film Script- "From Here to Infinia"*

How the fuck could Slade still be alive?

Fang had thought that bloodsucking bastard was long dead. Surely *someone* would have killed him, by now. Most likely Damien or one of Slade's own idiot followers. The list of possibilities was endless, though. That Vampire was the most annoying, arrogant, meddlesome asshole ever born. There should have been a line around the block of supernatural beings waiting their turn to behead that douchebag. Instead, he was wandering free in Infinia, gathering more followers by the day.

Fang slammed through the echoing hallways of the Obsidian Fortress, his cape billowing behind him.  The entire palace was constructed of glassy black rocks.  It loomed over the green lands of Infinia like a tombstone.  Jagged and dark, it was designed to intimidate the weak followers of this weak land.  It showed them who was boss.

No one crossed the Werewolf King.  Lately, even his own men were wise enough to stay out of Fang's way.  He'd already executed a dozen of them just for being nearby.  When he was feeling testy, he needed an outlet for his frustrations and the Goblins were suitably breakable.  But after his justifiable burst of pique had left sixteen of them torn apart by wild dogs, he had his emotions back under control.

All of this just went to show that if you wanted something done right, you had to do it yourself.  Slade had ruined Fang's last homeland, but he wasn't going to get away with it again.  This time, Fang would see the Vampire dead and his stupid, blond head on a pike.  Since no one else was up to the task of defeating that bastard, Fang would personally perform the honors.

He looked forward to it.

For nearly a week, he'd been scouring the Endless Woods for any sign of Slade and he'd come up empty, though.  That ludicrously attired ass-hat had vanished.  No matter how many underlings Fang sent into the woods, there was still no trace of the Vampire.  In fact, there was very little trace of the underlings.  The infinite stretch of trees swallowed everyone who left the path.

But Fang knew Slade was still out there.  Plotting.  Pontificating.  Planning to steal his throne.  If he was going to defeat the Vampire, it was clear that more drastic methods were needed.

Fang checked to make sure he wasn't being followed and then stepped into a stone alcove.  Shoving aside a delightfully morbid tapestry featuring a wolf howling at a blood red moon, he opened a hidden door and headed down a concealed staircase.  Torches lined the walls, casting eerie shadows on the mirrored surface of the walls, as he descended into the bowels of the palace.

The Obsidian Fortress had been built on top of Infinia's most sacred spot. Fang was a big believer in choosing a home based on location, location, location. For generations, the Light Fairies harnessed the energy in the caverns, but they'd fled now. He had to make do with far less skilled assistance, so it was taking *forever* to discover the ancient spells. Werewolves weren't known for their patience.

"Did you find Slade, yet?" He demanded, slamming into the large chamber at the base of the stairs. It was the heart of the Fairies' magicks. The walls were made of thick, semitransparent crystal. It glowed with an aurora borealis of power; brilliant colors shifting deep within the white stone. It was said that all possible futures could be foretold in the patterns, if you knew how to translate them.

The Dark Fairy looked away from the changing colors. "I don't know his location, but he still lives."

Fang already knew that. Why was he paying this evil bitch to tell him things he already knew? Well, besides the fact that Fairies were the most beautiful of all supernatural beings.

He glowered in annoyance, but his body was already responding to the sight of her. With waist length golden hair and deep brown eyes, she looked like most of her kind. Except her angelic face held an underlying viciousness and her smile was all cruel edges. Dark Fairies and Werewolves often worked together, but this woman was particularly gifted at evil. He should probably try to remember her name, but it didn't matter. Her job was to help him control Infinia and to provide a warm body.

She gave him a knowing look, sensing his lust.

"You've seen nothing else?" He snapped. "Nothing at all to help us defeat Slade?"

She glided closer, covered in nothing but an ethereal blue robe. "Why do you worry so about this Vampire? You've killed so many of his kind, sire."

Fang shook his head, because she still didn't understand. "He isn't like the others. Slade is an overconfident, self-righteous idiot. But he *inspires* people.

That makes him the most dangerous kind of enemy."

"How so?" She untied the fastening of her robe, letting it fall to the ground. The woman spent more time naked than clothed. The ancient power in the cavern aroused everyone who entered the space and she seemed to thrive on the mindless lust. In the corners of the room, Cave Elves stirred. They were her sexual playthings and they scurried closer at the promise of a new game.

Fang let out a hissing breath as one of them dropped to its knees before her. Its wide mouth found the junction of her thighs and began lapping at her juices. Her head went back with an erotic moan, but her eyes stayed on Fang. She liked to tease.

Fang was so turned on by the sight that he didn't even protest when another Elf crouched before him. Spindly hands unfastened his belt and began massaging his erection. Ordinarily, he wouldn't allow such a low creature to touch him. Elves were just mindless servants, after all. But this room amplified sexual urgency and drove him towards release.

"Slade gets into people's heads with his naive jabber. He convinces them to risk all on hopeless dreams." The Elf sucked the hard length of him into its mouth and Fang's jaw clenched. "Slade's real power is his goddamn *optimism*."

"Then we'll find him and publically execute the optimism right out of his body." She whispered as the Elves worshiped at her body. "Show everyone who the real king of Infinia is."

"Soon it will be too late for that. The Vampires here are dead and forgotten, but if Slade survives much longer, he'll rally other beings to his side." Fang shoved deeper into the Elf's mouth, ruthlessly uninterested in its cry of protest. "His death will just make him a martyr. It will drive the rebellion to even greater heights."

"Well, then we'll have to break him. He must possess a weakness." The Dark Fairy bit her lower lip as more Elves cupped her naked breasts. Squeezing them hard enough to leave red marks. Offering them to Fang. "We just need to discover what he cannot survive without... and take it from him."

Fang slowly grinned. He pushed the whimpering Elf aside and crossed to the Dark Fairy. "Slade has a woman." He reported, because he'd already thought along similar lines. "A human."

As soon as it was safe, Fang had turned into his wolf-form to search for Slade's trail himself. He dared not go far into the Endless Woods, so he'd quickly reached an impasse. But he'd scented the woman and the fragrance of her still lingered in his mind. It was tainted and mixed with the Vampire's stench, but there was still something... *appealing* about the human's citrusy smell. Something that raced from Fang's nostrils straight down to his cock.

"Is she his Eternal-One?" The Dark Fairy asked in concern. "If he regains his soul, it could increase his power."

"He hasn't bonded with the woman," Fang would know if Slade had claimed her, "but those moronic brothers said Slade was fascinated by the human." Fang couldn't recall the siblings' names. He'd never been very good at caring what other people called themselves. Most of them simply didn't matter. "They said that he followed her like a puppy. That he seemed to *need* her."

"Need a *human?* Why would a Vampire need something so ordinary?"

"Not all humans are ordinary." Fang's eyes skimmed over the Dark Fairy's lamentably straight hair. The Whatever-They-Were-Called siblings had said Slade's woman possessed a headful of erotic toffee-colored curls. He couldn't get the image of them out of his mind. Why should the Vampire own such a gift? "Mortal women definitely have their advantages."

The Dark Fairy wasn't convinced. "Are you sure the Satyrs weren't lying about the Vampire's attachment to her?"

*That* was their name. Or it had been anyway.

"No one lies when they're on the rack. All four of the brothers told the same story before they died." Fang spun her around so she faced the crystal wall, gripping her neck and forcing her to bend over. He moved in behind her. "Slade cares for the human. She's his weakness, so we'll find her and steal her away."

The Fairy arched her hips back to rub against his pulsing erection. "And what horrific things will you do with this woman once you possess her?" She asked in a breathless voice.

Fang lowered his lips to her ear. "Do you want me to show you?"

"Oh yes." She loved pain. "Show me now and then, when I watch you do it to her, I'll know just how that bitch is suffering." His palm settled over her slim throat, squeezing tight, even as he slammed into her from behind. She cried out at the fierce invasion and tried to buck him off. "The human will fight you." She panted, trying to escape his grasp, just to piss him off. "It's their nature."

Fang quickly shoved her back into place, holding her still with his weight. In his mind, she was becoming the one he wanted. Her struggles sent his desire into overdrive. He would pin Slade's human beneath him, until the fight slowly faded and she accepted that she couldn't escape. Until he did every nasty thing he wanted to her small body. Until the gray eyes he'd heard about looked up at him, acknowledging him as her master.

The Fairy whimpered in submission and he nearly came, imagining the sound came from…

"Jane." He usually forgot all names, but the human's stuck in his mind. Already, he knew that it was special. *She* was special. Gods, he *wanted* her to fight, so he could make her submit. "Her name is Jane Squire."

The translucent stones of the cavern glowed brighter at the words.

The woman's brows drew together as if the sudden lightshow surprised her. She tried to pull back, watching the movement of color within the pale rocks. "Jane Squire's destiny is tied to the Vampire." She whispered. "I see it."

Fang couldn't have been happier to hear that. He pushed the Fairy back into position, so he didn't have to see her face and ruin the fantasy that he was taking *Jane* from behind. Slade's sweet-smelling woman at his mercy… Her luscious hair fisted in his hand… Her soft flesh vulnerable to his every twisted desire... Her voice panting his name and promising obedience...

The idea moved through his bloodstream like electricity. Fang's lust grew so intense that he knew he wouldn't be able to fully sate it until he took Jane in every position possible and a few that hadn't been invented, yet. He groaned, picturing the human's gleaming curls and desperate cries. She would beg and struggle and then finally relent to his demands. Meekly following his orders. Doing whatever he commanded. Bent to his will.

"Jane Squire does not come from this world." The Dark Fairy's gaze stayed on the mystical rocks. "Her land --Her *Chicago*-- is wondrous."

Fang barely heard the woman's yammering. "Jane." He ground out, pounding into the Fairy harder. Faster. Just saying the exotic name nearly sent him over the edge. "Jane." His grip tightened, wanting to punish the imposter in front of him. He could have any woman in the kingdom, but they all stank compared to the scent of Slade's human. *She* was the one he wanted. "Jane, Jane, Jane, *Jane*..."

He'd never seen the point in drawing out sex to please his partner, so it only took him a moment to finish. The Dark Fairy turned to glare at him as he came deep inside of her. Fang didn't care about her pleasure. She could find release with her Cave Elves later. They were all watching the heartless sex, desperate to join in the depravity. Fang had more important matters to deal with. He shoved the woman away, already forgetting about the interlude.

She glowered at him in irritation. "Frankly, my dear, I don't give a damn what the human calls herself. I just want her found." She gestured to the shifting patterns in the wall. "Slade cannot succeed without her."

"I know." Fang didn't need any mystical quartz to tell him that. He could *feel* it. From the second he'd smelled her, his instincts had told him that Jane Squire was the key. "Once she's in my possession, Slade is finished."

"In your possession?" The woman echoed. "Why take the chance on letting her live any longer than you have to? If we just kill her, Slade's quest is sure to fail. It's the smart play"

Fang had no intention of killing the human until he'd tied her to his bed and fucked Slade's scent right off her body. He was already getting hard again, imagining it. "How many wars have *you* won?" He adjusted his pants. "I know what I'm doing and I know the Vampire. He can't just *lose* the woman. We have to *take* her from him. That will destroy him."

The Dark Fairy rolled her eyes. "Fine. Then it's time you stopped screwing around and sent the big guns into the forest." She leaned closer to him. "Call in the Mages."

Fang considered the idea. "There is only one member of the Order left."

"You only need one, if it's the right one. They helped you eradicate Infinia's Vampire population once before and they will do it again. Send the last Mage into the Endless Woods. Make it *impossible* for Slade and Jane Squire to hide from your justice."

Fang slowly smiled. "Jane Squire will not hide for long." He agreed softly. "Her fate might be tied to Slade... but it will *end* with me."

# Chapter Seven

INT. MEGA-MYSTICAL DISCOUNT MAGICK SHOP- DAY

ROLAND bursts into store, his handsome face set into determined lines. He senses that something has derailed his epic quest. FANG is too busy obsessing over SLADE to even care about ROLAND vowing to kill him. No one is rallying to aid ROLAND'S cause. Even the other band members are pissing him off. JAMES THE ORC wants to rename the group "The Vampyre's Bytches" for Christ's sake! How are they supposed to get chicks with a name like *that?*

ROLAND isn't sure what he's supposed to do next, but he's gotta think of something. Visiting the WIZENED ENCHANTRESS' shop might help him find answers. The old woman sells questionable Magicks at reasonable prices.

WIZENED ENCHANTRESS
(Looking up at Roland enters)
Store hours are three to midnight, boy. You know Infinia conducts business at night.

ROLAND
I don't have time to wait. Some Vampire named Slade is stealing my life. Do you have any anti-Vampires spells around here? Maybe some potions that the Mages used to hunt them? Something that could --like-- send a guy into a mystical coma for a couple centuries?

WIZENED ENCHANTRESS
(Shrewdly)
Blood of another Vampire will incapacitate him. And fortunately for you, I'm having a sale on the stuff. Inject the

Vampire with a vial and it'll buy you time to stab him in the heart with a blue diamond blade.
Blue diamond blades kill Vampires better than anything.
You got one of them?

ROLAND
(Uncomfortably tugging on his ear as he takes the vial of blood)
Yeah, I traded an amp for it last year, 'cause I thought it would be a cool album cover.
It's hanging on the wall of my shop.

WIZENED ENCHANTRESS
Then you're all set, aren't ya?
That'll be fifty-two gold pieces for the Vampire blood and the free advice.
And I don't take checks.

*Redrafted Film Script- "From Here to Infinia"*

      Seven days of living in Sherwood Forest with Slade had taught Jane several valuable lessons.
      One: The good citizens of Infinia definitely needed a new king. She'd known that Fang was evil, but the guy was straight out of a Freddy Kruger film. One after another, people told of being oppressed and tortured by the Werewolf. Families torn apart. Towns burned. Innocent miscellaneous beings slaughtered. It was no wonder the rebels were looking at Slade like he was some kind of savior. Any king would be better than Fang.
      Although --lesson two-- Slade had probably been an okay ruler of that stupid Vampire Isle. Jane saw the way the rebels reacted to him. As soon as he'd finished that speech, they were treating him as their leader. Granted he *told* them he was there leader... but they *believed* it. Why wouldn't they? *Slade* certainly believed it. He was already setting their rickety

village aright; organizing training for the "soldiers" and schools for the kids. Every idea he had, the people jumped to make a reality.

Slade considered it all his due. He was so sure of his path. So damn idealistic and passionate about everything. He could sway people with just the irrepressible force of his personality.

...And his amazing good looks. In fact, the guy's off-the-charts handsomeness was becoming kind of a distraction. More and more, Jane found herself forgetting that Slade was an irritating maniac and just noticing that he was so damn *shiny* it burned her eyes.

And that he was kind of sweet.

And not quite so dumb as he seemed.

And that he *occasionally* made her laugh.

Jane blew out an aggravated breath. She didn't need any big, Vampire-shaped complications in her life. It was a lot easier to just focus on valuable lesson number three: Life without indoor plumbing sucked.

Jane stood under the freezing deluge of the waterfall and missed her lousy apartment's lousy shower. Even three minutes of hot water was better than none and there was *none* here in Infinia. It was no wonder half the population chose smelliness. Jane refused to give up bathing, so the frigid waterfall was her only choice.

The damn thing was at least a hundred feet high, so she couldn't stand directly underneath of it, but there were small off-shoots that worked well enough. The force of the cold water beat against her skin. Miserable as the temperature was, the surroundings were surprisingly picturesque. The Endless Woods was so green and nature-y. Everywhere she looked, it was like a National Park. Trees and rocks and clear, clean streams. It wasn't the *worst* place in the world to be lost.

Except Jane wasn't *in* the world. At least not *her* world. She was stranded in some crazy fantasyland, without water heaters.

She got through with her icy shower as quickly as possible, wrapping a blanket around her shivering body. She also refused to wear the Renaissance Faire clothing that seemed to be all the rage in Infinia this season, so she was stuck washing her khakis and Iversons' polo shirt again and again. They were still drying, which meant she was dressed in a toga for the next hour or so. Not that it mattered. Every single woman in this dimension was prettier, thinner, and way more ogle-worthy than Jane, so no one was going to try and sneak any peeks at her naked body.

Thinking naked thoughts just made her think of Slade, which pissed her off.

Damn it, she was *not* falling for that Vampire.

And why was the sun already going down? Jane glowered at the sky, as she headed up the path that led to the top of the waterfall and back to camp. Night was falling, again. The last of the warming rays faded behind the clouds. It was only light for about two hours a day in Infinia and that was her one Slade-free time. He had to stay inside when the sun was up. Otherwise, he was right beside her and she was getting way too used to his company.

They had to get out of the Endless Woods, before she forgot she detested the guy.

They couldn't defeat Fang and end this madness until they escaped from the forest. Jane had read that idiotic screenplay cover to cover at least a dozen times, though, and it didn't give any helpful maps pointing to an exit. The script really didn't mention much of *anything* important. Just a lot of questing and "my lording" and some bullshit about a Silver Sword.

Worse, it seemed to be... changing.

Every time she flipped through the pages, the words were a little different. Events shifted. New dialogue popped up. Old dialogue vanished. Roland starred in fewer and fewer scenes. It was like *From Here to Infinia* was being rewritten right before her eyes. She had to assume it was because of Slade. Infinia's derivative characters just couldn't compete with the Once and Future Vampire King. He'd begun appearing in the text, taking over the story just by being himself.

It was *Slade's* movie, now.

Jane wasn't sure whether that was a good thing or not. No one liked to be upstaged and Roland was kind of a whiner. He didn't appreciate Slade stealing the spotlight. Not to mention Fang. Except for some creepy sex montages with a Dark Fairy, most of his scenes were suddenly happening off-screen. She had no idea what he was up to. That worried her.

Jane needed to get home. Not that her miserable apartment really counted as a "home." Jane had never actually had a *real* home. But if she was ever going to see her lovely tenement again, Roland had to butt out of this story and Fang needed to die a Hollywood villain death. Then, Slade could marry Alla-ka-whozits and Jane could be alakazamed back to her real life.

So why was at least one step of that plan beginning to bug the hell out of her? She reached the top of the waterfall, wondering if she was losing her mind.

"Jane Squire!" Slade came bounding over, ducking through the trees and she was actually happy to see him. So yeah. *Definitely* losing her mind. "*There* you are! I awoke with many new ideas to share with…" He stopped short, as he caught sight of her. "Dear gods!" Caribbean blue eyes swept up and down her blanket-wrapped form. "You cannot be walking around like that, woman!"

"Why not?" She demanded testily. Picturing his wedded bliss with Princess Pinup put her in a lousy mood. And it wasn't like anyone here cared much about dressing for dinner. She was pretty sure they were having squirrel.

Again.

"*Why not?*" Slade repeated incredulously. "Because you're not wearing anything!"

"Please. This blanket covers so much even my Aunt Maybelline would've approved."

Slade didn't seem to hear that. His gaze went down to her bare feet, then jerked up to her completely covered chest and lingered for a beat. He gave his head a quick shake and looked over his shoulder, as if all sorts of spies could be lurking in the brush. "You must put your normal clothes back on. Scandalous as they are, they are far better than this."

Jane was starting to get annoyed. Every day, she had to hear him complain about "unseemly" pants and now this. "What would you know about 'normal' clothes?" She demanded. "You always dress like you're about to swashbuckle something."

Slade was wearing his usual open-throated, cover-of-a-romance-novel pirate shirt. No doubt laundry nymphs or washer-witches or some other idiotic, lovesick women fell all over themselves to clean it for him every day. Tonight, he'd added a sweeping, black coat to his ensemble, which topped off the whole *should've*-been-stupid-looking look.

…Except it wasn't stupid looking.

If God ever punished the world and allowed *From Here to Infinia* to be made into an actual movie, this was the exact outfit Slade should wear on the poster. No one could look as good as he did. It just wasn't fair, damn it.

He wasn't done bitching about her lack of fashion sense. "You must find other attire. Even your normal clothes are preferable. They are indecently alluring, but they are far better than *this*. You will tempt the men in the village even more than you usually do."

"Oh, you've *got* to be kidding me." Every word of that statement was crazier than the last and, considering Slade was the wellspring of all craziness, that was *really* saying something. "No one will even notice me with all the Miss America candidates around here. I promise you." Jane rolled her eyes and started past him. "I'm not sure what your deal is, but my clothes are wet and I'm not wearing a costume from *Camelot*, so…"

Jane stopped short when she ran straight into his huge chest. Slade had shifted into her path, so she couldn't get by.

Her eyes flashed up to his in surprise, no longer feeling cold. Heat spread through her system like a cyclone of fire. Being so close to him sent her heart pounding and had her breath catching in her throat. Slade's body pressed against hers and suddenly she saw his point about the blanket. Jane could feel the strength of him right through the fabric. She swallowed hard, staring up at him.

Blue eyes burned into hers, his jaw tight.

Holy Jesus, he was pretty.

Jane had never experienced anything like the helpless pull she felt towards Slade. He was unnaturally, impossibly, amazingly gorgeous. That was certainly part of the problem. But he was also a *fucking Vampir*e, and a crown-obsessed lunatic, and he'd ruined her life. All of that would trump good looks, if his face was his main attraction.

There was something deeper at work between her and Slade. Something that kept dragging her into his orbit, even when she knew it was a terrible idea.

"Jane." He whispered, like he felt it, too.

Which wasn't damn likely, since he was Prince Charming and she was the girl no one invited to the ball.

Jane jerked back, her eyes falling from his perfect face and settling on some random tree. For a desperate moment she cast around for something to say. Nothing brilliant sprang to mind, so she went back to the stupid blanket.

"Alright. Give me your coat." She finally relented, because she was willing to wear just about anything if it got her away from him faster. She couldn't think when Slade was so close.

"My coat?" He repeated, as if he'd never heard the words before. The guy seemed a little dazed. He stepped forward, closing the distance between them like he was on auto-pilot to get closer to her. "Why do you want…?

She cut him off, backing up another step. "Just give it to me."

She was close enough to the edge of the waterfall that Slade froze. He held up his palms, apparently worried that any sudden movements might frighten her into doing something stupid. "Jane, please be careful." He whispered. "The rocks are slippery and humans are far too breakable. I will give you whatever you desire, just do not fall."

"I'm *fine*." She glanced over her shoulder and winced a bit at the ledge directly behind her. Shit. That was quite a drop. She quickly looked away, again. "Look, I'll take off the blanket and put on your off-to-fight-a-duel-for-the-heroine's-fair-hand coat, instead. Will that soothe your offended sensibilities, Tim Gunn?"

Slade ignored her waspish tone. "So... you'll don my clothing?" He translated slowly, edging away to give her more room.

"Just until my stuff is dry. Alright? Problem solved." She stepped forward and breathed a sigh of relief to be on more solid ground. "Come on, hand it over." She gave her fingers an impatient snap.

Jane wasn't very surprised when he obediently shrugged it off. Slade was always a gentleman, even when she was bossing him around. Sometimes it was easy to believe that he'd been born in another time, when manners and chivalrous conduct mattered.

"I am pleased with the idea of you wearing something I own." He decided. "It is a strange sensation, but it feels... right." His voice grew softer. "Many things feel right when I am with you, Jane."

She refused to respond to that. Jane was a pragmatist. All the "rightness" he felt would fade real fast when he slipped a massive diamond onto Allandrina's manicured hand and won himself a kingdom. The thought made her teeth grind together.

"I'm not going to put the coat on with you watching, idiot." Jane made a "turn around" motion with her finger. "Turn around."

Slade obediently faced the other way and cleared his throat. "I sought you out because I had a new idea on how to defeat Fang that I wanted to discuss." He said, as if he wanted to fill the silence.

"Thrilling." Jane muttered.

"Yes, it's a very brilliant and complex stratagem. We -- uh-- must pour over each detail so we can...uh..." He trailed off, losing his train of thought. "So... Are you *completely* naked under that quilt?"

The man was unbelievable. "Is that something a king should be asking me?" Jane demanded.

"No! Of course not." He cleared his throat, again. "I apologize. It was an inappropriate comment to make to a lady."

"Uh-huh." His jacket was warm and comfortable and smelled like him. She should have stuck with the blanket. This was like being wrapped up in Slade's arms and that was the last thing she needed to cool her desire. "Just tell me your stupid plan to get us out of here." She grumbled. It wasn't his fault that she was so pitifully, helplessly attracted to him, but she still couldn't stop herself from glowering at the back of his head.

Jackass.

"Oh. Yes." He seemed to rally at bit. "Well, I was thinking of how we could defeat Fang. And it occurred to me that we should try to gain the Silver Sword."

"The Silver Sword that *Roland* has, you mean? Given to him by the Dying Old Knight Guy, as part of his prophesized fate or whatever?"

"Yes, the very one."

"Right. And you think Roland is just going to hand that over to you, huh?"

"Why wouldn't he? I am clearly the best candidate to defeat Fang. We shall find this boy. He will see my innate glory and incredible leadership qualities. Then he will give me the sword, so you and I can complete our grand task."

Jane couldn't believe that anyone was so clueless about human nature. She rolled her eyes and buttoned up the last of the coat's buttons. The damn thing fit her like a shroud, so he was sure to be happy. Even the ugly bracelet was better than this and she had no clue why she was even still wearing that hideous hunk of metal. For some reason she'd rather not examine too closely, she hadn't taken it off since he'd given it to her. She wasn't feeling so disgustingly sentimental about the coat.

She tied the belt with agitated movements and hoped the jacket didn't make her look as fat as she already *knew* it did. "Slade, no way is Roland just going to surrender Infinia's crown to you, no matter how awesome you are."

"I *am* vastly awesome." He agreed, because of *course* that's how he'd interpret that statement. "It is good of you to notice."

She tried again. "Roland's supposed to be the star of the movie. He's not going to want to give that up."

"Oh, Roland will surely do what's best for this kingdom. We just need to explain things to him and he will realize that *I* am the one destined for this glorious quest." Apparently feeling that he'd given her enough time to change, Slade turned back around. He smiled in satisfaction when he saw her dressed in his jacket. "This is *much* better." He decided. "See? You need and I provide. All is how it should be, no?"

"No, all is *not* as it should be, because I'm still stuck here in *World of Warcraft*. When all is as it *should* be, I'll be back in reality and the only Vampires in my life will be reruns of *Buffy*." She stalked around him and this time he let her pass.

"How can your mind still dwell on that silly realm of yours? I do not understand it. It is a world without heroes." Slade shook his head in annoyance and fell into step beside her. "No matter. You will come to your senses once we have the Silver Sword. Fang will be defeated and *then* all will be as it should be."

"Uh-huh." There was no sense arguing with him. Nothing she said would change his mind. Slade was stubborn as a mule when it came to that "destiny" bullshit. "Alright, so if you think my only way home is through Roland, then we'll have to find Roland. How do you propose we do that? We can't exactly walk out of this forest. It's a maze, remember?"

"Of course, I remember." He said, taking her literally. "But all mazes have a solution. We shall just have to work harder to find a way out. The rebels *must* know of one."

"They say they don't." She arched a brow. "And I believe them, given the fact that they're still here and not --you know-- *anywhere* else. Also, they're morons."

Slade flashed her a disapproving frown. "You should not insult our subjects, Jane."

"*Your* subjects. Not *my* subjects. I just work here." She rolled up the cuffs of his coat, trying to uncover her fingers. "Besides, it's not an insult if it's true. They're morons. More importantly, the screenplay says no one escapes the Endless

Woods once they enter. It repeats the line --like-- forty times. So, I don't see how we're going to just walk out of here."

"I dislike that cinema script. It lacks literary merit. I feel it best that we ignore the limitations it attempts to place upon us and blaze a path for ourselves."

Jane snorted. "Very inspirational."

It actually *was* a little encouraging. Slade would never, ever give up. It wasn't in his nature. The guy would keep charging ahead until he got *exactly* what he wanted. So far his crazy self-confidence had helped him travel across dimensions, put him on the shortlist for a supernatural crown, and won him the hearts and minds of the Infinian rebels. He would figure out a way to escape this forest, if only because he was eager for his climactic battle scene to begin.

Slade glanced down at her. "And you do not '*just work here*.'" He corrected. "I could not do any of this without you, Jane. We are partners." Vacation-poster-blue eyes regarded her earnestly. He *always* looked enthralled and intense and nauseatingly perfect. It was like he lived his eternal life basking in a permanent close-up. "Can you not feel the connection between us? Our fates are intertwined."

Jane scoffed at that idea, because what else *could* she do? Admit that she was becoming more and more attached to Kull the Conqueror? What would that get her, when she was standing in the unemployment line and Slade was married to his magical princess? "'Our fates are intertwined?'" She repeated. "Jesus, I already bought your little campaign speech. Let's not go overboard."

"It is the truth. We were brought together through providence. The sooner you accept that, the sooner you will be able to concentrate on our mission."

"Trust me, being stuck in the Wizarding World of Harry Potter has my full attention, alright? Just as soon as we can book a flight out of this forest and find Roland, I will be..."

He cut her off in confusion. "Book a flight?" He repeated. "I am unfamiliar with this tome."

"Not 'book' like a *book*. 'Book' like a *plane ticket*." From his blank look, she was guessing the Wright Brothers soared over Kitty Hawke post-1893. "We could fly out of here," she rephrased bluntly, "except we can't fly."

Slade made a dismissive sound. "Don't be silly, Jane Squire…"

"I'm not being silly. People in my time have machines that can…"

He kept talking right over her. "…Of course, I can fly."

Jane stopped short. "Huh?" She turned to look at him. "Wait, *what* did you just say?" She must have heard that wrong.

"I said of *course* I can fly. I am a Vampire, after all. It is one of our many gifts. For instance, we can use supernatural powers to shield ourselves from enemies, we are nearly impossible to kill, we are wonderful dancers, and sometimes we can teleport."

Jane stared at him. "And you can fly."

"And I can fly."

"So you could get above those trees," she pointed at the dense leaves over their heads, "and see which way we should go?"

Slade looked up. "Well… yes." He admitted.

Jane released a calming breath, trying not to scream. "I see. And you *haven't* done this yet, because…?" She let her voice trail off questioningly. As if maybe there was some *halfway reasonable explanation* for why he hadn't gotten them out of this damn forest days ago. As if that didn't solve one of their biggest problems. As if she wasn't two seconds away from beating him to death with a rock. "Did you not think of that?"

"I *did* think of it and I *can* fly." Slade explained. "But I can't fly, *right now*. It is a very taxing power and I am not at full strength."

"You look healthy to me." Massive understatement. She forced herself not to get distracted by his *overwhelming* healthy looking-ness. No small task, considering he was so fucking shiny it burned her eyes.

Jane sighed in frustration as they marched back through the rebel village. It still looked like Tarzan's summer place. There wasn't much she could do to change the idiotic set, although she'd certainly tried. She made sure Slade banned all the musical numbers and *Thunderdome* crap. No more Fred Astaire-ing and no more pointless MMA-fighting in cages made of branches and bones. Neither decision had gone over well, although no one bothered to blame Slade. The villagers waved, and smiled, and genuflected at him like he was Superman.

No one waved, and smiled, and genuflected at Jane.

She wasn't surprised. Slade was definitely the "good cop" half of their partnership. The villagers tended to watch Jane warily, possibly because she was always the one pointing out the obvious flaws in their rebellion. For instance, that their "weapons" were just sticks, which would have absolutely no effect on a Werewolf, and their "plans" *weren't* plans, because they never got around to actually planning anything except dinner.

Which was always squirrel.

Jane didn't worry about winning over the townsfolk, though. Slade was the one who dreamed of being Yertle, King of the Turtles. Jane just wanted to make sure the two of them survived his ascension. That was all that mattered.

...Oh, alright fine. It *also* mattered if the dorky rebels survived. That was kind of why she'd agreed to help, after all. She didn't want the villagers dead, which was exactly what would happen if they went after Fang without thinking. *From Here to Infinia* didn't care about people whose characters didn't even have names. Who would miss "Dirty Peasant Number 3" or "Screaming Woman in Hut?"

*Someone* had to look after the extras of this world and it looked like that someone was Jane. This might be a movie back in reality, but, here in Infinia, everything was *real*. It had taken her awhile to fully accept it, but it was the truth. This place was *real*. These people were *real*. And she needed to give them their best shot at survival.

Jane knew what it was to be an expendable part of the cast.

No one got killed off for dramatic effect in her film. She didn't care if it raised the stakes for the main cast or if these villagers weren't exactly going to change the world, *every* life meant something. *Everyone* contributed to the story. *Everyone* got a speaking part.

Even the stupid people.

For the past week, Jane had been preaching restraint, which seemed to baffle the brain trust of rebels. Especially since Slade listened to her and not them. For all his *numerous* failings, the Vampire consistently took her advice over everyone else's. Every decision he made, he ran past her. Jane's logical objections to suicide missions, and Slade's acquiescence to her complaints, frustrated the more hotheaded villagers. Now that they had a leader for their army, they were ready to ride to the Obsidian Fortress and throw rotten fruit at the gate. Jane stubbornly insisted that they come up with an idea that had a chance in hell of working.

Step one would be getting out of this damn forest.

"King Slade!" A bowtied Gnome popped his head out of a hut. He was *From Here to Infinia*'s "madcap scientist" character, forever creating anachronisms and eye-rolling stupidity. "The first phase of testing went better than expected. My wooden robots will be ready for the field in no time."

"Excellent work, Symon." Slade gave him an enthusiastic thumbs-up. "I knew you could do it."

Symon nodded happily and disappeared back into his workshop, which was somehow powered by a solar panel that he'd somehow made from leaves.

Slade glanced at Jane. "What is a wooden robot?" He asked in a quieter tone.

"I told you, I'm not dealing with Symon. Every fantasy movie has some guy with white hair and glasses who invented proto-steampunk bullshit. It's cheap and I refuse to engage." She shook her head and got back to business. "Now, what do you need to be at full Vampire strength and fly? Like kryptonite or something?" Or wait, that drained strength, didn't it?

"I haven't eaten in over a week." Slade shrugged, as if it was obvious. "I will have to feed."

Jane looked over at him. "On… blood?" She guessed, wrinkling her nose.

"Yes. Vampires need human blood to survive. Or the blood from our Eternal-One." He paused briefly to give an autograph to a beaming little boy with red horns. Slade tousled the kid's hair and glanced back at Jane. "Even if Melessa was in this dimension, I would not drink from her, though. So, human blood is the only option."

Jane tried to think of it like a specialized diet. Kind of like someone with a wheat allergy or who had to eat extra protein. "Well, I'm sure there are a ton of people around here who would be happy to open a vein for you. Just try not to kill them or turn them into Vampires, because…"

"I would never kill someone I feed from." He interrupted, sounding insulted. "And a bite alone isn't enough to convert someone to Vampirism."

"If you say so."

"I *do* say so." He paused. "There is a problem, though."

"What a surprise." Slade was nothing but one huge complication after another. "You know what? Don't even tell me about it. Vampire rules make my brain hurt."

Slade ignored that and told her anyway. "When a Vampire bites someone, the human experiences it like an aphrodisiac." He shrugged. "It is why I only bite women."

Jane blinked. "You sleep with the girls as you drain their blood? That is so frigging kinky. And not in a good way."

He began to look exasperated with her. "I do not sleep with them. They just inevitably find it pleasurable. If I were to bite one of the female rebels, her mate would be… unhappy with the results. Women find me nearly irresistible, even when I don't bite them. After I taste their blood, they are forever smitten with me."

Jane *really* wished she could argue with that narcissistic statement. It was hard to miss the truth of it, though. Especially when a woman with scales and neon yellow hair swooned at the very sight of him. The twit squealed his name like something out of *Bye Bye Birdie* and then collapsed to the ground in ecstasy. Her fellow yellow-haired creatures tried to bring her around. Well, the ones who weren't blowing kisses at Slade, anyway.

"Here's looking at you, King!" One of them shouted.

"Come up and see me sometime." Another offered in her best Mae West voice.

"Hasta la vista, Slade-y." A third one called, even though the line made absolutely no sense in this context.

God, Jane hated it here.

Slade cast his comatose fan an unconcerned look, disregarding the propositions. Apparently, he was used to insane spectacles. Why wouldn't he be? Every time he strolled through town it became a parade of his deluded fan club. Literally. The man had an actual fan club. "Also, I am not sure that most of these beings are exactly human, so their blood might not nourish me."

Jane saw where this was headed. "Well, you're not biting *me*. Are you crazy?"

"It will only take a moment."

"A moment where I'm *bleeding from the neck!*" She jerked open the rickety door to her hut. "I mean it. No way is this happening."

"It's painless. I promise." He ducked through the doorway after her.

"How would you know? Have you ever been bitten?"

"No, but..."

"Well, neither have I and I don't like the idea of some Vampire at my jugular. Is that really so hard to understand?"

"But it's not 'some Vampire.' It's me."

She looked over at him.

Blue eyes locked onto hers, holding fast. "It's just me, Jane." He repeated, softly. "I know it is hard for you to have faith in anyone, but --deep down-- you trust me. You would not be here if you had any doubts. I will take your blood, but I will not hurt you. I swear it."

She thought for a long moment, weighing her feelings for this guy. "How much blood?" She finally asked.

Slade's expression lit up. "Just enough to survive." He promised, looking eager to convince her that this was a good plan. "I cannot eat the things you do, but I still need sustenance."

"Like you're missing so much with the *à la carte* squirrel dishes every night." She crossed her arms over her chest, still considering her options. "You can't --like-- drink deer or something?"

"No. It must be human blood. You're my best hope."

"Do not try guilt-tripping me. It won't work." Except she already knew it was going to work. Damn it.

"This will help you, too. Your blood will restore my strength, so I can fly us out of here. It will save us both."

"We'll think of another way."

"There *is* no other way. Even if there was, this cannot be avoided for much longer. I am a Vampire. I will die without blood." He regarded her gravely. "Please help me, Jane."

Damn it.

Jane blew out an irritated breath. It was the "please" that did it. And the fact that he was so mind-meltingly handsome. And she did want him flying up there and finding them an escape route. Mostly, she just didn't like the idea of him being hungry, though. She'd been hungry too many times in her life to inflict that on Slade. It made no sense for him to go without blood when she could fix it so easily.

"Alright." Jane muttered.

Slade blinked at her easy agreement. "Alright?" He repeated. "Just like that?"

"What, you think I'm mean enough to let you starve?"

"No." He gave her a strange smile. "You would never let anyone suffer, Jane. You have the softest heart I have ever encountered."

"I *don't* have a soft heart."

"Of course you do. I am just surprised that you did not make me beg a bit more. I was prepared for at least an hour of pleading, while you tried to recruit some other women to feed me."

"I guess I'm not that smart." Imagining him touching anybody else pissed her off to an unhealthy degree. If Slade needed to do some weird, sexual, bloodsucking thing, it should be with *her*, damn it. "But --hey-- if you want another donor, I can..."

"I want no one else." Slade interrupted firmly. The door slammed shut behind him, so he filled the small interior. "I only wish to drink from you, Jane."

"Eww. Don't say that. Call it..." Crap. No pleasant euphemism sprang to mind. "Never mind. Shit. Whatever. Let's just get this over with."

"Right now?" He urged, like a kid who couldn't wait for Christmas to come.

There didn't seem much point in putting it off. "You have something better to do?" Jane stomped across the dirt floor of her temporary home. It was furnished in a stylish way that any Puritan would envy. From the roughhewed log table, to the stained stone fireplace, to the uncomfortable mattress on the ground, it was a snapshot of why air-conditioning and television sets were *totally* the way to go.

Slade moved closer to her. For a second, his blue eyes glowed with a hunger that didn't seem like it had much to do with food, but it was probably just her imagination. "You will not regret this, Jane."

"Of course I will. I'm already positive that it's a bad idea, but what's one more bad idea this week, right? You can have an ounce or two, if that's what it takes." She jabbed a finger at his chest. "But if I catch Vampirism, I guarantee you're going to be my first victim."

# Chapter Eight

BACKGROUND NOTES FOR FANG'S MOTIVATION

Unlike most supernatural beings, Werewolves don't have destined brides. Their species is perpetuated by stealing the mates of their enemies. Luckily, they have *a lot* of enemies. It's the plus side of being the most hated supernatural beings in the universe. FANG has never been bothered by the idea that there is no special woman waiting for him, because he knows that he can take any woman he chooses.

And he's chosen SLADE'S human.

He has no idea what JANE looks like, but it's not important. Each rebel he captures and each spy who reports back to him, tells tales of JANE SQUIRE. She is a harridan. Bossy, pushy, annoyed with the rebels, impatient with SLADE. Yet, she is also loyal to the Vampire above all others and far too smart for anyone's peace of mind. All sides of the war are coming to fear the woman. No one can predict her and it frightens them. FANG knows the DARK FAIRY'S prophesy was correct. JANE SQUIRE is the key to the Vampire's success.

That's not the only reason he wants her, though.

At first --sure-- FANG was mainly interested in JANE because he assumed that she was SLADE'S Eternal-One. Now he's beginning to wonder if that is even true. How could this infamously difficult woman belong to the Vampire? In fact, when FANG finally tracks them down, SLADE will probably be glad to be freed of such a shrew. Vampires like their females vapid and weak. ...But Werewolves appreciate some seductive bitchiness. Forcing obedience is so much more rewarding than having it freely given.

Besides, there are whispers that JANE carries a book with her that can predict the future. The DARK FAIRY is desperate for it, claiming that it holds much power from the world of Chicago. FANG is dreaming about it, too. When you're struggling to hold onto your kingdom, a terrifying woman and a magickal book might come in pretty damn handy.

*Redrafted Film Script- "From Here to Infinia"*

Jane took a deep breath, trying to calm down. Her heart was pounding, already panicking over what she'd just agreed to. Why did she always go along with his insane ideas? She was pragmatic enough to know better, but Slade somehow overwhelmed her common sense.

He was like a Milky Way bar. You're in the checkout line and you *know* not to pick it up. You think you can ignore the shiny wrapping and just walk away. You're strong and smart and full of willpower… but somehow the candy still winds up in your basket.

"We're *not* having sex, Slade." She tacked on a little belatedly. "I mean it. Whatever aphrodisiac-y stuff goes on when you bite a girl, it isn't going to work on me. *No sex.*" It would be a huge mistake to get in any deeper with this guy.

He nodded, his expression dazed. "Whatever you wish." He murmured. He would probably agree to anything in order to have his dinner. "We must touch, though." His huge body shifted behind hers, moving quickly before she changed her mind.

And she should *totally* change her mind.

"Yes, fine. Touching. But nothing else." Jane's eyes drifted shut, feeling the strength of him pressed up against her back. One of his arms encircled her waist, drawing her against him. Oh wow… "Just --like-- what you *have* to do biologically." She got out unsteadily.

He nuzzled the curls at her temple as he lowered his head. "Only what is necessary." He whispered and Jane's insides took a sensual dip. That felt like it was more than just necessary. Slade's breath was hot on her throat and she was suddenly understanding the whole aphrodisiac thing.

Against her better judgment, her body melted into his. "Slade…" She whispered, unsure what caveat she was about to tack onto this terrible, terrible idea.

He didn't give her a chance to figure it out, either. Slade let out a groan at the sound of his name and then his teeth sunk deep into her flesh.

Jane's eyes went wide, flames tearing through her system. "Oh my God." She couldn't breathe. She couldn't think. All she could do was hang on. "Oh my *God*." Just that quickly, she was on the brink of the largest orgasm of her life. It was like Slade was stroking her in a thousand places at once. She instinctively began moving against him, feeling the hard length of his erection and *needing* it.

She'd never needed anything so much.

Slade gave a low snarl, gripping her tighter.

"Oh *yesssss*." Her head fell back against his shoulder, loving this. And hating it. The pleasure was making her crazy. It felt like he was licking every secret part of her. She couldn't process anything except the tension growing tighter and tighter. And tighter… "Oh please." Her hips undulated against his, needing relief. "Please, Slade."

The begging did the trick. Kings liked supplicants.

One of Slade's hands slid down her body, finding the opening in his jacket. He yanked the fabric aside, ripping off the buttons, so she was naked before him. She was too far gone to care. Slade's fingers moved like he wanted to memorize each inch of her skin as quickly as possible.

Jane arched into his touch, as his massive palm caressed her everywhere. She dimly recognized that she should've felt self-conscious about her size, but he seemed to like what he saw and she was having too good a time to care about anything outside of Slade's hands. He brushed the junction of her thighs and the grazing touch was enough to have her seeing stars.

It felt really, really, really right.

*Wrong.*

Jane's eyes popped open. "Wait." She gasped and caught hold of his wrist. She tried to focus through the sensual haze. This was a mistake. It wasn't supposed to feel so right. That was just going to lead to a broken heart. It was too big a risk to go any further with Slade.

…For some reason that she could no longer remember.

Slade pulled back to lap her skin. A bead of blood trailed down her neck and he licked it away. Jane shivered at the sensation, her body weeping for him. Pragmatism faded as quickly as it had appeared.

"Gods, you taste even better than you smell." He whispered. "How is that even possible?" His free hand tangled in her hair, gripping the curls with erotic strength. He angled her head to a more vulnerable angle and Jane whimpered with lust. "Do you want me to stop?"

"N-no." She panted. "Please."

"Good, because I don't think I can." He looked down at her naked curves and swallowed hard. "I need you too much." He bit her again, even deeper. Like he wanted more. Like he was past all control.

Jane gave up trying to resist. Some part of her knew this was a mistake, but she needed him, too. Her restraining palm slid free from his wrist, letting him continue south. Slade rewarded her with a pleased growl. His massive hand slid between her damp folds of flesh. He started a gentle massage, urging her legs apart.

All Jane's senses went into meltdown. She helplessly shifted her stance, giving him better access. He could do whatever he wanted, just so he'd let her come. She *had* to come or she was going to burn alive.

That surrender was what he wanted. Instantly, his long fingers were pressing inside of her. Jane let out a wail of desire as he thrust two of them into her tight channel. She went up on tiptoe, needing even more.

He wasn't giving her more, though.

He kept her like that for several centuries of time. Just milking every drop from her body and listening to her plead. Slade seemed as close to the edge as she was. His other hand left her hair and found her breast. Her nipple beaded against his palm, pressing deeper into his touch. He molded her flesh like he wanted to mark her.

"Mine." He rumbled and she nearly broke down in sobs.

Holy *shit*. Slade's idiot ex-wife had chosen some Werewolf over him in bed? The woman must have had the IQ of a really stupid brick. *Nobody* could be better at this than Slade was. It was a goddamn revelation. Jane suddenly saw what the fuss was about when it came to sex. Before, it had always seemed kind of lackluster, but now she finally got it.

Holy *shit*, did she get it.

Just when Jane was sure she was going to die of pleasure, Slade's thumb stroked the straining nub of her desire and she exploded. Hot, wet waves of ecstasy pulsated through her. It went on and on, washing away everything except the incredible sensations he'd created within her. She collapsed against him, breathing hard and unable to keep her head up.

Slade lifted his face from her throat, looking as stunned as Jane felt. His gaze locked on hers he coaxed every last tremor from her body.

Her eyes dazedly traced the perfect angles of his face and she gave a stunned smile. "Wow. You *are* the king." She whispered.

Then she sank into darkness.

***

He'd taken too much.

"Jane!" Slade grabbed her closer, lifting her limp body against his chest. Her head lolled against his shoulder, her toffee-colored hair sending off small sparks wherever it touched him. Gods, what had he done?

He should've stopped when he'd had enough blood to survive. He'd told her he would, but he'd been too greedy. Too lost in the incredible taste of her. And the feel of her. And the sensual sounds she made. She'd trusted him and he'd taken advantage, because he'd been helpless to let her go. He'd wanted her so badly that he'd become an animal.

For the first time in his life, Slade had lost himself while feeding. This not-so-ordinary little human set his whole system on fire. His body was still throbbing for release. It had been all he could do not to strip off his clothes and take her fully. He'd wanted to slam inside of her body until he was spent. And then do it again. And again. Until Jane knew exactly who she belonged to and so would everyone else who might think to steal her. He'd felt his Dark Instincts pulling him down, telling him that she was *his*. Telling him to claim every piece of her, so she'd never slip away.

That wasn't supposed to happen. Even with Melessa, Slade had stayed restrained and the taste of an Eternal-One was supposed to drive Vampires mad with passion. Slade's powerful self-control and innate honor had made it easy to resist drinking too much from his ex-wife, though.

Very easy.

Too easy.

The whole process with Melessa hadn't gone well. She hadn't liked being bitten and Slade never pressed the matter. Her blood had a bitter, unpleasant taste. He took exactly enough to keep him alive without having to drink from another.

They'd never even fully consummated their Eternal-Bond. That had become a sticking point at the trial. The Vampire King was supposed to Eternally-Bond with his mate by his thousandth birthday. That was one of the stupid rules of the kingdom and Slade had tried to bypass it. Bonding with Melessa had somehow seemed... worthless. His enemies had used his hesitation when they stole his land. He'd lost the crown, thanks in large part to his aversion to Melessa's blood.

It was nothing like Jane Squire's. Even knowing it was selfish, Slade couldn't get the sweetness of her out of his mind. No one else had ever tasted so good. Christ, how could he *ever* go back to the bland, tepid blood of others now that he'd had her?

It was as if she was made for him.

"Jane?" Slade laid her down on the straw mattress, working hard not to stare at her naked body. Jesus, she was beautiful. Hating himself, he quickly covered her with a blanket. His gaze traced over her pale face, instead. "Jane, open your eyes." He fumbled to remove her glasses. "You *must* open your eyes. I am your king and I insist you obey."

She didn't open her eyes. The woman never did as she was told.

Slade sank down beside her, wanting to cry at how still she was. His Jane was always so full of insults and confusing ideas and *life*. "Please, look at me." He smoothed back her incredible curls, marveling at their soft texture, and not even hearing his own desperate pleas. "*Please,* my One. You cannot leave me here alone. I *need* you. I need you so much."

Humans were fragile. He *knew* that. How could he have been so rough with her? So demanding? What if she didn't recover? The thought filled him with fear and the King of the Vampires feared nothing.

Slade rested his head on her chest, listening to the steady beats of her heart. If she would just awaken, he would make this up to her. He would never drink from her again. He would do anything she asked.

He just wanted her back.

He couldn't exist without Jane. She was the one part of the universe that he was completely sure of. The one place where he knew he belonged. All his doubts were gone when she was beside him. Every part of him *knew* they were supposed to be together. If he lost Jane...

Slade quickly rallied himself. No. He wouldn't lose her. There was a surefire way to bring Jane around: He would give her some of *his* blood. It could heal her and it was perfectly safe. He wouldn't have risked it if there was even a chance it would endanger her. So few humans survived the process of becoming a Vampire. But humans couldn't transition into one of his kind unless they took blood from two different Vampires and Slade was the only Vampire in Infinia. This plan would simply restore her.

Nodding with fresh resolve, he sliced open the pad of his thumb and held it to her lips. There was nothing for a beat of time. Then she swallowed a few drops of his blood. Jane's mouth slowly parted around his finger, pulling it deeper. Stroking it with her tongue. Small teeth grazing against his skin.

Slade's eyes crossed.

*Gods*. He was immortal and this woman was still going to be the death of him. Renewed passion slammed through his system and he wanted to beg. Images flashed through his mind. Hot, wet, dirty scenes of Jane sucking *far* more interesting parts of his anatomy. That fantasy had been growing more vivid by the day and now it threatened to consume him. She had no idea what she was doing, but his body didn't seem to care. He'd never wanted a woman more. He'd never wanted *anything* more.

Slade squeezed his eyes shut, breathing in her scent and trying to stay in control. Jane was coming around. That was all that mattered. It didn't take much Vampire blood to heal a small human girl.

She made a sleepy sound of pleasure, her beautiful eyes fluttering open. For a heartbeat of time, she didn't understand what was happening. Her gaze was welcoming and sensual. She licked away another droplet of blood and gave him a contented smile.

Slade's jaw clenched against a helpless groan. "Take as much as you desire." He leaned over her, his hand smoothing back her incredible hair. "Whatever you need, I will provide."

The desperate lust still pounded, but --beneath it-- something far greater swelled. He wanted to give her all he had. He always felt that way, but it was suddenly all so clear. As long as she'd stay beside him, he'd give her *anything*.

For two seconds it all seemed... right.

Then Jane processed what was happening.

"Jesus!" She gasped, jerking upright. His thumb fell from her lips, which filled him with an instant sense of loss. "*Jesus!* Did you just make me drink blood?!"

Slade nearly sighed at her appalled expression. Humans were so easily upset. "I had to." He licked the wound on his finger closed, savoring the taste of her on his skin. "It was the only way to bring you around."

"Then you should have let me sleep! I don't *drink blood*, you moron."

"I was concerned." He reluctantly shifted back from her. "Things got out of hand during the feeding. I took too much and you passed out."

"I don't think that was just from blood loss." Jane muttered, rubbing her forehead. Silence hummed for a beat, both of them remembering how she'd come apart in his arms. Her gaze slipped to the front of his pants and then quickly away. "It got *super* out of hand." She agreed with a gulp, hitching the blanket up around her. "You were right about the aphrodisiac part."

"I am Slade, King of the Vampires. I'm always right. But Jane, this was a very strong reaction to be simply..."

She cut him off. "There was some supernatural weirdness going on, messing with my head. That was *totally* the problem." She nodded like she was trying to convince herself. "And on top of that, you're so... And I got so..." She cleared her throat. "And you're *still* so..."

"I know." He was *very* aware of his current state of arousal.

"At least, nothing too terrible happened... Except the part where you fed me *blood*."

"I told you, I needed to heal you. Vampire blood has medicinal properties for humans."

She still looked wary about it. "It doesn't turn me into a Vampire, does it?"

"No. I give you my word."

"Good." She gave a nod, not meeting his eyes. "Well --I mean-- this is a little awkward, now. With the orgasm and all. But it was to help you to eat and now everything's fine. No harm done. We'll just go back to our normal, quasi-normal relationship and we'll forget this even happened. We're both adults and we're just moving on, right?"

"It may take a few moments for me to *move on*." Slade shifted uncomfortably.

"Oh." She glanced back down at his bulging trousers and then averted her gaze with a blink. "Well, that's your problem. I'm not sleeping with you, after you *fed me blood*." She decided in a firm tone. "No way." Her eyes tracked over to his erection again, like she couldn't help herself. "Sex would be a massive, *massive* mistake." She bit her lower lip. "Really, really... massive."

Slade sighed. "I would not ask you to share my bed." He knew she would refuse. The woman would never sleep with a man unless she had total faith in him and she did not give her faith easily.

Her attention snapped to his face. "You wouldn't, huh?" She shook her head, apparently irritated. "No, of *course* you wouldn't ask me. Kings and servants don't consort."

"That's not what I..."

"I mean, what would your soon-to-be-fiancée Allandrina say if you started screwing the help?"

Slade frowned, annoyed that Jane would say such a thing. "You are not just *the help*. Didn't we discuss this by the waterfall? You are being..."

Jane cut him off. "Forget it. This whole blood drinking thing was a mistake. I don't even know why I agreed to it, except I'm losing my mind." She began searching around for her spectacles. "Look, we can't do this again. You're just going to have to go hungry until you're safely in your witchy-bride's arms and I'm going to sit here, being sexually frustrated, until I meet up with my Prince Charming. Deal?"

"*What?*" Slade's scowl grew deeper. "Wait. When are you planning to rendezvous with another prince?"

She had mentioned the mysterious potentate before, but Charming governed no land Slade knew of. And if Slade hadn't heard of a place, it was sure to be small and dreary. Jane couldn't *possibly* be interested in the low-level ruler of a forgotten world. Someone of her quality could do so much better.

Jane paused in the act of putting on her glasses. Her head swiveled to squint at him like she was baffled by his question. "Huh?"

"Is Prince Charming why you wish to get back to your precious supermarket?" She spoke of mating with this man, so they must be close. He must be someone she had faith in and fully trusted. Someone she missed. Slade's temper began to spark. "Is he waiting there for you?" Did Jane *love* this other monarch?

His Dark Instincts snarled at the thought.

Jane gave a short laugh. "Christ, sometimes I *do* remember why I keep you around. You say crazy stuff and it's kind of adorable." She pinched the bridge of her nose, not even noticing Slade's mounting anger. "Sure, why not? Right now, Prince Charming is no doubt scouring Iverson's Grocery Store for my damsel-y self. He's been after me for years, but --you know-- a gal like me has gotta sow her wild oats, before she settles down in her enchanted castle."

Slade couldn't argue with that logic. It still pissed him off, though. His own sexual frustration fed into his rage. Jane refused to sleep with him, because she wanted some royal pretender from her own world. "So this Prince Charming is just a *human?*"

Jane stopped snickering at his disdainful scoff. "Hey, *I'm* just a human." Her eyes narrowed. "At least, I'd *better* be a human. Because, if you turned me into a Vampire, so help me..."

"I told you, I didn't turn you into a Vampire." Slade interrupted dismissively. "I just don't see how we can go through all of this together," he waved a hand around to encompass their epic journey, "and you'd still think of returning to your ghastly Chicago."

She rolled her eyes. "Yeah, because the Endless Woods has *such* great amenities. What's wrong with me for missing little stuff like refrigerated food?"

"Our stay here is only temporary. Soon we will have all of Infinia and I will gladly share it with you. The rubies and the flying horses and the magicks." He nodded, willing her to see how much he had to offer. "This whole kingdom will be *ours*, Jane."

She studied him for a long moment, her face growing

somber. "And Allandrina's."

Damn it, why did Jane dwell on the princess? Slade kept forgetting the other woman even existed. "Allandrina will be there, too, I suppose. Somewhere." Slade wasn't about to deal with her more than necessary, though. They'd have to work out boundaries, like in any other business arrangement. Maybe they could split Infinia, so they'd each oversee half. That seemed fair. She could have some castle far away and he could be with Jane. "But, she is just a means to an end. You and I are supposed to rule this kingdom *together*."

Jane gave him a strange smile. "Slade, I don't want a kingdom." She said quietly. "To be honest, all I've ever wanted is a *home*. I'll help you win this war, but then I have to go. I have to find my *own* home." She shook her head. "This world can't be it."

She was serious.

Jane didn't want to stay with him.

It felt as if a centaur had kicked Slade in the chest. He'd thought she'd see reason. He'd been so sure. But no matter what riches and glories he offered, Jane would choose her backwater dimension and some second-rate sovereign over being Slade's partner. Over being a key part of his magnificent destiny. Over being his best friend in this or any other world.

*The woman was out of her goddamn mind.*

Slade got to his feet, pain like he'd never known eating a hole inside of him. Melessa leaving him was *nothing* compared to this rejection. He wasn't even sure how he managed to stay standing. Jane's words sliced deeper than any blade, making it feel as if his insides were bleeding out through his skin and leaving him empty.

"*Fine*." He bit off, unable to look at her. "Settle for your small and ordinary life, if that's all you dream of for yourself. Squander our only chance for greatness. *I* have far bigger plans."

"You always have big plans, Slade. That doesn't mean they're going to work."

"At least I *try*. You take no risks and will have no tales to tell, because you are afraid."

"That isn't true!" She vehemently shook her head, like she was trying to convince herself. "It just *isn't*. I'm not afraid. I'm *pragmatic*. There's a difference."

"Call it whatever you wish. It still means you base all your decisions on fear and on what you believe is impossible. I make mine based on *hope*. On what I wish to create with you beside me. Hope that there are heroes in this world and that I can be one." No matter the doubts that plagued him, Slade wouldn't believe that he was a failure. He *wouldn't.*

"You make your decisions based on *fantasy*." She retorted. "Any random thought that enters your head, you believe. You know what happens to people who think they can be heroes? They *die*, Slade. You would've been killed fifty times over, if it wasn't for me!"

"And you would stagnate in your boxed-in world if it wasn't for me!"

"I *liked* stagnating in my boxed-in world. I was *safe* there."

"You were *wasted* there. There is so much *life* in you, yet you refuse to live it. Given a choice, you will do *nothing*, rather than chance disappointment. How is that a worthy existence?"

"It's better than the alternative! When I take a chance, I'm *always* disappointed. You should understand that. Your wife cheated on you... Your people fired you... Your grandmother turned against you... Everyone you know has let you down."

"You haven't. Not even once."

She stared at him, not having an answer for that.

Slade kept going. "You have taken a chance and followed me, thus far. It frightened you, but you did it. Have I disappointed you? Have I let you down?"

"No." She admitted. "Not yet. But..."

He cut her off. "Not *ever*. I wish to remain with *you*, Jane. Having you beside me has been..." He trailed off, shaking his head. How could she want someone else? Couldn't she feel what was between them? How special it was? "You and I *belong* here. Side-by-side. I know it and so do you."

"No." She whispered. "I won't stay with you, Slade. I *can't*."

Slade's jaw tightened, stifling a flinch at her refusal. "*Fine*." He snapped again and headed for the door. He wasn't giving up. He would *never* give up on Jane. But she was in no mood to see reason and he was too hurt to find the right words. "Ignore your destiny, if it makes you feel safer. Embrace a hollow future. Plan your return to that uninspiring human *prince*." He looked back at her, wounded pride talking. "I will stay here and be *king*."

# Chapter Nine

EXT- EDGE OF THE ENDLESS WOODS- NIGHT

FANG'S Goblin forces have surrounded the vast forest. They should look all slimy and gross, kind of like the lizard-guys from V. FANG stands at the top of a hill, talking with DALLYN, the last of the Mages. DALLYN is a tall, beautiful woman, wearing a tight leather outfit. She has the body of a Victoria's Secret model, a cool kind-of-Russian accent, and she's a ninja. Is she good? Is she evil? It depends on the recommendations of the focus group, but either way she'll make one hell of an action figure.

DALLYN
(In a kind-of-Russian accent)
Fear not, King Fang. My magicks will make it possible to safely enter the forest's maze.

FANG
(Irritated)
If magicks could unlock the mysteries of the Endless Woods, why didn't some other supernatural being solve them long ago?

DALLYN
(After a long pause)
...I have no idea. But I'm sure it all makes sense.

FANG
(More irritated)
I doubt it. I swear to the gods, something weird is happening lately.

> DALLYN
> (Ignoring his complaints)
> You wait here, King Fang. I know Slade and he is far too crafty to be caught in just any trap.
> I have planned this very carefully.
>
> FANG
> (Super irritated)
> I'm sick of planning.
> It seems like all I ever do is *talk* about my evil schemes and hire evil henchmen.
> I want to actually *do* something evil.
>
> DALLYN
> I don't think that happens until the finale.
>
> *Redrafted Film Script- "From Here to Infinia"*

Slade stared at the campfire, trying to make sense of his life.

Everything *should've* been perfect. Infinia was a beautiful land, just as he'd hoped. He was making inroads with the rebels and already gaining a loyal following of loyal followers. Once he got the Silver Sword and defeated Fang, his epic destiny would be assured. He'd finally have his crown and all would be as it should be.

So, why did it all feel so futile?

It was Jane's fault. How could he focus on anything when she was sitting in her borrowed hut, plotting to leave him? Every step he took towards the throne was actually a step away from Jane. She would go back to her pathetic prince and her drab little world, never thinking of Slade, again. How was he supposed to enjoy his success knowing that?

With Jane at his side, he felt as if he'd already won some glorious battle. Like things finally made sense. Like he could do anything.  Like he was *home*.  Meanwhile, she couldn't wait to go back to her life without him.

The woman was obviously under some kind of spell.

His eyes narrowed in sudden thought.  Actually, a spell *would* explain much about her stubborn refusal to stay in Infinia.  Perhaps this so-called "Charming" used some enchantment to enthrall Jane.  Perhaps her inexplicable attachment to the bastard was the result of magicks.

Slade's mood improved as he pondered those implications.  Jane would be displeased if he killed the man she loved without good reason.  But if that asshole prince had somehow hypnotized her --which he *obviously* had-- then Slade had a viable reason for the slaughter.  Afterwards, Jane would see that he'd had no choice but to rip out Charming's heart and feed it to him.  She would probably even *thank* him for saving her.

"Slade," she would whisper, her luminous gray eyes glistening with tears, "you've rescued me from that stupid, hideous, small human.  How could I have ever imagined abandoning you for such a poorly-endowed fraud?  Please forgive my inexplicable lunacy and let me stay with you forever."

Then Slade would take Jane into his arms and he'd breathe in the citrusy fragrance of her hair.  His hands caressing her warm curves, as she pressed against his body.  She'd look up at him with caring and mischief, and everything would be perfect.  When Jane smiled like that, Slade felt like they were the only two people in the world.  Like he was finally the hero he'd always dreamed of being.  He'd tell her things that he'd never told anyone and she'd tell him things, too.  Because she trusted him.  Because they were partners in everything.  She'd slowly sink to her knees and her mouth would...

"King Slade?  Don't you think that is a wise plan?"

Slade jolted at the sound of his name.  He looked around, surprised to see the rebels all looking at him expectantly.  Shit.  Had they been talking this whole time?  What had they been discussing?

He didn't want to seem inattentive to their concerns.

Over the past few days, Slade had changed his views on what being a king really meant. He'd made mistakes on the Vampire Isle and he wasn't going to repeat them here. Ruling wasn't just having a castle and waving at commoners. It meant being a part of something. Jane taught him that. Since he'd started listening to her advice and engaging with the rebels, they'd become more and more vocal. It was almost as if they were coming into *focus* somehow. They even had names, now. Slade didn't completely understand how it happened, but he liked the changes and he knew Jane was responsible. How could she want another man? Didn't she see how much Slade needed her?

It was obviously Charming's fault. The prince needed to die.

"Uh... I was contemplating very important stratagems and missed that last part." He told the waiting rebels. It was strange for Slade to converse with peasants, but he wasn't finding it nearly as horrible as he'd feared. Some of the beings had reasonable suggestions, when you gave them a chance. "What were you saying?"

Konrad, an Ogre with a shedding problem, was more than happy to repeat it. "I said that now is the time for us to attempt the Corpse Road. It's the only chance we have to get out of here."

The other rebels looked concerned about that idea. They must have been bickering over Konrad's plan for some time. Slade had no idea why and he didn't particularly care. "There is another way out of the forest?" He surmised.

Konrad nodded. "Yes, your majesty. I'm sure of it."

Everyone else glowered at him.

That was wonderful news! Jane had been right. Listening to the villagers was *really* paying off. Flying to freedom would only take moments and Slade clearly needed longer than that to get through to Jane. It would be better to walk. Ideally, she would have to remain by his side for days. Delaying his inevitable victory meant more time with her, so Slade had to stall.

"What is the Corpse Road?" Granted, it didn't sound

like a street Jane would enjoy traveling upon, but she *was* eager to escape the Endless Woods. If he could find a way out, she would surely be impressed. ...And if that way out meant Jane was stuck with him, so much the better. Given time, she would see that he was the best possible monarch a girl could have.

The best *partner*.

"If the Corpse Road was a viable escape, none of us would still be here, Konrad." An older guy named Neville snapped. He had horns and a face like a seahorse. "Do not speak such foolishness."

There was a general murmur of agreement.

Konrad wasn't giving up. "The path is cursed, it's true. But, now we have King Slade to lead us. He will see our way through the danger, Neville."

"And risk his own grand life in the process!" Neville shot back. "Your ideas are not the stuff dreams are made of, Konrad. It's folly to even mention them. *There is no way out of this forest*. Attempting to traverse the Corpse Road will kill..."

Slade cut him off. "What is the Corpse Road?" He demanded again. He did not recall that name in the script.

The rebels exchanged more troubled glances.

"It's a trail that leads to death." Neville finally said. "It's hidden, with none but the dead knowing where it starts." He lowered his voice as if something sinister might be listening from the trees and he didn't want it to overhear. "You don't want to attempt that path, your majesty. No one has ever survived the trip. Better to stay hidden here in the forest."

"Kings do not hide." Slade scoffed. "At least, not for long." The very idea was ludicrous. "We will never defeat Fang unless we face him. And to face him, we *must* leave these woods and find the Silver Sword."

"Each soul that falls dead upon the Corpse Road rises again as a Shadowman." A Pixie named Andra whispered. ...Although it didn't seem possible for her to know such a thing if no one had ever come back from the road to tell the tale. "They haunt the ground and attack trespassers, making ever more of their deadly kind."

"I do not fear ghosts."

"These are not just ghosts, majesty. They are *Shadowmen*. They steal the souls of everyone who crosses them."

The other rebels made signs of prayer.

Perhaps Slade should read the *From Here to Infinia* script again, because he had never heard of beings called Shadowmen, either. Jane was forever telling him that the pages were changing and he should pay more attention to the "film" unfolding around them. Slade just didn't see the point. He'd skimmed the tome and seen that events had been altered, but the shifting story was only to be expected. Whatever had been written before was obsolete now that he was here. Once he had the Silver Sword and escaped these woods, he would...

"Slade?"

His head snapped around at the sound of his name and the scent of her skin. Jane. Seeing her, the world made sense again. His irritation melted into longing, as she drew closer. If she would just stay with him, he would give her whatever she wanted. They were supposed to do this *together*. Why did she not understand that?

Her clothes must have finished drying, because she was back to wearing them. Slade frowned. Pants were simply not decent on a lady. He'd tried explaining that to her, but she laughed at him and did as she pleased. At least half the rebels were staring at her khaki-covered legs. He sent them all a warning look and they quickly averted their eyes.

"Are you ready to fly out of here, yet?" Jane demanded, marching over to join him. The woman was clearly annoyed. He was used to that.

"We may have another option." Slade got to his feet. "The rebels tell me there is a path leading out of the Endless Woods, after all."

"Since when?" She demanded skeptically. "Why hasn't anyone mentioned it before now?"

"It is hidden."

"Hidden?"

"That road is fraught with horrors beyond imagining, milady." Neville intoned like some medieval prophet predicting their doom. He was clearly hoping that Jane could talk Slade out of the plan.

"Don't call me 'milady.'" She told them that fifty times a day but they never listened.

The rebels all respected Jane. She intimidated them, but Slade had noticed that they often went to her when they wanted someone to intercede with his more controversial rulings. It didn't bother him, since he liked it when the woman got involved in village life. It showed Jane cared about their quest. Besides, she was almost always right. Slade wasn't sure how that worked exactly, since *he* was always right, but he couldn't argue with the facts.

"Someone explain to me what's going on." Jane ordered, turning her attention to the peasants. Melessa would've swooned before she talked to these grimy rebels, but it never occurred to Jane to avoid them. She thought everyone should have a voice and that everyone was important. Slade loved that about her. Though she tried to hide it, Jane truly did have a soft heart.

"Where did this path come from?" She persisted impatiently.

Andra watched Jane with a mixture of hope and fear. "Neville speaks the truth, milady. No one has ever stepped foot upon the Corpse Road's horrible surface and survived to reveal its location. To travel it is certain death."

Slade flinched. He'd been hoping to avoid telling her most of that. *All* of it, actually.

Jane very slowly turned back to him. "*The Corpse Road?*"

"Frightening names are often given to lovely places in an effort to discourage tourists." He ventured.

"Well, it worked because I'm discouraged. We're flying out of here, Slade. Start flapping your arms or whatever."

"But... I cannot." It would ruin everything.

"What do you mean you *cannot?* You told me you could fly, remember? You said all you needed was my blood."

"I *can* fly. ...But not in Infinia." Lying to Jane was difficult, but what choice did he have? Slade needed more time with her, so he could convince her to stay. "My powers are somehow suppressed in this land." He shrugged. "We are stuck on the ground."

Jane's eyes narrowed. "You're lying."

Damn it, the woman was so inconveniently smart. Slade refused to back down. This was too important. "Why would I lie?" He asked, unable to meet her eyes.

"I have no idea, but I have yet to see *anything* that you couldn't do once you decided to do it. You know what that tells me?" She jabbed a finger into his chest. "It tells me that you could get your cute ass airborne, if you tried. Only you're *not* trying, because you don't *want* to try."

"I *have* tried and it is impossible."

The rebels looked back and forth between them like spectators at a tennis match, staying out of the fray. It was often that way. The village considered Jane his queen and Slade did nothing to discourage the idea. This obstinate woman was his future. Regardless of whatever ridiculous feelings she had for Prince Charming, *Slade* was the one she was supposed to be with. It was so obvious to everyone but Jane.

Still, ruling Infinia with Jane would be far different than ruling the Vampire Isle. Melessa had never argued with him the way Jane did. It was a refreshing change to have someone else assuming part of the responsibility and offering fresh ideas. Slade *liked* having another person care about the kingdom and its people. ...Usually. When his partner wasn't so bent on wrecking his plans, anyway.

"You're doing this on purpose, aren't you?" Jane accused. "You're *deliberately* dragging your feet, for some crazy reason."

"I have no idea what you're talking about." Slade cleared his throat and stared at a random rock formation like it held the mysteries of the universe. He was not gifted at deceit, especially not with Jane's luminous gray eyes watching him so closely. "I'm simply telling you the truth. We must use the Corpse Road. There is no other choice."

Jane's temper exploded. "I don't want to use the Corpse Road! Who the hell would want to use anything called the Corpse Road?! Maybe you're okay with living in *Quest of the Delta Knights*, but I'm *not!* I just want to get this nightmare over with, so you can marry your stupid princess, and I can forget I ever met you!" She gave him a frustrated shove and stalked passed him towards the trees.

Slade frowned as something new occurred to him. "Are you upset that I plan to wed Allandrina?" He demanded hurrying after her. That idea was sheer lunacy. The princess barely even registered in his mind. "Jane there is no need. That woman is *nothing* to me. I have never even met her."

"Then it's even *worse* that you'd propose."

"But she will not care for me, either. I've explained that it is a business…"

Jane cut him off. "Besides, it doesn't matter *who* you marry, because I'm not going to be here to see it." She waved a disparaging hand. "Go ahead and say 'I do' to some girl, because you want a damn castle. I'm sure it'll work out *great* for you. It did last time, right?"

"I *did* know Melessa!" Slade protested indignantly. "When a Vampire meets his Eternal-One, he instinctively knows her on every possible level."

"Really?" Jane stopped walking to pin him with a glare. The two of them were isolated by the forest now, which suited Slade fine. No man could ogle her… except him. "What level *instinctively knew* she was going to screw Viktor the Werewolf in your bathtub?"

Slade's jaw ticked.

She arched a smug brow at him.

"That was a low blow, Jane Squire." He finally said. "Melessa's betrayal was unprecedented among Vampires. No one could have predicted her actions. She was my Eternal-One, after all. My destined mate."

"Oh, she was not." Jane rolled her eyes. "'Cause if she *was*, she wouldn't have fucked around on you."

Slade blinked at that glib response.

"Face it," Jane continued, "on some level you knew she wasn't the right girl for you. You only married Melessa to retain control of the Vampire Isle, just like you're only proposing to

Allandrina to get Infinia. All your weddings are about real estate. You said yourself you care about business and not romance."

Slade *had* told her that, but he hated that she'd listened. The words made him seem so shallow. "Melessa *was* my Eternal-One." He snapped. "She *had* to be. All the signs pointed to it."

"If you say so."

"I *do* say so. And while Allandrina is simply a means to an end, that doesn't mean I am incapable of deeper feelings. I care for you very much." There were no words for what he was coming to feel for this woman. "You *know* this, Jane."

"Yeah, the situation was real clear to me when you basically suggested I become your royal mistress."

"*I never said that!*" Slade roared, his voice echoing through the woods. "I have never even *thought* of the situation in those terms!" He wanted Jane to stay with him, because he could no longer picture an existence without her. Why did she have to make everything sound so sordid?

She snorted. "Oh right. Sorry. I *couldn't* be your mistress, because you would never lower yourself to actually sleep with the help, right?"

He leaned closer, pushed to the brink by her refusal to see the truth. "If you wish, I will show you once and for all how very idiotic that statement is." Slade snarled, grasping her wrist. He tugged her hand forward, so it was pressed to the front of his trousers. "Being around you leaves me in a constant state of readiness, so just nod your head and I'll be inside of you. Would that convince you of my desire?"

Jane's eyes went wide as she felt his erection, automatically trying to tug away.

He wouldn't let her go. Instead, Slade stepped closer, pressing her hand tighter against him. "You know full well I would have us both naked the *second* you gave consent. You can *feel* how much I want you, Jane."

She swallowed, her fingers resting on the bulge of his manhood. "You want *me?*" She blurted out as if the idea had never occurred to her before.

Gods, dealing with the woman drove him mad. How could she be so clever and still miss everything important? Slade kept his gaze locked on hers. "I have never wanted anyone the way I want you, Jane Squire."

Releasing her wrist would've been the gentlemanly thing to do. Instead, he urged her hand lower so she was cupping more of him through the fabric of his pants. The silver bracelet moved beneath his grip. The fact that she still wore his gift made him even more aroused.

She bit down on her lower lip and he nearly groaned. Jane's fingers slowly traced the size of him, her thumb brushing against the tip of his shaft. Slade's whole body jolted at the sensation. Her gentle explorations were going to kill him. He rocked against her palm and she instinctively tightened her grip.

Slade stared down at her and she stared back.

*Now,* everything was perfect.

God, he'd never felt anything like the connection he had with Jane. Whenever Slade looked into her eyes, he felt as if he was on the verge of some fantastic discovery.

That baffling mixture of aching tenderness and crazed hunger built within him, again. He was swamped with the seemingly contradictory desires to shield her from everything and to possess every inch of her body in a thousand shocking ways. He wanted to talk to her and make her smile. He wanted her weeping from desire. He wanted her turning to him for comfort and protection. He wanted her to know that she belonged with him and that he would destroy any other man who sought to claim her.

He wanted *everything*.

She was... everything.

Jane gazed up at him and Slade lowered his head to kiss her.

For a moment, it seemed that she might let him. Jane's mouth parted, her body softening into his. She leaned up almost imperceptibly, as if she wanted to meet his lips halfway. It was all exactly as it *should* be.

...So, of course, Jane had to go and ruin it. The woman was just determined to complicate every step of their lives.

"No!" She jerked back, glowering up at him and breathing hard. "I'm *not* kissing somebody who plans to get engaged to somebody else. I'm not touching him, either." She yanked her hand free, which made Slade want to curse and cry and destroy small planets.

"Jane…"

"*No.* You want this kingdom and you're willing to trade yourself to Allandrina to get it." She shook her head with the inflexible morality of someone truly good. "But I'm *not* going along with it. I'm better than that." She met his eyes. "So are you, Slade. You're so much *better* than this sleazy plan. I wish you could see that."

Slade froze. In a blinding flash of insight, he realized that Jane was once again right. His plan to wed Allandrina *sounded* sordid, because it *was* sordid. It was something a Werewolf might plot. How could he possibly do such a thing and still call himself an honorable man? If Slade proposed to another woman that he did not love, he would never respect himself.

Worse, *Jane* would never respect him.

She wouldn't stay, if she didn't respect him.

Slade looked away from the purity of her gray eyes, his mind whirling. He wasn't sure how it had happened, but he couldn't ignore the truth. Keeping Jane was the only thing that mattered. She meant more to him that any throne. Allandrina and Infinia and the future he'd sought versus this one small human…? That was no choice at all.

It would *always* be Jane.

"Why must you confuse everything?" He muttered, surrendering to the inevitable.

The thought of giving up another kingdom was very vexing. They were difficult to come by. It would no doubt take him weeks to find another. In fact, on second thought, he wasn't going to just give Infinia up. He was Slade, King of the Vampires, so he'd think of a way to claim Infinia *without* Allandrina. It was possible, but much more difficult.

Also, more time consuming.

Not only would the war be longer, but Allandrina

would surely not be in the mood to help send Jane back to her own dimension. Not after Slade conquered her lands, took over her castle, and didn't marry her. Without the princess's magicks, he had no idea how to get Jane home. She would be stranded in Infinia forever.

He smiled at that thought.

Jane was the only woman in Infinia immune to his many charms, but he could change that. Somehow. When Slade wanted something, he found a way to get it. And he wanted Jane. With more time, he *knew* he could win her over. If she could never return to her dismal world and her dismal prince, Slade would have nothing *but* time with her. She'd spend the rest of eternity right beside him. Sooner or later, she'd *have* to start caring for him.

Actually, this wasn't such a bad idea, after all.

"Are you laughing at me?" Jane demanded, seeing his sudden grin. "Because, I'm right about *all* of this, Slade. About you and me and Melessa and Alla-What's-Her-Face..."

"I am unamused by this entire conversation, I assure you." Slade assured her. "And while you might be right about *most* things, you are definitely *wrong* about Melessa." He refused to budge on that point. "She *was* my Eternal-One." He was positive that his ex-wife was the woman he'd been waiting a millennium for. She *had* to be.

Didn't she?

"Then why didn't you love her?" Jane asked, feeding into Slade's most secret doubts. "Why didn't she love you?"

"Something obviously went wrong between us," he admitted, "but I *know* what my Dark Instincts told me and they are never wrong. When I looked at Melessa, I *knew* that she would lead me to my destiny."

"Only she didn't." Jane countered. "I think you were both more interested in the idea of *ruling* together, than of really *being* together."

"On Melessa's side, I'm sure that's true. But I *know* what I felt and it was the call of fate." Slade crossed his arms over his chest. "What else would it be? Believe me, I did not marry her for her conversational skills."

"How about for her cup-size? You said yourself she was the most beautiful girl in the universe."

Slade squinted. "Did I really say that?" He must have been delusional. Honestly, it was a struggle to even recall the woman's face.

"Yes, you really said it! You think I'm making it up?"

"Fine." Gods, why did Jane have to remember every stupid word he'd ever uttered? "Perhaps I *did* say it, but I was wrong. Melessa may have been pretty, but only in a very expected sort of way." He flicked a dismissive hand. "I did not look at her and see something new each day. I never woke up with her image at the forefront my mind. There was nothing… *extraordinary* about her."

Not like with Jane.

"Nothing extraordinary about Melessa." She muttered. "But she helped you secure your kingdom, so you proposed anyway."

"That was *not* why I married her. I grow tired of you saying such a thing."

"You grow tired of me saying the stuff you'd rather not think about."

He arched a brow. "I suppose your feelings for Charming are entirely based in love and have *nothing* to do with his crown?" He'd much rather discover more about Jane's beau than rehash ancient history about his ex. Melessa had never been very interesting.

"I can honestly say that I've never even *seen* his crown."

"It is probably very small. And fake. And small." He paused. "Has Charming shown you anything *else?*"

"Like what?"

"Like…" He hunted around for some way to casually ask if she'd slept with the bastard. He probably didn't want to know, but he *fucking wanted to know*. Images of her kissing that barely-royal human filled his mind. Her hair brushing against Charming's skin, her beautiful body opening for his, her smile warming every piece of him. Slade told himself he was in control of his Dark Instincts, but it wasn't true. He would slaughter any other man who touched her.  In his heart, he knew it.  Jane was *his*.

Her eyes narrowed.  "I *know* you're not asking if I've slept with Prince Charming.  Because that's none of your business, Slade."

Shit.  She was right and that pissed him off even more.  "Of course not.  I was asking... about... his castle.  Have you seen his castle?"

"No."

"Then he's lying about having one."  Slade decided.  "If a man truly has a castle, he shows it to the woman he wants."  God knew, he would be showing Jane the Obsidian Fortress as soon as he'd claimed it.  Maybe that would impress her.

She made a face.  "For your information, I know for a *fact* that Prince Charming has a big, pink castle in Disneyland."

"You've been to this land of Disney?"

"No, but I've seen it on TV."

Slade snorted.  "Oh, the picture box is filled with lies.  I saw a program on that screen which claimed Bigfoot was eating campers in some forest.  Only he is a vegetarian, so I *know* that report was fabricated."  Slade nodded smugly at Jane's eye roll.  "Your alleged 'prince' is no doubt lying, as well."

"I guess we'll see when he rides up on his white steed and sweeps me off my feet."

Slade's teeth clenched.  He'd never been so sexually frustrated, the only woman he wanted longed for another man, and he *still* missed his royal horses.  The very last thing he wanted to hear was Jane admiring Charming's herd of thoroughbreds.  "I owned an entire *stable full* of white steeds back on the Vampire Isle."  He told her tersely.  "They were the envy of the realm."

"So you've said.  A lot."  Jane didn't seem awed by the news.  "If I were you, I'd be sorrier about losing the giant butterflies.  They sound way cooler."

Aha!  *Now* they were getting somewhere.

"Charming does not have giant butterflies?"  Slade smirked.  "Mine will come whenever I call.  What kind of king lacks a loyal swarm of giant butterflies?"  He gave a dismissive scoff at the very idea. "But then, Charming's *not* a king, is he? He is a mere *prince* and giant butterflies are discriminating creatures. They only seek out the *truly* worthy." He arched a brow. "You should take heed of their wise example."

"This 'Prince Charming' joke is becoming less funny." She muttered and shook her head. "Whatever. We're getting way off track. Let's get back to the you-flying-us-out-of-the-enchanted- forest plan."

"I told you I cannot fly." Slade would not backpedal on that deception. Not when she was still obsessed with leaving him. It offended his intrinsic nobility to lie, but he would gladly suffer the degradation before he lost Jane. He would endure *anything* to keep her. "We will have to use the Corpse Road."

"Your creepy henchmen say that it's a bad idea. No one even knows where that path."

"So we shall find it. And our devoted followers are not *henchmen*. Or creepy."

"That one guy has three eyes and an extra elbow, Slade. It's creepy."

"That is a female." Slade corrected. "Mrs. Zagn'2!x. She bakes wonderful bread."

Jane squinted at the pronunciation. "Uh-huh." She sighed again. "Look, all I'm saying is that we need to get out of here and your 'devoted followers' just told us that Corpse Street *isn't* the way."

"They are an overly cautious group. Do not worry. I can protect you from whatever small ghosts lurk on the path." Slade smiled confidently. "They are easily defeated with…"

She cut him off. "Ghosts?" Her brows drew together. "Hang on, like actual *ghosts* live in this place?"

"Ghosts do not 'live.' They haunt."

…And kill unsuspecting travelers, if Neville was to be believed. Best not to mention that part.

"They *haunt?*" Jane looked appalled. "Holy shit! I'm not going on a path *with freaking ghosts haunting it!* You must be out of your mind to even suggest that, you lunatic!"

"It *is* called the Corpse Road, Jane. What did you think dwelled there?"

She didn't appreciate that logic. "You got us into this, so you *fix* it, Slade. Find us another way out!"

He liked it when she called them "us." Slade and Jane were an "us." Jane and any other man were *not*. Her eyes sparked in beautiful shades of silver and her impertinent demands had his whole system aflame. No one but Jane ever issued him orders. For some reason, he found that so attractive. He found everything about her attractive, actually. It was almost as if she was made for him.

Like *she* was the destiny he'd been searching for.

Slade's head tilted, on the verge of a great revelation. "Jane..."

His words were interrupted by the lightning storm. A fantastical bolt of electric orange burst from the cloudless sky and arced downward. The unnatural power impacted the ground with a gigantic crash, igniting the trees in the distance. Flames jumped fifty feet in the air, illuminating the sky. Then another lightning bolt struck. And another. And another. Until the forest was burning in every direction.

At the rebel camp, screams and panic erupted. Slade's followers began frantically running towards the river to escape the encroaching flames. Someone had set the entire Endless Woods ablaze.

"Oh my God!" Jane gaped at the chaos. "What's happening?"

There was only one species capable of this level of destruction. They were hunters of the Vampires. Remorseless killers, who'd been eradicated in all civilized realms. He should have known that the few who remained would join forces with the Werewolf.

Slade looked down at Jane, his jaw set in a grim line. "Fang has called in the Order of Mages." He intoned, waiting for the true horror of that statement to sink in. Her beautiful face would no doubt pale with the realization that they were about to encounter one of the deadliest enemies in the supernatural world. He just prayed that she wouldn't faint in terror.

Jane squinted. "Who the hell is that?"

# Chapter Ten

INT.- DRUNKEN DRAGON TAVERN- DAY

ROLAND is brooding. Everything seems to be going wrong for him lately. The anti-vampire supplies he bought from the WIZENED ENCHANTRESS haven't helped, because he has no idea where SLADE even is. Worse, over the past week, ROLAND has ceased to matter. All anyone can talk about now is the vampire. Even his musical gig was canceled, because everyone else in the band was too busy talking about SLADE to care about rehearsal. ROLAND'S glorious fate has been derailed, all because of that blood-sucking asshole. He must find a way to stop SLADE before it's too late. In the meantime, ROLAND finds comfort in sharing his thoughts with the pretty bartender. And in drinking a lot.

ROLAND
(Drinking a lot)
I don't get it, Tegan. You were here when the Dying Old Knight Guy gave me the Silver Sword. I'm the one who's supposed to defeat Fang, not this Slade douchebag. The dude is a total fucking nobody, man.
What does everybody see in him?

TEGAN
(Sighing dreamily)
Well, he's *amazing* looking, for one thing. His hair is like someone bottled the sun and sold it as shampoo...

ROLAND
(Cutting her off in surprise)
Hang on, you've met Slade?

### TEGAN

*Well, yeah. He and his trusty squire were in here last week. It was the same night the knight gave you that sword, actually. They left right before you arrived. They were really interested in finding the rebels.*

*Redrafted Film Script- "From Here to Infinia"*

"Oh for gods' sakes… The Order of the Mages." Slade repeated in a less foreboding tone. "Their kind hunted Vampires for millennia, before my grandmother defeated them at the Battle of Gothmoreia."

"Your grandmother the cat?"

"Yes! She is a powerful warrior and mystic. I've repeatedly told you this"

"Uh-huh."

Slade wasn't satisfied with her blank tone. "Surely you've heard of Gothmoreia." He prompted. "It is the greatest battle, in the greatest war ever waged."

"If you say so."

"I *do* say so. *Everyone* says so." He shook his head. "Your education is sadly lacking in some areas, Jane Squire."

"Feel free to write a letter of complaint to the Chicago Public School System, if we survive this." Jane muttered, her eyes on the huge fire crackling their way. "So these Mages are trying to barbeque us on Fang's orders?"

"So it would seem. Of course, the fire is not our most pressing concern."

"It's not? Do I even want to ask what *is* our most pressing concern, then?"

"Mages can control electricity."

"Electricity?" That didn't sound so dire. "Oh. Is that all?"

Slade gave another dramatic sigh. If Jane didn't know better, she'd swear he was disappointed that she wasn't adequately impressed. "Electricity isn't as common in most worlds, as it is in yours." He pointed to the charges igniting the sky. "The lightning is quite frightening to most people. And Mages can travel on the bolts. Each strike allows them to move to a new position, searching for their prey."

Jane made a face. "I swear that's ripping off some sci-fi movie, but I don't remember which one."

"The Mages are the stuff of legend, so they are no doubt the subjects of many of your 'movies.'" He glanced down at her. "Today, *we* are their prey. They will find us and attack. Whatever you do, don't touch them. Their entire bodies are electrified. If you land a punch, you will die."

"Yeah, that part's a little scarier." Jane allowed. "Are you *sure* you can't fly us out of here? Because it would be *really* helpful if you could fly us out of here."

"We cannot attempt it with a Mage nearby. Flying is a delicate balance. The storm would knock me from the sky." He paused and then quickly tacked on. "Also, I cannot fly in Infinia, so the point is moot."

"You're a terrible liar, but I don't have time to kick your ass." Jane headed towards Slade's hut, shaking her head in annoyance. "If you refuse to fly, we'll have to do this the hard way. Be warned, when we die and become ghosts, I'll *definitely* be haunting you throughout eternity."

Slade hurried after her. "Where are you going?

"To get that stupid movie script. Since I'm not about to fight Dynamo, we have to find the Corpse Road. It's the only way out and the script might be able to tell us where to find it."

"You wish to run?" Slade looked outraged.

"Of course I wish to run. Why would we stick around to get cremated, if we can just amscray?"

"I am unfamiliar with whatever language you are speaking and thus unable to adequately address that question."

Jane ignored that and stomped inside Slade's hut without bothering to ask permission. Those useless rebels had given him the biggest and fanciest house in the village. It was still just made of sticks and straw, though, so any Big Bad Werewolf was going to be able to blow the damn thing down. Jane did not plan to be around when that happened.

"Jane?" Slade persisted, ducking through the doorway after her. He stood there, posed like Captain America. "Sooner or later, we must face Fang. How else will we win the kingdom?"

"I'm kinda hoping for a game show." She absolutely didn't notice that he took up all the space in the room. Just like she didn't stare over at the bed for a beat and imagine doing all kinds of things to him that would screw up this movie's PG-13 rating. Because Jane Squire didn't long for what she couldn't have.

It was part of being a pragmatist.

She stalked over to the rickety dining table and grabbed the red manuscript lying on the rough surface. Sure enough, *From Here to Infinia* had changed again. Every edit just seemed to get worse, so that wasn't exactly welcomed news. She began fanning through it, looking for some mention of the Corpse Road.

"Good news, there only seems to be one Mage. Bad news, she's some psycho named Dallyn, who spends three pages monologuing with Fang about eradicating the evil Vampire menace."

"Dallyn?" Slade scowled. "She still lives?"

"You know her?"

"Yes. She is one of the most dedicated hunters. She hates all Vampires, but most especially me."

Jane made a face. "Why does everyone have a vendetta against you, Slade? I mean, aside from the obvious reasons of your personality and behavior."

"In Dallyn's case, I once resisted her dubious charms at a particularly raucous supernatural ball. She has been holding a grudge for centuries."

"Oh." Jane instantly decided the bitch needed her batteries yanked.

From the crappy dialogue, Dallyn seemed like the typical scantily-clad, vaguely-foreign villainess who populated Hollywood films. Jane refused to be intimidated by some cheap refugee from *Underworld*. She was escaping this inescapable forest and she was taking Slade with her.

"Well, we're not going to stick around and let you two get reacquainted." Jane scanned the script. "Right here!" She triumphantly pointed to the scene heading on one of the new pages. "Exterior: Entrance to the Corpse Road- Night. Fang stands *by the waterfall* and reads the note. See?" She slammed the folder shut and arched a brow. "That wasn't so hard, now was it? Grab your sword. We're leaving."

"I do not wish to leave. I wish to stay and fight. I defeated Fang once and I shall do it again."

"Yeah, well, you're not 'doing it again' right now." Slade didn't seem excited to pack clothes or food, but he did pick-up the golf bag. God knew why he kept lugging the thing around, but whatever. "We don't have a plan, we're armed with sporting goods, and your not-so-brave troops have dashed off into the trees." She made a face. "Actually, that's probably for the best. They'd just get themselves hurt."

"We've been training! They are much improved at battle tactics." He hesitated. "I should have stressed that fleeing was not the best strategy for annihilating one's enemy. Perhaps they are confused."

"Perhaps they are dumbasses." Jane muttered. "Not that it matters. This whole world might be actually happening, but it's still running by movie rules. I'm betting it will stay that way until the finale, and I seriously doubt the decisive showdown between you and Fang happens in the second act. You don't even have Roland's stupid sword, yet. No way will either of you be annihilating each other today."

"Fang shall not defeat me on *any* day." Vampiric gentleman that he was, Slade held the door open as she passed, but he was still annoyed by her refusal to stay and die. "I am a *king*."

"A king? Wow, you're kidding. If only you'd said something *before*."

"Sarcasm does not change the truth." Slade told her, sounding miffed. "Besides, you said yourself that the cinema script is changing. The balance of power could shift, if we are not vigilant."

"That would probably be a *good* thing for us, since

we're currently on the low end of the power teeter-totter. You know how I can tell? Fang's got Mages who can control lightning and *your* fearless troops are hiding in the underbrush."

Slade didn't appreciate that recap. "I have power from fate itself guiding me. It is my *destiny* to win this land."

"And it's my destiny to *not die* helping you win it."

Now he looked pissed. Not at the monsters attacking them, but at Jane. "You should have more faith in me." He informed her, as if she'd somehow hurt his feelings.

Jane sighed. He was so touchy about all that fate crap. "Look, I one hundred percent believe that you're going to kill Fang. Okay? Just not when he has us on the defensive and the woods are on fire. Can we please finish arguing about this later and concentrate on evacuating the…?"

Slade cut her off. "No. I do not mean you should have more faith in me as a king or soldier. I mean you should have more faith in me as a *man*."

Jane glanced at him in surprise.

Slade regarded her seriously. "I know it makes you uncomfortable to rely on me, but I am a thousand years old and have fought in countless battles. You can trust me to know what I am doing." He shook his head. "You will not die helping me, Jane. I'll let Infinia fall before I risk you. Trust me and I will not disappoint you."

She tore her eyes away from his steady gaze and cleared her throat. "It doesn't make me uncomfortable to rely on you," she lied, "I'm just not used to it."

"You think I will fail in our quest."

Jane winced at the blunt phrasing. "I know that you'll win this war." She reiterated. "And I think you're probably the most honorable person I've ever met. You're a little insane, but in a very comic book-y way. You're stupidly brave and stupidly honest. You take stupid risks, because you think it's the right thing to do, and you always believe the best of people. Even the stupid ones. I admire that about you. I do." She nodded, willing him to understand. "But I'm *none* of that stuff."

"Jane, that is not true."

"It *is* true. I'm a pragmatic, cynical, suspicious loner. I always have been. My feelings aren't about *you* being untrustworthy. I've just never had a lot of faith in *anyone*. It's how I'm wired."

Slade stared down at her, the irritation on his face softening to compassion. "Have you always been alone, then?"

"I'm not alone. I'm *independent*. There's a difference." It was just hard to remember that difference when she spent every holiday watching infomercials on her couch.

Slade seemed equally skeptical. "You were trapped in your world, with no one to shield you from the darkness." He deduced. "It makes it hard for you to trust. I blamed myself."

"I blame you for a lot of things, but not for that. Why is my rotten childhood your fault?"

"I should have come for you, Jane. I should have protected you. You were just born too far away for me to know of you." He blinked suddenly, as if someone was shining a bright light in his eyes. "You were born too far from me." He repeated in a distant tone. "*That's* why I had to leave the Vampire Isle." His lips parted in amazement. "My gods... *You* are why I am on this path."

"Oh no, this whole disaster is *your* fault, not mine." That part she could absolutely blame him for. "I was minding my own business, stocking shelves, and you showed up to wreck my life."

Slade disregarded that. His head tilted to one side, an odd expression passing over his face. "Saving Infinia isn't my only chance for greatness." He murmured. "*You* are my only chance, Jane. I'm supposed to save *you*."

"I don't need saving." Jane paused as she passed Symon the scientist's workshop, her eyes narrowing. "Hang on." She took a quick detour, ducking through his doorway and looking around. She hated it when fantasy movies stuck in primitive versions of modern technology, but maybe the Gnome had created something useful.

No machine guns or tanks popped out at her. Not even a fire extinguisher. In fact the whole hut was empty except for a large wooden lever in the middle of a table. It looked like a light switch, but she had no idea what it powered. Symon had painted one side red and one side green. Off and on. Jane considered her options and then flipped it to green. Sketchy inventions always worked in fantasy movies, so she might as well take a chance. At this point, what did she have to lose?

"Jane?" Slade stuck his head in the door. "Please. You must listen to me."

"Not to beat a dead Werewolf, but *this* is where listening to you has gotten me so far." She pushed passed him, stalking back outside and waving a hand around the smoldering forest.

"This is *destiny*. You don't understand." Slade sounded like he was finally piecing together some complicated puzzle. "I followed my instincts to my true fate. *That* is why we are here. It was meant to be."

There was just no talking to him sometimes. "Well, congratulations. Some of us don't have the universe planning our glorious futures and handing us pretty crowns, though, so we have to look out for ourselves." She headed towards the waterfall.

The lightning strikes were getting closer. That was probably a bad sign. The rest of the camp had emptied out, everyone scattering into the forest. Hopefully none of them would burn to death in their blind panic to escape. The rebels weren't the brightest crayons in the box, but Jane didn't want to see them charred to cinders.

Slade seemed almost in a daze as he followed Jane to the river. "Gods! You were right all along, Jane. Why did I doubt it? You are always right."

"Wow, you just said something that made sense. If this place has newspapers, we could alert them."

Slade didn't seem to hear that. "Melessa was not my Eternal-One. Of *course* she wasn't." He shook his head. "Did I *always* suspect that? I must have known. Or maybe I *couldn't* know it, because I wasn't meant to yet." He didn't even notice as lightning struck nearby and another tree went up in flames.

Jane did.

She winced at the destruction, glancing towards the raging stream. "Seriously, do you think it's safer to risk the fire and stay on dry ground, or risk the lightning and wade into the water?"

She might as well have been talking to herself. Slade was lost in his own thoughts. "It all makes sense, now. The unappetizing way Melessa smelled… The empty feeling when I touched her… The lack of connection I felt… She could *never* be the one I was waiting for, could she?"

He didn't seem to need an answer, but Jane gave him one anyway. It was *way* more satisfying to focus on Slade's crappy love life than on their current crappy situation. "Yeah, your Vamp-y instincts totally misfired when they set their sights on your ex." She muttered. If she ever met Melessa, she planned to deck her right in her perfect face. "I'd probably start ignoring them, if I were you. They keep landing you in trouble."

Jane reached the top of the waterfall and began moving faster through the brush, scouting for something that looked like the Corpse Road. She figured there would be corpses or a road to mark the path, but so far she wasn't spotting either. Damn it, how were they going to get out of this mess?

"No, my Dark Instincts told me that Melessa would lead me to my destiny and they were correct. I see that so clearly, now." Slade looked stunned. "All happened as it was *supposed* to happen, because I am here with you, Jane."

She scoffed at that revisionist history. "I told you, I don't need anyone to save me."

"Maybe *I'm* the one who needs saving." He somehow moved fast enough to get in front of her.

Jane gave a surprised yelp, as she slammed into his massive form. "What the hell are you doing? Is it *really* so hard for you to pay attention to our impending death scene?"

One huge hand snaked out to grab her arm and anchor her against his chest. It was a nice place to be, but they didn't have time for this. She gave an experimental tug on his grip, but he wasn't letting go. He stared down at her, his face intent. Jane's heartbeat picked up in a way that had nothing to do with the mortal danger they were in and everything to do with the incredible feel of his incredible body.

"I mean in, Slade." She got out breathlessly. "Focus on our escape and not…"

He cut her off, again. "You are my destiny, Jane Squire." He whispered and his lips found hers. This time, he didn't give her time to evade him. His mouth sealed over hers…

And just like that, Jane forgot everything.

Forgot the fire burning towards them, and the vengeful Werewolf plotting their deaths, and Slade's destined bride waiting in the wings, and the scorned Mage headed their way. Forgot everything except the Vampire who'd upended her life.

For one incredible moment, it was all swelling music, and spinning camera angles, and happily-ever-afters. It was standing at center stage and knowing the handsome prince was all yours. It was everything Hollywood always promised about kissing and more.

So much *more*.

Jane's toes curled in her shoes, her fingers fisting around the fabric of his shirt. Holy *God*. She'd known that Slade would taste incredible, but *this*… This was even better than she'd imagined. And she'd imagined it a *lot*.

She dragged him closer, taking things to an even higher level. The guy didn't need much urging. Slade dropped the golf bag so he could wrap both arms around Jane. His lips slanted across hers, taking everything she had. One big palm tangled in her hair, his hand caressing the thick curls like he wanted to feel every single strand. Jane undulated against him. When he'd taken her blood, it had been mind-blowing. Having him so clearly want her for more than just dinner made things even better, though. Her mouth opened under his, drowning in sensations. A bomb could've gone off and she would've ignored it. All she cared about was staying right in this moment with Slade.

For the first time in her life, Jane was home.

When he finally pulled back, she let out a distressed moan. "No, wait." She didn't want it to stop. It had all been *right*. Like she was finally where she belonged.

"Jane." He touched her cheek, his eyes traveling over her face. "It's always been *you*." His perfect teeth gleamed in a dazzling smile. "I should have felt it from the first. I *did* feel it, I just didn't understand what it meant." He shook his head. "Forgive me, my One. I've been such an idiot."

"You're always an idiot." She got out, barely processing his words. Reality was beginning to intrude. What had just happened? Was it some kind of Vampire aphrodisiac thing, again? It had to be, right? Nothing normal could feel that spectacular. "Wait, *what* am I forgiving you for? Are you sorry about kissing me? Because, I'm... *Shit!*" Her words ended in a shout as Slade was blasted out of her arms.

The lightning bolt slammed into the ground beside them, blowing them apart. Jane hit the ground, seeing stars. She must have blacked out for the second time that evening, because the world went dark and silent. She only managed to come to when she felt the heat of the fire.

*Too close.*

Instinctively, she knew the flames were coming towards her. Jane had to move. She wasn't sure that she could do it, though. Her eyes wouldn't open and her ears were ringing from the explosion. All she could hear was the roar of the waterfall.

...And Slade's uncharacteristic cursing. The guy was using four-letter words so vile that she didn't even recognize them. That wasn't like him. Slade might utter an occasional oath, but he was usually too much of gentleman for this level of enraged swearing.

"*Jane!*" He bellowed.

She jolted at the sound of her name in the middle of his obscenity-filled rant, becoming more alert. Was he calling her? Why was he calling her?

"Jane, don't do this! You *can't* do this. *You cannot leave me!*"

"Your human is as good as dead, Vampire." A woman taunted in a kind of Russian accent. "Soon you will join her."

There was the sound of swords clashing and a flash of

orange sparks. Jane focused for a second and saw Slade dueling with a woman in a leather leotard next to the riverbank. It had to be Dallyn. There was another burst of electricity. Jane realized every time their blades met, Dallyn was using her powers to shock Slade. The Mage's powers easily traveled through metal.

Slade didn't seem to care. "Whatever happens to my Eternal-One, you will suffer a *thousand-fucking-fold!*" He roared back. "*Now get out of my way!*"

His Eternal-One? Oh great, was Melessa here? That was *just* what this movie needed. If Jane could've opened her eyes for more than a second, she would've rolled them. Forget it. She was just going to say unconscious and...

"*Jane, you must wake-up! I will die without you!*"

Jane's lashes popped open at Slade's words, the haze evaporating from her mind so quickly that it left her dizzy.

Slade was about to die, unless she did something. Did *what?* What the hell was happening? Was he hurt? Could she get to him in time?

*Shit!*

Jane quickly took stock, trying to assess her injuries. Nothing felt broken or severed, but that could be the adrenaline talking. Hell, what did it matter? Slade needed her. There was no choice but to get up.

Jane raised her head, giving it a clearing shake. She was seeing three of everything, but at least she was upright. Slade and Dallyn continued their duel. He seemed okay for the moment. Well, considering at this particular moment he was fencing over a hundred foot drop, anyway. Behind them, water rushed over the falls with unstoppable force.

Why did fantasy movies always stage fights next to waterfalls?

"*Jane!*" Slade shouted, again. He was in the middle of battle, unable to see that she was awake, but still yelling out orders. "You must run!"

Well, that suggestion actually made a lot of sense, but it wasn't going to happen. Not when Slade needed her.

"She cannot hear you, Vampire." Dallyn snapped, not

even glancing Jane's way to make sure of that pronouncement. Supernatural beings were always underestimating humans. Especially sturdy, independent girls, who everybody thought could only play the sidekick. "Say goodbye to your little friend!"

Oh Jesus, they were misquoting *Scarface*, now? *From Here to Infinia* was seriously running out of ideas. Jane dragged herself to her knees.

"Your woman will die in the flames and you deserve to lose her, Slade." Dallyn pressed on with vengeful relish. "Who would choose such a pedestrian creature over someone as magnificent as *me?*"

Jesus, it was like Dallyn was just *daring* Jane to kill her.

Firming her jaw, Jane's gaze fell on Slade's precious golf bag. The golf bag that Amalie, the Witch, said they'd need on this quest. Now seemed like a good time to test that theory. A prop like that didn't get introduced to a film unless it was going to matter, right?

"*Jane will not die!*"

Damn right she wouldn't. Jane somehow found the strength to stand up.

Dallyn wasn't as convinced by Slade's bellow. "Forget it, Slade. This is Infinia-town."

Dear God, the stupidity just never ended.

"I am a *Mage*." Dallyn continued. "A goddess in any dimension I grace. Yet, you prefer the company of that drab human! A Vampire King --The hero of his people-- and a disgusting mortal. Just the idea makes me ill." Her tone was full of bitterness. "I do not understand what spell Jane Squire could have woven over everyone to make her seem *remotely* worthy of attention. Even Fang seems obsessed with her!"

"What?" Slade demanded, his face getting even grimmer. "How does he know of my Jane?"

Dallyn smirked, sensing that she'd finally struck a blow. "Werewolves salivate at the thought of possessing Vampires' Eternal-Ones. You know that. Fang's men say that ever since he caught her scent, he's talked of nothing but your precious human."

Now would be a *really* good time for Slade to point out

that Jane *wasn't* his Eternal-One, so there was no need for a werewolf to kidnap and rape her.

Instead, King Helpful slowly shook his head. "No one will take Jane from me." The words were deadly serious. "I have sought her too long to lose her now."

Dallyn gave a harsh laugh. "You already *have* lost her, you fool. Be glad that I've killed her quickly. Fang wanted her alive and surely death is preferable to what he had planned."

Super. Because, this whole thing wasn't freaky enough. Jane reached out to grab one of the golf clubs. As she turned, she spotted a sign pinned to the tree in front of her.

*Corpse Road Entrance.*

An arrow pointed down a narrow path that had appeared out of nowhere.

"Oh screw you, movie." Jane cast a glare towards the sky. "Is that the best you've got?"

These bastards had no idea who they were dealing with if they thought she'd run off and leave Slade behind. Even the hero of the film needed some help, now and then. Jane Squire wasn't some Red Riding Hood, waiting in the woods for Prince Charming to come and save her. She might not be the star, but she'd choreograph her own fucking fight scenes.

Slade's blue eyes locked on hers as she moved towards him. Desperate relief filled his face when he saw she was okay. "Jane." He whispered the word like a prayer.

Dallyn used his momentary distraction to strike. There was another flash of swords and the Mage drove Slade towards the rushing water. She pushed him to the edge of the rocks at the top of the waterfall. One more step and he'd topple over the edge. Jane wasn't sure even a Vampire could survive a fall like that.

"You were stupid to bring that mortal slut here, Vampire." Dallyn chortled, reaching one lethal palm towards him. Electricity arched between her fingers, eager to fry him. "You should have kept her locked away in her own dreary world. No ordinary human can survive this land."

Slade didn't try to evade her deadly palm. He didn't have to. "My human is far from ordinary." He murmured, his gaze still on Jane.

Dallyn realized what was about to happen a second too late. She turned, her mouth opening in a silent scream of denial as Jane slammed the nine iron into her skull.

The Mage's powers would've incinerated wood, scorched flesh, or electrified swords, but the golf club had an insulated handle. Dallyn's electrical powers traveled through the metal, the rubber grip not conducting the charge to Jane's skin. It was the perfect weapon for beating Slade's bitchy stalker.

Jane swung the club like she was going for a homerun at Wrigley Field, smiling with satisfaction as Dallyn cried out in panic. Without her zappiness fixing the fight, it was just about which of them was stronger. Too bad for Dallyn she'd been cast to look good in a leather bathing suit, not for her muscles. Size mattered. Jane hit her again and the impact sent the smaller woman flying backwards into the river.

Mages' magicks really should've come with a warning not to go swimming. The water came alive with short-circuiting, orange lightning. Dallyn shrieked in agony, her own energy turning against her. Her body was cooked alive in the broiling water, even before she was swept over the falls. Her blackened form disappeared in the torrent.

All over the Endless Woods, the terrible fires winked out and the ominous claps of thunder faded.

It was over.

Jane let out a long breath, glancing at Slade. "Okay, you were right about holding onto the golf clubs." She admitted. "They did come in handy."

For once, the King of the Vampires didn't remind her that the King of the Vampires was *always* right. Slade just stared at her, like he was in a trance. It wasn't like him to pass up a golden opportunity for gloating. Maybe he'd hit his head.

Jane frowned in concern, looking him over for injuries. "Are you hurt?"

"In my entire life, I have never felt such joy." He said quietly. "Thank you for existing, Jane Squire. I had given up hope."

Well, that was kind of dramatic, but at least he appreciated the save. About time he showed some gratitude for all the shit she put up with. "You're welcome." She muttered, staring over the waterfall. "I don't think we were supposed to kill Dallyn that easy, though. That probably means she's still alive."

Slade seemed to rouse himself from his amazed stupor. "No being could survive a defeat like that."

"If that were true, there would be a lot fewer cheesy sequels filling Cineplexes every August." Still, there wasn't anything they could do about Dallyn now. Jane heaved an irritated sigh. "Whatever. Let's just move onto the next act before something else goes wrong." She glanced over at the script, which had fallen to the ground a few feet away. "But first, I have to leave a message for my new admirer."

# Chapter Eleven

EXT- ENTRANCE TO THE CORPSE ROAD- NIGHT

FANG stands by the waterfall and reads the note. The piece of paper is pinned to a tree. It seems to be part of a play. It details an odd scene where FANG is reading the page of a script, which has been pinned to a tree. While reading about himself, reading the page of a script, which has been pinned to a tree. While reading about himself, reading the page of the script, reading about himself, reading the page of the script, which has been pinned to a tree. ...And so on and so on and so on, until his eyes begin to cross.

It is dizzying. Like looking into two mirrors at once so you see an infinite army of identical yous, all lined up on top of each other.

The tales of the magickal book were true. He has no idea what kind of powers could have accomplished such a thing, but he knows that it is not the work of the Vampire. SLADE is too honorable and righteous to gloat. This taunt is from the human. JANE has left a message for him, scrawled across the paper in red river mud and displayed where he was sure to find it.

JANE'S NOTE<br>
(In close-up)<br>
Give it up, asshole. I already know how this story ends.<br>
Spoiler Alert: You get neutered.

FANG slowly smiles and his eyes glitter in anticipation. He knows now that fate *does* exist for Werewolves. That there *is* one special woman for him. JANE SQUIRE isn't meant for

SLADE. This mocking little bitch is all his.

FANG
(Crumpling the note in his hand and turning to his men.)
Whoever brings me Jane Squire gets a really big castle and a hot date with the princess.

*Redrafted Film Script- "From Here to Infinia"*


The Corpse Road was lined with wild flowers.
On either side of the twisting path overgrown fields stretched as far as the eye could see. It all looked harmless and still. Almost dreamlike. As if everything in the beautiful landscape was peaceful, and tranquil, and you were the only one for miles. As if there was nothing to worry about except finding the perfect spot for a picnic. As if Monet might wander by later, painting haystacks and colorful blossoms.
Jane wasn't fooled.
The environment was designed to lull you into a false sense of security. The strange vegetation grew tall enough to provide cover for all sorts of badness. That was why the gentle breeze blew *juuuust* enough to hide any movement in the vast meadows and why the fragrance of the multi-colored blooms tried to seduce you closer. This whole misadventure was doomed and even the plant life knew it.
Jane looked up at Slade. "Nobody who goes into those fields is coming back out."
"I am getting a similar feeling." Slade's Caribbean blue eyes scanned the waving grasses, his jaw tightening. "Do not leave the path." It was a royal decree. "No matter what happens, stay on the gravel."
"Like I really planned to go off hiking with the ghosts." Jane retorted. Even when she knew he was trying to look out for her, it bugged her to follow orders. With the Goblins stationed in every other direction and Slade refusing to fly them out of there, she didn't have a lot of options, though. "Any

chance you can do that teleporting thing you were talking about?"

"No. Those magicks only work in the heat and the weather here is quite mild."

"*Heat?*" Well, that was typically random and stupid. "God, I can't *believe* I let you talk me into this." Grumbling anti-Vampire sentiments under her breath, she continued down the Corpse Road. "I hate this plan even more than all the other plans I've hated."

"Great heroes must prove themselves through hardship, Jane. It will all be worth it when we have our kingdom."

"I don't believe in heroes." Jane reminded him. "And this kingdom belongs to you and *Allandrina*, not me. I told you, I'm just along for the ride."

The "kissing Slade and seeing fireworks" debacle made it *super* clear that she needed to get out of this place as soon as possible. Every minute she was around the jackass was another minute she was falling deeper under his spell.

"According to the rebels, Allandrina was not much of a ruler, even before Fang took over. She is not interested in helping Infinia's people." Slade glanced at her. "Really, if anyone should be queen of this kingdom, it should be *you,* Jane. You care for them far more than Allandrina does."

Jane laughed at that, realizing that he must be joking. "Yeah, I'm totally cut out for a crown. I'll have to telecommute from the Windy City, though, because no way am I staying in Hyrule even one second longer than I have to."

Slade flashed her a brooding glance. He was unusually pensive, like something was weighing on his mind. Maybe he was still annoyed that she'd left that "Fuck You" letter for Fang. Slade hadn't thought it was such a good idea for Jane to draw more of the Werewolf's attention, but she'd been too pissed off to care. Girls from the Southside didn't cower from bullies.

"You still wish to leave Infinia?" Slade demanded.

"Just as fast as I can click my ruby heels together, pal."

He looked down at her battered Nikes in confusion. "Is your footwear enchanted?"

"No, of course it's not... Oh, never mind." Jane sighed. "*Yes*, I'm still leaving. The fact that a psychotic Werewolf now wants to make me his girlfriend, just makes my travel plans out of this dimension sound all the sweeter. You and Princess Toadstool can rule the Mushroom Kingdom on your own. I just want to get away from Bowser."

Slade's jaw ticked. "I will deal with Fang." He promised quietly. "You do not need to fear him."

The flatness of his tone caused Jane to stop walking and focus on his serious face. Slade was always so positive and cheerful. She liked that about him. His exuberant optimism was the exact opposite of Jane's relentless practicality, so it felt like a breath of fresh air. Seeing him in this dark mood confused her.

"I know you'll beat Fang." She assured him, in case that was what he was so worked up about. "I'm just angry that there's been a script change and now he's apparently obsessed with me, for some reason. Villains in the movies get obsessed with the *heroine*, not the sidekick. It doesn't make any sense."

"You are not a sidekick." Slade's celestial eyes burned into hers, the perfect blue glowing like the heart of flames. "And I'm not just going to beat Fang. I'm going to *kill* him." It was a vow. "Now that Fang has your scent, he's a threat to you. I will eradicate *all* threats to you, Jane, in this land and every other."

"I can eradicate my own threats. I think I proved that at the waterfall." She arched a brow. "Besides, you can't make this all about me. You were *already* going to kill Fang remember?"

"Well, now I am going to kill him *more*. *Everything* has become about you. Fang and I both know that." He shook his head. "The Werewolf thinks to take you from me and I will die before I lose you. There is *nothing* that will pry you from my side."

Jane stared up at him, mesmerized by his intensity. No one had ever cared so much about keeping her around. "Gee, that doesn't sound stalker-ish, at all." She whispered, because it was a better option than ripping off his clothes. "You're not planning on locking me in a dungeon or something, are you?"

Slade relaxed slightly at her sarcasm. The side of his mouth curved upward. "You can go anywhere and do anything you wish, Jane Squire." One of his massive palms cupped the side of her cheek. "You will just never have to do it alone."

Wow.

Jane swallowed hard and ducked away from him, before she melted into a puddle. Putting some distance between them would be a *very* smart idea, right now. Slade was way too good at telling a girl without a home just what she secretly wanted to hear.

She started walking a little faster, trying to think. What had they been talking about? The Werewolf, right?

Right.

She seized on that. "Anyway, to kill Fang we still need the Silver Sword. And to get the Silver Sword, we have to find Roland. Any idea where Infinia's favorite tween might be?"

Slade cleared his throat. "I believe the script last mentioned him listlessly sitting in an empty room, bouncing a rubber ball off the wall."

"Steve McQueen should come back from the dead and kick his ass." She rolled her eyes. "Whatever. We'll track Roland down, drag him from his parents' basement, and force him to participate in this insult to film-making. It's about time that dingus start pulling his own weight."

"You always have a very determined attitude, Jane." Slade cleared his throat, again. "I'll certainly need that kind of indomitable spirit, when it comes time to rule Infinia. I do not think I could do the job half so well without you beside me. Your heart is often too soft…"

"I do *not* have a soft heart!"

He kept talking. He *always* kept talking. "…But you put the citizens here first and your ideas are almost always correct. I believe it is your destiny to help save this kingdom. Not just from Fang, but from all the challenges yet to come."

"No way. That's *your* job."

"We are *partners*. We must do this together. My track record with leadership on the Vampire Isle is spotty at best. I need you. *Infinia* needs you. Whatever awaits you back in your world cannot be more important than the welfare of thousands."

"I'm not staying here, Slade." Jane reiterated firmly. She wasn't about to help him and What's-Her-Witch whip Infinia into shape. No way was Jane sticking around to clean the castle, while they planned their goddamn honeymoon cruise. "You'll have to find someone else."

"There is no one else." He said with absolute certainty.

Well, he probably had a point about that. Infinia wasn't exactly filled to the rafters with competent employees. "Yeah, speaking of which, I have to say that I'm still a little bit pissed at your precious rebels. Remind me why we went looking for them in the first place, if they were going to surrender at the first little werewolf attack? Talk about *useless*."

"It's disappointing that they didn't try to stand against Fang's forces, but..."

"Disappointing?" She interjected incredulously. "We came looking for their help and now we're about to be killed by ghosts. *That's* disappointing."

"I know." He sighed. "I blame myself. I have not inspired them to greatness."

Jane looked up at him. "That's not what I meant." She made a face. "Honestly, I like picking on the blockheads, but I was serious earlier. It's safer for them if they're not involved. You're the only one who can defeat Fang in the finale. Extras in fantasy movies are just around for the body count. The little guys shouldn't have to die, just so the stars get a big battle scene."

Slade beamed like she was the most special part of the whole universe. "You see why I need you so much? You are the best person I've ever known, Jane Squire."

"Oh please..."

"It's true. You care for people as a true ruler should. This is what I was trying to tell you. *I* am not supposed to rule Infinia. *We* are supposed to rule Infinia."

"That's ridiculous. You'll lead just fine on your own."

"No. You teach me so much. I am a better man for knowing you."

Jane was uncomfortable with the praise. "Yeah, well, it's good you got to know me before I'm eaten by ghosts, then."

"I will let nothing harm you, my One." He assured her softly.

Jane really wished he wouldn't say things like that. Or smile like that. Or really do *anything* like he did it. The guy was so shiny, he made her forget all the reasons she didn't believe in fairytales.

"Anyway, the line for the throne is kind of a moot point, because I don't think we're getting out of this place alive." She muttered, because she needed to focus on something besides gawking at him. "*From Here to Infinia* is trying to kill us. This scene wasn't even *in* the earlier draft of the screenplay." She waved a hand at the empty field around them. "The whole movie is getting made up as we go."

Slade scanned the deceptively picturesque landscape. "Is it so surprising that the script is changing? You said yourself that our actions have altered things."

"This isn't just a couple of new sets or some characters losing screen time, though. We've descended into chaos! There are so many different drafts, no one even knows what they're doing anymore. I'm an *actress*. I like it when people know their damn lines."

Slade didn't seem to have a reassuring answer for that. "One day, I would like to see you on the stage, Jane." He finally announced. "Or on the picture box."

"Sure." Jane nodded, going along with the new topic. It was better than dwelling on their imminent demise. "Just try not to blink or you'll miss me. I don't exactly get the leading roles."

"Well, you should." He seemed genuinely interested in her career as a glorified extra. "Which was your favorite character to portray?"

Jane thought about that for a beat. "Truthfully? As much as I bitch about it, I liked being Clarissa on *Dracula, Ph.D.*

That was the part I had the most fun with."

"Why?"

"Well, I was Johnathan Harker's long lost wife. I appeared just in time to ruin his wedding to Mina, the naive Psychology student. Dimitri Dracula, the vampire professor in love with Mina, resurrected my corpse to break them up. *Very* dramatic stuff."

He nodded, still listening. Slade always focused on her like he was fascinated, even when he couldn't possibly understand half of the words she used. The guy had been born in another world, but he still gamely tried to follow the plot of a nighttime soap opera. "You must have been magnificent in the role."

"Well, it was only for six episodes. See, Mina was my therapist, because I had amnesia from being brought back from the dead."

"The undead do not get amnesia. Zombies have no thoughts, at all."

She decided to ignore the supernatural director's commentary. "Mina was *also* the identical twin of the psychotic vampire Domonique Montgomery-Montgomery, who killed my character off again and then tried to frame Mina for my death."

"Psychotic Vampires are rare and horrible creatures, not to be trusted."

Jane smiled. "Exactly. Don't worry, though. Domonique got staked in season three." She hesitated. "I just wish we could've ended my storyline better. I just *died*, with no great closing scene, ya know? It felt unfinished. Clarissa deserved more." She shrugged. "Still, it was fun to have so many angsty lines and to be in the middle of the action. That was the closest I'll ever get to a starring role. I usually just get to stand in the background."

"You should have more confidence in your abilities. I have no doubt you are an extraordinary actress."

"Critics and Jonathan/Mina shippers don't tend to agree."

"Simply point out the ones who've offended you. I

guarantee, their final words will be apologies for how very, *very* wrong they've been."

Jane glanced up at him with a huge grin. He was teasing her! "Why, King Slade, you old charmer! That's the sweetest thing you've ever said to me." It was a bad idea to flirt with him, but she couldn't help herself. He was just so damn awesome.

Slade's gaze fixed on her happy expression, something untamed moving behind his eyes. "Jane, I am a Vampire of many talents, but subterfuge is not among them." He said hoarsely. "I cannot go on this way."

Jane reacted to that out-of-the-blue announcement with the kind of sparkling repartee that any screenwriter would be proud of. "Huh?"

Slade glanced away with a shake of his head. "I must share my revelation, though I fear you will not welcome it."

"Um… Okay."

He sighed, wearily. "For nearly twenty minutes now, I have held back my words, but I find I no longer can sustain this charade. I thought perhaps it would be better to let you realize the truth on your own, but you are taking far too long." He flashed her an expectant look, like he was waiting for her to apologize for not reading his mind.

Except Jane still had no idea what he was talking about. "Slade, I have no idea what you're talking about."

He frowned at that news. "How can you not know? I think *I* knew from the first. My Dark Instincts recognized you from the minute we met. Really, it explains so much."

"What does? The fact that you're insane?"

He made an expansive gesture with his hands, as if she was being completely unreasonable. "It's like you are *deliberately* ignoring the truth."

"*I have no idea what you're talking about.*" She repeated in exasperation. "For real, what the hell is your problem now? Because…"

"My problem is *you*." He interrupted at a roar. "*You* are my Eternal-One and you seem determined to deny it!"

Jane stared at him.

Oh dear God. He was hallucinating. Was it the Corpse Road? Was it somehow messing with his mind?

She chewed her lower lip, trying to decide the best way to help. "Slade, sweetie, you should sit down for a minute." She reached over to take hold of his arm, guiding him towards a flat rock on the side of the path. "Just take deep breaths. We might have a serious problem here."

"I *know* we have a problem." He crossed his arms over his chest. "*You* are the problem. I said as much, not two minutes ago."

"Slade, *I am not the problem*." She shouted, on the verge of a major freak-out. "The fact that Fang is coming after us? *That's* the problem. The fact that we have to reach the end of this road soon or you're going to be stuck out in the open when the sun comes up? *That's* the problem. The fact that you're becoming delusional? *That's the fucking problem!* So just shut-up and let me deal with this, okay?"

"Delusional?" He squinted like maybe she was the one hallucinating. "Explain how I am delusional."

"You think I'm Melessa." She told him bluntly. "Maybe you should put your head between your knees and see if that helps."

"I know you're not Melessa! Have you gone mad?"

"No, but *you* might be. You're calling me your Eternal-One." She patted his shoulder, trying to reign in her panic.

Okay. She could figure this out. Somehow.

No matter what happened, she had to keep Slade safe. In the meantime, it did no good to yell at the poor guy. She needed to look out for him until he recovered. That was what best friends did for each other and she abruptly realized that the big doofus was the best friend she'd ever had.

"I'll take care of you." She touched his shiny hair, pushing it back from his forehead. "Don't worry." She gave him a tender smile. "Everything will be fine, alright? I'll get us out of this."

"Jane, you *are* my Eternal-One."

She barely heard that, trying to estimate the distance to the edge of the vast field. Maybe she should risk cutting across it. If it got Slade help quicker, she'd...

"Jane!" Slade interrupted her planning with an impatient frown. "Are you listening to me?"

"What?"

"I said, you *are* my Eternal-One."

"What?" She repeated vaguely and then turned to look at him in surprise when she actually processed that statement. "Wait, *what?*"

"You. Are. My. Eternal-One." He carefully spaced each word. "I tried to tell you, but you don't seem to understand. It was never Melessa. It was *always* you."

Jane gaped at him. For once, she couldn't think of a single thing to say.

Slade took her silence as encouragement. "It's why so much seemed to go wrong for me earlier this year. Only nothing went wrong, at all. Marrying Melessa and then losing the Vampire Isle, *had* to happen so I could come to your world." He nodded like it all made perfect sense. "Everything was designed to bring me to your side. *You* are where I belong. You and I are *one*."

Jane blinked. Come to think of it, there was only one possible response to that gibberish.

She burst out laughing.

Slade scowled as Jane doubled over in hilarity. "You find our shared destiny amusing?"

"I find the idea of *having* a shared destiny amusing." She wiped her eyes and jerked a thumb towards the fields. "Alright, come clean. Have you been smoking some of these weeds?"

His jaw ticked. "Is it because of Prince Charming? Do you not wish to acknowledge your connection with me, because of your inappropriate feelings for him?"

"Inappropriate? Wow. You must have watched a more interesting cartoon than I did."

"Any feelings you have for another man are *wrong*. I do not accept them." He arched a brow. "And I suspect that Disneyland is a squalid and miserable place. I have not heard of it and I have heard of every kingdom worth hearing about."

"I think Mickey's team of super-lawyers can have you thrown in jail just for saying that." Jane shook her head. "Seriously, is this some kind of weird royal rivalry thing, where you want to prove your scepter is bigger than Charming's?" Since Slade was planning to marry a princess, she'd enjoyed pretending that she had a royal fiancé of her own, but enough was enough. "Because, there's no need. Prince Charming doesn't exist, you moron."

"Doesn't exist?" Blond brows compressed. "Why do you keep speaking of him, then?"

"Because he's *Prince Charming!* He's the perfect man that little girls dream about. Then we grow-up and realize a guy on a white horse isn't going to charge to our rescue, no matter how many movies tell us otherwise.

Slade began to look more cheerful. "You mean... you just *invented* this man?"

"*I* didn't invent him, he's a fairytale. One of our most famous stories. He's the ideal husband." She shook her head. "*Everyone* knows that, Slade. I mean, how could you not realize I was messing with you? Do you *really* think some handsome prince would wander into the grocery store and decided *I* was his dream girl?"

...Except that seemed to be exactly what was happening, didn't it?

Caribbean blue eyes regarded her steadily and things suddenly seemed a lot less funny.

Jane felt her heartbeat speeding up. Her amusement faded into something like terror. "Slade, come on. You're not serious about this..." She began.

He cut her off. "So, you aren't planning to marry another man?" He still seemed halfway convinced that Charming was going to show up with a glass slipper.

"I'm not going to marry *anybody*." She deliberately stressed the "anybody" part, so he'd know it included "any *Vampire*," too. "I mean it. I'm *not* your Eternal-One. That's not even up for debate."

"Oh, I don't plan to debate it."

Jane decided to interpret that in the best possible way.

She could hear her heart beating in her ears. "Good, so I think we should forget this whole thing ever happened. You're just… confused."

"No, Jane. I'm not confused, at all. You are my Eternal-One. There can be no debate, because it's empirical fact. And now you tell me that there is no other prince in your life, so all of our problems are solved." He beamed at her, like he'd singlehandedly solved world hunger.

Jesus, he *was* going crazy.

"*My* problems aren't solved. Not even close." She shook her head. "Your problems aren't solved *either,* if you stop to think about it. All you want is Infinia, remember? Even if it *is* true and I *am* your Eternal-One --which I'm *not*-- I can't give you a kingdom, Slade. Only Allandrina can do that. It's why you're planning to marry her!"

Slade frowned. "I do not know why you continue to worry about that woman. I have already decided I cannot marry Allandrina."

Jane refused to be relieved over his change of heart. "Since when?" She demanded. "Six seconds ago?"

"Since you made it clear that you would never tolerate the plan. And you were right, as you usually are. I was a fool to even consider such a cold transaction." He sighed. "My only excuse is the divorce left me hardened to the idea of romance. I had given up on finding you."

"You think you were looking for *me?*"

"I know I was. My Dark Instincts all told me when I'd found you, but bitterness blinded me to the truth. I am ashamed of that. My plan to wed that princess was an insult to you and our connection. Forgive me, Jane."

Jane stared at him. "You want me and not Allandrina?" She finally asked, knowing it was a mistake to be so delighted by that fact.

"Of *course*. How can you even question that? Even before I realized we were Eternal-Ones, you were the only…" Slade trailed off and blinked as if a new idea occurred to him. "Wait, did you create this Prince Charming, because you were upset over my supposed feelings for *Allandrina?*" He seemed thrilled. "That is a ludicrous --yet encouraging-- idea. I forgive you for lying. Jealousy is a good sign."

"*You* forgive *me?!*" It felt like all she could do was echo the utter craziness he was spouting.

"Of course, I do." Slade gave an arrogant nod. "I was going insane, picturing you with another man. Just as you were upset that I would stupidly consider marrying another woman." He smiled the kind of smile that made her want to punch him. Repeatedly. "It is actually very sweet. But I promise there is no need for you to concern yourself about Allandrina. I never even *met* the woman, Jane. She means nothing to me. Nothing at all."

"You are the most egotistical idiot in the world! This isn't about me being jealous! I don't care *what* you do."

"You do not mean that."

"Yes, I do!" She shouted, even though he was right. "Sleep with every tiara-wearing twit in the land, if it makes you happy. I just want to go back to my old life, lock myself in my apartment, and be safe and alone forever."

Slade rubbed the back of his neck, apparently irritated that she wasn't rushing off to buy *Vampire Brides Magazine*. "You cannot be alone." He complained. "Without you, *I* would be alone and that is the last thing I desire. You are needlessly complicating this wonderful news. We are Eternal-Ones."

"Bullshit."

Slade sighed at that succinct answer. "You are always so difficult to reason with."

"*I'm* difficult?"

"Yes! You have fought me every step of our journey."

"*Your* journey, Slade. I've been a really good sport about you dragging me into *Army of Darkness*, but it's never been about *me*. This whole becoming-a-king plan is about *you*. Just like this Eternal-One thing is about *you*. And what *you* want and what *you* think." She waved a hand. "You've never asked me what *I* want. Not even once."

He seemed baffled by that. "If I asked you what you want, you would tell me things that I do not wish to hear. You would tell me that you plan to leave me and not be my Eternal-

One."

"*Yes.* That's exactly what I'm telling you!" This couldn't be true. There was just no way someone like Slade wanted *her.* It was another one of his loony ideas that would lead to badness and heartbreak. "This whole thing is ridiculous. Just sit there and try to regain your normal *kind of*-sanity, while I figure out what to do next."

"I do not understand your attitude. I *expect*ed it, but I don't understand it. Many women would be *thrilled* to have me as an Eternal-One."

"Many women *have* been your Eternal-One and none of them were thrilled." She retorted. "You got it wrong with Melessa, right? And didn't you tell me that you thought Damien's wife was your Eternal-One, before that?"

"I was tricked into believing Karalynn was mine! I was influenced by a magick book and not thinking clearly. Many of the words I spoke to her were not even my own. There was a *spell* that fogged our reality!"

"If you say so."

"I *do* say so! Yes, I was wrong about other women in the past, but I am *not* wrong about you. Even you must sense the bond between us, Jane."

She shook her head. "I don't." And, even if she did, she would never, ever admit it.

"You *do.*" He insisted. "You *have* been a good sport about our journey, Jane. And I know you well enough to know that you are *rarely* a good sport."

"Way to woo me, ass hat."

"I am simply being honest. You would *never* be this accommodating with another man. We both know that."

She turned away, unwilling to consider the truth of that statement. Every conceited word out of his conceited mouth annoyed her. "You're twisting this around." She snapped. "You're my ticket out of this dimension. *That's* why I've been sticking with..."

Slade cut her off, catching hold of her arm and swinging her back around to face him. "You would have left anyone but me *days* ago." He continued passionately. "You would have used those golf clubs to kill any other man who brought you to this realm against your wishes. You would never, *ever* have fed another Vampire. Not Jane Squire, cynic and loner. You've only done all this because of me. Because I'm *me*."

"You're admitting that it's your fault? Good! I totally agree."

He ignored that too and kept going. "You did these things, because --deep down-- you know that we're supposed to be together. You *want* to be with me, Jane. We belong with each other and you know it."

Jane shook his hand off, adrenaline pouring into her system. "No."

Slade regarded her like he was seeing her for the first time. "That's it, isn't it?" For someone who worked hard at acting like an idiot, he was always so annoyingly perceptive. "That's why you're fighting so hard to leave. You already *know* you're mine. You've known longer than I have and it frightens you."

Frightened? She was fucking *terrified*. What if this was all a trick? What if it *wasn't?* "I'm not yours. I'm not *anyone's*. I never have been."

"You *always* have been. You were born to be mine, Jane. It took me thirty years to find you, but I did it. There is nothing I wouldn't brave if it meant being together."

She took a step backwards. "We're not *supposed* to be together. You're supposed to be the hero of this movie and I'm supposed to be one of the damn extras. When have you ever seen the hero ride off into the sunset with an extra, huh?"

"That entire statement is faulty. You are *not* an extra. You do not even believe in heroes. And I would burn to ash if we went into a sunset."

"Because you're a *Vampire!* You live on magical islands, and you have giant butterflies as pets, and you're so frigging shiny it hurts my eyes. *I'm* a normal person and normal people don't get mixed-up with Vampires! We do normal things and live normal lives."

"You have had more fun with me than you ever did in

your 'normal' life." He retorted. "*This* is the existence you were meant for. Standing at the middle of the story, not hiding in the background." He waved an expansive hand. "Your whole face lights up at the memory of six weeks when you had an almost-leading part on that *Dracula* show! You *loved* it, but you were scared and so you gave it up. This is the same thing, Jane. Don't you see that?"

"I didn't give it up! That was just a short term role, Slade. It wasn't meant to last."

"It might have lasted, if you'd taken the chance. You said yourself that Clarissa's story was unfinished." He watched her closely, still seeing far too much. "I know you, Jane. Did you even *try* to stay on the picture box?"

No. But she'd wanted to...

Jane swallowed, because deep down she knew he had a point. She should have fought harder for Clarissa. The writers killed her off without even a final scene. Jane *had* been scared to take a chance and try to change things. What if she tried to stay and they didn't want her? No one ever wanted her.

Slade's voice was deep and sure. "You and I can write our own story, Jane. Together, we can do anything. Have faith in yourself. Have faith in *me*."

Jane squeezed her eyes shut. Slade was about a million times more important than any acting job. Putting her faith in him would be like stepping of a bridge. Her fingers instinctively curled, like she was trying to cling to an invisible railing. Thirty years of stark pragmatism had her hanging on for dear life. She couldn't do this.

She *couldn't*.

"You're not going to confuse me, Slade. I won't let you. You can talk me into all kinds of shit, but not *this*." Jane kept edging away from him, wanting to increase the distance between them. Being near Slade messed with her head. Right from the beginning, he'd been able to slip passed her defenses and drown out logic. He could make her believe the impossible. "I want to go home and you can't convince me to stay."

"I don't have to convince you of what you already know." He said simply. "You are in love with me."

Jane saw red at that matter-of-fact response. "*Why would I be in love with you?* Huh? You've done nothing but wreck my life, you maniac!"

"I'm your Eternal-One!" He roared back. "You *must* love me. It is part of our bond."

"I *don't* love you and I will *never* be your Eternal-One! Go sell that crap to the next girl on your endless list of possible fiancées, because I'm not interested!"

Slade flinched.

Jane shook her head, too upset to even process the devastated look on his face. If she let him, he would destroy her. Betting on Slade would end up with her having *nothing*. She knew it. "I can't do this." She whispered out loud. "It's too big."

"Jane, please." He held out a hand. "I know you're afraid, but I can be a good mate for you. I swear it."

"No." It was a denial of this entire situation. "There's no way. I can't take a chance like that. Are you crazy?"

His face changed. For the first time since she'd known him, Slade looked defeated. "You mean you can't take a chance on *me*." He corrected quietly, dropping his palm. "I'm not worth it."

It was exactly the opposite.

Jane backed up even more. "You're just too big a risk." She told him, her voice unsteady.

If she handed him everything and he let her down, what would she have left? Slade was too important to her already. If she gave anymore and he walked away, she could never recover. And everyone *always* walked away. She had to be smart. Be a survivor. It was better to have nothing than to gamble on such a crazy, shiny, impractical longshot.

Right?

So why did she want to jump off that bridge and trust that he'd catch her?

Jane was so frantic that she didn't pay attention to where she was going. In her panic, she inadvertently left the Corpse Road. Her feet came down in the too-green grass at the edge of the path.

Instantly, she knew she'd made a massive mistake. She tried to scramble back onto the gravel, but something blocked her. An obstacle now stood between her and Slade. Her hands flattened against the invisible wall that had been erected, dread filling her. Once you left the safety of the road, there was no way back on.

"Jane," Slade shouted, "you will be alright!" He tried to reach through the barrier and grab her, but it didn't work. He could touch her arm, but he couldn't pull her back through. She saw concern cloud his features, as he tried to figure out how to help.

"Do *not* come out here." She ordered, reading his mind. "I mean it. There's no sense in both of us being screwed."

Slade's grip tightened on her arm. Even though it was pointless, he wasn't releasing his hold. "You are *not* screwed, Jane. Just give me a moment to come up with a plan to rescue…" His voice trailed off, his attention fixed on the endless vegetation behind her.

She whirled around and immediately spotted the problem. Something moved in the tall grass. Something dark and big and headed her way. The figures looked almost human, but their bodies swirled like small tornadoes. The shifting, twirling forms bore down on her, red eyes glowing amid the black smog of their faces.

Shadowmen.

Oh Christ…

Jane's gaze flashed back over to Slade. There was no way she was getting out of this alive and, if her death scene was coming at the hands of some cheap visual effects, she'd die looking at him. Slade was the final image she wanted to take with her. With a start, she realized that even if she died in her bed, seventy years from now, her final thoughts would *still* be of him. Crazy as it sounded, Slade was *it* for her. She knew that. She'd known it from the beginning.

Her Prince Charming.

"I'm sorry." Jane murmured and knew she was apologizing for not being brave enough to tell him how she actually felt. "Slade, I... *Stop!*"

Her words ended in a shout of alarm. Apparently intent on proving he was the stupidest Vampire in the universe, Slade silently stepped off the trail.

Jane's jaw dropped in horror. He'd left the road! Once you left the road, it was all over. Mutant ghosts were set on devouring them and he'd just deliberately put himself at risk.

"You fucking idiot!" She instinctively tried to push him back onto the path. "I *told* you not to come out here." She swore when the invisible barrier kept him from crossing back onto the gravel. "Goddamn it!" She gave his shoulder a frustrated shove. "I *told* you I'm not your Eternal-One. It's completely pointless for you to sacrifice yourself for me. It's not worth it! Why in the hell would you...?"

Slade cut off her rant, his eyes on the Shadowmen. "Because you're Jane." He said, moving in front of her. "Even if you never accept our connection, you will still be *Jane* and that is worth *everything*."

She stared up at him, having no idea what to say to that. There *was* nothing to say. The guy was a colossal lunatic, but he was also something more. Something a whole lot rarer than a Vampire and much more important than a king. Something that came straight from the core of him and that nothing could ever change.

Slade was something Jane had never believed in, until that very moment...

An honest-to-God hero.

# Chapter Twelve

INT- ROLAND'S BLACKSMITH SHOP- NIGHT

As he has for several scenes, ROLAND restlessly bounces a rubber ball off the wall. He isn't sure what to do next, so he isn't doing anything. It seems like the easiest option and ROLAND likes easy. The camera stays on him as minutes tick by. It's not very interesting, but at least it shows the audience that ROLAND is thinking.

What is he thinking about? Well, if he goes looking for SLADE, he knows one of them will perish. Is confronting the vampire worth the risk? Honestly, this quest thing is getting old. Does he *care* about ruling this dumb kingdom enough to die for it? The whole place is kind of lame, ya know? ROLAND'S an *artist*. He doesn't do –like-- taxes and laws and shit.

Maybe he should just let FANG and SLADE duke it out for the throne, and save himself the noise. Seriously, ROLAND'S young and handsome and he's got a horse. He could go off and have rocking adventures someplace tropical. Maybe even start a *new* band. A *better* band. (JAMES THE ORC sucks on bass. Why is he the only one who sees that?) For realz, ROLAND could write some hit songs. Meet some babes. Go bungee jumping. He doesn't need all this freaking pressure, man.

Those philosophical thoughts cause ROLAND to pause and consider something new. Hang on… If he walks away from Infinia, SLADE will get to nail the princess. Oh hellz no! ROLAND'S eyes cut over the pin-up spread of ALLANDRINA on the wall. All she's wearing is a tiara and a come-hither *smile, and ROLAND suddenly recalls his earlier voiceover. That chick does have a killer rack. And she's sure to thank-you-fuck the guy who saves her from FANG. No way is he just handing her over to the Vampire. If anyone gets a piece of that sweet ass, it's gonna be ROLAND.*

*He's the damn hero of this quest, bitches.*

*Redrafted Film Script- "From Here to Infinia"*

 

The Shadowmen came closer and Slade wasn't sure how to kill them. He could defeat regular ghosts, but he had never even seen this type of creature before. They didn't seem to have a permanent shape. They moved like an encroaching fog, only with clawed hands and feral eyes. There would clearly be no reasoning with them and it would no doubt prove difficult to wound a being made entirely of smoke. He had no idea where to even begin.

From out of nowhere, the doubts struck. The insecure thoughts that he refused to even acknowledge most of the time screamed louder than they ever had before. The voices that told him that he could pretend with everyone else, but they knew he was really a failure. He wasn't smart enough. Wasn't worthy enough. His own people didn't want him. His grandmother had forsaken him. His Eternal-One thought he was a joke. He was *nothing*. Slade was about to screw everything up and Jane would pay the price.

He was supposed to be the greatest warrior ever born. He was supposed to win any battle he entered. ...Except he always seemed to lose the ones that mattered.

"I can't believe you did this." Jane hissed at him. "You were safe on the damn road and you deliberately left it. You have the IQ of a comatose fruit fly, you know that?"

"You would prefer I stand by and watch you die?"

"I would prefer you *survive*." She sounded incensed. "I'm *still* going to die, but now you'll be joining me. Do you think I want that? Huh?"

Slade's mind was racing. "Neither of us will die today, Jane Squire." He vowed... only he had no clue how he could keep that promise.

The Shadowmen were drawing closer. They seemed to appear right out of the ground, changing positions instantly. Their misty bodies materialized in torrents of air, surrounding Jane and Slade. A terrifying howl went up as they closed in; the victorious cry of predators about to feast. The ghostly appendages reached for them, wanting to pull them deeper into the grass.

Jane's fingers found Slade's and he glanced at her in surprise. In what was very possibly their last moment alive, she linked herself to him. Jane Squire --the prickliest, least sentimental, most contrary human ever born-- planned to die holding his hand. She might deny their connection, but the truth was so clear. Deep down Jane knew it, too.

They belonged together.

Her palm tightened on his and Slade felt his heart turn over in his chest. A strange clam came over him, driving out his doubts. No matter what, he could not lose to the Shadowmen. He *wouldn't*. His whole world was at stake.

Slade's eyes narrowed in determination. The creatures moved too quickly to outrun and they had no heads to lop off. Dashing across the field would be suicide. Returning to the Corpse Road was impossible. So, there was only one choice.

Slade grabbed Jane closer, sweeping her up into his arms. "Hold on to me."

She gave a startled yelp as he lifted her against his chest, her arms circling his neck. "What are you doing? You can't pick me up. Only thin girls get picked up. You're going to throw your back out and the monsters are going to..."

"Jane, be quiet and *hold on*." Slade interrupted. With a surge of power, he propelled them straight up into the air.

"Holy shit!" Jane clutched him in a death-grip, her eyes the size of plates. "You're flying!" She looked down like she couldn't believe it. Clearly, few beings in her world could leave the ground. Why did she miss such a magicks-less place?

"Oh my God, you can actually *fly*, Slade!" She shook her head in astonishment. "I *knew* you were lying about Infinia blocking your powers."

He supposed it would be too much to ask that she'd forget that ridiculous deception. The woman had the lamentable habit of recalling every stupid thing he uttered. "Right." Slade cleared his throat. "I apologize for the untruth. It was wrong of me."

Jane's gaze stayed locked on the thwarted Shadowmen far below. "Well, Superman-ing me away from certain death is a great way to say you're sorry." She spared him a quick glance. "Just don't drop me."

"There is no chance of that happening." Slade held her close, breathing in the scent of her hair. She was safe. He couldn't believe that he'd actually done it. "I will never let you fall."

She swallowed, her constrictive grip lessening to a merely suffocating one. For Jane, it was an incredible show of faith. "Thank you." She whispered. "I had no clue how we were going to get out of that one. The next time I start complaining about one of your idiotic ideas, feel free to remind me of this moment."

Slade gave a serious nod, shocked that it had been so easy to escape the Shadowmen. The more he thought about it the more amazing it seemed.

"You okay?" She prompted, staring at his profile. "You look kind of weird."

"I expected to fail." He said honestly. "When it's important, I always seem to fail."

"*Fail?* You are the most absurdly successful..."

Slade cut her off. "No, it's true." He'd tried to deny it or pretend otherwise, but he knew in his heart that he was a disappointment. He'd always known. "The Vampire Isle exiled me, because they did not want me as their king. My grandmother practically disowned me. Rather than battle Fang at my side, the Infinia rebels fled at the first sign of danger. My own Eternal-One says she does not love me."

"Slade..."

He interrupted her again, not wishing to hear her pity. "I am not blaming you." No one had ever really loved Slade, so he wasn't even surprised by her lack of feelings. Hurt but not surprised. He'd hoped that it would be different. Maybe for a second he'd thought it could be, but Jane was so damn extraordinary and he was never quite enough. Not for anyone. "My point is, when something is *important*, I am guaranteed to screw it up."

"Slade." Jane lifted a palm to the side of his cheek, her eyes tracing over his face. "How could you *ever* feel insecure? You're brave, and smart, and handsome. Hell, you can even *fly*. You're as close to perfect as a guy can get."

"Except you do not want me."

And Jane leaving him would be a defeat from which he'd never recover. Usually, he'd just sigh over his lack of success, pick himself up, and go on. Despite everything, Slade was a naturally optimistic person. No matter how many times he failed, he always looked on the bright side. Not even losing his homeland had quashed his positive outlook for long. But there'd be no "going on" without Jane. Without Jane, his life would just… stop.

Dark Instincts stirred, hissing at him to do whatever it took to keep her.

Vampires *never* gave up their Eternal-Ones.

In retrospect, he'd been an idiot not to realize how ridiculous his relationship with Melessa truly was. The woman had been as much his Eternal-One as a puddle was the ocean. When she left, all he'd felt was a bruised ego and a massive amount of relief. If Jane had tried to divorce him, he'd end the universe. She owned everything inside of him and more.

Beautiful gray eyes stared up at him. "It's not that I don't want you. It's *me*. I can't…" She stopped mid-word, something catching her attention back towards the tree-line. "Okay, I hate to contribute to this movie's dialogue thievery, but… Infinia, we have a problem."

Slade turned and immediately saw the army. Black banners flapped in the breeze. Armor glinted. Hundreds of Goblins marched forward in relentless formation. Fang's men had reached the edge of the Endless Woods and they were starting straight across the field. Clearly no one had warned them about staying on the road.

Jane shook her head. "It's going to be a bloodbath once the Shadowmen see…"

She didn't even get to finish the sentence before the screaming started. The ghostly creatures swarmed the Goblins. Black mist swirled around Fang's henchmen, dragging them downward. Desperate Goblins tried to fight them off. Swords swung out, passing right through the thick fog of the Shadowmen. Arrows and axes were equally useless. No matter what they tried, the Goblins couldn't stop the onslaught.

As usual, Jane was right. It was a bloodbath.

One at a time, the Goblins vanished. It was as if the grassland opened up and swallowed them. The survivors fled back to the Endless Woods, but most of them didn't make it. The Shadowmen devoured them as they retreated. The ground turned to quicksand, pulling them under and slowing their steps. Within two minutes, half the force was gone.

Jane shuddered. "I am *so* glad you can fly right now."

A bloodcurdling howl cut through the night. "Vammmmmpirrrrre! Come out and plaaa-aayyy!"

Slade's gave a low growl, his gaze unerringly finding the source of that idiocy. Fang was standing in the safety of the trees. He didn't give a shit about his slaughtered men. His lupine gold eyes were fixed on Slade.

No.

Fixed on *Jane*.

The Werewolf was staring at Jane with a mesmerized look on his face. Even over the distance separating them, Slade could see Fang's wild hunger for her. He was too far away to pose a threat, but supernatural beings had excellent eyesight. Jane's hair blew around her face, the curls dancing, and the Werewolf was entranced. Slade knew the feeling, but it still pissed him off.

He bared his teeth and shifted Jane, so his body was between her and Fang. He did not want the other man even looking at her. Slade's Dark Instincts surged closer to the surface, wanting to destroy any threat to his Eternal-One.  His mind whirled for some way he could kill the bastard without endangering Jane.

"Not until we have the Silver Sword."  Jane told him.  "Don't be reckless."  It was uncanny the way she could predict what he was thinking.  Or maybe *not* so uncanny, considering that she was the other half of him.  Of course she could read his intentions.  They were destined to be at each other's side for eternity.  "Please, Slade.  Let's just get out of here."

Slade's attention stayed fixed on Fang.  "You will not be safe until he is dead."

The Werewolf moved forward, so the toes of his boots were right on the edge of the field.  It was as close as he could get to her without being attacked by the Shadowmen and the barrier infuriated him.  "You can't keep me from my woman, Vampire!"  He bellowed.  "I'll claim her, if I have to tear this whole kingdom apart!"

Slade's fangs sharpened.  Goddamn it, no other man got to call Jane "his."  "I will see you *fucking dead* before I let you touch her!"  He roared back.

"That sounds like the kind of dignified dialogue I'd use."  Jane said quietly, but Slade heard the tension in her voice beneath the dry words.  "Fang didn't take a hint from that note, did he?"

Slade's arms tightened around her.  "He cannot hurt you, my One.  I won't allow it."  Jane's personality made her a force of nature.  Strong and sure.  But compared to a Werewolf or Vampire, she was so damn vulnerable.  It would take no effort at all for a supernatural being to break Jane's small body and rob the universe of her light.

Slade abruptly realized that he'd been wrong to bring her to this land.  He'd complained that she took no risks, but he'd *never* intended to place her in harm's way.  That was the last thing he wanted.  He'd been too arrogant in thinking he could keep her safe.  Infinia was no place for such a delicate creature.  Jane had been far safer in her own ummagickal world, surrounded by weak humans, noisy technology, and ice cream cartons.

"This really is all your fault, you know." Jane groused, as if reading his mind, again. "Fang thinks I'm your Eternal-One, so he's planning to hurt *you* by hurting *me*."

"No." Judging from Fang's face, this went far deeper than revenge. "The Werewolf wants you, because he wants *you*, Jane. And once his kind settles on a mate, nothing dissuades them short of death." His jaw ticked. "Luckily, I intend to slaughter that son of a bitch, so the problem is easily solved."

Lurching movements in the forest suddenly caught Slade's attention. Wooden automatons lumbered from behind Fang's line. Their arms outstretched, their stiff legs unbending, they looked like a bizarre, mechanized mixture of trees and humans. At first Slade assumed they were some new monsters Fang had enslaved. Then the Goblins started retreating from these creatures, too. Shadowmen in front and the wooden men behind, Fang's army descended into chaos. Soldiers ran screaming in every direction.

"Remember when you asked me what wooden robots are?" Jane asked softly. "I think *those* are wooden robots."

"I take it you are the one who activated them, when you detoured into Symon's workshop as we fled the village?"

"Seems that way." She smiled at him. "I didn't really read the instructions, though. I just flip a switch to see what happened."

Slade's mouth curved, adoring her.

"Kill them all!" Fang bellowed.

The mass of his army fled, but his private guard remained. His most trusted and highly-trained soldiers shielded him, trying to drive the robots back. This was a staggering defeat for the Werewolf and Slade hadn't even had to raise a hand. It was beautiful.

Fang cursed violently. He craned his neck, trying to spot Jane through Slade's protective grasp. "Give me the human and I'll give you Princess What's-Her-Name." He offered desperately, sensing that he was nearly out of time. "It's an even trade, Vampire."

Jane Squire would never duck behind anybody. No

way. In her mind, death by Werewolf was no doubt preferable to admitting weakness. But she instinctively moved her head so Fang couldn't see her face through Slade's shoulder. Her fingers twisted in the fabric of his shirt, hanging on like she wanted to be as close to him as possible.

Slade's breath caught in wonder.

She trusted him to protect her.

It was the first time Jane had ever believed in him as a man. Probably, it was the first time she'd ever believed in *anyone*. His optimism about their connection returned in a rush. If his independent Eternal-One could rely on him, then anything was possible. In that second, he knew he could win her over completely. ...Assuming they survived this.

"It's alright." Slade murmured and turned his back to the enemy. Strategically, it was a stupid move, but it made Jane feel safer and that was all that mattered. "I have you, my One."

"I want to get out of here." She whispered, again.

"The woman *you* want, for the woman *I* want." Fang persisted, still trying to get a good look at Jane. Goblins and robots battled around him, but he didn't even glance in their direction. "You take the princess and I will take Jane Squire. Your honor will be assuaged. I'm not going to harm the human. You know that's not what I want from her."

Oh, Slade knew full well what the bastard wanted from Jane. Fang could sense she was the greatest treasure in this universe. His animal instincts were trained on claiming her as his own. Slade would die first. He started flying towards the opposite side of the field, frustrated that he had to leave Fang alive, but not willing to subject Jane to this any longer.

"Maybe this Werewolf talisman thing-y is busted." Jane muttered. "He doesn't seem repelled."

"That is not how the bracelet works..."

Fang cut him off, frantic that Jane was leaving his sight. "The princess is a centerfold, you know." He tried. "Quite the supernatural beauty. And she'll legitimize your quest for the kingdom. You need her, if you're going to claim Infinia, Vampire. And I need Jane Squire. She's destined to be my mate. I can *feel* it." He sweetened the pot. "I'll even throw in my favorite pegasus. I recall your fondness for horses, Slade. Be smart and we'll both leave here winners. Make the pragmatic choice, for once in your life."

Jane glanced up at Slade, her expression concerned. "Don't believe him. He's doing all this to trick you into going over there. I can't *possibly* be what this is about. Guys do *not* get obsessed with me."

"I am."

Jane blinked at him in surprise.

How could she still not understand? "I am beyond obsessed with you, Jane. You are every thought in my head and every beat of my heart. My best friend. My Eternal-One. My *partner*. Do you honestly believe I would *ever* give you to Fang? Do you think so little of me?"

"No." She looked hypnotized. "No, of *course* not."

Slade wasn't appeased by her quick answer. "You *are* what this is about. I told you that. Fang wants you, because he knows you are extraordinary. He is not a fool." Slade shook his head. "But there is no prize that I would *ever* trade you for, Jane. Not Infinia. Not a pegasus. Not my own life. I will kill and die to keep you at my side. No matter the cost, I will always see you safe. You should *know* that."

"I *do* know it. I'm sorry. Really. I didn't mean…" She trailed off and gave a strange smile. "I'm just not used to someone caring about me. I'm used to being nonessential to the plot." Her hands came up to cradle his face. "Or maybe I'm used to hanging out with pragmatists instead of heroes."

"You do not believe in heroes, so…"

She lifted her lips to his and Slade forgot to be irritated. She was kissing him! Jane had never instigated anything between them before. She'd never thought he was worth the risk. Shock and delight flickered through Slade, but they were quickly overshadowed by desire. He would never get enough of the woman's taste.

"*Jane.*" His mouth opened over hers, hungry for more. "You are the most essential part of my life. I would not…"

An arrow slammed into Slade's arm cutting him off.

"*Open fire!*" Fang screamed at the Goblins, a bow clutched in his hand. The projectiles wouldn't kill Slade, but the Werewolf was too angry to care. "Forget the robots! Bring down the Vampire!"

Jane screamed in panic. "*Slade!*" She tried to examine the wound, her fingers soft and searching. "Oh my God, you've been *shot!*"

Slade quickly overpowered her efforts to help, knowing what was about to happen. He dragged her arms in front of him, so every part of her body was shielded by his. He curved himself around her as more arrows rained down. Slade didn't even try to get out of their path. If he moved, it would expose Jane as a target. A single arrow could be deadly to a human and now she was inches away from hundreds of them.

Everything that was *Jane* was housed in this small, mortal form. What had he been *thinking* to bring such a delicate creature to Infinia? Gods, he'd been so fucking selfish! Slade surrounded Jane and prayed the onslaught wouldn't harm her.

She was already struggling to get free. "*Are you out of your mind?! What are you doing?!*"

He ignored that, holding her still. He felt the arrows piercing his back and shoulders, disrupting his magicks. Despite his best efforts, so many projectiles hitting him at once knocked him from the sky.

"*NO!*" Fang bellowed, realizing his mistake. "Stop shooting! The Shadowmen will kill my woman!"

Slade barely heard him. Half-a-second before he slammed into the ground, he turned his body to protect Jane. Still holding her against his chest, he hit the field on his back, the arrows breaking off and tearing more of his flesh. The impact created a ten foot furrow in the dirt and left Slade dizzy with pain, but he didn't have time to assess his wounds. The Shadowmen were already moving towards them.

"Slade!" His grip loosened enough for Jane to get her head up. Anxious gray eyes met his. "Are you okay?"

"I'm fine." He got out, not sure if it was true. "We have to go." He staggered to his feet and picked her up, again.

He could see the end of the Corpse Road now, but the Shadowmen were right on top of them. Clawed hands reached out for them, trying to drag them down. Slade pushed himself into the air, narrowly evading capture.

"Jesus! Slade, *stop!*" Jane tried to stanch the bleeding. "You're hurt too badly."

"If I stop, we'll die." Pure determination had him flying towards the boundary of the field. Injuries had drained too much of his power. He wasn't sure he could make it.

He saw the green grasses shifting into blackened rocks. *Forty feet.* Saw the boiling red pools that could only be the Magma Pits of Maldondorr. *Thirty feet.* Saw the Shadowmen keeping pace beneath him, fighting each other for the blood that dripped from Slade's body and expecting him to fail. Like he always failed, when it was important. *Twenty feet.*

Too far.

His strength was fading fast. He wasn't going to make it. They were so close, but Slade could feel himself beginning to blackout. He'd *known* his earlier victory against them had been too easy. He'd *known* that he'd blow it in the end.

"I'm going to lose." He wasn't aware he'd whispered the words out loud until Jane responded.

"No, you're not." She took a deep breath like she was trying to center herself. "A pragmatist would lose, but you're better than that. You're Slade, King of the Vampires. You can do anything."

He looked at her in surprise.

*Ten feet.*

Ten feet between Jane living and dying. Ten feet and she'd be safe. She met his eyes, trusting him, and all the doubts faded away. In his entire life, she was the only thing he was absolutely sure of. Jane was his Eternal-One. And the Eternal-One of a woman like this could surely keep going for ten more feet.

Slade's gaze stayed locked on hers as he somehow got them past the field.

The staggering relief he felt sapped the last reserves of his energy. Slade tumbled to the ground again. He automatically shifted to protect Jane, which was fortunate since this landing was even less graceful than the last one. The best he could say about it was he somehow avoided the magma pits and most of the bigger rocks. His arms shielded her head, her delicate body cushioned by his. He skidded to a halt in the black gravel, Jane clutched on top of him.

Less than a second later, a perfect face hovered above his. "You are totally crazy." Jane whispered, her voice awed. "But you are the only real hero I've ever met."

At which point Slade knew he wasn't a hero, at all. Almost losing her to the Shadowmen... Fang's unceasing attempts to steal her away... Nearly dying... All of it pushed his Dark Instincts to the breaking point. They screamed at him to do whatever it took to claim this woman. *Now*. And, for once, he was going to listen to their ravenous urgings.

...Just as soon as he could sit up.

# Chapter Thirteen

EXT- EDGE OF THE ENDLESS WOODS- NIGHT

ROLAND has followed the river into the Endless Woods. With the curse on them (somehow) lifted, he isn't afraid to venture into the darkness of the trees. If TEGAN was right, then SLADE is hiding here with the rebels. Unfortunately, ROLAND has been searching for hours and there's no sign of his enemy. As much as he wants a live-and-in-person chance to see ALLANDRINA topless, ROLAND is getting tired. And hungry. And bugs are biting him.

This quest is *totally* harder than he thought it would be. Damn it, he's got stuff to do, ya know? ROLAND is thinking about saving himself a lot of trouble, and just going home to jack-off to ALLANDRINA'S picture instead of rescuing her. ...Then he sees the woman.

She's washed up on some rocks by the edge of the stream. Her body is broken and burned and she is clearly close to death. She's still super-hot, though. ROLAND has a thing for gals in S&M outfits and she's dressed in a leather leotard. He scampers down the embankment to check on her breasts. Um, make that *pulse*.

                    ROLAND
   Hey, you okay, mysterious and sexy stranger?

                    DALLYN
      (In a wheezy, dying -but still kind of
        Russian sounding- voice)
   No. The Vampire has killed me.

                    ROLAND
Now he's killing chicks with big boobs? God, he's such a *dick*.
                I'm going to make Slade pay.
                      Where is he?

                    DALLYN
                  (Still wheezing)
The Vampire and his bitch human left the Endless Woods,
          after they pushed me over the waterfall.

                    ROLAND
                    (Confused)
Yeah, but if it happened *after* you went over the falls, how
          could you possibly know that they left...

                    DALLYN
          (Reaching up to grab his stylish tunic)
Death is upon me, boy! Stop with your mindless questions
              and focus on what's important.
The Vampire is on the Corpse Road. You must stop him from
                  completing his quest.

                    ROLAND
              (Nervously tugging on his ear)
The -uh- Corpse Road? No offence to the dying, but that
            sounds pretty gross. I don't think...

                    DALLYN
              (Wheezing her last breaths)
Circle around and cut Slade off at the Magma Pits of
                     Maldondorr.
      Go forth and prove you are... king of the world.

DALLYN spreads her arms LEONARDO DICAPRIO-style and
then dies. (Note: OMG, we MUST get LEONARDO
DICAPRIO for this movie. That would be so cool.) The camera
pulls back in an overhead crane shot, implying her upward

*ascension, because attractive people should always go to heaven. Though he's just met her, ROLAND is deeply affected by the death of someone with such a smoking body. Um, make that indomitable spirit.*

*ROLAND*
*(Throwing back his head and screaming out in manly pain)*
*NOOOOOO!*

*Redrafted Film Script- "From Here to Infinia"*

Jane was surrounded by a wasteland of lava straight out of *Return of the King* and she didn't even notice. Slade was hurt. That was all she could process.

What was she supposed to do? Jane wasn't a doctor. The only time she'd ever even *played* one had been in some stupid local TV commercial when she was twenty-three. Her only line had been, "My patients love the great taste of Geno's Pizza." Why would a doctor be advertising a pizza restaurant? The role hadn't made any fucking sense! Goddamn it, if she'd tried out for better parts, this wouldn't be happening. If she'd become a regular on *Grey's Anatomy* or something, she would have picked up some medical pointers. As it was, Jane was useless. She didn't know how to help Slade. How could she…?

Jane's frantic thoughts skidded to a halt, as she stared down at her hands. They were covered in blood. Slade's blood. He was losing too much blood.

Vampires needed blood.

Her eyes desperately glanced around, falling on a jagged piece of obsidian. That looked sharp enough. Jane grabbed the stone, yanking open the front of her shirt. "Alright." She could do this. Without giving herself time to think, she sliced open a long, shallow cut on her neck. Actually her hands were shaking so badly, that she missed and it was more like her collarbone, but it would have to do.

"Slade?" She lifted his head, bringing it to her torn

skin. "Slade, sweetie, you have to drink."

He certainly wasn't fighting the idea. Slade gave a low groan, his mouth opening against her wound. His tongue slowly tasted the flowing blood. Following it as it pooled onto the top of her breast. His teeth grazed and then...

"*Oh God!*" His teeth sank into the delicate globe and Jane's whole system went into meltdown. It wasn't the time to jump the poor guy. He was *hurt*, for Christ's sake. But her body didn't seem to realize that. When Slade bit her it was like being dropped headfirst right into the middle of the best sex *ever*. Her libido just wanted more. Jane's hand clenched in his hair, her eyes squeezing shut, as she tried to keep control.

Slade *wasn't* trying to keep control.

Not at all.

He fed with insatiable greed for a long moment and then slowly lifted his head to look at her. ...And Jane knew she was in trouble.

Those Dark Instincts he was always going on about were running the show. Slade's eyes were half-crazed with lust and hunger. His body was healing fast, but he sure wasn't thinking clearly. "Jane." He rasped and began tugging at her clothes. "Now."

Her chances of spontaneous combustion reached one hundred percent. "Slade, you're injured." She tried to push his hands away from her bra and get him to focus. "Hang on. You're not yourself. You can't..."

Or maybe he could. Slade ripped the scrap of lace right off of her and then moved on to her khakis. "Have to have you now." He sounded guttural. "Can't wait."

"We're outside." There was nobody around, but it was still pretty scandalous. At least to Jane. A certain Vampire seemed fine with it. "Slade, someone could see."

"Don't care."

He held her against him, even as he stripped her naked. The guy had incredible dexterity for someone so recently shot. Jane had no idea how he moved that fast. Not that she was exactly trying to fight him off. Her body was screaming for him. She *loved* that he was so intent on making love to her. But this wasn't like him. He was usually such a gentleman.

Jane tried to remember how to breathe as the hot air of the magma pits blew across her exposed nipples. "Later, Slade. We can do this later." Sleeping with him had always been inevitable, but he was too hurt for this kind of activity. What if it caused permanent damage? What if they did this and then he snapped out of his caveman mood and regretted it?

It didn't *seem* like he was going to regret it, though.

The guy was as aroused as she was. She could feel it.

Slade caught both of Jane's wrists behind her back, dragging her forward so she was straddling him. His fingers rubbed against the links of that ugly silver bracelet. He always checked to see if she still wore his gift and he always smiled when he felt it. His free hand found his belt, freeing his massive shaft. He probably would've taken his shirt off too, but there was still an arrow holding it in place.

"Now." It was an order.

The guy always had a one track mind. Typically, it was fixed on getting his stupid crown. Right now, it was all about having her do hot and dirty things to his *incredible* body.

Jane whimpered at the feel of him straining beneath her. If she sank down Slade would be inside of her and it would be… incredible. She tried to tug her wrists free, but he wasn't letting go. She should've known he'd want to dominate in bed. Kings liked obedience. Jesus, she *really* liked this, too. She had no idea she was into bondage until she met up with the Vampire. She wanted him to hold her down and make her beg.

Still, she made one last effort to get through to him. "Listen, when you're better, I *promise* you can do whatever you want to me, okay? I'll happily go along with all kinds of kinky shit. I swear, Slade."

"Now, Jane." He arched his hips to brush her core with the crown of his erection.

She bit her lower lip, trying to stay strong. He wasn't going to go any further until she okayed it. Not even in his current frenzy. She completely trusted him in that. So she could just refuse and then…

His forehead dipped forward to rest against hers. "Please, my One." He breathed. His lips found hers, coaxing and sweet. "I need you so much."

Oh shit. There was no way she could resist that.

"Now." She surrendered and slowly lowered herself onto him. Her eyes stayed locked on his as she eased down. "Tell me what you want and you can have it, Slade. You know that. Just don't hurt yourself."

His hand came up to tangle in her hair, holding on like she might try to slip away. "Not want. *Need*. I need all of you."

She slid forward at the harsh command, taking him even deeper. Her eyes dipped down as her body yielded to his. She wasn't a submissive person, but this game was jacking up her desire to even greater heights. "Like that?"

"*Yes.*" His head went back, his expression rapturous. "Mine." His jaw locked, his voice darker than she'd ever heard it. "*Finally.*"

God, she could orgasm just from his rasping tone. Sex with him was so good, she couldn't believe it. It just wasn't possible for something to be this fucking *incredible*. "Yours." She panted, knowing that was what he wanted to hear. And it was completely true. Who else could ever compare to this man? "Are you sure you're okay to do this?"

Blue eyes burned into hers. His free hand stopped touching her long enough to reach over his shoulder and yank the arrow from his back like it was a splinter. "The wounds won't kill me." His lips found hers again, tossing the arrow aside. "But if I can't have you now, I will die."

Only Slade could get away with dialogue that cheesy. Jane chuckled and kissed him back, starved for the taste of him. "So have me. You're the king, remember? You can do anything you want."

Oh, he liked that remark. Slade shifted his hips, driving into her as deep as he could go and she cried out. He gave a snarl of pleasure at the sound. "You are my soul, Jane. It's not just something that you give me. It's *you*. It's the way I feel about *you*."

"Uh-huh." Jane was barely listening to him. She

couldn't focus on anything except the heat. She could feel Slade throbbing deep inside of her and she *had* to move. She was so close to release that she could taste it, but he was holding her still. "Please." She whispered needing more.

"Please *what?*"

"What?" She couldn't think. He was so big that he stretched places she hadn't even known existed. She bit back a sob. If he would just *move*, she could...

"Please, *sire*." He breathed into her ear. "That's how you address a king, Jane."

Jane's gaze flashed back to his in surprise and Slade had the audacity to smirk. He was teasing her. God, that was adorable. "You're supposed to be a hero." She reminded him breathlessly, playing along. "A hero wouldn't say something so kinky to a damsel in distress."

"Are you in distress?" Now that he was inside of her, he seemed calmer, like he was reassured. "Don't worry. I'm fair to *all* my subjects. My Eternal-One insists on it. She has a very soft heart." He lifted her slightly and then dropped her down again, eliciting a moan of pleasure. "In fact, every bit of her is soft."

"I'm going to get you for this later, you know." She gasped.

Slade looked thrilled to hear that. "Gods, I hope so. But right now, you're so tight, Jane. I can feel how close you are. Just two little words."

He wasn't going to relent. She loved it. "Please, sire." She asked seductively.

"Again." Slade released her hands to grip her hips, guiding her movements. Rewarding her with several deep strokes.

This game was turning her on so much she might just die. "Please, sire. More."

"Yes." He lowered his face to the curve of her neck, his fangs scraping against her hammering pulse. His teeth sank deep and Jane almost blacked out from ecstasy. His hands came up to squeeze her breasts together, measuring their weight. It didn't take a mind reader to know that he was planning to do all kinds of unchivalrous things with them.

The hero of this movie was going *bad*.

It was incredible.

Jane tilted her head so he could have better access and rode him up and down. "Slade, I'm going to come." She couldn't hold on much longer.

"Not yet." He shifted again so she couldn't get the last bit of friction she needed. "Not yet, my One. It has to be together."

She bit back a curse as he stopped her release. "Are you sure you're not the villain of this movie?"

"I am about to be." He lifted his head, his eyes still not completely clear. "Wizard-Warlocks need consent before they claim their mates. Vampires do not." He lifted up a piece of obsidian from the ground and made a small gash in her palm.

A drop of blood pooled and Jane blinked. "Hey, what are you…?"

"You do not wish to drink from me, so this is the only way. Don't worry. It will heal in a moment." He sliced his own hand, much deeper than he'd cut her. "I did not want to do it this way, but the Dark Instincts are beyond my control. It is the best way to protect you. The only way."

Jane's eyes widened, panic fissuring through her sensual haze. Hang on, was he doing that Eternal-Bonding thing? Could he do that? "You can't do that!"

"I *can* do it." He assured her. "No one can stop me from claiming my Eternal-One. Not even my Eternal-One."

Definitely *not* Hollywood love scene dialogue.

So why was it making her feel safe? Like maybe Slade wasn't going to make her jump off that bridge, after all. Like maybe he was going to climb up to meet her. He slammed their palms together, so their blood joined, and Jane yelped in surprise.

…Or maybe he was going to push her off.

"I'm sorry." He told her, not sounding sorry. "I will not lose you, no matter what I must do."

"It won't work." She frantically shook her head. "I'm *not* the heroine."

"Then we are a perfect match. I told you, I am not feeling much like the hero."

"You're not *acting* like it, either. This is crazy, Slade!"

He shrugged, unrepentant about his sudden heel-turn. "If you're right, and you are not my Eternal-One, then nothing will happen and you can gloat about how smart you are." He dipped his head to nuzzle the curls at her temple. "If *I'm* right, then you and I will be linked forever." His voice got deeper. "And Jane?"

"Yeah?" She got out, her eyes glazing over. It was really, really hard to concentrate on arguing when he was inside of her, but as soon as she'd recovered her normal brain functions, she was going to clobber him.

"I am Slade, King of the Vampires." His teeth grazed her ear. "I'm *always* right."

She sucked in a quick breath as he took control of their pace. Supporting most of her weight, he thrust into her, again and again. Her mouth opened in a silent scream. He *was* going to shove her over the edge, only she had no idea what was down there. "*I can't, Slade!*"

Slade stopped. Their bodies were still intertwined, but he wasn't moving. No matter what either of them said, he could never be anything but a hero. She could see the strain he was under, but he wasn't going to push her.

…And that was enough to calm most of her fears.

He waited. "Do you want me to continue?" He finally asked, as seconds ticked by.

Did she want him to continue?

Jane swallowed. "You don't understand the risk you're asking me to take." She whispered, trying to think. Damn it, she wanted to be brave enough to jump. She just didn't know what would happen if she let go. Could she really do this? What if it all went wrong?

Slade's hand was still clasped to hers, their fingers locked. "There *is* no risk." His voice was low and desperate. "Even if we somehow *weren't* Eternal-Ones, you are still the only woman I would *ever* want."

"But the kingdom…"

"Means *nothing* compared to you. I am completely and totally in love with *you*, Jane Squire. Just you."

What did he just say?

Her damp eyes flew to his, shocked by the calm pronouncement.

Slade seemed amused by her astonishment. "Did you not notice my feelings? Everyone else has, I assure you. I am not a subtle man."

She gaped at him. He loved her?

"You have consumed me from the second I first saw you in that grocery store and nothing will ever change that." His free hand touched the side of her face. "You are not taking a chance with me. We are a *sure thing,* no matter what this ritual does. Just have a little faith."

Jane stared at him. Slade stared back, waiting for some kind of response. Too bad for him words were totally beyond her current capabilities.

"This is the part where you tell me what you want." He prompted after a long moment. "You say I don't ask you that enough and you are right. It isn't egotism, though. It's fear. I am always worried that you'll tell me good-bye, so I try to push ahead and drag you with me. I will not do that anymore. It's your choice, Jane." He eased away from her. "Do you wish me to stop? Because I will stop if..."

Jane jumped.

Yanking him back, her mouth sealed over his. Her hands grabbed his body closer, trying to be careful of his wounds, but mostly just wanting him as hard and deep as he could go. She was plummeting towards the unknown, but she wasn't afraid. Hell, why would she be? Wherever she was headed, Slade was going with her and he wasn't going to let her go splat.

"Oh, thank gods." Slade groaned, kissing her back like he was wild for her. "Releasing you may have been beyond even my strength. You are so beautiful and I am so in love with you, Jane. Do not ever leave me. I would be nothing without you." He pistoned inside of her and the words washed over her and there was no way Jane could hold back.

"*Slade!*"

Her orgasm was powerful enough to drag him down, too. Slade gave a roar as he erupted inside of her, his arms tightening around her body, like he'd never let her go. Jane arched towards him, as waves of pleasure crashed through her system. The wonder of it went on and on. It was like nothing she'd ever experienced. As the wracking pleasure eased into small aftershocks, she looked at Slade...

...and knew she'd come home.

He wasn't exactly a cute little bungalow with red shudders, but he was right where she belonged. *He* was the place she'd been looking for. She'd been an idiot to doubt this guy.

Slade, King of the Vampires, was always right.

Jane's dazed eyes met his and she saw him smile. She felt something in her palm, the blood they'd shared growing hotter, but she barely noticed. Whether or not they bonded didn't matter nearly so much, now that she knew the truth.

"Slade, I..."

She didn't get to finish her words. A dark shape moved behind Slade. Not one of the ghostly Shadowmen, but a person. A guy with emo hair and a tunic embroidered with the words, "I *AM* the Band, Bitches."

"Do you feel lucky Vampire?" He shrieked, lunging forward.

Roland. There was no one else it could be.

Jane saw the glint of metal in his hand and her heart stopped. He was going to stab Slade! "*No.*" She cried.

Slade spun to face the kid, instinctively shielding Jane, but there wasn't enough time for him to defend himself. Roland lifted his arm, preparing to attack Slade, and Jane didn't hesitate. Her hand shot up behind Slade's back to protect him from the weapon. It sank into her arm rather than Slade's neck. But instead of the searing agony of a severed limb, she felt the small prick of...

...a needle?

Hold on, did Roland inject her with something? Jane looked down at the tiny hole in her skin. "He gave me a shot."

She said vaguely, already feeling the mysterious liquid moving through her system.

Slade grabbed her arm to examine the damage. The jagged edge to his breathing told Jane that this film was about to become a tragedy. He let out an inhuman bellow, lunging at Roland.

"Shit!" Roland tried to scamper away. "Dude, I didn't know you had a chick with you! It wasn't supposed to go this way." He blurted out, as if this was all some wacky sitcom misunderstanding. "For realz, I didn't mean to stick *her*, I was aiming for *you*." He tried to evade Slade, while studiously *not* looking at Jane's naked body. "Seriously, my bad. Let's just have a do-over and…"

Slade grabbed Roland by the front of his stupid tunic, lifting him right off the ground. "*What the fuck did you give her?!*"

"Calm down, man!" Roland's eyes were huge with fear. "It was an accident! I didn't even see her! It's *your* fault! You're so big, you blocked her with your stupid back when…"

Slade gave Roland a furious shake, as Jane grabbed for her clothes. "*What did you give her?*" He repeated at a roar. "*Is it poison?*"

"No! It's just some Vampire blood! I swear. The Wizened Enchantress said that it won't harm a human!"

The color drained from Slade's face, so Jane was betting the Wizened Enchantress was full of shit. He dropped Roland like he forgot the boy even existed and dashed back to her side. "Jane, what have you *done?*"

Roland sprawled to the gravel with a grunt. "Hey, that hurt, man!"

Jane ignored him. She swallowed hard, staring up at Slade. "You were lying about Vampire blood being medicinal, weren't you?"

"I would *never* lie to you. Except about small things like when I can fly." His words were coming out way too fast. "I swear, I did not think you would ever be exposed to *another* Vampire's blood, in addition to my own. That will trigger a transition. I didn't foresee it, but I *should* have. I am so sorry, my One."

"Transition? Like to a *Vampire?* I don't want to be a *fucking Vampire!*" Worse, Slade thought Vampires were God's gift to the supernatural world and he'd never suggested this transition thing before. If he didn't want her to become a Vampire, there was a reason.

...Like maybe humans didn't come through the process so well.

Pain was already eating through Jane's body. "Am I going to die?"

"No!"

The way he shouted it meant "yes."

Fucking typical. The sidekick *always* died in fantasy movies. This never would've happened if she was the heroine. Jane *knew* living happily ever after with Slade was a longshot. So much for the King of the Vampires always being right.

She felt herself getting dizzy and reached out to steady herself on Slade's arm.

"Jane!" He grabbed her closer, holding her against him. "Don't do this. Please, don't leave me." His voice cracked, tears welling in his celestial eyes. "I will fix this. Somehow I will fix this. *Please,* Jane. Just hang on."

Jane looked up at him and realized... She wasn't a pragmatist, after all.

Not anymore. Maybe Slade was wrong about their Hollywood ending, but he *was* right about everything else. She should have risked more. She should have gone out for the parts she really wanted, instead of just settling for the extras. She should have believed in fairytales. Jane had lived her whole life so afraid of failure that there was no way she could succeed.

Until Slade.

Because of him, she wasn't dying with any regrets. None. Maybe she'd been afraid for most of her thirty years, but she'd pulled it out in the end. She'd taken a huge, crazy, illogical chance on this Vampire. ...And it had paid off better than she could've dreamed. Knowing Slade helped Jane feel brave and strong and whole. He challenged her to be the best person she could be and pushed her to have faith in herself.

With Slade, she was a star.

"It's alright." Jane touched the side of his face. "I'll be a Vampire or I'll die trying." Not exactly a great set of choices, but *un*dead sure beat *real* dead. "Either way, I wouldn't have changed *any* of it, Slade. Not one second." She gave him her best shot at a smile. "Not even this one."

He shook his head, his eyes wild. "*I* wish to change it! How could you risk yourself like this, Jane? Do you think I would want that? *Ever?* Why didn't you just let him inject *me?*"

What a bunch of stupid questions for a smart guy to ask. "Because I am completely and totally in love with you, too, dumbass." She muttered and then the world went dark.

# Chapter Fourteen

INT. OBSIDIAN FORTRESS- NIGHT

PRINCESS ALLANDRINA stares into the mirror of her vanity. She is amazingly beautiful, with a lush body and a face exactly like ANGELINIA JOLIE'S. In fact, (ideally) she's being played by ANGELINA JOLIE. Hopefully, ANGELINA JOLIE is reading this script and is super-happy to be offered a part in this movie. (Hi, ANGELINA!) Anyhow, everyone in the kingdom has always been in awe off ALLANDRINA'S overall amazingness.

Until lately.

Lately, it seems that she doesn't exist, at all. Lately, all anybody cares about is JANE SQUIRE. ALLANDRINA hears the name being whispered all over the castle. JANE SQUIRE. JANE SQUIRE. JANE SQUIRE. It's like a broken troubadour. ...And it pisses ALLANDRINA off. When will ALLANDRINA have some attention? What does she have to do, invent neon and point a big, blinking arrow at her head to remind everyone that she's here? Clearly, something will have to be done, if this tale is ever going to get back on track.

*Redrafted Film Script- "From Here to Infinia"*

 

"*No.*" Jane collapsed and Slade's world bottomed out. "*Jane!*" He laid her limp body on the gravel, frantically assessing her still form.

Shit! What could he do? There had to be something. He had to *do* something!

"Uh-oh." Roland gazed down at her, looking dim and

troubled. "Is she dead? 'Cause she looks dead."

"If she dies, so will you." Slade didn't even bother to glance at Roland as he delivered that threat. All his attention was on Jane. This couldn't happen. He wouldn't allow it.

Roland glanced at him. "She's --like-- your girlfriend?"

"She's my fucking *soul*."

"Oh. Shit. Sorry, man. I thought you were into Allandrina."

"Stop talking or I will kill you, right now." Slade's mind raced, trying to come up with a way to save Jane. Goddamn it, a villain would be able to think of something. Damien or Fang would no doubt devise some brilliant scheme to cheat death and save their woman. But Slade didn't know how to come up with fucking *schemes*. He'd been raised to be a hero. If it wasn't for Jane urging patience and restraint, he would have stupidly charged at Fang days ago. It was just who Slade was. He only knew how to get a sword, stand up, and face his enemies.

But how did he fight against *this?*

He couldn't. Jane had the blood of two Vampires in her. There was no way to stop her from transitioning. Which meant there was only one chance in a thousand that she would survive this.

No.

*No.*

"Dude, do you know you got a bunch of arrow holes in your back?" Roland asked as if he was just noticing. "They're --like-- closing up, though. It's kinda weird."

Jane's blood was healing him. His blood was inside of her too, healing the cuts and bruises that she'd endured. But it wasn't enough to bring her back from the edge of death.

*NO!*

"You cannot do this. Jane!" Slade gave her a shake, trying to rouse her. "You cannot leave me. You must fight!" The woman was the most obstinate creature ever born. She would never just surrender. She'd been knocked out before and she came around. She could do it, again. Jane Squire could do anything. "Jane, you must *fight!*"

"You should use CPR." Roland recommended, hovering like a vulture.

Slade was desperate enough to try anything. Even something suggested by someone he planned to rip apart with his bare hands. "What the fuck is CPR?"

"I'm not sure. I don't think it exists in Infinia. But it would really be useful, right now."

Slade truly was going to murder the boy. He might've done it at that very moment, except something so much more important distracted him.

Jane stopped breathing... and so did Slade.

"*JANE!*" The roar came straight from the soul that she gave him. He couldn't go on without her. He didn't even want to. Without Jane, the whole world might as well wither into dust. He loved her. Not just because she was his Eternal-One, but because she was *Jane*. Cynical and softhearted. Fearless and wary. A mass of contradictions and curls that came together to form something *perfect*. She couldn't die. She *couldn't*. Jane was *everything*.

Slade went into a complete meltdown, the Dark Instincts screaming inside of him. Tears were running down his face and he didn't notice.

Roland looked weepy, too. "Man, this whole thing was a *huge* mistake. I don't even *want* to be king. I'm not sure what I was thinking, ya know? I'm supposed to be a rock-god, not a politician." He swiped at his nose and sorrowfully gazed at Jane. "She was totally kinda hot, too. I wouldn't kill a hot chick. That goes against everything I believe in."

"*Shut up!*"

"Do not worry, Slade. All will be well."

Slade was so frantic, he barely heard the familiar voice. Nothing registered outside of Jane. She was so still, like she had already left. Like she was already *gone.*

*Oh gods please don't let her be gone...*

It wasn't until the newcomer tried to pry Jane away from him that he really noticed her. His head snapped up with a snarl, coming face-to-face with an elderly woman. To most people she was known as Dawnyah-Zanabriah, the legendary shape-shifter and prophet.

To Slade she was just Grandma Dawn.

His grandmother was a gray haired woman, who always acted like she was the smartest person in the realm. Hell, she probably *was*. She was also stronger than she looked. His grandmother tried to drag Jane closer to her, even as her magicks automatically created new clothes for them to wear. His grandmother was sort of a prude, so their half-nakedness was sure to freak her out.

Slade couldn't care less. He jerked Jane back from her determined grip, the fabric of Jane's new flowy dress flowing around him. Grandma Dawn *loved* flowy dresses. "What are you doing here?" He bellowed.

If Dawn answered, he didn't hear it. Slade couldn't think. Couldn't function. He just instinctively clutched Jane tighter as his grandmother tugged on her arm. He wasn't letting her go.

"I can help your Eternal-One." Dawn met his eyes levelly. "You know I can, Slade. Just let me see her."

"*Are you out of your mind?* You abandoned me when I needed you most and now you think I'll give you my...?"

Dawn cut him off. "I looked into my crystal ball and saw your true path. *That* is why I ensured that you would be deposed. *Everything* I have ever done has been to aid you, Slade. To help you find your true destiny. And you *have,* if you'll just let me help her."

Slade stared at his grandmother, breathing hard. Her words closely mirrored the thoughts he'd been having. Maybe she hadn't betrayed him, after all. Maybe she'd foreseen that Jane was his only chance at finding happiness. It made sense. Without Jane, his life would be empty. That was why she *had* to start breathing again. She was the only thing in his whole life that mattered...

"Please!" Dawn pulled on Jane's arm again. "I haven't much time in this realm. Listen to me and I can fix her!"

Slade's attention sharpened, finally processing her words. He needed a miracle and his grandmother held untold power. Although Jane scoffed at the idea, Dawn's people really did come from some distant world beyond the stars. His grandmother was one of the most powerful women in the universe. Surely, she could save a tiny human girl.

"Fix her." He implored, allowing his grandmother to tug Jane closer. "I'll do anything. Just bring her back to me."

"She's not breathing." Roland interjected, as if maybe they *hadn't fucking noticed that*. "It's hard to fix dead."

"She is not dead yet, Grandson."

*Slade* wasn't the one who'd said such a pointless thing, so why was Dawn addressing the answer to him? To offer reassurance, maybe? He couldn't be sure, but it didn't really matter. He barely even heard her. Everything was a meaningless roar of white noise in his head. All he could hear was the echoing silence where Jane's heartbeat should've been.

She was still alive, though. His grandmother was right about that. Slade could feel it, too. Some small part of Jane was hanging on. She wanted to stay with him.

Dawn picked up Jane's limp fingers and dropped them into Slade's palm. "Your bond will be what saves her, Slade. She does not want to leave you and her will is strong." She pressed their hands together, chanting the strongest healing spells of her ancient people. "Reach for her and guide her back. She will follow you out of the darkness."

"That's not going to work." Roland complained. "I'm telling you, we need to figure out the CPR thing, because…"

Slade tuned out the rest of that gibberish. All his life he failed when it was important, but he would not allow those doubts to weaken him now. Not when failure meant Jane would die. He closed his eyes, reaching for her. All his powers were concentrated on the tiny sparks of life still within her body. She was fighting and he threw all of his strength into helping her. If Jane faded from the world when they were fully linked, she would take him with her. Slade didn't care. Ever since he'd met her, the woman had been trying to slip away. If she was determined to leave, he would go, too. There was nowhere he wanted to be, except beside her.

He was so deep that he could feel the all the invisible strings that tied them together. The millions and billions of tiny ways they were Eternally-Bonded. It was beautiful. Like looking into the heart of magick itself. Their blood and the mating had completed the ritual, but their true connection was so much deeper than that. What he felt for Jane went down to the core of everything Slade was.

She truly was his soul.

*Jane, this is not the way our story ends. Come back to me or I will follow you wherever you lead. You are my partner. My home. I will be by your side, in this world or the next.*

For a moment there was nothing.

Then Jane gave a gasp, her heart resuming its rhythm. She was back!

Slade's eyes popped open, relief flooding his system and making him dizzy. "*Jane!*" He wasn't through panicking, quite yet. Not until he knew she was safe. "Look at me! Open your eyes and look at me, Jane!"

Her gaze fluttered up to his and he saw recognition light the perfect, fathomless gray. Her mouth curved ever so slightly. Then her head slumped to the side and she was unconscious, again.

Dawn grabbed his shoulder before he could experience a full breakdown. "Your Eternal-One will be alright. She's survived the hard part of the transition. Now, her body must heal. You must allow her to sleep."

Slade gave a jerky nod and forced himself to sit back from Jane's still form. His gaze stayed focused on the steady rise and fall of her chest. "She is so small." He whispered. "But, she is the biggest part of my world. I am her fate and she is mine."

Trumpeters sounded in the distance, signaling that Fang had regrouped and was advancing. Perhaps he planned to circle around and use whatever route Roland had taken, or perhaps he was just forcing his troops to charge across the field, again. The Werewolf had lost at least half of his force, but he would sacrifice every man if that's what it took to reach Jane.

"We have to get out of here." Slade said. The sun was rising and Fang was approaching. He needed to get Jane to safety.

Roland ignored that, squinting down at Jane. "So is she a Vampire, now?" He asked in confusion. "'Cause she still looks the same."

"Humans who transition do not physically change, they just gain Vampiric powers." Dawn paused. "I think."

Slade glowered over at her. "You *think?* You just said she would be fine!"

"And she will! But so few humans survive the transition, it is difficult to be sure what will happen when she first awakens." She touched his shoulder. "The important thing is that she is alive, Slade."

He closed his eyes. "I know. I do. And I will do whatever it takes to ensure she adjusts to this change." Jane was the only thing that really mattered. He reached over to hug his grandmother. He had been wrong to ever doubt her love. In the end, she had given him *everything*. "Thank you for helping her. I can never repay you for all you've done."

"You don't have to. Your woman has a great destiny, Slade. Even if she refuses to acknowledge it." Dawn smiled. "Besides, to help her is to help you. And I will always help my grandsons."

Grandsons? Plural? Dawn had only *one* grandson. Unless...

"Is To'kel back?" Damien had killed Slade's evil cousin, but there was always a chance that traitorous bastard had found a way to return. He automatically glanced around preparing for attack.

"No, not To'kel." Dawn looked over at Roland. "My *other* grandson. *You* Roland."

Slade and Roland exchanged a sideways glance. "What?" They chorused.

"It is a long and fascinating tale." Dawn assured them. "Possibly suitable for a prequel of some kind. You see, I was married to Adonolo, King of the Enchanted Realm of Melody. Our daughter was your mother, Harmony, who married Stone, King of the Vampires, and had you, Slade."

"I know all that, but..."

Dawn kept talking. "When you were a baby, Harmony was lost in the Sea of Silence and it swept her to Infinia. Here, she met Roland's father and, knowing her old life on the Vampire Isle was lost to her forever, she moved on. She eventually married him and they had Roland. Then they were killed by the Werewolf. I saw it all in my crystal ball long after it happened, but I know it is the truth."

Slade blinked at that ridiculous story. Not only was it unsupported by all previously known facts, chronologically infeasible, and mystically impossible, it also meant that this moron next to him was his...

"Brother!" Roland turned his huge eyes on Slade. "At last, we have been reunited!" He flung his arms around Slade, hugging tight. "This is the happiest day of my life." He mumbled into Slade's shoulder. "I've always wanted a big brother. You can totally beat the hell out of everyone who's mean to me. Like this asshole Orc names James."

"Get away from me." Slade shoved the boy aside, glaring at Dawn. "This is preposterous."

In his head, he could already hear Jane mockingly saying something like, "Of *course* the kid is your long lost brother. Fantasy movies *always* have some magical person show up and do a long lost brother reveal." And thinking about Jane meant thinking about the fact that this little shit almost *killed* her.

"I will never accept this." He shook his head. "Roland harmed my Eternal-One! I have a duty to decapitate him and then chop his body into as many pieces as possible."

"But, it was a total accident!" Roland insisted. "The Wizened Enchantress gave me the Vampire blood to stop you from stealing..." He stopped mid-word, his eyes cutting back over to Dawn. "Hold on." His brows compressed in deep thought. "You look different, but the voice is the same. I recognize it." He spun back to Slade. "*She's* the Wizened Enchantress. *She's* the one who gave me the blood, in the first place."

Slade gasped in outrage. "*Grandmother!*"

Dawn winced. "Well, I knew it would all work out in

the end." She defended. "This is your path, Slade. I was just doing my part to move you along it and bring you boys together." She patted his cheek. "Now, I love you, pumpkin, but I have to go. Traveling between realms is hard work for a Were-cat and I have fencing club in the morning."

"You set all this into motion and now you just plan to leave?!"

"I must. But don't worry. You've got everything well in hand, just like always. I have never doubted you, even for an instant." She smiled over at Roland. "It's so wonderful to see you two together at last. Your mother would be so proud of you both."

Roland nodded happily. "Especially of me. So, I'm really a prince, right?"

Slade sighed in irritation. "Grandmother, I cannot be expected to tolerate this moron."

She ignored that and kept talking. "Remember, our true fate is never just handed to us. We all must forge it for ourselves. Oh, and watch out for the Dark Fairy. That bitch wants your cinema script and you won't like what she intends to do with it. Toodles, boys." With that, she disappeared in a fog of sparkles and magicks.

…Leaving Slade sitting in the gravel beside the lava pits with an unconscious, newly Vampired Eternal-One, a "brother" he didn't know and already detested, and a Goblin army on their tail. He had no idea what to do next. Staying there meant death. Flying again so soon was impossible, especially with the sun rising. He could not outrun Fang for long with Jane incapacitated and he would never leave her behind. This was an untenable situation. Anyone with a brain in their head would be terrified by the lack of options and…

"This totally explains my rockingly awesome band, ya know?"

Slade's eyes slowly slid over to Roland. "What?" He growled.

"If Mom came from the Enchanted Realm of Melody, it's no wonder I'm so musically gifted! It's like a genetic superpower." He smirked. "That ass hat James the Orc is going to be soooo jealous. I can't wait to tell him."

Yeah... Now was a really good time for the decapitating-and-chopping part to begin.

The Dark Instincts took control again, howling with satisfaction as Slade lunged at Jane's attacker. His frustration found a worthy outlet. Slade grabbed Roland by the neck, wanting to squeeze his bones into powder.

"Dude!" The boy flailed around, but he wasn't going anywhere except to whatever afterlife awaited idiots. "Let go! I'm your little brother."

"I don't *have* a brother. And even if I *did*, I certainly wouldn't have one for long *after he hurt my Eternal-One!*"

"What part of 'accident' are you not getting, huh?! Besides she's *fine*. Grandma said so, remember? Don't be a dick about it."

Slade's grip tightened.

"You're supposed to be the hero." Roland gurgled. "Heroes don't pop-off the skulls of their little bros."

Son-of-a-*bitch*.

Slade released the kid, shoving him backwards. Not because of Roland's whining words, but because of *Jane*. She should be Eternally-Bonded with the hero of the tale, not a murderer. He would be the Eternal-One she deserved, no matter how tempting it was to toss Roland into some magma and watch him liquefy.

"Give me the Silver Sword and go home." He ordered, jabbing a finger at Roland. "Jane would not want me to kill you, so I will ignore my better judgment and let you leave here with your head." He paused. "Actually, she probably *would* want me to kill you, at first. Then, she'd quickly change her mind and try to make it seem like she was grudgingly allowing you to live as a favor to *me*, even though *she* was the one who wished to keep you breathing." It was just the way the little softhearted cynic operated. "So, I will just cut to the end of the argument and let you survive, *for now*. But don't. fucking. push me." He accentuated the final words with a deadly glare that even Roland seemed to understand.

The kid shrank back. "I don't want to go home. I

wanna stay with you." Roland nervously tugged on his ear and Slade recognized the gesture from the earliest recesses of his childhood. His mother had often done the same thing. "You're the coolest guy in this whole kingdom. Who *wouldn't* want to hang out with you? That's why I was so pissed earlier. Everyone --like-- *likes* you and nobody really notices me. I mean, I get it. But..." He trailed off with a gloomy shrug. "Whatever."

Slade frowned down at him, refusing to soften. "What do you want from me?"

"Well, I was thinking that maybe we could work together."

"Work *together?*" Slade repeated dubiously. "I don't think so."

"We'd be an awesome team! Why not?"

"I can think of many reasons, the primary one being that you just tried to murder me."

"That was before I found out we were brothers." Roland retorted. "Now, I'm totally on your team."

Slade snorted at that idea. "You will flee at the first sight of danger."

"Probably. But I might come back at the end, just when you desperately need help and you've nearly forgotten about me." Roland nodded in encouragement. "I think that might be kinda my thing. I'm the comedic, plucky, anti-hero guy. What do you say? Can we team up?"

Slade stared at him for a beat, once again thinking of what Jane would want. "I'll consider it." He decided reluctantly. "In the meantime, give me the Silver Sword, so I can kill Fang."

"I can't. The Silver Sword is back at my blacksmith shop."

"You don't have it *with* you?" Gods, but the boy was hopeless.

"Why would I have it with me? I don't have my blue diamond blade here, either. I told you, I didn't come here to kill you." Roland rolled his eyes. "Honestly, I was kinda still working out the details of my plan, but I sure didn't need that stupid Silver Sword. It's kind of embarrassing to carry around something about *this* small." He held up his thumb and index finger to show an inch of space. "Seriously, if you're planning to slay the Werewolf, you're going to need a bigger boat. ...I mean knife."

"There is no other weapon that can kill Fang. We'll have to go back to your shop and get the damn thing."

Roland cast a doubtful look towards the sky. "It's quite a hike to town and it's almost dawn. I think you'll fry by the time we get there."

"We're not walking." Slade scooped Jane into his arms and got to his feet. "The magma pits provide vast amounts of heat."

"So?"

"So if there's heat... I can teleport."

Roland blinked. "Wow. You are *so* damn cool."

# Chapter Fifteen

INT.- ROLAND'S BLACKSMITH SHOP- DAY

When SLADE teleports them to the blacksmith shop, FANG *is already there.* It's not a plot hole; it's an exciting twist!

Trust me, no filmgoers will question it when the Werewolf is somehow lying in wait for SLADE, JANE, and ROLAND. Seriously, have you seen *Eragon?* Audiences will accept *anything* in a fantasy movie. And if anybody does start whining about "logic," we can use the Blu-ray commentary to explain all the problems away. Maybe Fang used the Dark Fairy's magicks to zap himself back to town. Maybe he flew the Pegasus there super quickly. Maybe there was a time traveling DeLorean. We can tell them all kinds of shit, because the excuses are built right into the genre!

Anyhow, ROLAND takes off running as the Goblins swarm SLADE. The kid skedaddles out of the shop, dashing through the streets of the village. No one bothers to chase him. All their attention is on the Vampire. SLADE kills twenty-six Goblins, but it's hopeless. They number in the thousands. (Well, at least a hundred. A bunch of Fang's men died at the hands of the robots and Shadowmen. Besides, we don't want to pay *too* many extras and, logistically speaking, how big can a blacksmith shop really be?)

SLADE fights bravely, protecting JANE'S unconscious form. The scene is very heroic and doomed. Those are the buzz words the cinematographer needs to keep in mind: *Heroic and doomed.* Lots of close-ups of SLADE'S heroic and doomed face. FANG chortles, sensing that victory is at last within his grasp. The Goblins subdue SLADE, binding him in enchanted golden rope. Within the unbreakable coils, no magicks can be used. Slade is captured!!!!!

And everyone watching in the theater begins to wonder if this film is becoming one of those award show darlings, where the lens are all soft focus and the hero dies at the end.

*Redrafted Film Script- "From Here to Infinia"*


Jane heard the shouting before she even opened her eyes. Had she been knocked out, again? Seriously, *again?* What was this --like-- three times in one movie? Jesus, maybe she really *was* the heroine. Only heroines fainted so much. *Such* a fucking cliché. She really should start a letter writing campaign to improve female roles in sword-and-sorcery movies. This was getting ridiculously sexist and repetitive and painful.

The argument grew louder, drawing her attention from her aching head. The sentences were fragmented, but she recognized Slade's voice and that had her growing more alert. Was he okay? He didn't sound okay. Her fuzzy brain tried to piece together the meaning of the words, wondering why he was so upset.

"...can't be here." He was insisting at a bellow. "...impossible... you were just at the Corpse Road. This is the movie's doing and I will not be cheated..."

Another man was talking, too. Sounding dazed and unconcerned with Slade's anger. "...more beautiful... thought she'd be... Imagining that hair wrapped around me..."

"...one curl and I will tear your fucking..."

The second man laughed. It was a self-assured mockery of true amusement. "You are defeated, Vampire! ...tried to take my woman and now she's..."

Fang.

Jane's heartbeat sped up as she realized that the Werewolf had found them. Everything came flooding back, including the fact that she was probably now a Vampire. Great.

It was better than the "being dead" option, but not by much. An eternity of drinking blood and not getting a tan. She was *definitely* going to kick Roland's Justin Bieber-y ass, just as soon as they survived this mess.

Meanwhile, Slade and Fang continued their pissing contest. The love of her suddenly-endless-life was doing his very best to get staked. "*My* Eternal-One... psychotic bastard will never..."

"...train her to submit to *everything* I desire or..." Fang's voice changed, issuing orders, now. "Drag him into the sun to burn and bring the woman to..."

"Don't touch her!"

Jane forced her eyes open. She might be concussed and aggravated over her species-change, but she couldn't allow Slade to get himself killed. She had about thirty seconds to redirect this whole scene. Given the time crunch, there was only one plan she could think of and it was kind of a stupid plot twist. But, what the hell? This was Infinia, so stupid would fit right in.

Three deep breaths and...
*Action.*

Jane groaned, sitting up and resting a weary hand against her head. "What happened?" She pretended to look around in confusion, but mostly she was just taking stock of the situation.

She was in some Frontierland version of a blacksmith shop, wearing a poofy dress that looked a hell of a lot like Cinderella's. God only knew why, but it really didn't matter. She had bigger problems than fashion don'ts.

Slade was being restrained by Goblins. Given the number of headless bodies lying on the floor, he'd already slaughtered about twenty of their friends. Damn, but she was sorry she'd missed that part. Meanwhile, Fang was gazing down at her like she was a naked supermodel dropped into his hot tub. The rest of his creepy army stood around, just waiting to axe someone to death. No sign of Roland. Hopefully, Slade had killed the little rat.

Well, maybe not *kill* him, but at least maim him

severely.

"Jane!" Slade tried to get closer and the Goblins held him back. Five of them hit the ground as he plowed towards her, unable to match his determination. Several others clung to his back, barely slowing him down. "My One, are you alright?"

Jane looked right at him and made her face go blank. Slade would keep fighting --heroes never knew when to quit-- but there was no way he could win against these odds. Not without some help.

Time for *Dracula, Ph.D* to start.

"Who are you?" She asked in a voice that would've made any acting coach proud. It was perfectly in character: baffled, scared, and just a teeny bit accusatory. Her gaze cut around like she was seeing everything for the first time. Which she kind of *was*. "Where am I?"

Really, she could take a guess. This had to be Roland's place, since he was the only blacksmith in the movie. Her eyes grazed over the tools and horseshoes covering the walls, lingering on the hooks for a long moment. Huh. That was interesting.

Slade gaped at her. "*What?* Wait, you don't know who I *am?*"

"No. Am I supposed to?"

Under different circumstances, his utter astonishment would've been cute. Right now, Jane just felt bad about tricking him. She *had* to pull this off, though, which meant she couldn't break character. She was about to prove all those TV critics and internet bloggers wrong, and give Clarissa the final scene she deserved.

More importantly, she was going to save Slade's life.

"*Yes*, you are supposed to know me! You *must* know me."

"I don't remember you." Jane gasped, her fingers pressing into her temples. "Oh *no*. I think I might have... amnesia." Damn, that wasn't her best read. She could do better. Jane squeezed her eyes shut like she was trying hard to access the forgotten details of her life. "I can't recall *anything*. Not even my own name."

Slade looked horrified.

Fang seemed confused. "What do you mean you cannot remember your name?" He crouched down beside her, his golden eyes traveling all over her face. "You are Jane Squire." He ran a hand over her hair, his fingers too rough as he fondled the strands. "I would know your scent anywhere. I will soon be bathing in it." He lifted her curls to his face and inhaled deeply.

Yeah... that wasn't creepy, at all.

Slade went for Fang, managing to slam a massive fist into the Werewolf's jaw. "*Do not touch her!*" He bellowed again.

Fang stumbled away from Jane, as the Goblins dragged Slade back. "Vampire bastard." Fang swiped a hand under his bleeding nose. "*You're* the one who defiled her, not me." The Goblins held Slade still, while Fang started ruthlessly beating him. "You think I don't smell you all over her?! You think I don't know you turned her into one of your pathetic kind?! You think I can't picture all the things you did to her body? The body that belongs to *me?!* She is *mine* and you will never..."

Jane covered her ears and started screaming.

She had a really great scream. It got her a lot of voiceover work during Halloween. Everyone turned to gape at her as she let loose with the shrillest, most terrified cry she could muster. It went on and on and on.

Fang and Slade were so surprised they stopped fighting.

"Jane!" Slade tried to rush to her side, but the Goblins held him back. "My One, please stay calm. You will be alright. I swear it."

Fang forgot about torturing Slade and headed back over to her. "Why are you screaming, woman? Is it because you remember the Vampire? Does seeing him hurt upset you?" He grabbed hold of her. "Do you *care* that he's about to die?"

Up close the Werewolf was dazzlingly handsome and icy cold. Jane couldn't have hated him more. Just being near him turned her stomach. Jane wanted to cringe away from his touch and rush over to Slade.

...But, she didn't.

Saving Slade meant she had to keep going.

"Of course I don't care about him! You just said he made me a *Vampire!*" She threw her arms around Fang. "It's like I'm trapped in a nightmare. Please don't let him hurt me, anymore. I'll do anything you say, if you'll only keep me safe."

Slade's jaw dropped.

Fang liked the pleading. She could feel his arousal pressed against her. His growing desire made her flinch, but hopefully he'd just chalk it up to fear over the memory loss.

"Take your fucking hands off of her." Slade snarled at Fang. "Jane," he began to look desperate, "this man is dangerous. Do not trust him. You must try and remember the truth."

"I *can't*. It's all a blank." She swallowed, her eyes filling with tears. Clarissa was always a crier. She moved away from Fang to lay a prostrate wrist against her forehead. Kind of overdone, but all the best actors pushed the limits. "Oh God! Please tell me what's going on."

Fang looked over at Slade for a diagnosis. "What's wrong with her?" He demanded. "What have you done, Vampire?"

"It must be the transition." Slade sounded appalled. "Grandma Dawn said she wasn't sure how it would affect you, Jane, but I never imagined *this*."

His grandmother? Had *From Here to Infinia* really called in Cat Woman as a *deus ex machina?* Grateful as Jane was for the assist, that twist was even dumber than this amnesia crap.

"The transition causes amnesia?" Fang threw his hands up. "It just keeps getting worse!" He restlessly paced around. "What else does it do?"

"I don't know! Hardly any humans survive it." Slade ignored Fang's frustrated cursing and focused on Jane. She could see his mind racing for a solution. "Jane, you will be alright. I swear it."

Jane responded with more tears. "Why can't I remember?"

"I don't know, but I will find a way to get your memory back."

"You will do nothing except die in the sun, Vampire." Fang spat out. "*I* will care for my woman. It is obvious that you have done nothing but harm her. I am not surprised. Your whole species is thoughtless and stupid."

Slade disregarded that, too. He somehow managed to slam two Goblins together, so their skulls collided with a sickening crack. Momentarily escaping the others, he knelt in front of Jane. "My One, try and recognize me." His palms cupped her face. "I am *Slade*. I am," he paused, trying to settle on words she would accept in her current state, "your husband."

Yes, he certainly was.

Jane stared into his eyes and saw her whole future staring back. A future that *no one* was going to steal. Without meaning to, she reached up to put her hand over his.

Triumph briefly lit his features. Then more Goblins rushed forward to pull him back from her. This time it took twelve. The whole time Slade struggled against the onslaught, his attention stayed on Jane. "Jane, I love you! You said you loved me, too. Try and remember!"

She somehow managed to look away from him and blink up at Fang. "Is the Vampire telling the truth? Is he my husband?"

That line prompt was all the Werewolf needed to get on board with Jane's new script direction. "No." Fang gave an eager smile. "*I* am your husband, Jane Squire."

"*No.*" Four Goblins hit the floor as Slade fought. "Jane, do not listen to him!"

Fang disregarded the commentary and helped her to her feet. "I am Fang, King of Infinia and you are my mate." He ran his hands over her body and Jane couldn't even look at Slade. If she did, he was going to see that she was terrified. "My beautiful, obedient mate."

Clarissa wouldn't call him an asshole, so Jane didn't either. "If you're my mate, what was I doing with him?" She pointed at Slade. "That's what you're saying, right? That I was at the mercy of this Vampire, for God knows how long?"

"He kidnapped you and I have spared no expense in getting you back. You have caused me much worry."

Slade got free again and stalked forward. The guy just would not quit. It was the hero thing again. Thank heaven he had unheroic Jane Squire to save him, because he was totally not helping this situation. "Fang is *lying*, Jane. Look into your heart. I *know* you sense our connection. You must."

She did sense it.

Even if the amnesia had been real, Jane would *still* know this man was hers. The Eternal-Bond thing had sewn them together in ways that she couldn't explain, but it went even deeper than that. The love Jane felt for him went straight down to the core of her.

...So it was nearly impossible to back away from Slade when he approached.

Luckily, she was one hell of an actress and she was giving the performance of a lifetime. Jane made her body moved closer to Fang, her hand coming up to rest on his arm. "He's crazy." She whispered in her most traumatized voice. "Please, Fang, don't let him hurt me."

Slade's eyes nearly bugged out.

Fang smirked, his arms coming around Jane and pulling her closer. "Do not worry. The Vampire won't ever touch you, again. He won't be alive long enough."

Being held against Fang nearly made her gag. He smelled wrong. He felt wrong. He *was* wrong. Jane had no idea how she could keep this up. Just to give herself some room, she shoved him back. The Werewolf might say he wanted an obedient mate, but she was betting the script was right and he wanted to *force* compliance. Her resistance was just turning him on more.

"The Vampire had *better* not be alive for long." She snapped. "I expect you to make him pay for this, husband."

"This is just not *possible*." Slade sounded like he was about to lose it completely. A mass of Goblins was wrapping him in some kind of glowing rope and he barely seemed to notice. "Jane, you cannot believe him! You are the smartest person I've ever met. *Think!*"

She wanted to give him some kind of sign to reassure him, but she was afraid that Fang would see it. Besides, Slade would try and stop her if he understood her plan. The guy wasn't so great at subterfuge and he would battle an army before he let her put herself at risk.

Jane turned back to frown at Fang. "How could you let me get kidnapped by a Vampire, anyway? What kind of mate are you?"

Fang blinked at her biting tone. "Well, I did not…"

Jane kept going. Clarissa had always been an unreasonable bitch. It was the main reason Jane liked her. "And now you say you're going to kill him, --which you *should*-- but how are you going to make him *suffer?*"

"I am going to stake him in the sun. Aside from blue diamond blades, that is the most effective weapon against Vampires." He paused. "Blue diamond blades can cut through all magicks, you know. They are rare in this land, but they can break through many enchanted…"

"That's it?!" She interrupted the random exposition, with an aggrieved scowl. "You're just going to leave Slade here in the middle of wherever-the-hell-we-are with no one to *see?* What kind of message does that send to our enemies? That they can just kidnap me and you'll give them all a quick death?" She arched a brow. "Or do you *like* the idea of having other men abducting me? Is that it? Do you get off on imagining me helplessly submitting to some depraved Vampire's twisted fantasies?"

Just as she'd anticipated, that set him off.

"Of course I don't want you fucking Slade!" Fang roared. "Are you out of your goddamn mind? *I* am the one you submit to. *I* am your mate."

"Jane, I swear to the gods, if you do not get away from him, I will not be responsible for what happens." Slade warned in a dark voice. The glowing rope must have incapacitated him somehow, because he couldn't seem to break free. That didn't keep him from trying, though.

"Save your threats, Vampire!" Jane cried with

dramatic zeal. Clarissa was also a dramatic kind of girl. "My mate will *never* allow you to hurt me."

"I wasn't threatening *you*, Jane! I would *never*..."

"Don't threaten her!" Fang shouted talking right over Slade's objection and backing up Jane's version of the dialogue. Once you started working off a new script, your costars didn't have much of a choice except to adapt. "Christ, I thought Vampires prided themselves on caring for women, but now I see you've been terrorizing her this entire time."

"He's a bully." Jane nodded. "And he must have *forced* me to become one of his wretched kind. I cannot wait to see him suitably punished. Dragged before our people and publically executed for his crimes."

"All my enemies will be suitably punished." Fang caught her chin in his grasp, slightly suspicious of how well this was going for him. "Including *you*, mate, if you think to betray me." He looked over at Slade. "As long as she knows the *truth*, though, she is safe from my wrath. Isn't that right, Vampire?"

Slade's eyes narrowed, understanding that threat. Fang wasn't trying to hurt Jane, because she seemed to be buying his lies. Slade wouldn't risk the Werewolf turning on her. Not even if it meant he was going to be drawn-and-quartered, or whatever *Braveheart* inspired tortures Infinia had up its sleeve. He leveled a furious glare at Fang, but he stopped trying to jog her memory.

God, she loved that guy.

"Why would I betray you, Fang? Unless... you don't want me anymore." More tears spilled out. "Do you blame me for becoming a Vampire?" Jane didn't wait for an answer, before she started wailing in Clarissa's most irritating whine. "You *do*, don't you? I don't remember what happened, but I *know* I wouldn't have gone with this horrible man willingly."

Fang was really buying this bullshit rewrite. "Jane, you are being stupid. The fact that you are a Vampire is disgusting, but it is not your fault. I know he forced you."

She kept crying. "*Please* don't give me back to Slade. I want to go home with *you*."

"Of *course* you will come home with me."

Jane gave a hopeful sniff. "Really? You still want me?"

"I want you so much it makes me crazed." Fang's fingers clutched at the fabric of Jane's fairytale dress, like he wanted to rip it off her. "Gods, I cannot even *think* of giving you up. You are the destiny I was not supposed to have. I am going to claim every inch of your body, while the Vampire watches."

Jane suppressed a shudder as Slade cursed viciously in several languages she didn't know. "But how can you make him watch if he's dead?" She asked, going with the new direction. "Can't you keep him alive for a while and make him suffer?"

Fang frowned, considering her words.

She wasn't surprised. Hollywood black hats couldn't just kill the hero outright. No, the villain's master plan needed to be a complicated, grandiose scheme featuring volcanoes and lasers and maybe a lion. With a little push, of *course* Fang was going to default to that kind of bad guy reasoning. His natural impulse would be to chain Slade to a wall and explain every step of his plan. It was just how films worked. For once, Jane wasn't complaining about the plot device. If she was living in a movie, she could at least take advantage of the loopholes.

"We shall take the Vampire back to the Obsidian Fortress." Fang decided, his lust and his need to humiliate Slade overcoming his good judgment. He stared down at Jane, his breathing fractured. "But if this is a trick to save the Vampire, it will not work." He warned. "It won't be beauty kills the beast."

*King Kong*. That misquote almost seemed reasonable, considering this was quickly becoming a horror flick. "Does it seem like I want to save that jackass Vampire?" Jane gave her hair a toss. "Please. Just how good an actor do you think I am?"

Slade froze, his eyes cutting over to Jane. "Oh my *gods*..." He wheezed. "*Clarissa* had amnesia."

"Who the hell is Clarissa?" Fang demanded.

Shit.

"How should I know?" Jane scoffed. "I don't even remember *myself*, you think I remember somebody else?"

Slade quickly put the pieces together and, predictably enough, he didn't like her plan. "Jane, goddamn it, you cannot do this!"

Ignoring Slade's dawning comprehension and the Werewolf's wary confusion, she hurriedly changed the subject. "Let's get out of here, Fang. Do you have something I can cover myself with? If I'm a Vampire now, I can't just stroll outside."

"Yes, of course." Fang swept towards the door. "Wait here and I'll fetch you a cloak." He snapped his fingers at the Goblins. "Find a blanket for Slade. He rides with us."

The Goblins fell all over themselves searching for a quilt, which gave Jane a few precious seconds to talk to Slade. She stepped closer to him and lowered her voice. "You said you wanted to see me on stage. Well, *that* was Clarissa's grand finale. Once you're untied, I expect some loud clapping."

Slade didn't seem ready to applaud. "This is too big a risk, Jane." His wild blue eyes stayed locked on hers. "Stop it *now*. I will gladly burn in the sun before I *ever* let him touch you. You *know* that."

"Calm down. I have Fang under control." That was a lie, but, for the first time ever, Jane didn't mind taking a risk. She'd gamble anything if there was a chance to save Slade's life. "When a girl from the Southside is touching a guy she hates... she's playing him, sweetie."

"And what are you going to do when Fang gets you to his fortress and locks you in his bedroom?" Slade hissed back. "Have you thought that far ahead?!"

She was seriously trying not to. Being alone with the Werewolf terrified her. If Slade saw how scared she was, he was going to really freak out, though. A lifetime of hiding behind a confident façade had her projecting strength she didn't feel. "Don't worry. I'm only willing to take method acting so far. Before things get too creepy, you'll have figured out a way to get that enchanted knife over there and cut your glowy ropes."

Slade blinked, his eyes flashing over to the wall. Right there, between a weird looking wrench and a pin-up of some girl who looked like a blonde Angelina Jolie, was a sapphire-colored weapon.  It hung on an innocuous hook, but the star-effect that gleamed off the damn thing made it as prominent as Chekov's gun.  Films didn't spotlight props like that unless you were supposed to notice them.  Especially not this close to Fang's heavy-handed foreshadowing about blue diamonds' anti-magickal properties.  Jane hated stilted dialogue like that in movies.

Usually.

"That is a blue diamond blade."  Slade whispered.

"I figured as much.  Can it cut through those shiny ropes?"

Slade glanced at her, his expression intense.  "Yes."

"Good.  Now, Fang's going to notice if I take it."  It wasn't like she had many places to hide an illuminated knife in her gauzy dress.  "So *you* have to do it.  Sandbag the Goblins, palm the blade, and get free.  Then just wait for an opening to escape."

"Without you?"  His eyebrows slammed together.  "*No.* I will save you if I have to kill every Goblin in the…"

Jane interrupted his protest.  "Do you hear me arguing?  You'd *better* come save me.  You think I want a wedding night with the Wolfman?"  She rolled her eyes and marched after Fang.  "You'd better find a white horse, buddy.  If I'm suddenly the heroine of this crappy movie, I expect some epic goddamn rescuing from my Vampire Charming."

# Chapter Sixteen

INT. JAMES' PARENTS' GARAGE- DAY

JAMES THE ORC is a gigantic, orange creature with a collection of tattoos and a purple goatee. (Note: We might have to CGI him, with some kind of motion capture thing. Then JONAH HILL could do his voice. And --bonus-- he's friends with LEONARDO DICAPRIO, so JONAH could finally convince him to be in this movie. LEO's people still aren't returning my calls.) Anyway, JAMES' life is pretty uncomplicated. He's committed to the band, he hates ROLAND, and he dreams of one day getting a date with TEAGAN. Contrary to ROLAND'S opinion, JAMES is also pretty good on the bass. He is jamming out to some White Snake songs when ROLAND barges into the garage.

JAMES
Where the hell have you been? We were supposed to meet and vote on band names, dingus.
How do you expect anyone to take us seriously if we don't even have a kickass name to...?

ROLAND
(Panting for breath and cutting him off)
The Werewolf just kidnapped my brother!

JAMES
(Scoffing)
That's a terrible name.

ROLAND
It's not a suggestion for the band, you moron! It actually happened. Fang took my brother!

                    JAMES
You have a brother, now? Does he suck at lead guitar, too?

                    ROLAND
No, he's the fucking King of the Vampires! And he's the only
            hope we have of freeing Infinia.

                    JAMES
                  (Squinting)
Have you switched to hard drugs? Because that would explain
                    a lot.

                    ROLAND
        (Heading towards the band equipment)
Just shut up and help me find a radio. We gotta contact
   Slade's rebel buddies to come and save him.

                    JAMES
              (Suddenly interested)
Whoa, hang on... Somebody in this kingdom invented a
radio? Dude, that's awesome! Maybe we can finally get our
                  demo played!

        *Redrafted Film Script- "From Here to Infinia"*


    Somewhere between Jane concocting the (admittedly kinda hackneyed) amnesia plan and their arrival at the ominous portcullis of the Obsidian Fortress, *From Here to Infinia* stopped playing by typical, wide-release, bad movie rules. Instead, it pulled out some sort of art house, meta bullshit and screwed up everything.

    Granted it might've been a *tiny* bit Jane's fault for not ditching the damn screenplay sooner. But she'd been kidnapped by an egomaniacal super-villain and Eternally-Bonded to a Vampire today, so she was a little distracted.

Subplots and stupid props fell through the cracks when you were struggling to stay ahead of the latest weirdness in your life.

Jane didn't even remember dropping the script until she saw it in Fang's hands. It must have fallen when Slade took her to the blacksmith shop. Or when she was channeling Clarissa. Or when she was riding on Fang's frigging pegasus. Whenever it happened, the Goblins picked up the damn thing and gave it to their asshole boss. And their asshole boss read the damn thing, up to and including the part about the kinda hackneyed amnesia plan.

Obviously, Fang was not a happy black hat.

Especially not when he realized that Slade had escaped his evil clutches.

The awesome part about Eternally-Bonding with the hero of the movie --besides the incredible sex-- was that no dungeon could hold him for long. Jane knew Slade's jailbreak was filled with impossible parkour-y stunts and epic ninja moves. Because Slade *had* to know martial arts. It was like a perquisite for being an action star.

Not that Jane got to see any of them. So typical that *From Here to Infinia* edited all the best scenes. Maybe the budget got blown on the Werewolf effects.

Fang was so enraged by Slade's vanishing act that he began transforming right before her eyes. The sun must have set enough for his powers to emerge, because he was totally wolfing-out. His features elongated, fur sprouting from his skin. He dragged her into his room, throwing her towards the bed.

"You will pay for what you've done to me!" He bellowed.

Jesus, the dialogue was getting worse and worse.

Jane stumbled into the morbid chamber. It looked as if it had been decorated by Bram Stoker, with blackened weapons on the walls, heavy curtains covering the barred windows, and massive chains on the bedframe. The place scared her more than the Corpse Road. How the hell was she supposed to get out?

"What *I've* done to *you?*" Jane snapped back, trying to

hide her fear. "Are you kidding? You stalked me and shot arrows at me and kidnapped me, you moron! Not to mention that you're *trying to kill Slade!*"

Fang threw the script at her, letting out a howl of fury. "The Vampire deserves to die! This is *my* kingdom and you're *my* mate. He's trying to steal you both, like he always tries to steal *everything* from me! Do you think I'll let him win, again? *Do you?!*"

Jane dodged the flying folder. "I *know* he's going to win." She gestured to where the pages had landed. "So do you, if you've read the screenplay."

That was not what Fang wanted to hear. "Well, now that I know what happens, I can make sure I do things differently." He took a menacing step towards her, his features still changing. "Starting with how I handle you."

Jane edged away from him. If she was a Vampire, why wasn't she feeling any superpowers kicking in? Probably because she'd somehow become the heroine. Heroines in fantasy movies never got to do anything cool. Slade's job was to have supernatural adventures. Her job was to get kidnapped. Jane *knew* that Slade would show up to rescue her. He would come, no matter what he had to do. But she didn't have a heck of a lot of time to wait around for him.

Finding the screenplay had pushed Fang passed the edge of control. Maybe in the original version he'd done innocuous movie villain-y things like tie her to a chair or freeze her in carbonite, but now he was completely losing it. He wasn't going to wait for Slade to save the day. Determined to change his scripted fate, Fang planned to attack her right that minute. Jane's heart was pounding out of her chest, as she tried to think of a way out of this mess.

"How can you possibly be on the Vampire's side?" Fang bellowed, still fuming about her "betrayal." "You're supposed to be *my* mate! Do you have any idea what Slade did to me?! All the indignities I've suffered? We have been enemies for longer than you can imagine, all culminating on that fateful day on the Vampire Isle."

…And that's when the flashback started.

For real. It was an actual flashback of Slade and Fang battling on some tropical beach. Like something out of *Game of Thrones*, the two of them fought across the shoreline. Swords flashed in slow motion. Artfully sweaty hair fell around intense faces. Jane had no idea if the images were projecting into her mind or into the bedroom itself. Somehow she was seeing Fang's memories, though.

God, this movie sucked.

Flashback-Slade gained the upper hand and shoved Flashback-Fang into the sand. "You're beaten, Werewolf!" Blue eyes flashed cold fire as he loomed above him. "I hereby banish you from this land forever."

"NO!" Flashback-Fang and real-Fang screamed at the same time.

Jane realized she'd better do something before the movie decided to reveal that Fang was Slade's long lost brother or something. It was about the only cliché they'd missed, so far.

Taking advantage of the flashback's trippy distraction, Jane advanced on Fang. *From Here to Infinia* probably would've written her character helplessly screaming or fainting, again. It never got sick of the fainting. Luckily, Jane was a hell of a lot more practical.

While Fang was caught up in angsting about his past, Jane punched him. She didn't stop to think about it, she just plowed her fist into his morphing face. It was shock more than her self-defense abilities that had him stumbling backwards. He must have expected her to politely wait for the floorshow to end before fighting back. Or maybe he didn't anticipate any resistance, at all.

Too bad, asshole.

The bed was behind her and Jane used Fang's momentary surprise to scramble backwards over the mattress. She landed on the other side, wondering what the hell she was going to do next. Nothing brilliant was springing to mind, but fuck it. She'd figure it out. She was a sturdy pragmatist from the Southside of Chicago, not some weepy princess.

"You *bitch!*" Fang bellowed, still holding his nose.

Black hair sprouted on his hands, his fingers getting longer and more gnarled. "You're just making it harder on yourself! I'm a *Werewolf!* You don't stand a chance against me and we both know it."

Werewolf.

Jane's eyes narrowed, recalling Slade's words back in the woods when she'd asked him if Fang needed a full moon to change: *"No, of course not. Just the night. He will not change in front of his men, though. The transition leaves him vulnerable for several moments."*

Jane slowly smirked. Pissing Fang off was triggering his transition... And the transition would leave him weak. Her eyes fell on the ominous looking weapons on the wall. That one would do nicely. She headed over to grab the handle of a gigantic mace, yanking it free of its hooks. "Villains don't win in movies, jerkoff. At least, not in mine."

Fang didn't care that she was now armed. Why would he? She was half his size and she didn't have the Silver Sword, so it wasn't like she could kill him. He vaulted over the bed, seizing hold of her arm. "I'll teach you to obey..." He didn't get to finish that hackneyed threat. Instead, his hand clamped down on her wrist, directly on top of the bracelet.

His scream was the stuff of nightmares.

Jane hadn't taken the stupid hunk of silver off since Slade gave it to her, which, now that she thought about it, was kind of telling. Granted, there wasn't exactly a line forming of handsome guys presenting her with jewelry, but would she *ever* wear something so ugly if anybody else had given it to her? Hell no. She wore it because it was Slade's. She'd never really believed in its supposed powers, though. So Jane was pretty surprised, when it turned out that Slade was right. Again.

The damn bracelet *was* a Werewolf repelling talisman.

Fang let out an agonized bellow of pain the second he touched it. The silver burned into his flesh, filling the room with the noxious smell of smoldering fur. He wrenched his palm back and Jane could see the engraved pictures of victorious Vampires scorched into his skin. He stumbled back from her, his free hand gripping his injured wrist, smoke rising from his hand.

Jane didn't give him a chance to recover. She swung the mace as hard as she could, catching him in the knee. Fang fell to the ground with an enraged roar, his clawed fingers reaching for her and dragging her down with him.

*Goddamn it!* Fight scenes in movies always looked a lot more graceful than this. Jane kicked at his face as they toppled to the stone floor.

"The Vampire isn't coming to save you." He hissed, hauling her towards him as she fought. "You're all mine, Jane Squire."

Pure luck had Jane hitting his bleeding nose, again. The heel of her shoe slammed into the cartilage and he reared back with a vile oath. She slithered under the bed, grabbing the *From Here to Infinia* script as she passed, and popped out the other side. "I don't need to be saved, dickhead. I'm not that kind of heroine."

Fang was fully changing now, shifting right in front of her eyes. He couldn't follow her, because his bones were snapping and his body reshaping itself. For a few precious seconds, she had a window of escape.

Except she couldn't quite remember how to run.

Holy *shit*. A wolf like creature was taking the place of Fang's human form. Jane gaped at the transformation, trying to process it. He wasn't becoming some cute, fuzzy wolf cub from Yellowstone. He was morphing into a massive hairy monster, with the same hatreds and thoughts that the human version of Fang possessed.

Lupine gold eyes fixed on her in animalistic fury and far too much intelligence. He was some horrible *Island of Dr. Moreau* experiment, with the awareness of a man and the strength of an animal. His features were a horrific mix of both, his body twice its normal size. Jane sure wasn't about to wait around for the rest of his mutating parts to snap into place.

Shaking her head, she backed towards the door, the script hugged to her chest. "Stay away from me." She warned. "In fact, you should get out of Infinia, while you still can. If I can't kill you, Slade *will*. That's the only way this story ends."

Fang bared his jagged teeth at her and Jane bolted into the hallway.

She only had a few moments before Fang was after her. She needed to find Slade, but she had no idea which way to go. Jane raced down random hallways, looking for an exit. The entire fortress was a maze. She tried to find a staircase or even a window, but all she saw were rows of locked doors. It felt like she was back in the Endless Woods, hopelessly lost and going in circles. Where the hell was a cellphone when you…?

A hand shot out as she passed, grabbing hold of her and dragging her into one of the rooms lining the twisting corridor. Jane opened her mouth to scream, but a massive palm covered her lips.

Within two seconds, she was trapped in a darkened closet with a huge man. In the tight confines, she was pressed between the wall and his aroused body. There was no way she could miss the evidence of his desire.

Or mistake who'd kidnapped her.

"Slade." Jane tugged his palm from her mouth and beamed up at him. "'Bout time you showed up."

\*\*\*

"I am upset with you, Jane." Slade growled, bracing his palms on the wall behind her, so she was caged between his arms. The words were the most massive understatement ever uttered. "You have ten seconds to improve my mood."

She shook her head. "Calm down. I had it all under control."

"He fucking could have raped you and murdered you a hundred times over!"

"He didn't, though. I'm fine."

Slade wasn't appeased. "What the hell were you *thinking?*"

"I was thinking about saving your life. And it *worked.*" She arched a brow. "If anything, *I* should be the one who's annoyed. Where have you been? Sightseeing?"

"In the *dungeon*. I killed thirty-three Goblins and a

dragon to get to you, so it took a while."

"A dragon! Wait, the movie *edited out* a dragon? That is *so* annoying. We have twenty scenes with Roland's terrible band, but no screen time for a *dragon?* What the hell is wrong with this picture?"

Slade didn't respond to that. He was still trying to get his heartbeat back under control. God, every moment Jane had been out of his sight, he'd been tortured with thoughts of what might be happening to her. It had seemed like an eternity. When he'd heard her coming down the hall, the relief he felt left him dizzy. It was quickly followed by anger, which was why he'd used his powers to commandeer this closet and lock them both inside. He needed to talk to his errant Eternal-One.

He needed more than talk.

Jane was still fixated on Slade's jailbreak. "I've been *waiting* for a dragon to show up, too. It's a fantasy movie, so I knew it was coming. I can't believe I missed it. Are they really huge, fire-breathing monsters?"

The woman was going to be the death of him. "*Five* seconds to improve my mood." He reported. "And, to answer your question, dragons are *not* huge, fire-breathing monsters. Well, they do breathe fire. But they are mostly just green-skinned assholes with wings, who hire on to whichever cause pays the most rubies. I am rarely happy to see them."

"Well, I'm happy to see *you*." Jane assured him, grudgingly moving on. "I suck at being a damsel in distress. I was waiting for you to rescue me, but things went to hell, so I rescued myself."

"I was coming!"

"You were taking too long. I got impatient." She arched a brow. "Besides, I hate movies where the girl has to be saved all the time. It's patriarchal crap."

"Two seconds to improve my mood." He didn't touch her, but his erection made it pretty clear what he wanted. "You need to start calming me down. Now."

Gray eyes met his. The woman was a brilliant actress. He could sense her growing desire, but her voice stayed perfectly innocent. "Oh, I don't think it's such a good idea to do what you're suggesting, sire." Even as she said it, her hand traveled down his body, unfastening his pants.

"Kings don't make 'suggestions.' We issue commands. Touch me, Jane."

"Yes, sire." She freed his erection, her fingers wrapping around the width of him. She gave a small hum of pleasure as she felt his size.

"Gods." Slade's eyes squeezed shut, his hand coming up to tangle in her beautiful hair. "Stroke me." Her fingers obediently danced along the surface of his skin and he groaned. "That's it." He helplessly thrust against her palm. "That's it, my One."

Jane's grip got tighter, her breathing coming faster to match his own. "Is your mood improving, sire?" Her lips found the column of his throat, her tongue tracing over his flesh. "Because, it certainly *seems* to be looking up."

Slade almost chuckled at that dry remark. Irritated as he was, the woman never ceased to delight him. He wasn't done complaining at her, though. "Fang had his hands on you, Jane. I cannot *stand* that he had his hands on you."

"I didn't want him to, but I had to protect you, Slade. It didn't go too far."

"It *did* go too far. What if I couldn't get to you and you couldn't escape on your own? Did you think of that?"

Her eyes flicked up to his, revealing the anxiety she'd been hiding. "Yes."

Slade's chest tightened at the quiet admission. It was the first time Jane had ever openly admitted any vulnerability. In a way, it was more intimate than having her fingers on him. A deeper show of trust. "I am sorry, my One." He whispered. "I should have been there sooner."

"I told you, I like being able to save myself. That's important to me. I can be independent and still be in a relationship with you." She paused. "But --honestly-- you *were* a key part of my escape. I only got away because of your bracelet and because you told me that Fang would be weakened when he shifted. He grabbed my wrist and the bracelet burned him. That pissed him off and I escaped when he was trapped between bodies."

The tenderness Slade felt switched into incredulity. "You pushed Fang until he *transformed into a wolf?!*" Like one of those picture box programs, his imagination showed him graphic, full-color visuals of all the brutal things a fully transitioned Werewolf could've done to her small body. "Do you *want* to die? Is that is, Jane?"

"What else could I do to get away? He's bigger than I am and he wasn't going to stop." She swallowed. "Slade, he wasn't going to stop. I was *so* scared. I did the only thing I could think of."

Fuck... That was all it took for the tenderness to come back. Slade dropped his forehead to hers. "I was never more terrified than I was today. Without you..." He trailed off, because there was nothing he could say to finish that thought. Without Jane, there *was* nothing. "My heart cannot take the strain of your ideas."

His words seemed to reassure her. Jane leaned up to kiss him and he groaned at the perfect taste of her. "But I have *soooo* many good ideas." She teased.

"Show me."

"Of course, sire." She breathed against his lips. "Tell me what you desire and it's yours."

There was one thing he'd been imagining since they met. "Get on your knees."

She hesitated, her tongue touching the corner of her mouth. "There's not much room in here."

"Kings don't listen to excuses, they just want results." He began nudging her downward. "Please, Jane." Vampire males were always dominant during sex and their silly "sire" game just made it easier to demand compliance. "We're not leaving here until I've had your mouth wrapped around me."

Jane liked that answer. She grinned at Slade and sank down so she was kneeling before him. His manhood jerked at the feel of her warm breath. Her tongue flicked out to lap a bead of moisture from the tip and the top of his head nearly came off. Content to take her time, she licked along the shaft, refusing to take him deeper until he begged. She was torturing him and it was glorious.

"More, Jane." He ground out when he was close to his breaking point. He tugged her head closer. "Open your mouth and take all of me. Please."

Gray eyes sparkled with desire. "Yes, sire." Her lips sealed around him, sucking him deep… and time stopped.

Slade's head went back, his teeth grinding together to hold back his roar. His hips instinctively moved, his hand tangled in her hair to guide her. "Christ, I've imagined this for so long. When we met, you were kneeling in the supermarket aisle and I started picturing your lips around me. I knew it would be like this." His eyes closed in rapture as she suckled him harder. "Only it's better than I ever dreamed."

Jane gently nipped his straining flesh and he nearly lost control. He might have, except he heard voices on the other side of the door.

"Find them!" Fang's tone was deeper than usual, the words infused with a wolf-like snarl. "I don't care what it takes!"

That asshole had the worse goddamn timing in the world.

Jane froze, her eyes flicking up to Slade's face. The woman had outsmarted Fang at every turn, but underneath her bravado, she was still frightened. How could she not be? The Werewolf had terrorized her. It was a wonder she could function, at all. Most people would be in a state of hysteria if they faced what Jane had.

Slade quickly dragged her to her feet. "It's alright." He could see her fear and he knew he had to fix it. "You're alright. I swear it."

"He's in his wolf form. Can he smell us?"

"Not through my magicks." The wolf form would make killing Fang harder, though, especially since Slade still didn't have the Silver Sword. That idiot Roland had run off before he told Slade where it was hidden.

Jane nodded. She clearly expected Slade to stop their fun… Which he was absolutely *not* going to do. At the moment, Slade couldn't go after Fang without risking Jane, but he could wipe the Werewolf from her mind forever. She would never think of that bastard without remembering this moment.

Her mouth parted in surprised as Slade lifted up the hem of her skirt and craned his neck to admire the view. "What are you doing?" She hissed, trying to yank the fabric back down.

"Find my woman before the Vampire does!" Fang continued ruthlessly. "I don't want that damn, dirty ape putting his paws on her."

Jane blinked as Slade smiled and very deliberately put his paws *alllll* over her. He backed her up against the wall and tugged down the neckline of her dress, so her breasts popped out over the top. They filled his hands, her nipples beading against his palms. Slade lowered his mouth to lap at the tight points. "*My* woman." He breathed.

Jane's fingers tangled in his hair, unsure whether to hang on or push him away. "Slade, we *can't*."

"Of course we can. The Werewolf is practically daring me." His lips traveled along the valley between her breasts. Gods, he couldn't wait to feed from that spot. He was going to spend the next century or two drinking from every millimeter of her perfect skin. "I love your body."

"You're about to start loving it to itty-bitty pieces. There are armed men right outside, hoping to find us and hack us apart."

"I told you, they cannot hear us. My magicks are surrounding us." Nothing would be able to sense them through the barrier Slade had constructed.

"But..." She drew in a sharp breath as Slade's hand left her breasts to explore under her dress, again.

Slade really needed to thank his grandmother for creating the outfit for her. It was so much more convenient than Jane's favorite, too-revealing pants. His palm slipped beneath the edge of her underwear, gently parting the damp folds of her body.

"You see why I like skirts?" His thumb started a slow massage.

She glowered at him, even as her cheeks flushed with

arousal. "You cannot *possibly* be getting off on this."

He grinned at her outraged tone. "Actually, I'm wagering that *you* will be the one who gets off first." Jane's mouth curved in reluctant amusement and Slade knew he had her. It was never hard to convince the woman to follow him, just as he was always eager to follow her. Their paths only led to each other. "Have faith in me, my One. I won't let you come to any harm."

Jane made a small sound of pleasure as he slipped a finger inside of her. "It's very kinky to be having sex with people two feet away." She warned, but she didn't try to stop him. "It's totally going to piss off parents' groups and movie censors."

"They're just jealous."

"Search *everywhere*." Fang continued. "The Vampire probably has her pinned down someplace, completely at his mercy."

Slade caught Jane around the waist, lifting her up and pinning her against the wall. "Feel free to start begging for mercy." He offered softly. "I don't mind a bit."

The anxiety had faded from her eyes, replaced with passion. "You're a crazy, reckless egomaniac."

"But so damn charming about it."

She beamed at that playful remark. "You really are my Prince Charming, Slade. I knew it from the minute I saw you."

"If the Vampire gets inside of her, I will see all of you dead." Fang thundered. "I mean it. I will execute *every one of you*."

Jane's gaze locked on Slade's, already knowing what he was going to do. She silently slipped off her underwear and dropped it to the floor. For a woman averse to taking chances, she seemed very willing to bet on him. It was humbling. Slade eased Jane's legs apart and she opened herself to him. It was the most breathtaking sight he'd ever seen.

"Now." She whispered.

Slade surged into her, his teeth grinding together at her breathless cry. Jesus, it was beautiful. *She* was beautiful. Jane was tight and hot and he would die a thousand times over before he parted with her. He buried his face in her hair. "Only think of me, my One. Only think of this."

Jane wrapped her legs around him. "I love you." She gasped. "Slade, I love you so much."

Oh *fuck* yes.

More Goblins stomped by outside, Fang still shouting orders. Slade braced his foot against the door, so they wouldn't be able to open it, even if they tried. Which none of them did. Slade was making sure of it. His goal was to take every threat that Fang leveled at her and turn it into something fun, and beautiful, and loving. And it seemed to be working.

Jane undulated against him, a blissful look on her face. "*Slade.*"

"He's probably feeding on her!" Fang shrieked.

Slade smirked. For half a second, he was almost grateful to the bastard. He bent his head to bite the side of Jane's neck, drinking deep.

*His.*

Jane's eyes drifted shut in pleasure, giving him everything he wanted. "Of course, I don't recall Prince Charming doing *this* in the fairytale."

"Princes are children. I am a *king*." Considering the circumstances, Slade couldn't have been more pleased with how this had turned out. Jane arched into his forceful thrusts, a seductive moan leaving her, and Slade almost exploded. He would never get enough of her.

"Find Jane Squire!" Fang was seething at his inability to recapture his quarry. "I want that bitch back and tied to my bed within the hour! I will fuck every hole in her body, and then gouge some new ones and fuck them, too!"

Jane flinched, shocked out of her sensual haze.

Fang was just outside their door now. It was taking most of Slade's self-control not to charge out there and pummel the Werewolf, even if he was killed in the process. That bastard would die *today*... but Slade had to be smart about it. Strategic. He didn't have the Silver Sword and it would do no good to go on a suicide mission, leaving Jane unprotected.

Besides, soothing Jane was just as important as

avenging her. Slade needed her to see that she was safe. That he would *always* keep her safe. And if he was dead and unable to reach her, she could protect *herself*. Because Jane Squire was the smartest, strongest, most extraordinary person he'd ever met.

"It's alright." Slade cupped her cheek, meeting her eyes. Her fright twisted his heart. "Fang's been dead from the minute he targeted you, Jane. I'm going to stab him through the heart before daybreak, so do not concern yourself with him. I will never let anyone harm you and live."

She relaxed against him, gray eyes meeting his. "I know. You're my hero."

"No. I am *in love with* the hero."

She looked startled. "Me? Hang on, you think *I'm* the hero of this story?"

"I know you are. You have saved me in every possible way. Inside of you beats the bravest, softest heart I've ever encountered." He dropped his head to kiss her, coaxing a response from her body. "You can do *anything*, Jane."

Her arms circled his neck, dismissing Fang from her mind. The woman who had faith in no one, put all of her faith in him. Slade smiled against her lips, adoring her.

The troops were moving away. Slade had known they would. The doorway was small and they weren't very bright. More importantly, he was camouflaging the entrance with his powers, so it became invisible. None of them could even see the door, let alone open it. If there had been a chance this would endanger Jane, he would have stopped long ago. He would never risk her safety. The woman meant more to him than anything else in the universe.

"You are my soul, Jane Squire." He whispered.

"And you're mine." Her hand came up to touch his face. "You are the very best part of my life, Slade." She bit her lower lip as he began moving faster. "Please. I need…" She shook her head, not finishing that request.

She didn't have to.

He knew exactly what she wanted, even if she didn't. Sexual hunger and the hunger for blood were inextricably linked in Vampires. Newly transitioned Vampires would be starved for both. Slade's desire spiked to almost unbearable levels at the idea of her drinking from him.

"It's alright." He pressed her face into his neck. "You need and I provide. That is the way it should be."

She made a small sound of denial. "No. Wait. Ew. I can't drink *blood*."

"You can, my One. You *want* to."

Jane swallowed. "But I'm…"

"A Vampire." He finished for her. "It's perfectly natural. Believe me, I *want* you to feed from me. I certainly love feeding from you." Gods, he could still taste her sweetness. "Take what you need and I'll let you finish." He thrust into her wet depths and she gasped, right on the edge. "There's no risk, Jane. Not with me."

She looked towards the door. She hadn't been shy about making love to him with others nearby, but drinking his blood so close to them seemed to worry her.

Slade found her modesty adorable. "I will keep you safe." He promised, again. "You know that. Give me what we both want."

Jane took a deep breath and stopped fighting. Her teeth grazed his neck, trusting him, and there was no way to hang on. Slade's mouth opened in a silent roar as she bit deep, his body erupting into hers. His orgasm triggered her own. Jane convulsed around him, crying out against his skin. Her mouth stayed at his throat, her tight sheath milked him dry, and it was the greatest moment of his life.

Slade struggled to remember how to breathe, as the last of the footsteps faded away. "The feelings I have for you cannot even be described in your language." He gripped the back of her head, urging her to drink more. "Do not *ever* risk yourself for me, again. I could not bear it, Jane. I nearly lost my mind when Fang took you away."

She lifted her face to kiss him. "In my language, the feelings I have for you are crazy, incurable, do-*anything*-for-him *love*. There's nothing either of us can do to change that, so get used to me protecting you."

He sighed. "I preferred it when you avoided risk."

"I didn't." Jane pulled back to frown at him. "Did I hurt you?" She examined his neck, but the wound was already closing. Vampire bites healed quickly. "I didn't mean to do that."

"I meant to do *everything* we did." Slade stopped her panicked inspection, catching hold of her hands. "I am *fine*. Are you sure you're alright?"

"Are you kidding? I've never felt better in my life. We finally had sex without me passing out afterwards. Being a Vampire just might be the best health plan ever." She tilted her head, like something new occurred to her. "Hey, am I going to be able to fly?"

"Yes, but only if you keep your strength up by feeding from me."

She swallowed at his provocative tone. "Well, the drinking-blood thing wasn't quite as terrible as I'd imagined. I could probably manage it, every now and then." He leaned down to nuzzle her temple and she drew in a shaky breath. "Or maybe even more often than that. For now, though, I just want to get out of here. If Fang finds you, he's going to be pissed. Especially if he figures out what we just did, right under his nose."

"He will not find me. I will find *him*."

"Slade, I don't want you to…"

He interrupted her protest, setting her on her feet. "I warned Fang what would happen if he touched you. I will see him *dead* and the threat to you removed. Then, we will leave this kingdom, go back to your world, and…" He trailed off, because he didn't have the next part quite figured out yet. It didn't matter. Just so he was with Jane, Slade was happy.

She blinked up at him as he adjusted her clothes and smoothed back her curls. "You want to leave Infinia? Why?"

It seemed fairly obvious. "Where you go, I will follow. You said you wished to return to Chicago, so I will be at your side."

"Yeah, but what about the people here? They need you."

"I need *you*. With Fang dead, someone else can rule. Allandrina, perhaps. You said yourself it should be her kingdom."

"And you said yourself that she's a lousy leader. Why isn't she the one fighting Fang? Why are her citizens being murdered and starved, while she does nothing to stop it?" Jane shook her head. "That witch has superpowers, but she's been hiding out this whole movie, letting other people suffer. How can she rule Infinia, if she expects us to do all the heavy lifting?"

"Roland, then." Slade offered. "I have discovered that the boy isn't totally useless, after all." He paused, realizing she hadn't heard the news. "Oh, he is also my younger brother."

Jane stared at him. "You've *got* to be kidding me."

"No. It's true. My grandmother appeared to explain it all."

"She *appeared?*"

"She traveled to Infinia just long enough to tell me of Roland's true identity. I was as surprised as you are."

"I'm not *surprised*. Not about you getting a brother, anyhow. This is a fantasy movie. Of *course* it would pull out the long lost sibling cliché. The hero always gets a long lost sibling. It's a rule of the genre."

"I expected that you'd say something like that."

"I totally guessed it was going to be Fang, though." She mused to herself. "I was thinking a fraternal-version of Luke and Vader, but it seems we're doing pure Luke and Leia."

"*Fang?* My brother? He is a Werewolf and I am a Vampire. It is *impossible* for our species to be related."

"Yeah, because this film's *so* above retcons." Jane sighed. "Whatever. Roland's definitely the better of our lousy options. Not by much, but I'll take what we can get." She arched a brow. "Speaking of lousy family members and *Star Wars* films, when your grandmother Obi-Wan-ed into this land, did she explain why she turned on you?"

"Yes." Slade met her eyes. "She foresaw my destiny lay far from the Vampire Isle. With *you*, Jane. She forced me to leave, so that I would find *you*."

Her mouth curved. "I guess I have to forgive her for

being mean to you, then."

"She gave me the most valuable gift of my life." Slade assured her. "All she asked in return was that I not harm my new sibling. So, I resisted the urge to kill Roland. Instead, I am considering a bargain to work with the boy."

"Really?" She made a show of looking around. "So where is he?"

Slade hesitated. "I am not sure. He fled the blacksmith shop when Fang arrived."

Jane let out an irritated sound. "Very inspiring for a future king. Jesus, maybe Fang *would've* been the better option." She rolled her eyes. "Look, kid brother or not Roland isn't capable of ruling this realm. That guy probably can't even comb his stupid, hipster hairdo without detailed instructions."

"Well, his hair *is* very complicated. But he said that he might return at the last minute to provide us with some sort of plucky and comedic assistance. He believes that is his true role."

Jane wasn't moved by that defense. "Well, I hate to leave out Han Solo from the mix, but that kid is no Han Solo. Face it, Slade, you can't leave Infinia. The kingdom needs you and you need to be here."

Slade had no intention of being anywhere except beside Jane. That meant going back to Chicago. Since he wasn't going to change his mind, he changed the subject. "Neither of us will go anywhere unless we defeat Fang. We must get the Silver Sword."

"Agreed. But even if we somehow get our hands on it, how do the two of us take over a whole castle? It's going to be hard to stab Fang if he's surrounded by hundreds of Goblin bodyguards. I have no idea how we're going to defeat them all."

Slade smirked. "Luckily, I have something that pretenders to the throne and their minions do not. Something that can help us win our war. Something that only a *true* king can possess."

Jane stared at him for a long moment. "Oh Jesus… You're about to say 'giant butterflies,' aren't you?"

# Chapter Seventeen

EXT. OBSIDIAN FORTRESS-NIGHT

Giant butterflies swoop in from the sky!

SLADE has called for his faithful pets' assistance and they heed his request. They are like gossamer stealth fighter jets, zooming to the rescue. Their multicolored wings glisten, as they silently soar above the Obsidian Fortress. It is an imposing and sparkly sight. (Note: These giant butterflies are going to be a marketing bonanza! I can already picture the plush toys, and lunchboxes, and maybe a Saturday morning cartoon of their adventures.)

But it is not just the pterodactyl-sized insects that have come to save the day. Infinia's rebels sit astride the beautiful bugs. ROLAND'S radio message has rallied SLADE'S followers and they eagerly attack FANG'S palace, dropping into the courtyard from the giant butterflies' backs. More people are there, too. TEGAN and JAMES THE ORC and KONRAD THE OGRE and countless others who are fed up with FANG'S oppression.

The Goblins now face an army of pissed-off peasants. Even FANG'S private guards have to race into the mêlée, leaving him alone. War rages for Infinia, both sides knowing that this fight will decide their future. Rain pours down, because rain always makes a battle scene more cinematic. It's very edge-of-your-seat awesome.

> ROLAND
> (Leaping from the lead butterfly, his sword raised over his head)

> Fight for this land! Fight for Infinia!
> And, for God's sake, somebody find my brother, because I
> have no fucking clue what to do next!

A beautiful blonde woman rushes into the fray, her beautiful eyes on ROLAND. He instantly recognizes the beautiful ALLANDRINA, whose ample cup-size is even more impressive in person. The beautiful princess throws her arms around him, like she's been waiting for him to arrive.

ALLANDRINA
Roland, thank God you've finally arrived!

ROLAND has no idea how she knows his name, since they've never met. Maybe she's a fan of his music. Whatever the reason, a hot chick is pressed against him and he's not complaining.

This has been a super-cool day. He's on the winning side of a kickass fight, he's found a rockin' big brother, and now the princess is totally --probably-- going to sleep with him. Being ROLAND is *awesome*.

ROLAND
(Patting her back, as she clings to him.)
There, there. I'm here, now. Everything is okay.

ALLANDRINA
(Pulling back to look up at him with watery brown eyes)
No, it's *not* okay, brave Roland. Do you have the Silver Sword with you?

ROLAND
Yeah, I brought it so Slade could kill Fang, but...

ALLANDRINA
(Cutting him off)

*Then we must hurry! You're the only one who can save me from this monstrous fate.*

*Redrafted Film Script- "From Here to Infinia"*

All movies needed their climactic fight scene to happen in some suitably atmospheric place. For *From Here to Infinia,* it was the glassy, black battlements of the Obsidian Fortress. Torrents of rain washed down, making the open sides of the parapets slippery and dangerous. The roof was illuminated by lightning strikes, the sheets of water reflecting the eerie light. It was deserted and creepy and ideal for an epic showdown.

"This is not good." Jane muttered, trying to spot an escape route.

She looked over the steep drop to the battle far below. Slade looked up, trying to spot the giant butterflies. Maybe that was why they fit so well, despite his eternal optimism and her diehard realism. Jane looked down and he looked up. Sure they focused on different things, but between the two of them, they were seeing the whole picture.

Of course, this particular picture wasn't so great.

They were trapped.

"The giant butterflies have already gone." Slade reported. "We cannot use them to reach the ground."

"First I miss seeing the dragon and now I miss the giant butterflies. This movie is really beginning to piss me off." Jane pushed the wet hair out of her face and gestured towards the courtyard. "At least your training seems to have paid off with the rebels, though. I think they're going to win this thing. They *did* listen to you, Slade."

"I think they listened to *you*, actually. All the things you told them about fighting for what they believe in and standing up for themselves. They took it to heart, Jane. There are no more extras in this story. They're taking control of their own destinies."

"We're both inspiring, I guess. Too bad we're also screwed." She flipped through the script to see if it gave any hint on where they should go next. The rain had the pages sticking together and the ink running, but she kept scanning for clues.

The two of them had been endlessly circling the upper stories of the fortress, trying to discover a way down. Slade insisted that the stairs had moved since he'd escaped the dungeon and Jane knew he was right. It didn't matter how hard they searched, they would only find what *From Here to Infinia* wanted them to find. For instance, the exit to the roof... which had locked tight behind them.

In order to reach the end, the movie needed to make sure everyone was in the right place. That meant funneling them towards the grand finale. The rooftop was a direct rip-off of the *Beauty and the Beast* cartoon, right down to the gargoyle statues. Obviously, *something* was about to happen. A film didn't invest in an expensive set unless it was going to stage some big scene. All Jane's instincts told her that they needed to get out of there before all hell broke loose.

"We should do that flying thing and float ourselves to another time zone." She suggested for the third time.

"I told you before, Vampires cannot fly in storms. And it is not hot enough to teleport, so we must come up with another way."

"Well, we have to do *something* or..." Jane stopped short, her eyes locked on the last sight she wanted to see. "Aw shit."

Fang stepped out of the shadows, the rain plastering his dark fur against his skin. "Heeeeere's Fang-y." He snarled out in his best Jack Nicholson impression and hurled himself at Jane.

For once, Jane didn't complain about the mangled dialogue. She was too busy stumbling sideways. Slade pushed her out of the way, putting his body between her and danger. The Werewolf tackled him, an enraged bellow leaving his throat. Fang and Slade collided like a thunderclap, knocking themselves off their feet.

Jane's eyes widened in horror. "Slade!"

In his wolf form, Fang was bigger than Slade and fury

gave him extra strength. His clawed hands wrapped around Slade's neck. "You invade my land, and you take my woman, and *you think I'll let you get away with it?!*"

"*My* woman." Slade snarled back. His Dark Instincts had taken over again, his fangs and claws gleaming. He slammed a fist into Fang's face, knocking him backwards. "*No one* touches her, you son-of-a-bitch." They still didn't have the Silver Sword, so it was impossible to kill Fang. That didn't seem to slow Slade down. "*No one* takes her from me." He somehow got on top of Fang, beating him with an unwavering focus. "*And no one fucking frightens her!*"

Fang roared in fury, freeing himself through brute force. "You stole everything from me once before and it won't happen again!" He plowed a shoulder into Slade's midsection, sending them sliding across the wet surface of the roof. They hydroplaned to within a foot of the drop-off, neither of them paying attention to the precipice. "I'll see you dead this time!"

"Slade!" Jane rushed forward. "Don't fall!"

She'd only taken two steps when she heard something ridiculous and unmistakable: The duh-duh-*daaaah* sound effect, warning the audience of coming danger. The three notes were universally understood by moviegoers everywhere. They sounded when the monster was oozing from the swamp or the villain was about to strike his fatal blow. They were the words "Oh shit" expressed through trumpets.

Jane didn't know how that stupid score could be heard inside the film, but it didn't matter. Something terrible was about to happen. *From Here to Infinia* said so and she believed it.

"Slade, we have to get out of here!"

He didn't seem to hear her desperate cry over the pounding rain. Slade heaved Fang away from him, trying to maneuver back onto solid ground. "I gave you a second chance, Werewolf. At the end of our last battle, I let you start again in another world. Look what you did with that opportunity!" He waved a hand around to indicate all of Infinia. "You enslaved this kingdom and its citizens, and now you're surprised when they fight back?"

"*You're* the one fighting me." Fang blocked Slade's progress, keeping him trapped by the edge. "But that's about to end. Once you're dead, I will have *everything* that's mine. The peasants will stop their rioting, the kingdom will bow to my rule, and Jane will worship *me* as her true mate."

Slade gave an honest-to-God laugh at that boast. "If you believe that, then you have not met my Eternal-One. There is *nothing* that will make her submit to you."

"What about *me?*" A new voice demanded over the pounding rain. "Isn't anyone going to mention *me?*"

Jane spun around and realized why the portent-y music had sounded. Behind her stood a stunning and pissed off woman. Her long hair flowed down her back, her Bunny Ranch body covered in a nearly transparent gown. Given the fact that she looked a hell of a lot like the blonde Angelina Jolie in that centerfold picture, she had to be Allandrina.

Princess. Witch. Topless model.

Surprise villain.

Crap.

Jane totally should have seen this one coming. It was *such* a stupid plot twist.

"You're fools. All of you." Allandrina stepped forward, dragging Roland with her. She held Slade's long lost brother in front of her like a shield, the Sliver Sword clutched in her manicured hand. The point of it was aimed right at his jugular. "Do you think I'll allow any of you to steal my future?"

Jane spared Slade a quick frown. "I told you the whole premise of this story was sexist." Not that Allandrina was doing so much to promote gender equality. Jane turned back to the renegade lingerie ad and shook her head. "Look, this is just bad film making. You were barely *in* this movie, so how can we be invested in you suddenly going rogue? If you were supposed to be the secret bad guy, you should have been in *way* more scenes before the big reveal."

"I was in plenty of scenes until *you* came along and stole them all." Allandrina hissed. "Nobody puts Allandrina in a corner."

"Oh for God's sakes, you didn't even have any lines,

until now!"

"I did, too! Ask Fang. He's been my costar this whole time."

"Costar?" Fang scoffed. "Please. I don't even remember your name, woman."

"I am *Allandrina*, Princess of Infinia, and the strongest Dark Fairy who's ever existed!"

Jane's brows soared. "*You're* the Dark Fairy?" She'd read some of the full frontal encounters between Fang and the Fairy in that cave. The script hadn't included a lot of context, but it had stressed the nakedness and depravity. Jesus, she could've gone forever without putting a face to the writhing. "I thought you were a Witch."

"That's what I *want* people to think. My kind are hunted here, while Witches are adored." She snorted. "If I were really a Witch, I wouldn't be stuck in this shithole dimension. With their powers, I'd have fled to a better world long ago. For years, I had to pretend to *care* about this dumpy kingdom. When Fang arrived, I began to see there was another way."

Slade made a face. "I told you Dark Fairies were often the lackeys of Werewolves, Jane. You see? They are powerful, but cannot think for themselves."

Allandrina pushed the Silver Sword against Roland's neck and the kid gave a panicked squeak. "Bro, can you not piss her off, please?" He begged.

"I am no one's lackey." Allandrina snapped. "This is all *my* plan. I helped the Werewolf gain power, so I could drive the Light Fairies from this realm. Now their magicks are unprotected and I will harness them for my escape. *Finally*, I will flee Infinia and go someplace *worthy* of a true princess." She smirked. "Can you guess where I'm going, Jane Squire?"

"Hell?"

Allandrina pursed her lips at the snarking. "Close. To your very own Chicago."

"Wait, you want to go to *my* world?"

"Of course. In a land without magicks I will have absolute power. Also, I believe you have martinis there. That alone is enough to sway me." She shrugged. "Now, all I need is that script of yours. Witches created it, after all. With those pages to guide the connection and the Light Fairies' powers, I can leave Infinia forever."

...And do her damnedest to ruin Earth once she got there.

Jane's jaw tightened.

"You'll never get away with this, Allandrina!" Roland squawked, trite to the end. "I'm *totally* not sleeping with you, either. You blew your chance with me, babe. And that pinup shot was airbrushed. I can tell."

"Shut-up, Roland. In every version of the tale, you're a moron." Allandrina held out her free hand to Jane and gave her fingers an impatient snap. "Hand over the script."

"No." Not the wittiest comeback for a heroine to use, but Jane wasn't in the mood to worry about quotable rejoinders. "Why the hell would I do that? I'm betting Slade and I can take you."

"Not before I kill Roland."

"Did you not get the pages where Roland tried to kill me? I'm not too worried about you stabbing him in the head."

"That was an *accident*. I wouldn't try to kill my long lost sister-in-law. I was trying to kill *Slade*, because I didn't know he was my long lost brother!"

Allandrina smirked, ignoring Roland's indignant whining and Slade's long suffering sigh. "I will give you another reason then, Jane Squire. The portal I open will allow *you* to pass through it, as well. No one else in Infinia will be able to return you to your world." She shook her head. "Believe me, I've tried *everything* to find a way out of here. I am your only hope."

Jane's jaw tightened.

Allandrina arched a smug brow, sensing she'd scored a hit. "Isn't that what you want? To go home? Help me now and I can see it happen."

Slade slanted Jane a concerned glance. "Allandrina is probably telling the truth." He said softly. "I do not know how to get you back home if she isn't a Witch. Infinia has strong barriers. Even my grandmother could not stay in this realm for long."

"It doesn't matter. There is no *way* I'm going to let an evil sorceress loose on Chicago. We have enough jackasses in the town."

He looked tortured. "But this could be your only chance, my One. We could both go through the portal and..."

Fang threw himself at Slade, interrupting the debate. No one had been paying attention to the Werewolf and Fang used their distraction to strike. He pulled out a blue diamond blade, holding it up so Slade could see the ominous glow. "You will not live to see any other worlds, Vampire!"

The knife slashed out, cutting Slade's arm. Blue diamond blades really were the one weapon that could harm Vampires. The small scratch wasn't fatal, but it burned Slade's skin like acid. He automatically staggered backwards... straight off the side of the roof.

"*NO!*" Jane screamed as he disappeared into the darkness.

"Brother!" Roland cried. Allandrina had to release her hold the kid, as he collapsed to the rooftop in a pile of deadweight and sobs. "*Why?!*" He shouted towards the heavens, throwing his head back and raising his arms in hammy despair. "*WHY!?!*"

Fang caught Jane around the waist, hauling her against him when she scrambled right to the edge to scan for Slade. "Stay back. Do you want to die, too?"

"He's not dead! I'd know if he was dead." She had to believe that. Jane's eyes desperately searched, but Slade had fallen through the thatched roof of some building below. It looked like a stable. "We have to get down there. He could be hurt."

"I *want* him to be hurt, you stupid bitch." Fang swung her around, leering in victory. "I hope you're right and he *is* still alive. I want him suffering. I want his whole body broken into little pieces of pain."

Jane's jaw clenched. "As long as he's breathing, he'll *still* beat you."

"Actually, I will beat *all* of you." Allandrina corrected. "So unless you want to join your Eternal-One, I suggest you hand over the script, Jane Squire."

"I suggest you bite me." Jane shot back, struggling against Fang's fierce grip.

"Fine." Allandrina shrugged. "We'll do it the fun way." She waved a hand towards the fortress' decorative gargoyles. Almost instantly, the stone monsters lumbered to life. Their gruesome faces pulling back in cruel snarls, their lifeless eyes glowing red, they sprang towards Jane.

*Fuck.* How was she supposed to fight a Witch, a Werewolf, and these rock-heads? She didn't have time for this. She needed to get to Slade.

"Call them off!" Fang held tight to Jane, as the creatures advanced. "Allandrina, are you out of your mind? Do you think I went through all this just to let you kill my mate with those piles of rocks?"

"Oh, so now you remember my name?" She snorted. "Don't worry, Werewolf. You won't be around to mourn your precious Jane. I'm going to kill you, too. You're the worst lover I've ever had …and I once slept with three sewer trolls!"

"Hey!"

Jane kept her eyes centered on the gargoyles. She had zero faith in Fang's ability to stop these freaks, so she was going to have to do it herself. There *had* to be a way. Getting through them was her only chance to help Slade, so she'd...

A noise cut through the air. Huge wings flapping. Jane looked up, thinking the giant butterflies had returned. Instead, she saw Slade, riding to her rescue on a white horse. Well, actually it was that damn pegasus, but close enough. The enchanted steed carried Slade back up to the rooftop, like something out of a fairytale.

Despite everything, Jane started to smile. Slade just *had* to dust off the gallant steed trope, didn't he? Goddamn, but he made the classics look good.

"Jane, are you alright?" He demanded, maneuvering the pegasus closer.

"He's alive." She whispered in relief.

"He's alive!" Roland cheered.

"He stole my pegasus." Fang complained.

"Kill him!" Allandrina screeched at the gargoyles. "Kill the Vampire!"

The stone monsters' extended their bat-like wings and launched themselves at Slade. They swarmed him, trying to knock him from the sky. Slade beat them back with his sword, his blade hacking through their stony skin. As they died, they crumbled into pebbles, the tiny bits raining down in explosions of gravel. Everyone gaped up at the clash. Forget the dragon and the butterflies, this was the *real* action scene. Slade was literally battling two dozen monsters at once and he was *winning*.

Still, Jane wasn't the kind of heroine who sat back and watched, no matter how awesome the show. She drove her elbow into Fang's midsection. If the Werewolf could take advantage of distractions, then so could she.

Fang cursed in surprise, his grip on the blue diamond blade loosening. Jane snatched it out of his hand and whirled towards Allandrina. Dark Fairies were magickal and *From Here to Infinia* had been *really* clear on the fact that blue diamonds cut through magicks.

"Let's see what *this* will do." She stepped forward and plunged the dagger into Allandrina's chest. The Dark Fairy let out a shriek of rage, flailing backwards.

Jane followed her down, intent on getting the Silver Sword from her hand. She slammed Allandrina's wrist against the rooftop. "Just give it up!" She was so frigging sick of all the mystical weapons in this place. They were going to finish it once and for all.

"Never!"

The woman was strong for a princess, especially one with a knife in her chest. She wasn't letting go of the blade. There was only one thing to do.

Jane deliberately dropped the screenplay. She threw it directly into Allandrina's line of sight. Allandrina gasped and forgot about Jane. She stopped fighting and blindly scrambled towards the folder, everything else ceasing to matter. All she cared about was reaching the sodden pages.

Jane easily wrenched the silver blade free from her fingers and tossed it up to Slade. "Here, sweetie. Let's end this stupid movie."

Slade gave her a slanting smile, his gaze fixing on Fang.

"This isn't over, Vampire." He backed away, golden eyes glowing. "I'll have my revenge in our next tale. You'll never be rid of... *shit!*" His threat was abruptly cut off as Slade seized him by the neck and dragged him into the air

The pegasus sailed upward, higher and higher, Fang's legs desperately bicycling for purchase. He tried to push Slade off the back of the stallion, but it was no use. Slade easily kept his seat, directing the pegasus just where he wanted it to go. Of *course* he was a wonderful horseman. It was all part and parcel of being a storybook hero.

"I *told* you what I'd do to you, if you touched Jane." Slade snarled.

"She's mine!" Fang bellowed back, still trying to kill them both by knocking Slade off the pegasus. "If I can't have her, no one will! I don't care what the magical book says. I'll be back again and again and *again*. Let me go or I'll make Jane suffer for the next millennium!"

Slade hefted the blade in his free hand. "Luckily, letting you go *is* in the script, you bastard."

He let Fang go... from about ten thousand feet and with the Silver Sword plunged into his heart.

Her Eternal-One seriously didn't play around when it came to finales. The Werewolf wouldn't be returning for *From Here to Infinia II*. Not even a movie could explain away his body's sickening crash into the pavement. It was like watching a watermelon dropped from a skyscraper.

Jane barely noticed the carnage. All her focus was on Allandrina, who'd grabbed the script and was mumbling some wordy incantation over the pages. "What good do you think that will do you, now?" She demanded. "You're bleeding out, Allandrina. If we don't get you to a doctor, you'll be dead before you..."

"It's too late for me." Allandrina coughed, staggering

to her feet. "The blue diamond magicks will see to that. But I'll make sure the Vampire pays before I go." She threw the screenplay down and held out a hand. Magicks arced and *From Here to Infinia* was consumed in a brilliant green fire that quickly morphed into a black hole.

At least, it *looked* like a black hole. Or what they looked like on TV, anyway. A swirling whirlpool of darkness and fog. It had to be a portal and, at the very center, there was an opening to another world. *Jane's* world. Looking through the vortex, she could see Chicago. The buildings, and the traffic, and the noise. The safety of familiar things. Popcorn, iPhones, reruns of *Downton Abbey*. It was all within her grasp.

"Dude, that is so cool." Roland breathed.

"Go, Jane Squire!" Allandrina shouted. Creating the portal was draining the last of her powers. Her whole form was withering into dust, the unstable magicks eating away at her. "I can't hold it much longer. Go back to your land. You know it's what you really wish."

"Jane!" The pegasus swooped down, Slade still astride its back. The gargoyles were preventing him from landing on the roof and he desperately battled through them. "Do not leave me!"

"Leave him!" Allandrina screeched. "Then the Vampire will have paid the ultimate price for all that he's done." She was fading faster now. "He ruined *everything* for me when he came here. I'll return the favor by taking his Eternal-One from his arms *forever*."

"Stop!" Slade slashed at the last of the gargoyles. "Jane, *please*. If you want to go back, I will go with you. I will do *anything*. Just don't pass through that portal alone. Please wait for me."

"I can't hold it open much longer!" Allandrina insisted. "Decide right now or you'll be stuck here forever, Jane Squire! What is your path?"

Jane slowly shook her head. Slade was on one side of her and Earth was on the other. Everything she'd ever known versus that lunatic Vampire. This really was her only chance. All or nothing. It was the kind of risk that had always terrified her. ...Until now. Jane looked between the options and smiled at how simple the choice was.

Only one direction led home.

She raced for Slade.

"*Noooo!*" Allandrina collapsed, her strength giving out as she was defeated. Her beautiful body vanished into nothing, her magicks stopped forever. The last gargoyles disintegrated and the portal winked out of existence. Before it evaporated, the vortex expanded, sucking who-knew-what out of Infinia and into Chicago. Then it contracted in a ball of smoke, like it had never been there, at all.

Jane didn't care. "Slade." She reached the side of the pegasus, as he touched down on the rooftop. "Are you okay? I knew that fall wouldn't slow you down for long, but it was such a long drop. Are you hurt?"

"Jane." He sounded like he couldn't believe she was really there. He held out a hand, seizing her palm and pulling her onto the saddle in front of him.

She settled on his lap, trying to arrange her legs around the horse's stupid wings and searching Slade for injuries. "Are you alright?" She persisted, worried about his odd expression.

"Yes." Slade's gaze soaked in her face for a long moment. Then his forehead dropped to hers, his eyes closing on a long sigh. "In a thousand years, I have never been so 'alright.'" He touched her hair, like he was still afraid she'd disappear. "You stayed."

"I've acquired a real taste for squirrel burgers." She teased. "Don't be an idiot. Of course I stayed. I could *never* leave you. You're the only place I want to be." She hugged him close, relieved that he was unharmed. "Besides, you told me that Infinia is my destiny, remember? And Slade, King of the Vampires, is always right."

His massive arms came around her, squeezing her tight. "I was right about *you*." He whispered. "You are a hero, Jane. You just saved my life. If you left me, I would cease to exist."

"I'm not likely to wander far. It turns out I'm a sucker

for a prince on a white horse."

He chuckled at that, pressing his lips to her temple. "I'm a king," he corrected, "and you --Jane Squire-- are my queen. My partner. My soul. You always have been."

She smiled at that and leaned up to kiss him.

"And that's a white *pegasus*, not a horse." Roland put in, interrupting Slade and Jane's beautiful moment. "White Pegasus. Hang on! Hold everything!" He lurched to his feet with an excited grin. "Wouldn't that be an *awesome* name for a band?"

# Epilogue

EXT. CHICAGO- NIGHT

AMALIE THE WITCH is pleased with the results of her latest matchmaking efforts. SLADE and JANE are finally together, Infinia is saved, and it's a happy ending for everyone. All in all, it's been another successful story. She's getting really good at this writing stuff! Time for a pat on the back and some hot cocoa.

She's just about to head off to bed with her favorite mug full of chocolate and marshmallows, when something outside draws her attention. Frowning, AMALIE heads onto the balcony and looks out over the skyline. It is a clear night, except for an unexpected swirl of dark clouds in the sky. They seem to be moving like a cyclone. Only it's not a cyclone. It's a...

                AMALIE
              (Horrified)
                Portal

...portal. ALLANDRINA'S vortex connects Infinia to Earth for a few precious seconds. Just long enough for the whirlpool of power to drag in some supernatural...

                AMALIE
           (More horrified)
            Hitchhikers.

...hitchhikers and deposit them in this new land. Who knows who they are or how they will adapt to modern day Chicago? Will any Vespas be safe? Only one thing is clear: AMALIE has a *big* problem on her hands.

AMALIE
(Squeezing her eyes shut in frustration)
Shit.

*End of the credits teaser- "From Here to Infinia"*

"There *must* be other Witches in Infinia." Slade leaned against the headboard and watched Jane brush her hair. "I will find them and they will be able to send us back to Chicago. Or maybe I can contact Amalie and she can help us return. No matter what I must do, I promise you, I will fix this, my One."

The two of them had appropriated one of the Obsidian Fortresses many bedrooms. Jane had nixed the idea of claiming Fang's creepy chamber, even though it was the largest. She planned to forget that the Werewolf ever existed and that meant *not* sleeping on his pillow. Instead, Jane and Slade settled on a room in one of the castle's turrets, with rounded walls and Once-Upon-A-Time décor. Jane thought it was perfect.

Except for the lack of a connected bath.

First thing tomorrow, they were starting a task force on "running water." Showers needed to get invented, pronto. *Someone* in Infinia had to be able to figure out how to get them to work. If they weren't all too hung over, anyway.

A party was raging in Infinia, the likes of which the land had never seen. With Fang gone, the whole kingdom was celebrating as if it was the end of *Return of the Jedi*. The rebels filled the courtyard and spilled out into the streets. Tegan was giving out free ale from the Drunken Dragon. Roland's band (newly christened "White Pegasus") was squealing music at octaves only monstrous bats could hear, triggering another dance number. Symon had programmed his wooden robots to walk in a conga line, which added a whole new layer of lunacy to the scene. Even the Goblins seemed pleased, if their God-awful karaoke was any indication.

Everyone was in a festive mood, except Infinia's new

king.

"Slade, would you please stop worrying. I don't *want* to go back to Chicago. I told you that." She frowned at him in the vanity mirror. "*This* is where you belong."

"No. *You* are where I belong, Jane. I wish to be where you are."

"Well, I'm *here*, dummy. Besides, you hate Chicago."

"And you hate Infinia."

"No, I don't."

"You say you do. Constantly. And I want you to be happy."

"I *am* happy. Honestly, being in this ridiculous place is the happiest I've ever been. I *like* to complain about all the stupid things that happen here. It's half the fun." She shrugged. "Besides, I'm pretty sure most of the egregious movie bullshit will clear up now that the screenplay is gone. The film is over, so things will probably be just *sort of* crazy, instead of *completely* crazy."

"And if they're still completely crazy?"

"Then I'm staying anyway. I'm a professional actress, so I'm trained for this sort of situation. *From Here to Infinia* wound up being way better than *Dracula, Ph.D.*" She arched a brow at him. "And there are worse happily-ever-afters than being queen of an enchanted realm, with my very own handsome prince. I'll suffer through the rest." She paused. "People aren't going to keep calling me 'milady' all the time, are they?"

"No. They'll call you 'your highness.'" He ignored the face she made at that irritating news. "And that is not the point. Infinia is far too dangerous for you."

"Really? Because, I think I'm kicking its ass. Did you see me take down that scrawny Fairy?"

"I *did* and it was impressive." He paused to appreciate the memory. "*Very* impressive. But you would still be far safer in Chicago."

"You clearly don't read the front page of the *Tribune*. Bad things happen everywhere."

"Very few Werewolves and Shadowmen and Mages

happen anywhere but *here*."

"I wouldn't be too sure of that. I think a lot of supernatural stuff got sucked through that portal at the end and crash-landed in the Windy City."

Slade reluctantly nodded. "I sensed the same thing. But Amalie is a Witch and she has Damien as a brother. She knows how to deal with disasters. *You* are the one I am presently worried about."

"I'm a Vampire, sweetie. I could *always* take care of myself, but now I'm --like-- superpowered and immortal. I have it all under control. Trust me."

"I do trust you." He said instantly. "I know you can do anything, Jane. But you are still so *small*."

"It's adorable you think that." Jane scoffed.

He kept talking. "If anything happened to you, I could not recover. I would not even want to. I will *gladly* live in your world if it means keeping you safe and happy..."

Enough was enough. "Look," Jane spun around, cutting off his concerns. "I've spent my whole life looking for a home, Slade. I'm not about to walk away now that I've found you. I'm staying right here and surviving for every single installment of this film franchise. You're *never* getting rid of me."

He was quiet for a long moment. "Promise?" He finally whispered.

"*Yes*. We're partners in this weirdness. *Forever*. That means mutual 'I dos,' and big white dress, and a cute little house in the country." She looked around. "Or I guess we're stuck renovating this ugly castle, actually. But I don't even care, just so we're *both* living here." She glowered at him. "Translation: We're living in Infinia and getting married. Deal with it."

Slade stopped arguing so fast it was almost funny. "Alright."

Jane blinked, a little surprised by his quick agreement. "Alright, then. Good. Wow, that was easy. I guess you do love me, because that was a fairly hostile marriage proposal."

"I guess you do love me, if you are willing to endure

Infinia and wear a big wedding dress, and tolerate the existence of my idiot sibling."

"Is that kid going to be living with us, by the way?"

"Probably. He seems to have imprinted on me like an orphaned duckling. I've been unable to shake him."

Jane rolled her eyes, because she had the feeling Slade wasn't trying real hard to get rid of Roland. He liked having a little brother. "Fine. We can keep him. And I'm okay with the Infinia part. Really. But a wedding dress…? I spoke without thinking on that one. We might have to negotiate."

He slowly grinned. "I do not wish to negotiate. I love it when you wear dresses. And you'll be happy to know that I look quite striking in a tuxedo."

"Oh, you would look 'quite striking' in a cardboard box." She headed over to the bed and arched a brow. "I hate to play the 'handsome prince' card again, but you are just *so. damn. handsome.*"

"Handsome *king*." He reminded her. "They just took a vote downstairs and I was the unanimous choice for ruler. Well, *nearly* unanimous. That James the Orc fellow is really an ass."

"*I* voted for you, sweetie. And not *just* because of the handsomeness." Jane shook her head. "For a lot of girls, that would probably be enough. But me," she shrugged, "I'm a reformed pragmatist. I want the whole fairytale. Kind, smart, brave, funny…"

"I will be anything you ask."

"Good, because I'm *really* picky about my kings and husbands. You might have noticed that I don't get swept off my feet by just any Vampire who wanders into the supermarket."

"I did notice that." Slade tugged her down on top of him. "I had to work very hard to win you over. I was quite disheartened at times. I thought you would never want me, as I want you."

"It was really a tough fight for you." She settled against him. "I resisted you for *at least* half-an-hour. I'm surprised you didn't give up in despair at that kind of rejection."

Being Slade, he took that seriously, convinced that she

really had tortured him by playing hard to get. "It was difficult, but I would fight for you forever, Jane." He let out a contented sigh, brushing a hand against her cheek. "From the beginning, I knew there was no one else for me. Every doubt in my head goes quiet when you're near. You have faith in me and it gives me faith in myself. It's a gift."

"Yeah, because you *really* need to work on your confidence."

"Are you claiming I'm arrogant, again?" He nuzzled the side of her neck. "That doesn't sound like something a besotted fiancée would say. I prefer it when you call me a hero."

"You *are* arrogant. And kind, and smart, and brave, and funny. And my very own hero. Even when you drive me nuts, I wouldn't change a single thing about you." She paused and fluttered her lashes at him. "...Except you'd be naked, sire."

Slade laughed at that suggestion. "You first." He drawled.

She loved it when he teased her. Jane obligingly unbelted her borrowed robe. "I'm going to need new clothes, you know. I hate that dress your grandmother apparently made for me and you ripped my khakis off, back at the lava pits. That leaves me with nothing but my bracelet." She held up her hand to show him the Werewolf talisman.

Slade kissed the inside of her wrist, his thumb brushing over the silver links. "With Fang gone, it is safe to get rid of this, you know." He murmured. "I know you do not like it."

"Get rid of jewelry? Do you know anything about girls? It could be a live snake and I'd never take it off. *You* gave it to me, dummy."

His mouth curved, pleased that she wanted to keep his gift. "I love you." He said simply.

"I know. It's why you're going to buy me pretty clothes. Andra from the rebel camp lent me this robe and some other stuff, but her personal style skews towards fur bikinis. *You'll* probably like it, but it's not really my taste."

"You need and I provide, my One. I will give you

whatever clothing you desire." He peeled the robe from her shoulders, letting out a low sound of pleasure at the sight of her body. "Later. Much, much later."

"Later, I desire *pants,* Slade. I mean it. I'll give in on wearing a wedding dress, but I have to have some jeans or heads will roll."

"One pair of pants."

"Twelve."

"Five."

"Ten. That's my final offer." She narrowed her eyes in mock ferocity. "Remember, I'm about to be your blushing bride. Be nice to me or I'll decorate the reception hall with orange and pink."

Slade adopted a noble expression. "All that matters is that you walk down the altar to me. For that privilege, I will give you closets full of scandalous clothes and I will patiently endure any color scheme you wish."

She smirked at his self-sacrificing tone. "Wow, this really *must* be love."

"It is." He ran a palm over her hair, his heart in his eyes. "You are my soul, Jane Squire. In every possible way. I will follow you anywhere. We really can live anyplace you wish. Decorate in any way you wish. Do *anything* you wish."

"Then I wish to stay right here in bed." Jane smiled brightly and leaned down to kiss her Prince Charming. "You're my home, Slade. And if movies have taught me anything it's that there's *no place* like home."

# Author's Note

This story is a sequel to *Not Another Vampire Book*. Hopefully, you knew that. When I first conceived *Not Another Vampire Book*, Slade was supposed to be the bad guy. I pictured him possessing the worst qualities of the worst romance novel protagonists, flipping the usual hero/villain dichotomy. I fully intended to have some fun, kill Slade off at the end, and never look back. But Slade wouldn't let me.

All my characters do things that surprise me, but few have ever surprised me as much as Slade. I saw pretty quickly that this guy wasn't going to do *anything* I expected. Within the first few chapters of *Not Another Vampire Book*, Slade's enthusiastic overconfidence and misplaced optimism won me over. I had to redraft the whole book to get him a happy ending.

Did he thank me for it? No. Slade *still* wouldn't shut up. If Damien got a book, *he* should get a book. It only seemed fair. He didn't *like* his happily ever after. He wanted something more. I ignored him for a long time. Ungrateful jerk. Besides, I had no idea what kind of story he could possibly have. Who would put up with that guy?

Then, one day, I was watching a particularly cheesy fantasy movie on TV and it suddenly dawned on me that *this* was Slade's ideal world. The knights and swords and monsters. *This* was what he wanted. To be a hero in the literal, King Arthur-y sense of the word.

Slade would need a heroine, too. I'd already given him a fairytale princess, though, and he wasn't very interested. Eventually, Jane Squire came along and I knew I'd found the right girl. Someone cynical enough to see through Slade's arrogant boasting and softhearted enough to love him anyway. With Jane around, things got done. Slade wanted to talk to her and she was willing to talk back. I never had to wonder what was going to happen next, because --in every scene-- he had some exciting new idea to share with Jane and she had some snarky new way to insult it.  Thus, *Vampire Charming* was born.

I enjoy creating these "story-within-a-story" books and hope to write more.  My tentative plan is to do Amalie's next.  Drop me a line to tell me what you think at: **starturtlepublishing@gmail.com**.

**Don't miss another exciting book by Cassandra Gannon**
*Cowboy from the Future*
**Available now!**

No doubt about it, Adeline Mulhaney's "Glamping Retreat" in Yellowstone National Park is the worst vacation ever. The campfire sing-alongs are bad enough, but when an earthquake strikes and she hits her head, things get even worse. Addy is somehow transported sixteen hundred years into the future. Only instead of the flying cars that Hollywood predicted, this future is filled with buffalo-sized lizards and laser-gun showdowns in the streets.

The icky locals might be content to worship the ruins of Mount Rushmore and fight bands of mutant Outlanders, but Addy is going home. Returning to the twenty-first century won't be easy, but she has a plan. The handsomest cowboy in this Wild West nightmare just happens to have superpowers and he's eager to lend her a hand.

Sort of.

Cade Westin isn't sure what to think when the strange redhead wanders into his saloon. Addy speaks in an antiquated language, wears bizarre clothes, and keeps asking for something called "coffee." The woman is crazy. But Addy's also the only person in town who doesn't ostracize him for his Voltyn heritage. Descended from genetically-engineered soldiers, Cade's people are feared and hated by the humans. Addy doesn't seem to know that, though. Soon, she's moving into one of the rooms above his bar and whipping his screwed-up brothers into shape. And driving him crazy with her bright smiles. ...And getting him chased by an angry posse.

Against his better judgment, Cade agrees to help Adeline find her way back to this mysterious "Why 'o Ming" place. But, when Addy's knowledge of the past puts her life in danger, not even wild Ghaa beasts can stop Cade from riding to the rescue. He isn't sure where the little lunatic comes from, but deep down he knows that she only belongs with him.

Made in United States
Orlando, FL
04 April 2025